An elven wizard on a quest for vengeance . . .
A knight on a holy crusade . . .
A young druid fighting to preserve her homeland . . .
A rogue repaying an old debt . . .
. . . and a band of warriors just trying to get out alive . . .

A foul demon struggling to escape her prison . . .
A power-hungry demigod plotting
to bend her to his will . . .
A sadistic priest waking a slumbering evil . . .
. . . and the Spider Queen weaves her webs
around them all

Join ... llains clash
... nds—

AGAINST THE GIANTS
RU EMERSON

WHITE PLUME MOUNTAIN
PAUL KIDD

DESCENT INTO THE DEPTHS OF THE EARTH
PAUL KIDD

THE TEMPLE OF ELEMENTAL EVIL
THOMAS M. REID

QUEEN OF THE DEMONWEB PITS
PAUL KIDD
(OCTOBER 2001)

KEEP ON THE BORDERLANDS
RU EMERSON
(NOVEMBER 2001)

The Temple of Elemental Evil

Thomas M. Reid

THE TEMPLE OF ELEMENTAL EVIL

Distributed in the United States by St. Martin's Press. Distributed in Canada by Fenn Ltd.

Distributed to the hobby, toy, and comic trade in the United States and Canada by regional distributors.

Distributed worldwide by Wizards of the Coast, Inc. and regional distributors.

Made in the U.S.A.

Cover art by Jon Sullivan
First Printing: May 2001
Library of Congress Catalog Card Number: 00-103750

9 8 7 6 5 4 3 2 1

UK ISBN: 0-7869-2616-3
US ISBN: 0-7869-1864-0
620-T21864

U.S., CANADA,
ASIA, PACIFIC, & LATIN AMERICA
Wizards of the Coast, Inc.
P.O. Box 707
Renton, WA 98057-0707
+1-800-324-6496

EUROPEAN HEADQUARTERS
Wizards of the Coast, Belgium
P.B. 2031
2600 Berchem
Belgium
Tel. +32-70-23-32-77

Visit our web site at **www.wizards.com/greyhawk**

To Al, Cheryl, David, Jerry, and Todd—
The Alliance lives in each of you,
and I cherish every moment we have been friends,
following the unknown path together.

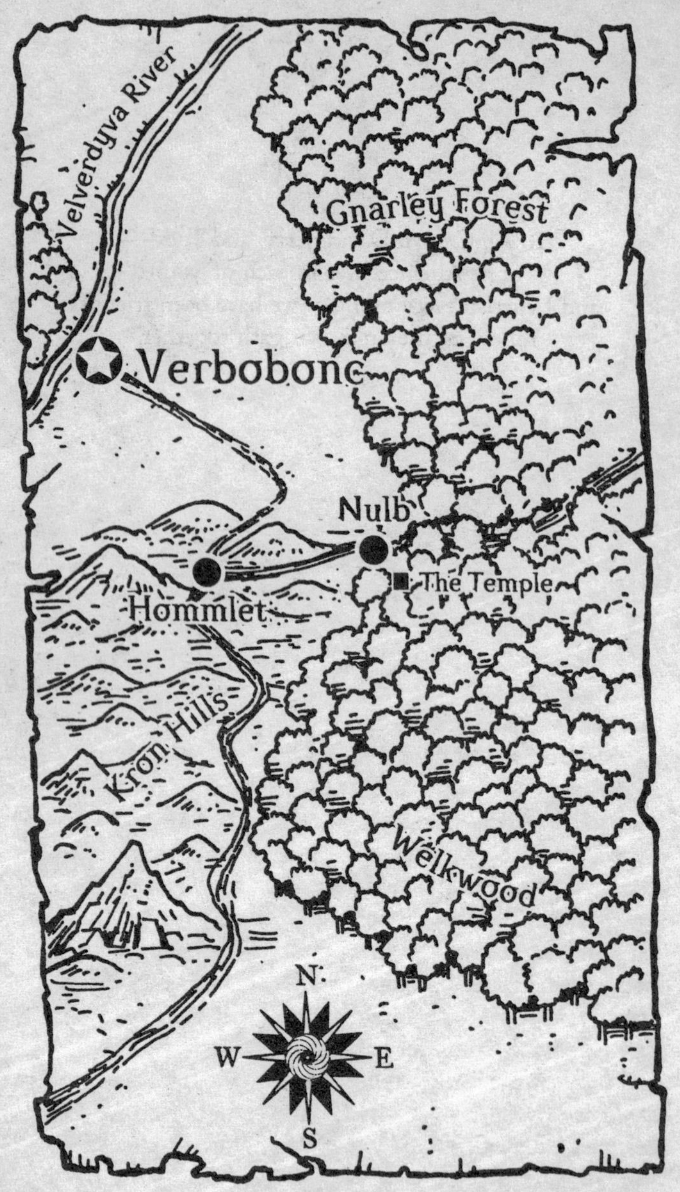
Velverdyva River
Gnarley Forest
Verbobonc
Nulb
The Temple
Hommlet
Kron Hills
Welkwood
N
W
E
S

Prologue

The smoke from two incense-laden braziers hung heavy in the air, giving the small but comfortable room a warm, pungent atmosphere. The dim light from the braziers, combined with the fire burning in the fireplace on the far wall, filled the room with long, flickering shadows. Dressed only in black silk pants, Hedrack, high priest of the Elemental Temple, reclined in his plush chair, his feet propped upon his writing desk. *Conquest, Obedience, and Command* lay open in his lap, but he paid little notice to the book. Instead, his attention was turned to the high, ermine-covered bed in the corner where his twin beauties lay.

Mika dozed, sprawled naked on her stomach atop the furs. Her face was hidden by the waves of ebony hair cascading across it. Astelle, sitting cross-legged on the bed next to Mika with one of the furs loosely draped across a shoulder, watched Hedrack. She leaned forward, one arm propped upon her knee, her chin cradled in her hand, and gazed at her master through heavy eyelids. A contented half-smile curved on her lips. Her own dark hair was thrown back, leaving her slender white neck and one delectable shoulder bare.

Hedrack watched Astelle's drowsy face for a moment, saw her lids flutter once, twice, as she struggled to keep her eyes open. Good, he thought. Always obedient. She would struggle to remain awake, to carry out any command he might choose to issue, knowing failure would be painful. Even with the threat of punishment, though, in her charmed state, either girl would jump to obey for the chance to please her master. Thus, he did not often have to punish.

And they pleased me well tonight, Hedrack thought with an inward smile. Always reward obedience, he reminded himself, re-reading those words on the open page before him. "Sleep," he told Astelle. She smiled, then slid down the bed and curled up beside Mika, throwing the fur across both of them. In a moment, her breathing matched that of the other girl, slow and steady.

Hedrack turned back to his book, intending to refocus his attention, when a small bell sitting upon his writing desk chimed once. He arose from his chair and threw a silk robe over his shoulders. The black garment bore a symbol of a jawless golden skull on the breast and a horned skull in red on the back. After donning his black silk slippers, Hedrack moved to the door, slipped the lock back, and opened it. He stepped into a large room furnished with a massive table and many chairs, then pulled the door shut behind him and locked it again. The high priest turned to look at the guard standing in this meeting room.

The creature, its two heads rising more than twice Hedrack's own height, stood straight, watching the man with no small amount of fear in its two pairs of eyes. "M-master," one of the heads said, while the other called out, "Lord Hedrack!" and the ettin bowed.

"Deus, Ahma," Hedrack replied, addressing each head separately. "How stands the watch?"

"The watch stands ever ready," Deus and Ahma replied in unison.

"Very good," Hedrack said as he turned and made his way out of the room. "No one goes in, no one comes out, as always."

Behind him, the ettin nodded and saluted, one hand to each forehead.

Hedrack moved into the hallways of his underground headquarters, walking with ease and confidence. Except for the occasional troll standing guard, the temple was quiet this evening. The high priest was in a good mood, and his thoughts strayed back to Mika and Astelle, awaiting him in his bed. As he made his way to the Greater Temple chambers, he found himself craving their embrace. Smiling, his steps quickened.

Hedrack passed through several more chambers and into a great room with many passages fanning out to either side. He made his way past these side halls and up a large set of steps to a dais. There, he passed through a strange, shimmering purple curtain that seemed alive, writhing and undulating as he pushed through it. He emerged in a smaller, private chamber with three altars. A faint pearly glow emanated from a set of descending stairs, and to either side black curtains blocked off small alcoves.

Settling himself between the three altars, Hedrack went to his knees and prayed. It was not long before he felt a presence in his mind, a strong and powerful personality that radiated beautiful, black malice.

"My Lord Iuz," Hedrack said to the presence inside his head. "I am your Mouth. I pronounce your wishes to the world you will tread beneath your feet. You called, my lord?"

Yes, the god replied, bathing Hedrack in his energy of hatred. *My loyal servant. How fares your progress?*

Hedrack smiled, for he loved bringing his deity good news. "My lord, things progress better than expected.

My commander in the field reports additional troops within the week, and many more soon to follow. He also sends fresh sacrifices."

Well and good, Iuz said, his grating voice reverberating through the high priest's mind. *We shall soon lay claim to the entire region, and that fat toad Belvor in Chendl will not know what to do when I come at him from both north and south. It will be a war the likes of which he has never seen.*

"It will be a glorious day, my Lord Iuz."

Any progress in finding her?

Hedrack nodded, having fully expected to be asked this question. "Only a little, my lord. The throne I spoke of before? I have discovered that she can feel me, and I her, when I sit upon it. We have begun a tentative communication in this way, and she calls for freedom, though she seems—how shall I say this?—not all there, as though she is in the midst of a deep slumber and only a part of her is aware of me. I have forestalled her, assuring her that you labor to free her. I think it satisfies her, for the moment. As you instructed, I have not sent diggers to search for her hidden chambers yet."

Excellent, my loyal one, Iuz replied. *However, I think it is time to find her and free her.*

"My lord? I thought you wished to leave her be. Did you not say that having the promise of her rather than the reality of her would keep the temples faithful to her and obedient to you?"

I did. But I have discovered activities on other fronts, powers that move against us. We no longer have the luxury of keeping her promise of power locked away. It is time we took it out and wielded it.

"Others, terrible one?"

Yes. He *has taken notice, and even now sends his servants to meddle. That is all the mustachioed fop in his silly hat will do, for the moment. But now that he takes an active interest, we must be ready for more from him.*

"You yourself said that it would be unavoidable to draw his attention, great Iuz. Has he meddled too soon?"

No, but we must not hesitate. Begin the digging. Find her. Awaken her, and also intercept his *servants. Destroy them. Send a clear message to any others he might think to send. Make them fear to come this way.*

"I hear and obey, my lord. I will catch them and send them into the very planes themselves."

Good. I want him to lose hope. Go now, and do these things.

"Yes, Lord Iuz." As quickly as it had come, the presence departed from Hedrack's mind.

The high priest opened his eyes and stood again, looking around the room. He spotted the descending stairs, the pearly white glow coming from below, and walked down them.

The gentle, pale illumination radiated from a column of light in the center of the room, suffusing the place. The walls of the circular chamber were entirely encrusted with precious stones, arranged to form the image of rich farmland as seen from the battlements of a great structure. Beings from every direction were bowing in homage to the viewer.

Hedrack moved to the center of the chamber and passed into the column of light. Inside, he found himself facing a silvery throne covered with more of the gems. This throne was completely bathed in the milky glow. Moving toward the throne, Hedrack took a deep breath and seated himself.

Instantly, the high priest felt the presence of her mind within his own. It was similar to the manner in which his own master visited him, but in some ways quite different. Where Iuz was aware and penetrating, she seemed sluggish, comatose. Hedrack tried to awaken her, to get her attention. She reacted slowly, as if she were engulfed in a sea of molasses, but she did respond.

You are back, she said, recognizing him from before. That pleased him.

Yes. I seek you. Your whereabouts. The Lord Iuz and I come to free you.

I am here. In this place.

But you must help me. You must remember how you got there.

It is difficult. I see . . . men coming. My beloved tells me to run. I flee . . . where? I can't remember. But there is something . . . golden . . . a key? Yes! A key! You must find the key!

A key? What key? What is this key? What does it do?

It will free me. You must find it!

Yes, I will. But where? Where is the key, and where is the lock?

A golden . . . it . . . is . . . key.

The contact with her shattered. She was too drained to continue with the struggle to remember, to stay conscious. Pursing his lips in a slight frown, Hedrack stood and left the column of light.

A golden key, Hedrack thought. And she remembered me. Perhaps there is progress. He smiled, feeling pleased. As he headed out of the gem-encrusted chamber, he considered whether he should order Barkinar, commander of the temple troops, to begin exploratory digging in an attempt to find her. No, he decided. Soon, but not yet. Still the temples rail against each other. I must force them to accept one another before I free her, then nothing will stand against us. Not this time. In the meantime, I will simply find out about this golden key.

Still smiling, Hedrack returned to his chambers, where his lovely Mika and Astelle lay waiting for him.

Ragged clouds hung low among the easternmost Kron Hills, drifting damply and obscuring the tree-lined ridges like the hoary, tattered wisps of Rao's beard, as though the god of peace were passing there. The drizzle-laden sky had deepened into the purple of dusk, and only a steely gray glow in the west still resisted the coming of night. Amid the rain-soaked oak and ipp trees lining the valley between those hills, two horses bearing riders plodded through the endless puddles of a deeply rutted road.

The rear rider, a stout staff of iron-shod wood tied across the saddle in front of him, shivered as rivulets of chill rain seeped through the heavy, oiled cloak he wore, trickling under the edge of his oversized hood and slithering maddeningly down his neck. For the hundredth time, he tugged the hood forward and hunched more tightly into himself, slumping further down into the saddle and trying to hide from the soft rain that had been pummeling him and his companion since midmorning. He sighed, saddle-weary after three days riding through the westernmost part of the Gnarley Forest, and clicked his tongue to his mount, signaling a sense of urgency that his posture belied. The horse snorted once and ignored the command for haste, its hoofs splashing incessantly through the shallow, muddy water.

"Lanithaine, please tell me we're going to reach this village tonight," the rider said to the figure ahead of him. "Tell me we're almost to this Hommlet." He shook the rain free of his hood once more.

"Yes, Shanhaevel," the man in front of him said over his shoulder. "We should reach Hommlet in another hour, at most." Then Lanithaine laughed. "You know, you've always told me elves have the patience to sit and watch a tree grow. You seem awfully eager to be where we're going. Yesterday, you were complaining that we should never have left the Gnarley."

"I just need a warm hearth and a dry bed," Shanhaevel muttered. "Of course, I'd much prefer if it were *my* bed."

Lanithaine laughed again, a rich, warm chuckle that glowed with genuine affection. "What? You don't want to spend another night huddled on the cold ground in the rain?"

"Oh, Boccob!" Shanhaevel snorted. "Don't be silly. Why be back home, warm and dry, when we can be out here, who knows where, traveling to a wide place in the road that isn't even on most maps?" He sighed again, thinking of home.

"Hmm, a roof over our heads *would* do me good," Lanithaine replied, his voice low and muffled now. "This weather seems to seep into my bones."

Shanhaevel could hear the weariness in his teacher's voice. "You still haven't explained to me why we're traveling to this place."

Lanithaine sighed. "Some tales are best left untold, you know."

Shanhaevel frowned, puzzled by his mentor's words. "What tale? What are you talking about?"

Lanithaine sighed again. "Something I had fervently hoped I would never *have* to talk about again, not with anyone. . . ." The older man paused for a moment, as if considering. "There is a wizard in Hommlet, an old friend of mine. Burne and I were very close, once. We survived a war together."

"A war? What war?"

"You might remember it. It wasn't so long ago, at least it would not seem so to you, I'd wager. A powerful temple—a walled fortress, really—had risen. It was a dark and horrific place dedicated to worship of the elements—and to foul demons, too. I left you for a time and told you to watch over the village while I was gone."

"I remember," Shanhaevel replied. "I heard the stories that came back with the traders. The army of the temple was soundly defeated, if I recall, and the temple razed. It was only a decade ago. I never realized you were a part of it. You never spoke of it."

"Yes. Well, it wasn't something I liked to think about, much less talk to others about. Not even to you. I hope you never have to experience such a thing.

"But I digress," the older man continued. "Burne and I rode together, serving the marshal of Furyondy himself, Prince Thrommel, who was in command of the army marching to oppose the temple. We were part of a special company, his personal retinue, in a manner of speaking. We had a special and very dangerous job. We were needed to counter the dark magic of the temple leaders and the fiends they served. As awful as it was, it was a glorious time, too." Lanithaine seemed lost in his memories. His voice was far away, in a younger day. "All the members of that company grew close under the prince. War made us more than just comrades. We became friends. Some of those friends of mine died that day." His voice grew dark and troubled. "But that's neither here nor now."

"But this is more than a social visit, isn't it?" Shanhaevel said. "You have some other reason for going to see this Burne."

"Yes. He needs my help with something we didn't finish during that battle, and it's time to finish it now. It's Burne's tale to tell, though. You'll see in good time."

"I hope his tale is worth sleeping on the wet ground," Shanhaevel grumbled, dissatisfied with his mentor's abrupt ending to the story.

"I'd rather be sleeping in my own bed tonight, too, but I made a promise, and I'm going to see the promise fulfilled." The older man sounded weary.

The elf looked at Lanithaine's back, hunched low in the saddle. The older man seemed even more stooped than he remembered. We should both be at home, Shanhaevel told himself, not out here in this mess. In his mind's eye, Shanhaevel saw Lanithaine, walking through the forest village of home with a stoop and a slight limp, smiling to everyone he met along the way. When did you grow so old? Where did those years go?

It seemed like only a few seasons since Lanithaine had taken Shanhaevel in, had begun to teach the orphaned elf child his craft of magic. Shanhaevel felt as though he had barely scratched the surface of his studies, that it was only a few short months ago he had tried his first simple cantrips. Lanithaine had worn a much younger face then, and there had been no stooped shoulders, no limp.

Lanithaine had spent most of his life with his pupil. The older man had devoted himself to teaching, and the student had been there since nearly the beginning. Older man, Shanhaevel thought with wry amusement. He's not really that much older—perhaps a decade or so. Not really old at all. And yet, Lanithaine *was* old. It made Shanhaevel sad to look at the man in front of him, hunched low on his horse as they rode through the rain and the last remnants of the day. He realized that their roles had reversed. Now he was taking care of the old man, looking out for Lanithaine just as Lanithaine had done for him years ago. We don't have many of those too-short years left to spend together, the elf thought. He'll be gone soon. I should make the most of the time we *do* still have left.

Shanhaevel forced his thoughts back to the present. He can't ride in the dark, the elf told himself. We'll have to stop soon, or I'll have to lead him. He shook himself, sending a cascade of droplets spraying into the near-darkness. At that moment, a vague half-voice, little more than a thought, intruded into his mind, and he realized it had been there for several moments, nudging him, trying to get his attention.

Bad things.

A branch snapped somewhere ahead, near the trail, and Shanhaevel froze, pulling his mount to a stop.

"Lanithaine, hold on," he called. As his teacher reined in, the elf listened, barely breathing.

Such a fool! Shanhaevel berated himself as he watched and waited. Letting your guard down to listen to nostalgic tales and to argue. *Where?* he thought, sending his silent question to the trees above, speaking to the mind that had spoken to him.

Hiding. In the trees.

The back of his neck prickled, but Shanhaevel heard nothing more, so he raised himself in his stirrups and shoved his hood back for a better look around. His eyes shimmered and glowed faintly, reflecting the faintest remnants of western light, revealing the unmistakable shape and lavender hue of his gray-elven heritage. Having stared so long at nothing more than the back of Lanithaine's horse and the muddy road, those eyes now scanned the purple gloom without difficulty, spying shape where there should be darkness, grayish light where only deep shadow should hang.

"What is it?" Lanithaine asked as he guided his horse beside Shanhaevel's.

"Ormiel spotted something ahead," the elf replied, his voice low. "He said there were 'bad things.' I don't see anything, but I heard a twig pop."

"You did? I haven't heard a thing."

"That's because you're as deaf as a newel post," Shanhaevel whispered, still watching. He saw no menace, but he caught scent of something—something foul. His horse must have smelled it as well, for it whickered and tossed its head.

"Shh," Shanhaevel whispered, running his hand along the horse's mane to calm it. He was straining to see and hear but was still unable to detect anything. Long moments passed, but there was only the patter of rain as it pelted the broad leaves of the ipps towering around him.

After a moment, Shanhaevel mentally commanded, *Show me.* From overhead, there was the briefest rustle, and as the elf looked up, a red-tailed hawk, its wings spread wide, glided down, shooting past his shoulder and ahead, following the road. It pulled up near a large tree perhaps thirty paces further down, settling onto a large branch about fifteen feet above the ground. As its taloned feet grasped the rough bark of the tree limb, it screeched loudly.

Here, it whispered into Shanhaevel's mind. *Hiding.*

The elf was just about to open his mouth and suggest that they turn their horses and head back the way they had come when he heard another fallen branch crack, and then there was the unmistakable sound of a bow being drawn tight. At the same time, something crashed out from the underbrush.

Fly! Shanhaevel cried as he heard the twang of an arrow, but the hawk was already in motion, lunging off the branch and diving low to gain speed rapidly, then gliding inches off the ground. It was past the two riders and up into the branches above in a heartbeat. The arrow lanced through the oak leaves where the hawk had been, slicing a few free of the branch and sending them floating wetly to the ground.

Shanhaevel caught a glimpse of several shapes swarming out from where they had been hiding behind the trunks of trees. The elf caught a glimpse of tall bodies with oddly shaped heads. A broad-bladed axe was in the hands of the nearest attacker, but Shanhaevel was already dismounting, tossing his staff down to the muddy road and cursing as he swung out of the saddle.

"Come on!" he growled at Lanithaine as he tugged the reins, swinging his horse around to use it as a shield between the two of them and the ambush. Lanithaine was leaning low in the saddle and trying to swing a frail leg back, but his horse was panicked, and with a frightened whinny it reared up on its hind legs and dumped its rider to the ground. Lanithaine toppled into the mud and rolled to one side.

"Run!" Shanhaevel shouted as he fought to maintain control of his own frightened mount, at the same time reaching to grab hold of the reins of Lanithaine's horse.

The approaching figures, fully a half dozen of them, had fanned out along the road and were closing. At least two wielded bows and were taking aim. Shanhaevel felt an arrow whisk past his shoulder, and he detected a soft grunt of pain from Lanithaine.

Dread filled the elf. Let him be all right, he prayed. Abandoning his efforts to control the horses, Shanhaevel released them both, letting them charge away in terror.

Lanithaine's mount reared and lunged forward, colliding with one of the creatures, which shouted what sounded like a curse.

Gnolls! Shanhaevel recognized the creature's language. This close to the edge of the forest? This near civilization? He shook his head and dismissed the thought as he spun toward where Lanithaine had rolled, seeking to aid the injured man—and went sprawling into the mud. He had stepped squarely on his own staff, and it had rolled out from underneath him. He landed awkwardly on both hands and wrenched one shoulder, while the other arm slipped in the slick dampness of the road and shot out from beneath him. He went facedown into the mud.

Shanhaevel rolled, sputtering and trying to wipe the mud free from his eyes with the hem of his cloak. Move! he screamed silently. The gnolls had to be almost on him. He managed to clean his face enough to open his eyes, just in time to see one of the gnolls looming over him with a huge axe raised high overhead. Gasping in near-panic, Shanhaevel felt for his staff as he scrambled to avoid being split in two.

Above Shanhaevel, the gnoll leered and hefted the axe even higher. *Boccob!* the elf prayed again as he rolled to the side. Time seemed to come to a near standstill as he kicked himself away from impending slaughter. No matter how hard and fast he tried to churn his legs, the gnoll was never far away, striding inexorably closer to him. A second creature moved beside the first and peered down at Shanhaevel, watching the elf with an ominous grin on its doglike face. The elf's cloak and clothes were now soaked in thick, wet mud and tangled about his legs and arms. He slipped again and flopped on his back, staring skyward as the gnoll hesitated, apparently savoring the moment.

The burst of light that shot across Shanhaevel's field of vision at that moment wasn't nearly as jarring as the concussive blast that accompanied it, leaving the elf flailing in the mud, blind and deaf, his whole body buzzing painfully. He panicked, although he knew what had happened, for he had seen Lanithaine's magical bolts of lightning often enough. Blinded, Shanhaevel had no idea if the gnolls had been felled by the bolt or were still standing over him about to carve him into tiny, mud- and blood-covered bits.

In his frightened floundering, Shanhaevel's hand smacked against something hard, and he instinctively closed his grip on it. It was his staff, he realized, and he pulled it to himself, gripping it for all he was worth and swinging it all about, hoping to discourage any potential attacks. He could still neither see nor hear, although both his vision and hearing seemed to be gradually returning.

After a moment or two, the elf realized that it was quiet. He could hear the slurping and sucking of the mud beneath his body as he twisted around. He stopped moving and listened. There were no sounds of battle, only the dripping from the surrounding trees and a faint rasping sound.

Shaking his head and wishing he could rub his eyes to try to restore his sight, Shanhaevel sat up and peered around as his vision returned.

"Lanithaine?" he called, worried that more gnolls might be nearby. There was no answer.

Shanhaevel scrambled to his feet, his eyesight mostly restored. Burned bodies lay everywhere. He moved among them, relieved to see that they were all gnolls. Then he spotted his teacher, slumped against the bole of a large oak, breathing in ragged, rapid gasps. Shanhaevel leaped across the distance between them and knelt down beside the old man.

Lanithaine's breathing was shallow, and Shanhaevel could detect a faint gurgling with each breath. An arrow had caught him squarely in the back and was protruding from his ribs in front. Shanhaevel leaned down, close to his teacher's face. He could see blood discoloring Lanithaine's lips.

No! The elf screamed silently. Why now? I have no healing magic!

"Lanithaine, talk to me," he said. Lanithaine opened his eyes and looked at Shanhaevel, although the elf knew that his own visage was nearly invisible to the man. *Good*, he thought. *Don't let him to see my fear.*

"You must go to . . . to Hommlet," Lanithaine rasped, his voice weak and moist. "Find . . . Burne. Tell him . . . what . . . h-happened."

"No, you're coming, too," Shanhaevel insisted. "I'm taking you there just as soon as I can get you on one of the horses."

Lanithaine reached up and took hold of Shanhaevel's arm with his hand. The grip was weak, and his teacher's fingers trembled. "No," the older man said, his voice softer still. "Can't breathe. Arrow . . . through . . . a l-l—"

Shanhaevel could feel the tears welling up in his eyes, because he knew what his teacher was saying, and he couldn't bear to hear the rest. He started to drag a sleeve across his face to keep the tears away, but his arm, his face, everything was covered in mud, so he simply let them fall.

"Go," Lanithaine said, the effort to speak clearly taxing him. He coughed, his body seizing up with spasms, and blood now stained his white beard. Shanhaevel could only hold the man, feeling Lanithaine's fingers dig into his arm. When the coughing fit subsided, the older man continued, his voice barely a whisper. "You . . . can . . . do this. Burne

. . . needs . . . you. Help . . . as . . . you wou—" The old man paused for breath. ". . . me."

"Lanithaine, no! *You* are my teacher. I can't—won't—serve another!" Shanhaevel, too, struggled to breathe, feeling as though he were suffocating. He felt helpless, and his master's words were ripping at his insides. The suggestion that the elf serve another was too much. It cut too deeply. The lump that formed in his throat nearly choked him.

"No . . . serve. *Aid.* For me. See . . . task . . . through." Another coughing fit gripped Lanithaine, and this time, it would not release him. As his breath grew more and more shallow, the older man gasped, his head sagging back, until the last cough was little more than a pitiful wheeze, and he sighed, lying still.

Unmoving, Shanhaevel crouched beside his master's body, his mind refusing to believe what was before him. It could not be. They were supposed to spend many more years together. This was not how it was supposed to end. He shook his head, trying to clear his vision of the face of his dead teacher, but he could not tear his eyes away.

"No," he insisted, and shook Lanithaine once, gently. He is just unconscious, the elf told himself. I can revive him. Not dead. Not dead!

"Noooo!" He screamed into the forest, loud and long, feeling his throat grow hoarse and not caring. He screamed it again and grabbed at the hated arrow, yanking it free from Lanithaine's body.

With his fist clenched around the missile, Shanhaevel lunged back and away from Lanithaine, unwilling to look upon his teacher's face any longer. His rage burned inside him now, white-hot anger that made him clench his teeth and ball his free hand into a fist. The elf whirled around, wanting, hoping to spot a gnoll on the road, one that might have escaped the death of Lanithaine's bolt of lightning.

There were none. If any had survived, they had vanished. Desperate, Shanhaevel peered around, listening. His breath heaved in his chest, and hot tears ran down his face, mixing with the mud caked there. He could feel his fists shaking from his rage. In fury, he gripped the arrow even more tightly, then flung it away and sank down in the road, his mind numb.

Bad things dead, Ormiel said, the thought vaguely coupled with a slight yearning for a mouse to snack upon. *Why still shout for the hunt?*

Shanhaevel raised his head and looked around. His vision was fine now, but the world seemed dull, muted.

Lanithaine is dead, he told the hawk.

Ormiel didn't answer, but Shanhaevel sensed the sorrow the bird felt, and the hawk cried out, a forlorn screech from the branches overhead that echoed into the night.

Damn, the elf thought, feeling the rage inside him reduced to a dull smoldering. Damn it all to the hells. He tried to wrap his mind around the meaning behind the words. *Lanithaine is dead.* The elf felt his throat tightening once more and refused to let it overwhelm him. Instead, he stood, peering around and focusing his mind on what to do next, shutting out, for the moment, his grief. He spotted one of the gnolls Lanithaine had slain.

Moving closer, he crouched down for a look, gathering in as many details as he could from the blackened, charred body. It was armed and armored—fairly well, too. Shanhaevel did not recognize the symbol emblazoned on the beast's black tunic. The cloth was burned, but the symbol seemed to be a flaming eye of orange. He made a mental note of it, wondering what tribes he might not be familiar with roamed this part of the Gnarley.

Gnolls this far west, Shanhaevel thought. Lanithaine said we weren't more than another hour, even on foot, from Hommlet, and there are easily half a dozen other communities scattered around, at least according to his map. Plus, we—*I*—I'm into the hills now, and the gnomes hold solid sway here. Why would gnolls risk ranging this far out of the deep forest? Maybe this Burne in Hommlet will know.

Do I go on, though? Why? What am I going to do there, just walk up and ask for this Burne? *Excuse me, Mr. Burne, but Lanithaine is dead, so I'm here instead.* They'll think I'm crazy. He shook his head in dismissal. I'm not going to Hommlet.

Yes, you are, Shanhaevel told himself. Lanithaine wanted it. He wanted you to go in his stead. The one thing Lanithaine would have hated the most about dying was leaving an obligation unpaid.

For a moment, the elf was angry again—angry with the wizard Burne, who had needed Lanithaine for whatever reason, angry with Lanithaine for coming to aid Burne and for dying, but mostly angry with himself for letting his emotions get so twisted around everything. The anger gave way to fresh sorrow, because he knew the reason plainly enough: It was Lanithaine's honor that was at stake, even in death, and Shanhaevel had cared too much for the man in life to taint that.

So be it, the elf told himself. I'll go for you, Lanithaine.

* * * * *

Shanhaevel stood a little way from the road, over the shallow grave he had dug for his teacher, studying the pile of rocks that covered the body and marked the site. To leave Lanithaine in this spot, here in the middle of nowhere, had at first seemed wrong, but Shanhaevel then remembered that, most of all, Lanithaine had loved the forest. After that realization, it had seemed like the only thing to do. The elf hung his head for a moment, closed his eyes, and recalled the happy times he had spent with this man, who had taught him of both magic and friendship.

Good-bye, Lanithaine. Rest. I will serve your cause. Only then will I go home. Not before.

Shanhaevel turned and strode away from the grave, pausing at the edge of the trees to listen and peer about one final time, wanting to remember this spot, this moment. The rain had stopped, but the sky remained overcast, and moisture still dripped steadily from the boughs overhead. Nodding in poignant satisfaction, the elf drew the hood of the heavy cloak over his head and moved out onto the road.

A few hundred paces up the path Shanhaevel found the horses, standing quietly. Now, with his walking staff once again tied across the saddle, Shanhaevel freed the reins, stepped into the stirrup, and swung up onto his mount. Despite the clouds, Luna, the largest moon had risen. She was nearly full and gave the overcast sky a faint glow, providing enough light for him to ride.

From the highest branches of a nearby tree, the hawk dropped like a rock, then flattened its dive and went gliding silently by. In the open area of the road, it climbed, banked, and turned, returning to circle the elf once before swooping in and coming to rest on his shoulder.

Shanhaevel stroked the creature's neck as the hawk bobbed its head in quick, jerky motions, eyeing him as if he were a morsel of fleeing food. Shanhaevel reached inside another of his many pockets and drew out a strip of dried meat, holding it up. The hawk eyed it for a mere second before darting its head forward to snag the snack. With his avian companion perched upon one shoulder, Shanhaevel began his journey, traveling for the first time without his teacher, his friend.

Riding along the center hump of the road to avoid the bountiful puddles that clustered in the wagon ruts, Shanhaevel took an easy pace, not wanting to be flung into the mud again should his mount stumble.

As he rode, Shanhaevel considered just how he should introduce himself to the people he met, especially this

Burne fellow. You don't want them to dismiss you as a green apprentice, he told himself. You should be cautious. You're not at home anymore. Don't trust anyone too quickly or easily. You need something that sounds impressive—subtle but impressive.

Shanhaevel considered his own full name, Shantirel Galanhaevel, which meant "child born of the shadow wood" in his native Elvish. Well, "whelp" is more accurate than "child," he reminded himself, but I'm certainly never telling anyone *that.* I can twist it around a little, make it sound more mysterious and powerful.

"I am the spawn of shadows, born of night's sweet fold," he said softly, testing the words. "I am Shanhaevel."

He liked what he heard. It fit his black mood.

After nearly an hour of steady riding, Shanhaevel realized the terrain had changed subtly. The trees that had lined the road all day were still there, flanking it as thickly as before, though the underbrush beneath them was now absent, replaced by short grasses. More importantly was the rail fence that cordoned the trees off from the road. It was someone's farm. As he swept his gaze farther ahead to spy the open pasture there, the elf caught the faint scent of woodsmoke with the barest hint of freshly baked bread. As if on cue, his stomach roiled. The body must eat, Shanhaevel thought, whether I'm interested or not. This must be Hommlet, and even if it isn't, it's as far as I'm going tonight. The road crested ahead of him to a low rise, and when he topped it, he spotted the thatched roof of a building peeping over the next ridge. To his left, beyond the split rails of the fence, was the unmistakable uniformity of an orchard, to his right was a sweeping pasture, and beyond it, in the distance, half-hidden by another line of trees, was a stone tower.

Gesturing toward the orchard, Shanhaevel whispered in the hawk's mind, *Go. Rest. Feed. Come again with the sun.*

Yes. Food for me. Sleep.

The hawk spread its wings wide, pushed free of Shanhaevel's shoulder, and flew toward the orchard.

Shanhaevel watched it go for a moment, then turned his attention back to the final step of his journey, eager to get out of the night to someplace warm. As he drew nearer the first building, a well-kept wood-and-plaster farmhouse with a sturdy barn beyond it, Shanhaevel saw lights in its windows and in several others beyond. A dog standing in the doorway of the barn loped halfway to the road, barking at his approach, and was soon joined by a second, both beasts warning the stranger away from their domain. When it became obvious to the pair that the traveler was passing on, they retreated back into the shelter of the barn.

Ahead of him, at what looked to be a crossroads, Shanhaevel could see a larger structure, two stories tall, with light spilling warmly from many of its windows. The smoke from the vast building's several chimneys carried the unmistakable smell of fresh bread, smoked fowl, and savory seasonings of many types. The elf's stomach rumbled again as he rode forward through the open gate and into the yard. The glow of two lanterns flanking the door shone brightly upon a large wooden plank displayed prominently overhead. The image—a smiling maiden, showing much of her ample bosom and holding forth a frothy tankard—was painted with no small amount of skill upon the plank, which glistened wetly from the rain and glowed in the light of the twin lanterns.

Shanhaevel untied his staff and tossed it down to the ground, then dismounted and began unbuckling the strap of both his and Lanithaine's saddlebags. When he had freed them, he flung both over his shoulder. At that moment, a strapping lad of perhaps sixteen years came out of the nearby stable. He walked across the yard to see to the care of the mounts. Shanhaevel dug a silver coin from his pocket and pressed it into the boy's hand. The young man smiled and took the reins.

"Welcome to Hommlet," the boy said as he turned to lead the horses to the barn, "and to the Inn of the Welcome

Wench. Mistress Gundigoot will have a hot meal, a room, and a bath"—the lad eyed Shanhaevel's filthy appearance before continuing—"waiting for you inside."

Grimacing, Shanhaevel nodded and stepped onto the porch and pulled the stout door open, letting both the dull buzz of conversation and the warm glow of lantern- and firelight spill upon him. After so long in the darkness, he had to squint a moment before stepping into the building. There was a pause in the chatter as he entered. Knowing that he was a sight, caked in mud as he was, Shanhaevel stood there for a moment, letting his eyes adjust and take in the place. Most of the patrons realized they were staring and resumed their conversations.

Shanhaevel found himself standing in one corner of a large common room filled with rough-hewn tables and benches. Perhaps a dozen folk sat in various spots, some alone and others together, dining, playing dice, or talking. Several massive tree trunks, their bark dark with smoke and age, supported the ceiling and the second story above. A huge fireplace with a lively, crackling blaze nearly filled the opposite wall, and several patrons, mostly farmers it seemed, had gathered near it to smoke their pipes and laugh.

Two young women, one with shoulder-length wavy blonde hair and the other a brunette with straight tresses that hung all the way to her waist, moved back and forth easily in the half-empty taproom, aprons and skirts swishing with the swaying of their hips. A slight smile curled up at one corner of the elf's mouth as he watched them serve the patrons.

A third woman, stouter and older than the other two, entered through a door behind the bar. She held aloft a tray in one hand filled with dishes, each containing a puffy pie with rich brown gravy dripping from the edges of the crust. In the other hand, the woman bore a large platter that held a hunk of white cheese and several loaves of rich brown bread.

The smell of the hot food wafted over Shanhaevel like a lazy summer breeze, and despite his sorrow, he realized he was famished. He leaned his staff against the corner, set his saddlebags down, and unfastened his filthy cloak. He slipped the hood back, shaking his hair free. A full mane of silvery locks cascaded down his shoulders in thick waves. The tips of his angled, pointed ears protruded through the hair, matching the narrow, swept-back features of his face.

The din of the common room grew quiet a second time, and Shanhaevel stopped in the middle of hanging the cloak on a peg near the door to peer over his shoulder, wondering what had silenced the room. Many of the patrons were looking at him, though most of them tried not to show it. Shanhaevel did a quick inspection of himself, wondering what else might be amiss besides the thick mud.

The blonde serving wench, frozen in the act of retrieving an empty platter, stared at him wide-eyed, her mouth hanging open. When she realized that Shanhaevel was staring back at her, she gasped and lowered her gaze, turning away to retreat toward the bar. Unfortunately, in the process of escaping the elf's attention, she bumped against one of the large tree-trunk pillars and lost her grip on the platter, which clattered to the floor. Everyone turned to look at the poor girl, and Shanhaevel was relieved to have the attention diverted elsewhere.

At that moment, the older woman with the meat pies spied Shanhaevel still standing near the door, his cloak half-hung, and strode out from behind the bar toward the two serving girls, scolding them severely in low tones and motioning them back to the kitchens. Her cheeks glowing, the blonde hastily dropped to one knee to retrieve the dish and then scurried to the kitchen, avoiding looking in Shanhaevel's direction. Sighing, the matronly woman turned to the elf, a wide and sincere smile on her face.

"Welcome, good traveler, to the Inn of the Welcome Wench. My apologies for Leah's rudeness. She is a silly girl who should know better than to leave a customer standing in the doorway."

Shanhaevel waved the woman's apology away as he watched both serving girls disappear into the kitchen. He finished hanging up his cloak and replied, "It's all right, although I've never seen people so amazed by someone covered in mud before. I may be a bit filthy, but you'd think they were looking at a ghost."

The woman laughed. "No, not the mud, good sir." She leaned in and spoke a bit lower, a more serious expression on her mien. "I suspect your, ah, *heritage* surprised Leah. We do not have many woodfolk visit us, even though we see many travelers pass through. I apologize. I will speak to her about such rudeness."

Shanhaevel blinked, puzzled, before he realized the woman was referring to his elven appearance rather than the fact that he hailed from the Welkwood. He shook his head. "Well, good mistress, there was no harm done that a seat by the fire and one of those savory-smelling meat pies won't put right." He kept the tone of his words warm. There was no sense taking his dark disposition out on her.

The woman's smile returned. "Of course, good traveler. But please, call me Glora. I'm Glora Gundigoot, and my husband Ostler and I run the Welcome Wench. Anything either of us can get for you, all you must do is ask. I suspect the first thing you'll be wanting is a bath." Shanhaevel grabbed his saddlebags as Glora turned to lead him deeper into the Welcome Wench.

"Actually, Goodwife Gundigoot . . ." Shanhaevel said as they crossed the room.

The woman threw a quick look over her shoulder. "Yes?"

"I'm looking for someone, a local. His name is Burne. Could you tell me where I might find him?"

Glora's eyes widened, but she covered her surprise quickly. "Ah, you're the one they're waiting for. I didn't realize— My apologies again. Master Burne and the others are waiting in the back room for you. It's this way."

The woman gestured for Shanhaevel to the back corner of the room, toward a door. The elf followed her, wondering just how many assistant wizards this Burne was going to need. As he followed the goodwife to the door, he noticed a trio of men sitting at a nearby table, staring at him, scowls on their faces.

The three were in the middle of a game, and their dress suggested travelers like him rather than local farmers. One, a hulking fellow with a scar across the back of one hand, openly wore a long dagger on his belt, while another, a wiry man whose golden-hued skin and blue-black hair marked him as Bakluni, was dressed all in crimson. He was almost completely bald except for a topknot and wore a slightly contemptuous smile on his face. As Shanhaevel and his escort passed their table, the third man, who was facing the door Glora was approaching, leaned out as though trying to gain a better view of what was beyond the portal.

Have they just never been muddy, before? Shanhaevel wondered, certain he did not recognize them. Maybe they've never seen an elf before. Boccob, what backwater place am I visiting?

When Glora reached the door, she knocked twice, pushed it open, and poked her head in. Beyond, Shanhaevel could see a good-sized room with a round table and several men sitting around it, thick pottery mugs in front of most of them and a sweating pitcher in the middle of the table. The smell of tobacco smoke wafted through the open door, and a thick haze hung near the ceiling. Glora said something in a low voice that Shanhaevel could not quite make out, then pushed the door open the rest of the way and motioned the elf inside.

"You go right on in, and I'll bring you some food."

Shanhaevel nodded his appreciation as he entered the room. It was cozy, with a fire built in a hearth on the opposite wall. A pair of decorative swords, crossed, hung over the mantle. Two lanterns hung from the ceiling to give the place plenty of light. Glora pulled the door shut as she hurried out. The elf stood near the door, facing the group of men. There were almost a dozen in all.

Shanhaevel cleared his throat, unnerved by the strangers who sat silently staring at him, and introduced himself.

"I am shadow—" he croaked in a gravelly voice, choking as he stumbled through his introduction. *Oh, Boccob! I sound like a frog!* He shook his head and tried again. "I am spawn—I mean, the shadow of spawns—"

No, idiot! He silently cursed as the men looked at him, obviously confused.

"You're who? Did you say 'Shadowspawn?' " one of them asked with a twinkle in his eye—a younger, clean-shaven fellow with a dimpled chin and a mop of unruly brown hair. "Shadowspawn," the man, barely more than a boy, continued. "That's got quite a ring to it. You must be a great hero."

The twinkle in the young man's eye grew brighter as several others in the room chuckled along with him.

"No," Shanhaevel said, disgusted with having just made a fool of himself. "Just Shanhaevel. It means 'shadow.' "

The mud caking his clothing only added to the ridiculousness of the situation, he realized. You've only made yourself out to be a buffoon, he silently chided. No more fancy speeches. Just talk. The elf blinked, knowing his cheeks were glowing red with embarrassment.

"I seek the wizard Burne, to serve in the stead of my late master, Lanithaine."

The elf stared at no one as he finished, not knowing which man was the wizard he sought and not certain he could hold anyone's gaze, anyway, feeling as foolish as he did right now. The sudden thought that this Burne character would find him unsuitable and send him back home with the obligation unsettled made Shanhaevel squirm.

One of them gasped at the elf's words. He was tall, muscular, and clean-shaven, with closely cropped straight dark hair. Shanhaevel could see that the man was dressed for traveling, complete with a shirt of mail. A second man, an older fellow with a thick pile of curly hair and rather large ears who was smoking a long-stemmed pipe, rose from his chair. Shanhaevel met the man's gaze despite his embarrassment, and saw with some surprise that he was rather short and paunchy, and his long robes seemed slightly too big for him.

"Did I hear you correctly?" the man asked, his face ashen. "Lanithaine is dead?"

Shanhaevel opened his mouth to speak, but the lump in his throat was back, so he only nodded. It was the first time someone else was aware of his teacher's death, and it freshened his pain.

"Oh, by the gods," the fellow replied, sitting heavily and gripping the armrests of his chair with trembling hands. "Our old friend," he half-whispered, lost in some private grief amid the solemn group of men sitting around him in the silent room.

"Yes. This is grave news, indeed," the first man answered softly, staring at his hands.

Blinking, the paunchy man with the pipe looked up at Shanhaevel once more. "How?"

Shanhaevel swallowed hard, trying to gain command of his voice. "Slain earlier tonight. By gnolls."

The room erupted in chaotic chatter.

"This is outrageous!"

"Tonight, you say? This is not good."

"That's the third sighting this week!"

It all came at once, a whirlwind of conversation, everyone speaking and asking questions. Finally, the man who had first spoken to Shanhaevel banged his mug on the table.

"Please, gentlemen! Enough!" When the room returned to order, the man sighed, his face grave. "Now, we all know that this does not bode well, and certainly, we will take steps to find out what is going on, but first things first, if you please." The man turned back to Shanhaevel. "My friend, I am Lord Burne. Lanithaine was a friend and a good man. I am deeply sorry for your loss."

Shanhaevel nodded his thanks, once again unwilling to trust his voice.

"I know of you," Burne continued. "Lanithaine mentioned you often. I was led to believe that you are capable. We need someone of your skill to ride with the company."

Shanhaevel swallowed in surprise. "The company? I don't understand."

Burne pursed his lips and explained. "We're forming a small expedition by order of his grace, the Viscount of Verbobonc. We need a wizard with some skill to be a part of it. Lanithaine did not mention this to you?"

Shanhaevel cocked his head to one side, considering. An expedition? Now that was something he never would have considered.

"No." His heart felt as if someone were squeezing it, but he swallowed the lump in his throat and held the other man's gaze. "I only know that the two of you served together in a war a decade ago. He said you were friends."

"Please, sit down," the wizard said, gesturing to one of the empty chairs surrounding the table. Shanhaevel nodded gratefully and slid into the seat, dropping his suddenly heavy saddlebags to floor beside him. Burne turned to make introductions.

"This," Burne began, gesturing to the man immediately on his right, "is Melias, sent to us by his grace, the king of Furyondy. He also rode with your mentor, and he is to be in charge of the company."

The hilt of a sword protruded above the man's shoulder. He nodded once at Shanhaevel and smiled. The expression held surprising warmth in it.

Shanhaevel returned the nod respectfully, still trying to sort this out in his head.

"I'll let Melias introduce his own companions," Burne said, indicating the two other fellows flanking Melias at the table, "for they arrived with him only today, and they are in his service, not mine."

Melias nodded again and pointed to the young man with the twinkle in his eye who had spoken earlier, teasing Shanhaevel about his botched introduction.

"This is Ahleage, our, um, scout, and this is Draga, who is a fair shot with that bow."

Shanhaevel nodded to each in turn, getting a better look at both as he did so.

Ahleage was dressed in a shirt of black leather, and as he rose and bowed, his movements were fluid and graceful.

Shanhaevel noticed both a short sword and dagger on his belt. When he sat again, he kept his chair away from the table, and Shanhaevel sensed that he was tightly coiled, a cat ready to spring up and away in a heartbeat.

Draga was slightly older than Ahleage, though not by much, Shanhaevel suspected. Also dressed in armor, the bowman was a rather hairy fellow, with tight curls of light brown hair on his head, several days' growth of beard on his face, big, bushy eyebrows, and forearms that were generously covered, as well. A bow stood in the corner behind him, unstrung at the moment, but Shanhaevel could tell that it was a weapon of some quality. A quiver of arrows rested beside it.

"The rest of these gentlemen are the village council," Burne said. "This is Lord Rufus of the Tower"—a graying, full-bearded man, one of the two who wore armor and weaponry and who had a reserved look to him—"and that's Canon Terjon"—a thin, middle-aged blond man, clean-shaven, his lips pursed in a no-nonsense frown. His robes were of the church of Saint Cuthbert. Burne gestured next to a man with a graying beard, a long braid, and a playful, warm smile. "This is Jaroo Ashstaff, a druid of the old faith."

Burne continued on his other side, indicating a powerfully built, completely bald man with grand, sweeping moustaches. "To my left, here, is Mytch, who runs the mill in Hommlet. Beside him is Hroth, the captain of Hommlet's militia"—a fellow with closely cropped white hair, one scarred, cloudy eye, and a large, hawkish nose—"Ostler Gundigoot, the owner of the Welcome Wench"—a bespectacled fellow with nearly white hair and beard, who was smoking a long-stemmed pipe similar to Burne's—"and finally, the lord mayor of Hommlet, Kenter Nevets"—a slight man with little of his dark hair left and somewhat watery blue eyes, who held an unlit pipe.

"Good evening and good health to you all," Shanhaevel said as he tried to gather his wits and mask his confusion. "As I said before, I am Shanhaevel, companion and student of the wizard Lan—"

"That's not what you said," Ahleage interrupted, chuckling, and Draga stifled a cackle of his own. "You said your name was Shadowspawn."

Shanhaevel's face flushed. He opened his mouth to retort, but Melias spoke first.

"Enough. I don't need—"

At that moment, the door opened and Glora Gundigoot entered, followed by the blonde barmaid, bearing a tray with platters of food, more mugs, and another heavy, moisture-coated pitcher. Shanhaevel noticed that the younger girl blushed as she caught Ahleage's eye, and she nearly stumbled as she came through the door.

"Just set it down and scoot," Glora scolded, "They have plenty to talk about without you lollygagging around."

Leah placed the tray on the table and turned to go, stealing a quick glance back at Ahleage.

"Shoo! Shoo!" Glora admonished, swatting at the girl with her dishtowel until she scurried out, and then the goodwife pulled the door shut once again. The smile on Ahleage's face remained for some time afterward.

Despite his unease, Shanhaevel wasted no time reaching for one of the platters of food. As he shoveled mouthfuls of hot meat pie in, using a crust of fresh bread to sop up the rich gravy, Burne reached for the pitcher and poured cold mead for Shanhaevel, then began refilling everyone else's mugs. Shanhaevel nodded appreciatively to the wizard before going back to the food in front of him.

Melias, Ahleage, and Draga joined in eating, but the rest of the gathered crowd seemed to have already dined, for they were content to sip their mugs. Burne tipped his back and took a long draught, then set the mug down and wiped his sleeve across his mouth.

"Now that you know everyone," Burned said, "perhaps Melias can explain why he is here and why the company has been formed."

The warrior nodded at Burne and finished off his own mug before speaking.

"Yes. Well, as most of you know, ten years ago a blight of evil assailed these parts, a festering sore in the form of a foul temple dedicated to the worship of things dark and elemental." An uncomfortable murmur rose up, and it was obvious to Shanhaevel that this discussion did not set well with some in the room. "The marshal of Furyondy, Prince Thrommel, raised an army to destroy this temple. Burne, Lanithaine, and I, among others, rode with the prince. At the Battle of Emridy Meadows, we scattered the forces of the temple. Most of their leadership was slain or captured, although a few managed to escape." Melias paused at this point, obviously troubled by this fact. Clenching both his fists and his jaw, he took a deep breath and continued. "The temple itself was thrown down. The prince's company, of which we were a part, was there to seal the place. However, recent activity in the area suggests that something may be stirring in or near the temple once again."

The room erupted into chaos for the second time that night, and it took quite a bit of mug-banging on Burne's part to restore the group to some semblance of order. Even after the men had quieted, many of the council members continued to mutter. Only the druid, Jaroo, and Rufus seemed unfazed by this revelation.

Hroth, the captain of the militia, spoke, and Shanhaevel leaned in, listening intently. "Are you telling me, sir, that the temple is growing again? Is that what this is about?"

Before Melias could answer, Burne explained. "Recently, there have been a rash of attacks along the trade routes near here, as everyone certainly knows." There was more mumbling, along with several nods of assent. "These attacks have been far too well organized to be attributed to the normal depredations of the tribes. Someone or something is leading them. It is entirely possible that whoever—or whatever—is behind this would like to see the temple rise again. We won't know for sure until we investigate."

"If your suspicions are true," Mytch, the miller, said, "we are no match for them. We're farmers, not soldiers. Oh, sure, we stand in the field once a month and march around when Hroth tells us to, but we're not up to fighting roving beasts on a regular basis. We need help."

"Mytch is right," agreed the mayor, whose soft voice seemed at odds with his position of authority. "This is how it started ten years ago, but we must not wait to act this time. The viscount must send an army immediately."

As the clamor for aid arose, Burne raised his hands for silence. When the room was calm, he said, "That is why Melias is here. Of all the old companions who rode with the prince ten years ago, Melias stills serves King Belvor in Chendl, primarily as an advisor to the viscount here in Verbobonc. The king and the viscount have agreed that Melias can represent both of their interests in this matter, and he thus has instructions to assemble a company to search the area—specifically the remains of the old moathouse south and east of here. Once we can determine the extent of the threat, the king and the viscount will act jointly, sending whatever aid is required."

Shanhaevel stopped eating and looked keenly at Burne. "That's why you summoned Lanithaine? To join this company? Surely you realize he was too old to go gallivanting around the countryside any—"

The wizard waved the elf to silence. "It was never Lanithaine who was to go on this expedition. I needed him here for other reasons, to help me research something related to this trouble. It was you whom we both intended would join Melias."

Shanhaevel's jaw dropped at this revelation. Why didn't Lanithaine tell me? What was he afraid of? This must have been what he was keeping to himself, but why?

Burne smiled at the elf as he said, "I know this must seem overwhelming to you. With Lanithaine's death, there are new problems to solve."

Nodding, Shanhaevel let all of this information settle, then looked up at Burne. "This moathouse? What is—or was—it?"

"An old stronghold in the swamps," Burne replied. "It was an outpost for the temple, a mustering point for troops. It was besieged and defeated shortly after the Battle of Emridy Meadows, once the temple itself had been defeated."

Melias cut in, looking somewhat pained. "You mentioned before that you were attacked tonight by gnolls." Shanhaevel inhaled sharply at the mention of the ambush that had slain his mentor. "How many of them attacked you?"

The elf grimaced. "Six of them. Lanithaine killed them before he died."

"Did they have any markings, any insignias?" Melias asked, his hands on the table in front of him.

Shanhaevel nodded. "Yes," he replied, "an eye, a flaming eye. Nothing I've ever seen before, but then, I've never been outside of—" He stopped suddenly, realizing he was about to admit that he had never left his home before.

"Those are the same markings mentioned by the other victims," Melias said to Burne.

"Yes." Burned nodded. "It seems as though they are spreading their activities farther afield."

"If Ormiel had not been keeping a lookout for us," Shanhaevel said, "I might have died, too."

"Ormiel?" Ahleage asked. "Who's that?"

Shanhaevel cringed, for he seldom liked mentioning his hawk companion to people.

"Ormiel is a friend of mine, a pet," Shanhaevel replied. "You will meet him tomorrow."

Shanhaevel realized he was clenching his jaw. The very thing Lanithaine was traveling to Hommlet to eradicate had instead brought about his own end. It should not have ended this way. *If only he'd told me!*

"Are you certain it was only gnolls?" Burne asked. "There was no one—or nothing—else with them?"

The elf shook his head, trying to keep his thoughts on the conversation at hand. "Not that I could see, although I was in fairly deep woods—and it was night, so something could have been farther back, out of my line of sight—but they seemed to be acting on their own."

"Hmm." Burne mused, scratching behind one large ear. "We must not delay, then. Melias and his company will set out first thing tomorrow."

"Aye," muttered the mayor, and several others nodded in agreement. "How can we aid you?"

"The company will need supplies," Melias said. "I have coin, of course, but the favor of the king and viscount will shine upon those who provide what we need at better than fair prices."

There was another round of murmuring, but it faded away as Burne cut in, "Most of what you will need must come from the traders. Rannos and Gremag keep their own council, and few seem able to sway them from their profits. Whatever else we can provide, we will offer at no gain to ourselves."

A few others muttered, but Burne's stare quickly silenced these.

"I could use a couple more stout bodies to round out the group. I need a healer," Melias said, looking toward Terjon, the priest of Saint Cuthbert, "and another strong arm, especially one who knows the land, would make me feel more at ease."

Terjon frowned, looking uncomfortable. "I do not think Calmert, my assistant, is much of the soldiering type. I can, however, provide you with a potion or two of curative magic. With Saint Cuthbert's blessing, of course." The priest smiled, apparently feeling he had done his good deed for the day.

Jaroo, the druid, snorted. "I can do better than that. My apprentice, Shirral, will go with you. I will send her at dawn. She will provide the healing you need, and she knows the land well for several leagues in every direction."

"My thanks, druid," Melias said, nodding.

Terjon glowered at Jaroo but said nothing.

A healthy bit of competition between the two faiths, Shanhaevel noted with a silent chuckle.

"My lad Elmo can join you," Hroth piped up.

A couple of other men grimaced, but they were careful to hide their expressions from the captain of the militia. "He's a good lad, and he swings a mean axe."

"I welcome him, then," Melias replied. "I thank all of you for your help. At first light, we will pay a visit to the trading post, and then the company rides forth."

There was general banter after that, and the meeting began to break up. Ahleage and Draga both excused themselves, Ahleage with a devilish grin on his face as he scurried through the door.

"So, how is that beef pie?" Ostler Gundigoot asked as the crowded room emptied, leaving only Burne and Melias still at the table. "I baked that myself," he added proudly.

Shanhaevel glanced at the thick pottery dish where the pie had been. All that remained were a few smears from where he had mopped up the gravy with wads of bread. He chuckled and smiled at the innkeeper. "It was delicious, and I could eat another two."

"I'll tell Glora to fetch a couple more for you," Ostler said. "I assume you'll be taking a room with us tonight?"

Shanhaevel glanced at Melias for some sort of guidance, and the warrior nodded, saying, "We've all got rooms here. Ostler will take good care of you."

"Then, yes," Shanhaevel said, "I would like a room for the night, please."

With that, the innkeeper turned and headed out, returning shortly with fresh platters of food.

As Shanhaevel began to put away his second helping, Burne smiled, a warm expression that reminded the elf of the way Lanithaine often looked. He glanced away, feeling sorrow washing over him once again.

Burne cleared his throat and spoke. "Lanithaine will be deeply missed, Shanhaevel. Melias and I both considered him a good friend and a staunch companion. He spoke fondly of you to me during the war."

"I wish I had known," Shanhaevel replied. "He never talked about any of this to me, and he never mentioned any of you. He merely rode off one day, telling me he had something to take care of and that he would be back soon."

Burne nodded. "He thought you could have ridden with us back then, you know. He just couldn't bear dragging you into a war. So he left you to take care of the f[illegible] in your village. He believed you more than able, even[illegible] then. If you are capable now of even half what he claimed you learned from him, I have no doubt you will serve our company well."

"I'm very flattered. Thank you. I will do my best." He suddenly felt a little embarrassed by both the praise and scrutiny. He hoped he would live up to everyone's expectations on this expedition. He realized that he had already decided to become a part of it, never bothering to take time to mull it over. Of course, he told himself, because that's what Lanithaine wanted you to do.

"Tell me," Shanhaevel asked, changing the subject, "what was it like to serve with the prince? I never knew Lanithaine had met royalty, although I recall now that he seemed quite upset when the news came to our village of Thrommel's disappearance."

There was a long silence at the table as both Burne and Melias stared at their hands. Neither of them seemed eager to respond, and Shanhaevel grew uncomfortable, wondering if he had touched on a taboo subject.

"I'm sorry," he began finally, "I didn't mean to—"

"It's all right," Burne answered at last. "You didn't know."

Shanhaevel frowned, puzzled, but he was loath to pry.

"I continued to serve with Thrommel after the war," Melias said, his voice low. "I rode with him as part of his royal bodyguard. I was a part of the hunting party that was with him the day he disappeared."

Shanhaevel could see that the soldier's knuckles were white where the man gripped the table. The elf swallowed hard, unnerved by the passion building in Melias.

Burne took up the tale when Melias seemed unable to continue. "There is evidence to suggest that the temple leaders who escaped us at the Battle of Emridy Meadows somehow orchestrated the prince's kidnapping. There's still more evidence that the prince is still alive, somewhere.

Melias has continued to serve the throne, even with the prince missing."

"I've spent the last seven years searching for him," Melias said. "I swore to his father, King Belvor, that I would." The soldier sighed and released the table. "But the trail grows colder. It's been seven long years."

Shanhaevel nodded, trying to grasp what frustration and disappointment Melias must be feeling. "I am sorry I brought up such a sensitive issue," he said, "but your loyalty and perseverance honors you." He bowed his head toward Melias, trying to show some sense of his respect for the man. Finally, he shoved back his plate. "But now, I am weary from three days in the saddle, and tomorrow comes early. I think I'm ready for bed."

"Yes, of course," Burne said. "Come. I'll get Ostler to get you a room."

As he arose from the table, gathered his belongings, and followed the other wizard and Melias out into the common room, Shanhaevel noticed the trio of men nearby, still sitting and watching. As Melias led the way across the floor toward the stairs, the stranger with the topknot stood up, his crimson robes swishing, and stepped to block the warrior's path.

"My name is Turuko," the main said with a deep bow and a smile. His Baklunish accent was thick. "These are my companions, Kobort and Zert. Word has spread that you seek wealth in the ruins nearby."

One of his companions, the one with the scar across the back of his hand, added, "We'd like in. What say we band together?"

Melias sidestepped the man to pass him. "We are not on a treasure hunt. Thanks, anyway."

The Baklunish man's smile faded, and he looked genuinely sad. "That is unfortunate, for there is much greater safety in numbers. It would be better for all of us to work together. In any event, we've been planning a foray there since before you arrived. Perhaps we will see you there." He smiled again and resumed his seat.

Without a word or a backward glance, Melias started walking again, leading the way to the foot of the stairs. Ahleage and Draga, who had been at another table enjoying a last mug before retiring, fell into step right behind him.

"You may have trouble with those three, I'm afraid," Ostler whispered as he led them up to their rooms. "They may try to reach the ruins first."

"They are of no concern to us," Melias said. "We will explore the moathouse, and if they try to interfere, we will deal with them then."

As the group reached the landing, the front door to the inn banged open, and a young man stormed in.

"Hommlet's under attack!" he shouted. "Lord Burne's tower's afire!"

“Damnation!” Ostler shouted as chaos erupted in the room.

Melias, Ahleage, and Draga moved toward the door, and before Shanhaevel realized it, he had fallen into step with them. He reached for his staff and gripped it in both hands as he followed them.

Out in the night, snow had begun to fall—huge, heavy flakes that fluttered to the ground, settling with a muted whisper, like fingers tapping softly against an overstuffed pillow. Other than that, the world was eerily quiet. The ground had already gained a thin covering of the stuff, a blanket of white that was quickly hiding the damp, muddy yard.

Shanhaevel faltered a step, surprised at this turn of weather. Snow? It's not that cold. Certainly, the ground's not cold enough for it to stick. He shuddered once, but there was no time to consider it further. A handful of villagers went rushing past, and just beyond a line of trees to the east, the orange illumination of flame hung in the night sky, diffused to a hazy glow.

Melias ran toward the main crossroads, with Ahleage, Draga, and Shanhaevel right behind him. He drew to a halt, his sword drawn, looking around as though he sensed something. Shanhaevel scanned the area, searching for signs of attack and listening for telltale screams or the sounds of fighting. At first, all he detected was a series of muffled shouts coming from down the road where the fire burned. Melias turned and started that way, and the others followed.

Shanhaevel spotted them first—forms drifting silently through the trees to the south. "Wait," he called softly, pointing. His stomach churned at what he saw.

The other three men stopped and turned back to the elf expectantly, not reacting.

"What is it?" Melias asked, his voice oddly disembodied in the curtains of snow.

"Over there," Shanhaevel replied, jabbing his finger in the direction of the figures, which were obviously creeping stealthily toward the middle of town.

"Elf, we're as blind as bats out here," Draga grumbled. "We don't have your sight. What in the nine hells do you see?"

"Shield your eyes," Shanhaevel warned.

Muttering a magical phrase, the wizard gestured toward the area of the woods where the figures were creeping. He closed his own eyes, but through his lids he still saw the sudden brightness. A number of throaty, guttural bellows issued forth from the woods, and Shanhaevel opened his eyes, blinking because the forest was filled with a blaze of fuzzy light, as though a lit lantern were hanging from a branch.

"There!" Shanhaevel said, pointing again.

This time, Melias and the others saw what he had spotted. A half-dozen creatures, large, furred beasts with ursine heads, were stumbling about with arms thrown across their faces to ward off the blinding light. Weapons hung loosely in their hands.

"Bugbears," Melias growled, grinning as he ran forward. Ahleage joined him, his short sword in one hand and his dagger in the other.

Draga knelt in the damp snow. He dropped the quiver by his side as he pressed his knee against his bow and flexed it in order to string it, then grabbed an arrow from the quiver. In one smooth motion, he had the fletching against his cheek, the bow forced out before him, and had sighted his first target. There was a solid twang as the bowman loosed, and Shanhaevel saw—and heard—a bugbear take the arrow in one leg. It fell to the ground, howling. Draga was already sighting along another arrow.

Melias and Ahleage, meanwhile, had closed with the creatures, who were recovering some of their sight and turning to face their attackers. Shanhaevel watched the battle begin. Melias was steady and true with his large blade, swinging it in a wide arc before him, clanging his weapon hard against the parries of the first bugbear he encountered. Ahleage was a whirlwind of feints and jabs, constantly spinning out of the way of a killing blow at the last instant and slicing at a hamstring or gut. Both men appeared capable, yet they were outnumbered, even though Draga had dropped two by this time.

Shanhaevel hesitated. He had no more useful offensive magic at hand, having prepared only a handful of practical spells earlier in the day. He had not expected to be engaged in a running battle. The light had helped, but now all he had was his staff. Useful enough for cracking an arm or rib, he thought, but how good against a bugbear? Despite his own misgivings, he started forward to help. Just seeing the hulking humanoids made his blood burn in anger.

Draga was beside him now, having tossed aside the bow when the fighting had gotten tight. Together, they threaded their way through the trees and headed off a bugbear that was trying to circle around Melias.

The beast snarled at them and turned to jab at Draga with its sword. Shanhaevel shifted around, flanking the creature. The trees made using the staff tricky, but when the bugbear lunged in again at Draga, the elf brought the iron-shod end of his staff up from the ground and caught the creature on the back of the elbow with a satisfying crunch.

Howling in pain, the bugbear whirled on Shanhaevel, hatred gleaming in its narrowed red eyes. Its wounded arm hung limply. Shanhaevel took a step back, but his blow had given Draga all the opening necessary. The bowman drove in with his own sword, running the blade deep into the bugbear's gut and up under the ribs, finding the heart. With a horrible, gurgling howl, the bugbear dropped to the ground, unmoving.

Shanhaevel looked up just in time to see another beast stagger away from Ahleage, who had just embedded a dagger in its throat. The wounded bugbear stumbled through the snow for several paces, its paws clasped around its ruined neck, then dropped to one knee and fell over on its side, shaking and gurgling. Melias stood over the body of another.

Behind the elf, the sound of battle still raged. Before he could turn around, he saw the surprise in Draga's eyes. Spinning, Shanhaevel discovered the last two remaining bugbears seemingly facing off with one another. He blinked, realizing the far creature was not a bugbear but a huge brown bear, reared up on its hind legs. The bugbear had dropped its weapon and was now warily watching the bear's huge paws, trying to anticipate an attack.

Draga stepped past the stunned elf to engage the bugbear when the humanoid suddenly stiffened and spasmed, a dagger hilt protruding from the base of its skull. With a shudder, the bugbear crumpled to the snowy ground and lay still. Shanhaevel caught Ahleage out of the corner of his eye and turned to see him rising from a post-throwing crouch. Draga did not lower his guard, however. He turned to engage the bear. The bear, still rearing on its hind feet, lumbered forward, and Draga raised his sword to strike.

In a blur, a figure emerged from the veil of falling snow and intercepted the bowman's blow. It was a human, Shanhaevel realized, who brought a scimitar up, parried Draga's strike, and shouted, "No!"

Draga stepped back, as surprised as Shanhaevel, and stared at the figure. It was a woman, though her features were masked in shadow.

"Easy, Mobley!" the woman said to the bear.

The bear settled down to all fours, rumbled one deep-throated whine at her, then sat down on its haunches as she scratched it behind one ear.

She turned, staring at Draga, and said, "There are more to the east, you big oaf. Go fight them and leave Mobley alone. And you"—she turned to Shanhaevel—"douse that stupid light. Go fling your magic somewhere else."

With that, she turned her back on them and padded back into the forest, with the bear ambling after her. The two of them were quickly obscured by the huge, feathery flakes that continued to descend from the sky and coat the ground.

Draga just stood there, stunned, then turned and looked at Shanhaevel, blinking. "Did you see that?"

Shanhaevel nodded.

"Who do you suppose she was?"

"I guess that would be Shirral, Jaroo the druid's apprentice."

"Oh, no," Draga breathed.

"Oh, yes," Shanhaevel replied. "She said there were more bugbears to the east."

Melias had joined the two of them, and he stared with the rest of them. "Let's go," he said. "Good work with the light magic, Shanhaevel. Well-timed."

Melias turned and moved back to the road, and Draga and Ahleage followed him. Shanhaevel hesitated for only a moment, looking back again to where Shirral had disappeared before he muttered a phrase and felt the connection with magical energies inside him loosen and dissolve, leaving the woods once more in darkness.

* * * * *

The rest of the battle had already been fought by the time Melias and his company arrived at the tower, which sat on a low hill on the east side of the village, guarding the road to Dyvers. It was the same structure Shanhaevel had seen when he had first arrived in Hommlet. It was actually intact, unscathed by the fire. What was severely damaged, however, was the scaffolding and forms beyond it, where Burne and Rufus were in the formative stages of erecting a good-sized keep adjoining the tower. The workers hired to erect the keep had managed to bring the fire under control, although several of them had been killed or had vanished in the attack.

Although the damage to the scaffolding and such was not total, the fire set the project back several weeks, Burne surmised. No one was sure if the fire had been lit to serve as a diversion for an attack in the village itself, or if the opposite had been intended. Members of the militia and some of the men-at-arms serving Rufus began to gather the bodies of the attacking bugbears. They wore the same flaming eye insignia that Shanhaevel had seen before. Something was definitely organizing the beasts and making them uncommonly bold, everyone agreed.

Shanhaevel summoned Ormiel, who had been awakened by the commotion and was none too happy at having his sleep disturbed. *Bad things were in the woods,* Shanhaevel projected to the hawk. *Are any of them still near where the people live?*

Ormiel flew around the village several times, swooping through the trees and soaring across the pastureland, but the only sign of the bugbears was their retreating footprints, which were slowly disappearing beneath the thickening blanket of snow. Shanhaevel reported as much to Melias, who looked at him askance.

"How do you know?" the warrior asked.

"Because my hawk told me. I mentioned him before. Ormiel."

"A hawk?" Melias said, obviously a little surprised.

"Yes," Shanhaevel replied. "Ormiel and I have a very special bond. I can talk to him and he to me, after a fashion. He patrolled the perimeter of Hommlet just now and says there's nothing in the woods anymore."

"Hmm." Melias grunted. "I've seen enough strange things tonight. If you say a hawk told you there's nothing out there, then I believe you. Let's get back to the inn."

Shanhaevel rested comfortably in a steaming bath, feeling the ache of three days of travel slowly seeping out of his body. More than once, Latt and Phip, the stablehands, returned with buckets of nearly scalding water to add to the tub, until the elf could barely stand the heat and told them that was plenty. A short time after that, Leah brought him towels and bade him goodnight. Listening to the sounds of the inn settling in for the night, he soaked a while longer and contemplated everything that had happened to him over the course of the long day.

He avoided dwelling on Lanithaine, instead trying to concentrate on what lay ahead of him. Joining an expedition to ferret out marauding bugbears seemed straightforward enough, and he was eager to exact some sort of revenge on Lanithaine's murderers, but there was something more to this, he knew. The snow had unnerved him, though he couldn't put his finger on why.

Sighing, he closed his eyes and contemplated what he would need to do to prepare for the journey tomorrow.

Finally, when the water had simmered to comfortable warmth but before it could grow cool, Shanhaevel finished the bath. Comfortably drowsy, he readied himself for bed. He stoked the fire, adding fresh wood, then doused the lamp and made his way to bed by firelight.

After crawling beneath the sheets and settling into the pillows, he let out a long, slow sigh, trying to relax his body completely. He lay there in the darkness for a moment or two, unable to avoid thinking about Lanithaine. He found himself imagining the body of his teacher, lying wrapped in his cloak beneath the pile of stones back in the woods along the road. How cold and hard that bed was, compared to the one the elf found himself in. How damp and lonely and disappearing beneath a covering of snow. . . .

Shanhaevel shook his head and shuddered as he tried to rid his mind of the morbid vision.

He heard a noise, a low thump from the room next door where Ahleage was staying. Before he could throw back the covers and climb out of bed, however, he picked up the low murmur of conversation. He could not make out the words, but then he heard a soft, feminine giggle, followed by a muffled squeal of delight.

Leah.

Shanhaevel rolled his eyes as a string of moans and giggles emanated through the wall.

"Boccob, please don't let them do that all night," he groaned, half smiling. Rolling over, he pulled the covers high then wrapped one of the pillows around his head, pressing it against his ear to block out the noise. It helped some but didn't shut out the sounds completely. For the moment, Shanhaevel forgot his grim musings about Lanithaine's grave. Soon enough, despite the tryst next door, or perhaps because of it, Shanhaevel was soundly sleeping.

* * * * *

In the small room off the main taproom of the Inn of the Welcome Wench, by the light of a single, dim lantern,

Burne and Melias conversed softly, planning the foray to the moathouse. A curling scroll of parchment rested on the table between them.

"You may prevail, yet, my friend," Burne said, laying a comforting hand on Melias's shoulder. "If what we believe is true, if the scattered priests are nearby, trying to raise the temple again, you may get the opportunity to discover the whereabouts of Prince Thrommel."

Melias nodded. "That must be the least of my worries, right now. If they somehow find her, manage to free her . . ."

The soldier left his thought unfinished, and for several heartbeats, the room sat in silence.

"That will be harder than you might imagine," Burne replied. "The old seals we placed on those portals are strong, still. They will hold. But we must find the key that is mentioned in the seer's poem," he said, tapping the parchment before him. "We must find it before they do, and finish this, finish it like we should have ten years ago."

"Aye," Melias nodded. "This time, there won't be anyone telling us to turn back. If only we hadn't lost Falrinth that day. We could have destroyed the demon, instead of trapping her inside."

"Yes," Burne agreed, "but what's done is done. He fell in battle, and we survived. We cannot go back and change history. We can, however, insure that the bindings we placed on the temple's portals will hold the demon inside forever. I will continue to try to learn what the key is. When I know, I will send word to you. Find the key and return here. I will know by then how to destroy it."

* * * * *

Shanhaevel awoke the next morning to find cheery light slipping around the edges of the curtains covering the window in his room. He stretched, feeling completely refreshed even after such a short night, for it had been spent in such a comfortable bed. He threw the covers back and dressed quickly, then parted the curtains to let in more light. He looked out. The day had dawned clear and sunny, and the eerie snow from the night before had almost melted away. From all appearances, it looked as if it would be a fine spring day.

The elf sat down at the table. Unbuckling one of his saddlebags, he slipped out a thick package wrapped in oil-skin. Unfolding the protective cloth, he noted with satisfaction that his spellbook was still dry. Uttering a few syllables of magic softly over the cover of the book, he carefully opened the tome and turned the pages, thinking. It was the first time he had gone through this exercise without consultation with his teacher, and it felt strange. After a few moments of careful deliberation, he settled on the spells he wanted for the day and began to memorize them.

Halfway through his studies, there was a light knock on the door. Shanhaevel crossed over and opened it. Melias stood in the hallway, a large leather backpack slung on his back and a coil of rope draped over one shoulder.

"Aren't you ready to go? The sun's been up an hour, now. I've already been to the traders for supplies." The man made a sour smirk that suggested the experience had been none too pleasant.

Shanhaevel gestured back at the table. "I'm studying. I shouldn't be much longer."

"Ah, good. Well, have you eaten, at least?" When Shanhaevel shook his head, the warrior frowned and said, "I'll have Glora send up some breakfast so you can eat while you work."

With that, Melias turned on his heel and headed down the hall toward the stairs.

"Fair enough," Shanhaevel called after him, then shut the door and returned to his spellbook.

A short time later, there was another knock, and Leah opened the door, bearing a tray with steaming porridge, more fresh bread, and cold milk.

"Just set it here." Shanhaevel pointed to a clear place on the table beside where he was working.

The girl's footsteps were heavy across the floor, and she practically slammed the breakfast tray on the spot where Shanhaevel had indicated. He glanced up at her.

"What is it?" he asked.

Leah blushed. "N-nothing, sir. I'm sorry. It's just that Paida is off somewhere, hiding or something, and I have to do all the work. Please forgive me, and don't tell Mistress Gundigoot of my rudeness." She curtsied and hurried from the room.

Shanhaevel looked up from his work long enough to watch her disappear, then shrugged and started in on breakfast while he finished his studying.

By the time Shanhaevel made his way downstairs and out the front door, walking staff in one hand, the rest of the company had already gathered. It was, indeed, a clear, bright morning, although snow still clung in the shade. The elf's breath was visible, whisked away by a mild morning breeze.

Shanhaevel hadn't taken four steps out the door before he noticed Shirral standing off by herself, bundled in a woolen cape of deep brown over leather armor. She leaned on a walking staff, facing away from him and down the road. Her golden blonde hair cascaded in gentle waves past her shoulders. She wore a curved scimitar at her belt, but she was twirling a sling in one hand.

Maybe it's time to make more proper introductions, Shanhaevel thought. *See if maybe the morning sun has done a little something for her disposition.*

When he altered his course to introduce himself, the druid heard his approach and turned to face him. He stopped dead in his tracks, stunned. Her narrow face bore the unmistakable swept-back look of the elves, and her partially pointed ears confirmed her heritage. But she was not full blooded, he realized. She had been born to mixed parentage, a half-breed of elf and human, which explained why he hadn't this noticed last night.

And she was absolutely beautiful.

Shanhaevel realized he was staring at her, and she looked right back at him, her icy blue eyes flashing in anger, her arms now folded across her chest. He shook his head, realizing his rudeness, and crossed the rest of the distance between them, preparing to introduce himself.

"We met last night," he said with a slight chuckle, "but we didn't get introduced. I'm Shan—"

"I know who you are. Jaroo told me."

Shanhaevel stood frozen, one eyebrow raised, taken aback by the druid's abrupt manner. "I'm sorry, I didn't mean to stare. It's just that I wasn't expecting—"

"A half-breed? Well, there's a surprise. No one ever does. But there you go. The world is just full of the unexpected, isn't it?"

With that, Shirral turned and walked several steps away, ignoring him as she tightened the straps on her horse's saddle.

Shanhaevel stood with his mouth hanging open for several moments before a shadow crossing in front of him brought him out of his stunned surprise. It was Ahleage astride a chestnut gelding, trying to reign in the frisky mount. Shanhaevel looked up at the young man and almost laughed out loud, forgetting his confrontation with the druid for the moment.

Ahleage's eyes were bleary and his face was puffy, as though he had slept with it buried between two pillows all night. Well, pillows of a sort, at any rate, Shanhaevel thought.

"Didn't get much sleep last night, huh?" Shanhaevel asked, smiling.

Ahleage blinked a couple of times, as though trying to absorb the elf's words, then he cracked a sleepy but smug smile and turned his horse away again, muttering something about needing eggs for a proper breakfast.

Shanhaevel shook his head in amusement and turned to find himself face to face with two more horses. A scowling Melias and a very large smiling man were astride them. Shanhaevel stepped back and caught himself staring again.

"Uh, hello there," he said, looking from Melias to the newcomer and back again.

"Hiyah!" The huge man said, smiling even more broadly. He leaned down and stuck out one big, meaty hand. His breath smelled of ale, and strongly at that.

Shanhaevel shot one puzzled glance at Melias, whose scowl deepened, and took the large hand offered to him, shaking it vigorously.

The captain's son, Shanhaevel realized with a start, remembering now the stifled groans during the meeting the night before. So, he's a drinker, is he? Shanhaevel mused. What's his name, again?

"I'm Elmo," the fellow said, as though reading Shanhaevel's mind. "You're an elf!"

"Yes." Shanhaevel smiled at the big oaf's forward manner, nodding. "I'm Shanhaevel. Good to meet you."

The man's smile was replaced by a deep, contemplative frown. "Those other two said your name was Shadowspawn," Elmo said, pointing over the elf's shoulder.

Shanhaevel didn't even have to turn around to know the big man was pointing to Ahleage and Draga. He rolled his eyes and tried to laugh. "Oh, they're just having some fun with you. Really, my name's Shanhaevel. They just like to call me that other name."

Elmo puzzled over this for a moment longer, then smiled and nodded again. "All right, Shanhaevel."

Shanhaevel took a moment to study Elmo's outfit. The man wore a shirt of chain mail, and he had an unstrung bow tied across his saddle. Shanhaevel's eyes widened considerably at the huge two-bladed battle-axe on Elmo's back.

"Are you any good with those?" he asked, gesturing to the weapons.

"Uh-huh," Elmo replied, then pulled out a fine dagger from a sheath at his belt. "This is my favorite. My brother Otis gave it to me!" he said, beaming with pride. He held the dagger out, hilt first, for Shanhaevel to examine. "Go on, you can hold it. It's beautiful, huh?"

Shanhaevel reached out and gripped the dagger. The blade felt amazingly well balanced in his hand, and just holding it gave him a small, unusual shiver, one he had felt only a few times before. He took a closer look at the weapon. Even in the brightness of the early morning sun, the elf's keen eyes noted the perfect edge to it. He spotted what he suspected was there—a tiny sigil etched into the blade near the hilt.

Magical, Shanhaevel thought in amazement. *I wonder if he even knows?* The elf looked up into the smiling face of the simple man, made a show of feeling the balance of the blade in his hand, then flipped the weapon around and passed it back, hilt first, to Elmo.

"Very nice," he said. "You should hang on to that."

"Oh, I will," Elmo replied. "My brother Otis gave it to me!"

Shanhaevel nodded, and Elmo smiled again. The man spurred his horse and trotted off to show Ahleage and Draga the dagger, leaving Shanhaevel and Melias to themselves.

"Goodness," Shanhaevel remarked. "He doesn't seem to be the brightest fellow in the village. But he looks like he can handle that axe well enough—if we can keep him away from the drink."

"Aye," nodded Melias, still scowling. "I would rather not have to watch him to make sure he stays out of trouble, but Shirral vouches for him, so . . ." The man shrugged. "I can't very well tell him to go home. We'd get run out of town, I suspect." He shook his head as if to clear it. "Come. We must be on our way. Where's your mount?"

Shanhaevel pointed as he saw Latt leading the pair of horses, one already saddled, out of the adjoining barn.

"Right here," Shanhaevel said, reaching for a silver to toss to the boy. "One to ride, and one for gear."

Melias raised his voice to get everyone's attention. "Come on! Let's get going."

The entourage gathered together and set out. Shanhaevel found himself riding next to Shirral. He wasn't sure what to say to her as they started up the road, but he certainly didn't want her scowling at him for the entire day, so he started by apologizing.

"I'm sorry for staring before," he began. "I didn't mean to make you uncomfortable."

"Forget it," the druid said, not looking at him.

When Shirral seemed unwilling to say more, Shanhaevel continued, "No, really. I was surprised, but only because I've been getting so many looks, myself."

Shirral did look at him, then, and her visage softened somewhat. After a moment, she said, "It's all right. I'm just a little angry with Jaroo for sending me off with the rest of you. I've got better things to do than traipse around the woods with a bunch of men."

Shanhaevel chuckled, drawing another scowl from the druid. "I'm not really here by choice, either," he said, trying to explain. "My late master and Burne were old friends, so I get to go on this expedition without being consulted. Believe me, I'd rather be back home."

Shirral looked at Shanhaevel, but she only grunted in response.

"Anyway," Shanhaevel continued, "last night. You and your friend really took us by surprise."

"Who, Mobley? He's harmless, most of the time."

"Except when there are bugbears about," Shanhaevel added.

"Yes, and idiots with swords smashing their way through the forest."

"Well, I don't own a sword."

Shirral looked at him, her blue eyes blazing. "And other idiots who sling magic around in the woods, lighting the place up like a Needfest tree. Neither Mobley nor I could see what was going on, you know," she said, rather indignantly. "Jaroo would have had my hide—and all of yours—if anything had happened to Mobley."

"I'm sorry," Shanhaevel replied. "I was trying to blind the bugbears, not you. We didn't even know you were there."

"Yes, well . . ." Shirral said, not finishing.

At that point, the entourage was approaching Burne and Rufus's tower, and they all got a better look at the damage from the fire the previous evening. Some of the blackened wood still smoked, and several sections of scaffolding were damaged beyond repair, but it didn't appear as bad as Burne had made it sound the night before.

"The turn-off to the old high road is just ahead," Shirral said as the group left the edge of town.

The road was flanked on both sides by woods now. At the junction, Melias headed off the main road to the right, with the rest following him. The old high road was little more than a game trail, overgrown and half hidden. Shanhaevel and Shirral were riding beside Elmo, and the three of them formed the rear of the procession. Farther up the line, Draga broke into a song, his voice high and smooth as the morning sun as he sang some ditty with a lot of nonsensical words Shanhaevel had never heard before.

"Jaroo tells me you have a friend," Shirral said. "A hawk?"

Shanhaevel turned and looked at Shirral.

"They got acquainted last night," Shirral said, realizing Shanhaevel was confused. "Jaroo told me he met your familiar after the bugbear raid."

Shanhaevel nodded and reached out with his mind. *Ormiel, are you there?*

Yes, came the hawk's reply. *Hunting mice.*

Come to me, the elf commanded, then smiled at Shirral and Elmo. "He's a steady friend and a good lookout. I've called him, so you can meet him."

Shirral smiled, and it was the first time Shanhaevel had seen her do it, he realized. It dazzled him, but he tried not to show it. Instead, he turned and looked at the road in front of him.

Ormiel appeared, swooping in from the trees behind the company. Shanhaevel smiled as the hawk circled the group and settled on his shoulder.

When the bird landed, Shirral gasped in delight, smiling as brightly as Shanhaevel thought imaginable. "Hello there, you magnificent beauty," she said, reaching up to stroke the top of Ormiel's head, smoothing the feathers softly.

Shanhaevel watched the druid, entranced and dazzled by her beauty. "Here," he said, reaching inside his pocket and pulling out a strip of dried meat, which he handed to her. "He loves these."

Carefully, Shirral held her hand up and extended the piece of meat toward Ormiel's beak. The bird eyed the meat without blinking. Then, in an instant, the hawk darted its head forward, snatched the meat from the druid's grasp, and began to consume it.

"What a gorgeous creature," Shirral said.

"Yes," Shanhaevel agreed, turning to see Elmo's reaction. The huge man was simply watching, an intent look on his face. "Ormiel is fine specimen," the elf added, then mentally spoke to his companion. *Watch the trail ahead today.*

Your mate with sky eyes speaks to me, Ormiel responded. *The big man speaks to me.*

Shanhaevel nearly choked at the bird's reference to Shirral, then he caught himself as the other half of Ormiel's claim registered. Big man?

"Ormiel says you're talking to him," Shanhaevel said, looking back and forth between Shirral and Elmo.

"He could hear me? Oh, that's delightful!" The druid said. She continued to stroke the bird's feathers and speak to it aloud in soothing tones. Elmo, however, said nothing, turning once again in the saddle to watch the path before him.

Not a mate. Only a friend. Shanhaevel projected. *What big man speaks to you?*

Big man with shiny feathers and bad air.

Shiny feathers means armor, but bad air? Oh! Shanhaevel realized. Elmo's breath.

"Ormiel says you speak to him, too," Shanhaevel said.

Elmo only smiled, not turning around. "Shirral talks to the animals. I just watch. Ormiel is a very nice bird, though, Shanhaevel."

Shanhaevel shook his head, wondering if Elmo had some sort of ability to speak with animals that he didn't know about. He watched the axeman for a long moment, but Elmo offered no clues. Dismissing this thought, Shanhaevel repeated to Ormiel, *Watch the road today for bad things.*

Yes. I watch. Watch and hunt. Sky eyes is very nice.

Shanhaevel looked again at Shirral, who was still enraptured with the hawk, seemingly very happy. *Yes. Thank you, Ormiel. She is very nice.*

Hedrack walked to one of the braziers that warmed his chambers. He pulled a burning taper from it, then crossed to the center of the room and dropped cross-legged atop a series of thick, plush carpets and cushions. Closing his eyes and uttering a few words of prayer to Iuz, he lit a single black candle in front of him and cast a spell. A moment later, the ghostly, vaporous image of Lareth appeared before him. As Hedrack made eye contact with his field commander, the apparition of the other man smiled and bowed.

"Most humble greetings, Mouth of Iuz," Lareth intoned, maintaining his bow.

Hedrack studied the figure for a moment, reminded with a tiny pang of envy how handsome he was considered to be. A mane of sandy blond hair framed a rugged face with compelling blue eyes. Lareth's broad shoulders and devilish smile always turned the ladies' heads, and the field commander knew it all too well. In fact, Lareth's assessment of his own beauty had made him slightly insolent of late.

Always with the handsome ones, the high priest thought, there are aspirations to rise above station. Durbas, the author of *Conquest, Obedience, and Command,* maintained that the occasional reprimand was absolutely necessary to remind a servant of his actual worth, to avoid instilling a false notion of favoritism and thus the mistaken belief that the servant might some day replace the master. Lareth was certainly one for whom this might be necessary.

"Greetings, Commander Lareth," Hedrack responded. "Rise and report."

Lareth straightened himself and began. "I will send raiding parties in three directions this evening, Hedrack." Hedrack frowned at the cleric's familiarity with him. "However, last night, our raid on Hommlet did not fare as well as expected."

Ah, thought Hedrack, the small failure I will exploit to remind him of his place.

"Yes?" The high priest said, furrowing his brow in displeasure for emphasis.

"A number of capable travelers stopping for the night in that village came to the sorry peasants' aid." Lareth sighed. "I lost fully half a dozen bugbears in the raid."

"You disappoint me," Hedrack said, glowering.

Lareth's eyebrows shot up in surprise. He was clearly not used to being so openly rebuked.

"I have charged you with recruiting fresh troops and with filling our coffers through your raids. I don't remember anything about having my army shrink through your mismanagement."

"My lord, I beg pardon, but this was an unexpected and unavoidable situation. I withdrew the moment—"

"Unexpected and unavoidable? It is clear to me that you are not giving your duties the attention they deserve. A competent field commander always gains reliable intelligence before engaging the enemy, and he always has not one but two contingency plans for *unexpected*"—Hedrack emphasized Lareth's own words back at him—"situations so that nothing becomes an 'unavoidable' *mistake.*"

"Of course, my lord," Lareth answered. "I beg your forgiveness in this, and I assure you that I will redouble my precautions."

Hedrack wasn't sure if Lareth's look of contrition was genuine or not, but he was convinced that the man had received the intended message loudly and clearly: Do not presume too much. A thought occurred to Hedrack.

"I have received warnings from Iuz himself that enemies move against us. Even now, agents of Cuthbert come this way. Perhaps these meddlers you mentioned are the very same?"

"I have reason to believe they are," Lareth replied, causing Hedrack to raise his eyebrow.

"Oh? And how is that?"

"My spies in Hommlet report that there is a company, led by an agent of the king himself, who is preparing to explore the outpost. I am setting up plans to deal with them."

Hedrack leveled his gaze at the other man. "Good. See that you do. And report to me when you have." He waved the issue away and changed the subject. "What of fresh sacrifices? When will I receive more?"

Lareth's charming smile returned in an instant. "I managed to snare a few last night, despite the unexpected opposition. I have sent a fresh batch of them to you this very day. I think you will be very pleased."

"Good, good," Hedrack said, nodding. "I look forward to examining them. Anything else to report?"

Lareth nodded his head. "I shall have no less than fifty new troops for you by the end of the month. And, if my reports are correct, another two hundred and fifty by the end of next."

"Excellent," Hedrack said, genuinely pleased. "We are ahead of schedule, then. Keep it up. And no more mishaps."

"I hear and obey, my lord."

The remains of the ruined moathouse sat to the left of the path, surrounded by a fetid bog and connected to the main road by a narrow causeway that was banked high to stay clear of the wetland around it. Most of the walls were still standing, although in places the stonework was a tumbled ruin, and the whole thing seemed ready to fall over into the bog at any moment. Timbers from what must have once been a second story jutted up in places, but they were blackened from fire. The entire structure was overgrown with vines and creepers, yellowish and sickly looking. The front gates were smashed and hanging askew, but a sad excuse for a drawbridge still spanned the gap between the pathway and the gate's threshold.

Melias studied the moathouse, as if considering. The rest of the company waited in the eerie quiet of the morning, the silence broken only by the deep croaking of frogs and an occasional fetid breeze blowing up from the direction of the marsh. Finally, Melias nodded, half to himself, and motioned for everyone to continue. Slowly, the company made its way down to the ruined moathouse.

Ahleage, sitting astride his horse next to Shanhaevel, coughed and held his nose. "Gah!" He groaned. "It stinks!"

"Shanhaevel," Melias called. "Would you please ask your hawk to reconnoiter the area? I want to know if there's anyone—or anything—about before we go inside."

Shanhaevel nodded. *Ormiel,* he projected, feeling for his familiar.

I am here.

Fly over the big broken man-nest. Are there any bad things? Any people?

From the trees off to the group's left, the hawk took flight, its powerful wings pumping as it rose into the air. It soared past the company, only a few feet over their heads, and winged its way toward the moathouse. Shanhaevel watched as Ormiel circled the place a couple of times and landed on a high parapet of a mostly intact tower near the front entrance. From there, Ormiel scanned the area, jerking his head this way and that.

No bad things. No people.

Shanhaevel shook his head. "Ormiel says nothing is around."

"Thank you." Melias turned in his saddle to face the rest of the group. "All right, stay sharp, everyone. Let's move."

With that, the warrior turned and spurred his horse forward, heading toward the side path that led to the front gate of the moathouse.

As he turned to follow, Shanhaevel thought, *Ormiel. Good job. Hunt now.* Ormiel took off from his perch atop the tower, searching for food.

The group reached the embanked path crossing over the swampy ground, where a slight breeze rustled the cattails. A bird of a type Shanhaevel had never heard before called from the trees. Shanhaevel studied the ruins, looking for any telltale signs that they were being watched.

Melias dismounted, signaling the rest of the company to do the same. He stood for a few moments, staring at the building. Finally, he turned to the rest of the group and said, "We leave the horses here. I want Ahlaege to take the lead. Check that drawbridge to make sure it'll hold us before we cross."

"Got it," Ahlaege said, already advancing along the causeway. The rest of the companions followed a few paces behind.

Before they made it even a third of the way across, something bounded out of the marshy ground to the group's right. Shanhaevel spun in time to see a huge frog, fully six feet long, land near him. As several more of the giant creatures plopped into the company's midst, the one nearest Shanhaevel snaked its long, sticky tongue out, latching onto his arm and pulling, and he was jerked off his feet toward the beast's gaping mouth.

Shanhaevel thrashed wildly with his staff, trying to beat the huge frog senseless. With one arm wrapped up by the beast's tongue, however, he found it impossible to wield the weapon effectively, and worse, he was still being pulled closer and closer to the frog's hungry mouth. In desperation, Shanhaevel used the staff to brace himself, digging into the ground with it and trying to resist the tug of the frog's tongue. It helped only a little.

"It's got me!" Shanhaevel shouted, barely keeping his voice from cracking in terror. "Somebody get it off me!" He flailed about, looking around, but the rest of the company was hard at work battling more of the frogs, although few of the creatures seemed as large as the one that had attacked him.

One of the beasts had a hold of Draga's leg and was pulling him slowly along the ground. Draga, sitting on his rear facing the frog, had his bow out and was firing arrows straight into the creature's head. Three or four shafts already protruded from the thing, and it was jerking and spasming in pain. Melias and Shirral worked together to kill another one with their blades, while Elmo dealt with a third by splitting it almost in half with his axe. Two more hopped out of the marsh even as the huge man dealt the killing blow, and one quickly had a hold of Elmo's leg with its tongue.

Shanhaevel longed to draw upon his magic, but he couldn't concentrate to cast the spell correctly. The frog pulled again and dragged him closer to its mouth. One more good tug, and he would be lunch. Desperately, he spun his staff around and sat down, feet facing the frog. When the creature tugged him a third time, he lined the staff up and tossed it into the slavering maw, crosswise, like a horse's bit. Then he quickly brought his feet up and braced them against either end of the staff, pushing with all his might against the frog itself.

The frog did not like this and began to thrash and shake its head. Shanhaevel found it tricky to keep himself balanced, but the brace held, although his arm felt as if it were being ripped from its socket, and his legs strained with effort. Quickly, before he lost strength, Shanhaevel reached inside his tunic with his free hand and pulled a long dagger from within. Laying the edge of the blade along the taut tongue of the frog, he sawed back and forth, slicing into the flesh.

Instantly, the frog loosened its grip on Shanhaevel's arm and jerked its tongue away. The elf kicked backward as hard as he could and rolled away from the frog, coming to his knees at the far edge of the embanked path. The frog tossed its head and pitched the staff to one side. Dagger still in hand, Shanhaevel rose to his feet. The frog leaped, its mouth open wide, and Shanhaevel took a half-step back, stumbling as he stepped beyond the edge of the path and onto the steep slope beyond. Slipping to one knee, he brought the dagger up to defend himself, treacherously balanced on the side of the embankment. The frog landed right in front of him, its cold, round eyes staring at its potential meal.

Shanhaevel raised his dagger to plunge it between those eyes, and suddenly Ahlaege was there, seemingly appearing out of thin air and bringing his sword down across the neck of the frog and severing its head. Shanhaevel flinched away from the shock of the sudden attack, and the frog's head bounced and rolled past him down the hill into the murky marsh at the bottom. Shanhaevel sighed wearily and slumped down, breathing heavily.

Ahlaege grinned at Shanhaevel as the sounds of battle died away around them. Laying his head back against the ground, the elf stared up at the cloud-flecked sky and caught his breath. His legs were shaking from the strain, and his shoulder was tender. He moved his arm in a swimming motion experimentally and was satisfied that it was not seriously injured.

Shortly, Melias announced that the group should move out, so they rolled the bodies of the frogs down the side of the path, letting the carcasses splash into the marshy water. When they were done, they prepared to enter the ruins once more.

Just as Ahleage started forward, there was a shout from farther down the abandoned road. Shanhaevel turned to look as everyone else unsheathed weapons a second time. It was one of the three men from last night, the one with the scar on the back of his hand, either Kobort or Zert; the elf wasn't certain which. He was running toward the group, waving for their attention as he did so.

As the man caught up to them, Melias brandished his sword and warned, "That's close enough."

The man stopped in his tracks, chest heaving, eyeing the weapon somewhat fearfully.

"Please," he panted. "Zert's hurt. He's . . . trapped, and I can't . . . get him out. We need . . . your help." The man pointed back the way he had come, breathing heavily.

Melias's eyes narrowed in suspicion. "What are you doing here?"

"We hiked out at . . . at first light this morning," the man explained. "Turuko, Zert, and I. We were going to dig . . . for treasure, like we told you."

"But you came from a different direction, just now," Ahleage said, a pair of daggers in his hands. "The moat-house is over there." He gestured with one of his weapons at the ruined structure.

Kobort nodded, still trying to catch his breath. "We went inside and found a way down into the cellars. There's a second way out, back over there," he pointed down the road, from where he had come. "One of the walls collapsed while we were exploring. It completely buried Turuko, and Zert's leg is pinned. I can't lift the stone by myself. Please, he's bleeding pretty bad."

Melias frowned, considering. "Have you noticed any signs that others have been here recently?"

Kobort looked surprised. "No one else is here. It looks like some bandits might have been camping in there." He pointed again, this time at the visible ground level of the moathouse. "They must have cleared out, 'cause no one's there now. Please, Zert's dying!"

Shirral strode back to her horse, mounted, and started forward. "Come on!" she called over her shoulder, sounding exasperated. "We can't just let him die."

Melias grunted in exasperation, but he remounted and spurred his own horse to follow, and the rest of the group fell in with him.

Kobort ran along beside them, saying, "Thank you!" over and over again.

"Just show us," Melias said.

Kobort nodded and pointed as they reached the bottom of the rise, pushing through some brush off the side of the road. Shanhaevel dismounted and tied the reins of his horse to the brush, then followed Melias and the others into the undergrowth.

Several paces off the trail, Kobort showed the group a partially concealed tunnel mouth, covered over with bushes. "In here," he said and moved inside.

"Wait!" Melias said, grasping Kobort's shoulder to stop him. "Unpack the gear," the soldier said to everyone. "If it's unstable in there, I want to be prepared." Turning back to Kobort, Melias asked, "How far back is your friend?"

Kobort scrunched up his face, apparently trying to think. "Maybe a hundred paces," he said at last, not sounding too sure.

"Didn't you have a torch or something?" Melias asked. "How did you find your way out?"

"Oh, I left the torch with Zert, so he wouldn't get scared," Kobort replied. "I could see the light here at the end of the tunnel, so I just felt along the wall with my hand and walked out."

Melias nodded, his lips pursed in a frown. "All right, let's get some lanterns lit and see what's what."

When the group was ready, Kobort led them inside the tunnel. It was long and straight, descending slightly as it ran. Kobort went first, followed by Melias. Ahleage and Draga followed the soldier, and Shanhaevel walked along beside Shirral. Elmo brought up the rear.

As the companions proceeded into the blackness of the passage, Shanhaevel frowned, thinking, Something isn't right. What is it?

After perhaps a hundred paces or so, just as Kobort had said, the group reached a point where the tunnel leveled out and ended. There were two doors, one directly ahead, and another to their right. The one to the right was standing open, and a second passage led off from it.

"He's in there," Kobort said, his voice echoing oddly in the passage. By the light of the group's lanterns, Shanhaevel could see that the man was pointing through the open door to the right. "Zert! I found help! We're coming for ya! Just hang on!"

In response to Kobort's calls, there was a weak groan from down the second passage.

"Shh!" Melias admonished. "Your shouting could bring down more of the place. Whispers only, from now on."

Kobort nodded solemnly.

"All right," Melias said, "Ahleage, lead the way. Check the entire place for weak spots, and go slowly!"

"Hey, you don't have to remind me," the man replied, starting forward cautiously.

Shanhaevel had to resist the urge to reach out and grab Ahleage. Damn it, he chided himself, what has you so spooked? He still couldn't put his finger on it, but something was definitely wrong.

With Ahleage in the lead, the group worked its way down the passage, which ran for about twenty yards before turning a corner. Beyond the turn, there was the faint glow of torchlight.

Shanhaevel tried to convince himself that his doubts were foolish, but the nagging feeling would not go away.

Ahleage reached the turn and went around the corner, everyone else close behind him. When Shanhaevel reached the bend, he looked around in surprise. At the turn, the passage opened into a room—a room filled with a large, crude wooden table surrounded by similarly constructed chairs. Crates and barrels of goods were stacked along the walls—foodstuffs, weapons, armor, and blankets—enough to supply a small army. A door was set into the wall to one side, but there was no collapse anywhere, and no one about. A lone torch crackled in a sconce on one wall.

"Zert's in there," Kobort whispered, pointing to a far corner, where Shanhaevel could now see a second room off the first.

Just then, it dawned on Shanhaevel: The frogs! Kobort had never mentioned his party being attacked by the frogs.

He was about to call to Melias when about half a dozen dirty, armed men rose up from hiding places on the far side of the table. A couple of them leveled crossbows at the group. At that same moment, another cluster, including a handful of gnolls, stepped out from the second room, brandishing swords. Each of the companions froze, although Draga immediately took aim with his bow at the chest of the closest man to him.

"Mother of Ralishaz," Ahleage snarled. "You bastards!"

Shanhaevel turned to where the man was glaring. Turuko and Zert were among the group of men on the far side of the table.

Only a heartbeat or two later, a third contingent of men appeared, coming up behind the companions from the corridor Kobort had led them through to get here.

They were surrounded.

Fool! Shanhaevel admonished himself. *It was right in front of me. Why didn't I see it sooner?*

"He lied," Shanhaevel said. "They never fought the frogs."

"What?" Melias snapped, his hands clenched in white-knuckled fists. "What are you talking about?"

"He said they went in through the front, but the frogs didn't get them. I should have realized it sooner. I'm sorry."

"Help, please help," Turuko said mockingly, an unfriendly smile on his face. "I've been buried alive, and Zert's leg is broken." He laughed, then said, "Lay your weapons on the ground and kick them away. Now!"

Melias growled in fury, but several crossbows were aimed in his direction, and he stayed his hand. Slowly, he pulled his sword free and set it on the floor. Following the soldier's lead, Draga relaxed his bow and tossed it away. The rest of the companions followed suit, and soon, all their weapons lay out of reach. Melias glared at Kobort, who had joined his companions.

Turning to the door, the crimson-robed Turuko called out, "Master Lareth, we have them."

A moment later, the door along the side of the room swung open wide. Framed in the doorway was a large man, dressed in shining plate mail with the flaming eye emblazoned on the chest plate. His face was hidden by a helm, but the malevolence that radiated from him nearly made Shanhaevel choke. In one hand, the man wielded a mace, and in the other, he held a staff. He stepped into the room and crossed to Melias. The soldier involuntarily flinched from the palpable evil emanating from the helmed figure, though he refused to back down.

"I am Lareth, priest and master of this place," the man said, looking from person to person before him, "and you are nothing before the might of the Elemental Temple. You will now die at my pleasure."

Then, in a single, graceful motion, the man struck, first hitting Melias squarely in the chest with one end of the staff, then swinging at Ahleage with the other. Ahleage leaped back out of range of the attack, but the blow against Melias sent a shower of sparks cascading over the warrior, who cried out for an instant in pain. That cry was short lived, though, for Lareth finished his attack by swinging the mace up directly in Melias's face. The warrior crumpled limply to the ground, his face a pulpy mess of blood, tissue, and shattered bone.

Shanhaevel found himself rooted to the spot, horrified by what he was witnessing but unable to move. The filthy, clinging feel of evil that emanated from this heinous man threatened to choke him. No one else seemed able to react, either.

Chaos engulfed the room as Lareth's troops surged forward, ready to cut down the disarmed prisoners where they stood. The remaining companions crouched defensively, pressed together, back to back. Ahleage had daggers in his hands. Shanhaevel flinched as several crossbows went off, but none of the missiles struck him—although one bolt whizzed by so closely that he felt the wind from its fletching as it passed his nose. He tried as best as he could to ignore the confusion welling up around him and concentrate instead on casting magic. In the back of his mind, he prayed it would be enough.

Shanhaevel spread his fingers wide and pointed them at Lareth, uttering a single magical phrase. The elven wizard engulfed the malevolent priest in great gouts of flame, spraying him with charring heat. Beyond him, the other ambushers flinched away from the scorching flames. Shanhaevel hoped that Lareth would be consumed or wounded enough so that he would back away from the fight. When the spell faded, the smell of smoke hung thick in the dim light of the room. Both companions and ambushers paused, staring in Lareth's direction.

The evil priest appeared untouched by the fire.

"Boccob!" Shanhaevel breathed in dismay.

Lareth laughed. His voice boomed in the place, echoing in the chamber, and the vileness of his evil washed over the companions like a foul vapor, turning Shanhaevel's stomach.

"Kill them!" he said and stepped forward to engage the elf.

Draga darted between Shanhaevel and Lareth. The bowman let out a ferocious roar and lunged forward, bullrushing the priest, grabbing him by the collar, and flinging him backward against the wall. Lareth grunted from the force of the blow, but he quickly shoved back, easily pushing Draga away from him.

Rolling to his side and away from that fight, Shanhaevel came up next to Shirral, who cried out in a language the elf had never heard before. She was instantly wielding a blade of fire in her hand, a glowing scimitar of flame.

Magic, Shanhaevel thought admiringly. *Magnificent!*

The druid and the wizard faced an advancing cadre of gnolls who were grinning and barking as they closed the distance. Every one of them held a large axe, and a few even had a shield. Shanhaevel began to cast again, hoping Shirral could keep the nasty humanoids at bay long enough for him to summon the magic. With the utterance of another simple enchantment, he gestured at the wall of menacing gnolls, and three of them slumped to the ground in a deep sleep, leaving the fourth still up, now dropping into a defensive crouch and eyeing the flaming blade in the druid's hand.

Get him, Shirral, the elf silently urged the druid, then turned to see how the others were faring. He nearly had his head taken off by Kobort, who had come up behind him, sword held high. Shanhaevel dived away, scrambling to stay clear of the furious Kobort, who had swung at the elf full force and was just now regaining his balance.

The man glared at Shanhaevel, nostrils flaring. "You're dead, tree-boy!" he growled, advancing again and swinging his blade back to strike.

Shanhaevel shoved one of the chairs toward Kobort and jumped away, desperately hoping the move would catch the thug off guard and buy him a second or two for a spell. He shouted a word of enchantment, aiming a finger at Kobort as the man kicked the chair away and came at the elf again. A bright flash of light, followed almost instantly by a second, darted forth from the tip of the elf's finger and streaked across the distance, slamming into the thug's chest.

Kobort gasped and fell back, dropping his sword and clutching his chest, which was smoking slightly. He stumbled and tripped over a crate, pitching down behind it.

Shanhaevel spied Elmo's axe lying on the floor and seized it. The heavy weapon felt awkward in his hands. He had often chopped wood for himself and Lanithaine, but this was a far different weapon—a much shorter haft and a wicked double head easily as large as his chest—and it was abominably heavy to the elf.

Steeling his courage, Shanhaevel closed the distance between himself and Kobort, the weapon in hand. The man was trying to rise to his knees. Shanhaevel lifted the axe as high as he could then brought the huge blade down hard on the back of the man's head. There was a sickening crunch and a spray of blood, and Kobort collapsed to the floor. He did not rise again. Shanhaevel gave a shuddering sigh and surveyed the rest of the battle.

Elmo was about to be cornered by Zert and another bandit, each of them holding him at bay with spears. The huge axeman had a crossbow bolt protruding from his thigh, and he staggered as he backed away, dodging the spear thrusts. Cursing, Shanhaevel ran forward, shouting. The two men turned to see what the ruckus was, and when they saw the elf running at them, axe in hand, they turned to receive his charge.

Perfect, Shanhaevel thought. He stopped dead in his tracks, dropped to one knee, and sent the axe sliding across the floor between the two bandits toward Elmo. In a single smooth motion, Elmo scooped the weapon up, even as Zert and his companion watched the axe slide by them. By the time they realized their opponent was now armed, it was too late.

Elmo slammed one blade of the axe into the chest of the bandit in a swift swing, knocking him off his feet and back two full paces, then turned to face Zert, who retreated a step, horrified. Before the thug could flee, Elmo caught him squarely in the hip. Zert screamed as he fell, and Elmo wasted no time closing in to finish him off. Shanhaevel stepped away from that fight and took stock of the rest of the company.

Amazingly, most of the ambush force was down. Shirral—her shoulder soaked in blood—Ahleage, and Draga were fighting with Lareth now. Without hesitating, Shanhaevel cast again, summoning two more of the magical missiles he had used against Kobort. Unerringly, the glowing green streaks of light shot across the room and hit Lareth squarely in the chest. The priest grunted and stumbled back a step, and Draga took advantage of the magical distraction to cut the man hard across the shoulder.

Lareth growled in pain and fury and knocked Draga away with his staff. Shirral darted forward, swinging her blade of flame at the priest's head. Lareth ignored the blow as it connected and rammed his staff into the druid's midsection. Shirral collapsed with a groan, but before Lareth could step forward to finish her, Ahleage was behind him, ramming his dagger into the small of the man's back.

Howling in agony, Lareth spun away, swinging his mace to fend off further blows. Ahleage had to roll away from the attack to avoid getting his skull bashed in.

Breathing heavily and with blood flowing from several wounds, Lareth backed away from Draga and surveyed his failed ambush.

"Finish them!" the priest growled, then gestured, and was engulfed in a cloud of palpable darkness.

"Bastard!" Ahleage shouted as he leaped into the magical blackness.

Shanhaevel hesitated, knowing it would be dangerous to join Ahleage in a blind fight. He'd likely plant a dagger in my ribs, thinking I was Lareth, the wizard thought, and he turned back to survey the room once more.

The only foe still standing was Turuko, who was now facing Elmo. The huge man was charging the Bakluni, bloody axe held high. Elmo brought his weapon down, but Turuko was faster. As Elmo swung, the Bakluni leaped into the air, topknot streaming out behind him as he dodged the swipe of the blade and kicked out with his foot, catching Elmo in the shoulder. The kick was hard enough to send the huge man sprawling to the floor.

Shanhaevel sucked air in through his teeth, amazed and dismayed, for he realized that Turuko must be a member of the Scarlet Brotherhood, a fabled order of fighting monks.

Here? the elf wondered even as he and his companions fanned out, ready to do battle. The Scarlet Brotherhood in league with the temple? Their battle prowess was legendary. Turuko would be deadly, even without weapons. Dismissing the thought for now, the wizard waited for an opportunity to attack.

Draga closed with the monk first, his sword in his hand. Shanhaevel grimaced and relaxed his grip on his staff, moving in to aid Draga. Elmo stood again, growling in fury, and brought his axe up once more, advancing.

Turuko moved as a whirlwind, surrounded by the three of them, his hands and feet moving like snakes. Shanhaevel tried to follow the Bakluni's movements, but Turuko was too fast.

The monk paused in his motions and smiled. "Yes, worthy adversaries, indeed. I had not expected—" he cut himself off, laughing in a placating manner. "But that is the first rule of combat, is it not? Never underestimate your adversary. Well, I shall not make that mistake again. Come, let's finish this."

He whirled around, leaping through martial forms, one after another—kicks and punches, graceful and lithe—demonstrating conservation of energy and motion. With each successive form, he landed facing a different opponent, ready to strike anyone and everyone who faced him.

Elmo was the first to lunge in, swinging his axe in a wide arc before him. Turuko dodged the attack and spun around, kicking Draga in his midsection before the bowman knew what had hit him. Draga grunted, stumbling back a step, but then he darted in again, jabbing his sword at Turuko while the monk was turned to face Shanhaevel. The monk dodged both attacks and sent a kick in Elmo's direction that barely missed the huge man's head. Elmo swung his axe again, but Shanhaevel saw that the big man was having a difficult time using the large weapon with his wounded leg and so many of his companions about.

"Bring your best!" crowed Turuko, smiling as he moved and dodged, gliding easily from opponent to opponent. "I welcome it."

"If you surrender," Elmo said, "I promise you will live."

"Ha!" Turuko laughed, spinning to kick Draga's sword from his hands and following through with a punch that caught the man on his jaw. It was a glancing blow, but Draga staggered back, breathing hard.

"If you attack, I promise you will die!" Turuko said as he dodged a swipe from Shanhaevel and a lunge from Elmo simultaneously.

There was a lull in the fight as the three men facing the monk stepped back, breathing hard.

Damn, thought Shanhaevel, wishing he had some appropriate magic left to aid in his attacks. Anything he tried to use now would endanger his companions, too. He adjusted his grip on his staff and found his center of balance again.

The three men circled Turuko, closing in to take the fight to him once more. Draga struck first this time, jumping in and feinting, then darting back out. While Turuko was still in the midst of repelling that, Shanhaevel stepped forward and tried to sweep the monk's legs, but he stepped back again before Turuko could land a retaliatory strike. They were working the monk more effectively now, feinting, jabbing, and making him spin and defend more strenuously than before.

After both Draga and Shanhaevel occupied Turuko together, Elmo came in high, his axe raised. Turuko sneered as he prepared to bend away from the attack, but at the last moment, Elmo released the axe, sending it spinning, and Turuko's sneer turned to surprise as the weapon went rotating toward his head. The monk ducked it easily enough, but Elmo had gone into a roll at the monk's feet and was now inside the Bakluni's reach. Turuko spun back to face the huge man, preparing to strike with a kick, but Elmo was too fast—*amazingly* fast, Shanhaevel later remembered thinking. Elmo snapped up and at Turuko from a crouch.

There was a glint of bluish silver in Elmo's hand as he embraced Turuko, and the monk went suddenly still, his eyes glazed over in surprise. He looked into Elmo's eyes, his own betraying the pain he felt. He opened his mouth to say something, but no sound issued forth, and then he sagged. Elmo let him slide to the flagstones, the huge man's dagger protruding from his chest.

Turning back to the one remaining foe, Shanhaevel saw that the magical darkness Lareth had used to escape had dissipated. Ahleage slumped against a wall, alive but holding his head, where a trickle of blood ran into his face. Of the dark priest himself, there was no sign. Shirral huddled over Melias. The warrior was sprawled on his back, his one good eye staring at the ceiling. He was still breathing shallowly.

Shanhaevel knelt beside Shirral and looked at Melias, trying not to let his horror show on his face. The druid had the soldier's hand in her own, but she was only crying. The others knelt down beside Melias, speaking soothing words to the warrior, but it was obvious to all of them that he was nearly gone.

"That bastard Kobort and his two companions had better be very dead," Ahleage said, struggling to his feet and joining the rest of them.

"They are," Elmo said, cradling Melias's head in his lap. "Lareth will join them soon, I promise you."

"I can't save him," Shirral growled through clenched teeth. She hung her head and sobbed. "My healing isn't strong enough."

Melias tried to speak, but his words were little more than a gurgle. Shanhaevel and the others leaned in, listening closely.

"K-key," Melias whispered, laboring to breathe. "Find . . . key. Pl-please."

His head slumped back into Elmo's lap, then, and his hand slipped from Shirral's grasp. His eye still stared at the ceiling, but it was unseeing now. With a final wet sigh, his last breath left his body.

Ahleage, the muscles in his jaw clenched and flexing, rose to his feet and turned away from Melias's body. He stomped to the other side of the room and paced. Draga stood off to the side, a respectful look on his face, but he said nothing. Elmo reached down and carefully pulled the warrior's cloak over his face. Shirral cried quietly.

What the hells do we do, now? Shanhaevel wondered, feeling the all-too-familiar and fresh ache in his chest. It's Lanithaine all over again. Only this time, everyone feels it. Is this all there is? Pain and death? If that's all we have to look forward to on this expedition, then I should just go home. There's no more reason to stay, anyway.

Except there was, the elf realized. There was Shirral. He sighed, unsure if he wanted to leave, and that surprised him more than anything. I didn't think I would hear myself saying that, he reflected. But there it was. The thought of leaving Shirral made the pit of his stomach roil. Still, the thought of telling her how he felt made it roil even more.

Instead of trying, the wizard laid a soft hand on Shirral's shoulder and squeezed gently. "You did what you could," he said softly. "Without your other magic, your blade of flame, we would have *all* died at their hands."

Shirral nodded but did not look up. "Jaroo has tried to get me to study more," she said at last, "to work on tuning my energy so I can cast more powerful spells. I never wanted to take the time, though." She sniffed and turned to look at Shanhaevel. "If I had, I would have had something to aid him." Her eyes did not sparkle now. They were clouded and red-rimmed with sadness.

He could only nod and say, "I wanted something last night, too—on the road, when Lanithaine died . . . something, anything, to keep him alive. I didn't have it. Sooner or later, we all discover that power isn't enough. Lanithaine often told me that power is not what defines us. It's what you do with what you have that makes you who you are. Right now, everyone else needs your skills. You still have the ability to help them. You need someone to tend to your wound." He gestured to the druid's blood-soaked shoulder.

Shirral looked at him for a moment, then nodded and replied, "I don't ever want to feel this . . . inadequate again." With that, she stood. Before she moved to aid the wounded, she looked back over her shoulder at him and said, "I led us here. I was the one who said we couldn't let Zert die. Melias wanted to be cautious, and I wouldn't let him. It's my fault."

Shanhaevel started to shake his head, to tell her that it was his fault, not hers, that if he had realized Zert's lie in time they would never have been ambushed, but she had already turned away again, and the words died in his throat. Sighing, he stood up and looked around, seeing what he could do to help.

Ahleage and Draga went from body to body, making sure there were no survivors. Shanhaevel realized the three gnolls he had subjected to his magical sleep were gone. They must have awakened and slipped away during the fight. Or they could be hiding somewhere, waiting until our guard is down. He told this to the others, cautioning them all to be careful.

Shirral administered to Elmo's injury, first. The huge man took a deep breath, then yanked the bolt free, grimacing from obvious pain. Muttering under her breath, Shirral laid her hands softly upon the puncture wound, and a soft glow emanated from the spot. A moment later, Elmo was up and testing his leg, walking back and forth with noticeably less of a limp. The huge man smiled at Shirral, but she was swooning, and he had to catch her.

"You've lost a lot of blood," Elmo said, lowering her to the floor as Shanhaevel rushed to her side, his heart pounding.

Not her, too! he thought in a panic as knelt down next to her.

"Shanhaevel, look in Melias's pack," Elmo ordered. "He had magical healing elixirs in there somewhere."

Shanhaevel moved quickly to the dead soldier and removed the man's backpack. Hurrying back to Shirral's side, he rooted through the gear, pausing for only a moment to peer at a finely worked scroll case before shoving it aside and continuing to dig until he found a small stopped bottle. Holding it up, he asked Elmo, "This?" to which the huge axeman nodded.

"Shirral, you have to drink this," Shanhaevel said, holding the bottle to the druid's lips. It smelled of cinnamon and ash, he noted as he carefully poured it into her mouth. As she sipped it, a soft, blue glow rose from Shirral, concentrating on her wounded shoulder. A few moments later, she was sitting up.

"Don't scare me like that," Shanhaevel told her. She looked at him quizzically but assured the wizard she was all right.

When Ahleage and Draga confirmed that there were no enemies still alive, Elmo moved over to Turuko's body and ripped the dagger from the monk's chest.

"We should pitch these"—he gestured at the dead

bandits—"into the marsh. Let the swamp eat them. And we must take Melias back to Hommlet. He deserves a hero's funeral. But first, we have to find out what we can about this Lareth."

"Fine with me," Ahleage said. He dropped down beside one of the bandit's corpses and began to search through the man's clothing. "First things, first. They won't be needing any of this stuff, anymore," he said, pulling a small pouch of coins free, "and it's small payment for what they cost us."

"I'll watch the entrance," Draga said, moving down the passageway out, "to make sure no one else sneaks up on us."

Shanhaevel stared at Elmo's back, somehow not surprised by the big man's sudden take-charge attitude. *I knew there was more to him than he's been letting on,* the elf thought as he followed him into the priest's lair.

Beyond the door was a lavishly decorated room filled with thick rugs, wall hangings, soft chairs, and a couch overflowing with overstuffed cushions. A brazier warmed the dimly lit room and gave off the odor of incense. As Elmo took more careful stock of the place, he and Shanhaevel discovered delicacies, fine wines, and an assortment of fine serving pieces, including a set of silver goblets that were exquisitely wrought. In a cabinet along one wall was an alabaster box filled with rare and valuable unguents, as well as an assortment of loose gems and jewelry.

By far the most important discovery was a small writing desk that also served as a shrine. Shanhaevel blanched upon seeing it, shuddering.

"Boccob!" he muttered. "That's a shrine to Lolth."

"I know," Elmo said. "We destroy that when we're through in here."

Shanhaevel spun to face the huge axeman. "How exactly

do you know that? You are far more than a drunken farmer's son. Admit it."

Elmo didn't look up from the sheaf of parchment he was beginning to go through. "Yes, far more, but it's not a tale for right now. Later, I will explain to you. Look at this," he said, changing the subject as he held up some of the papers. "Whatever we stumbled on to here today, it's much bigger than just these troops."

Shanhaevel stared at the big man for a moment longer, shaking his head in amazement, then turned his attention to what Elmo was trying to show him.

The papers held clues about Lareth's recent activities in the area. The records and letters were written by someone named Hedrack, obviously Lareth's superior, and they detailed plans for raiding caravan routes in the region. There was also mention of recruitment techniques, payment instructions for military troops, delivery schedules of various goods—armor, weapons, foodstuffs, and even slaves—and a long-term plan for the eventual destruction of Hommlet through the use of "elemental forces most powerful." Unfortunately, locations were left vague, as though this Hedrack did not want anyone to trace them back to him. It was clear nonetheless that Lareth served a very secretive and powerful organization that was somewhere close by.

"The temple," Shanhaevel surmised, sucking in his breath. "I'll wager my right arm that's where this Hedrack is."

"I think you're right," Elmo replied, nodding, "and I bet that's where Lareth went. Let's tell the others."

* * * * *

The companions deposited the bodies of the bandits in the swamp, wrapping the corpses in their bedrolls and weighing them down with rubble from the ruins so they would sink below the surface. Someone had wrapped Melias's body in his cloak, as well, and he now lay stretched out near the entrance to the tunnel, waiting to be hauled out to the horses.

"Let's go home," Shirral said when they were done, suddenly looking sad again. "It's getting late."

Elmo nodded in agreement and stood. "I'll get Melias."

Carefully, the huge man hoisted the body of their leader up into his arms and headed out into the afternoon. Ahleage and Draga followed him, carrying a small chest with the valuables they had recovered from the place.

Shanhaevel was alone with Shirral. The elf looked over at the druid, who was biting her lip thoughtfully.

"Shirral," Shanhaevel began, "what happened today . . . that wasn't your fault. The lie Zert told us was right in front of us—in front of me—and we still fell for it—all of us. Stop blaming yourself."

"At least you suspected. I was just a trusting fool. I talked him into going in there. I insisted on it, rode off with the man before Melias could argue with me. I was so damned sure I was right, and it cost Melias his life. I practically killed him myself."

"No!" Shanhaevel shouted. He took the druid by the shoulders and made her look him squarely in the eye. "Shut up! You did no such thing."

Shirral was crying now, big tears streaming down her face, but she said nothing, just bit her lip and looked away.

"We were doing what we thought was right," the elf continued. "The people who know you, who care about you"—he emphasized these last words—"know better. So should you."

Shirral looked at the wizard again, now, her blue eyes flashing as she deciphered the meaning of his words. "Care about me?"

Shanhaevel nodded, suddenly nervous. He covered it by saying, "Do you think Jaroo would blame you for what happened?" Would Lenithaine blame me?

She cocked her head to one side, as though realizing he was avoiding saying what he was really thinking. Yes, I care about you, the voice in his head said.

"I don't know," she said, and it was almost a whisper. "But he isn't the one who just died because of my foolishness. You should stop thinking about me that way and go home."

With that, she turned to leave. Shanhaevel let out the breath he had been holding.

"Wait!" he said, following her. They walked together out into the daylight. "Why? Are you saying there's no reason for me to stay? None at all?"

Shirral looked at him again as they reached the road. "I'm saying that I won't *let* there be one, not like this. Melias's death hurts enough. I couldn't bear watching someone I cared about die. I have my work with Jaroo. That's all there can be for me. It's safer that way."

As she finished, the druid sped up, moving up the road and leaving Shanhaevel behind. The elf watched her walk away from him, feeling a dull pain in his chest, then slowly turned and followed her.

Back at the top of the rise, where the group had left their horses, Elmo was tying Melias's body across the warrior's saddle. Ahleage and Draga were securing the chest of goods to the packhorse, the spare that had been Lanithaine's. Shirral was inspecting her mount, tightening a cinch here and there and shortening the stirrups more to her liking.

At that moment, the sound of a whinnying horse floated across the bog, and as one, the group turned, weapons drawn.

A powerfully built man approached along the path from Hommlet. He was wearing plate armor and sitting astride a horse so large and muscular that it was obvious it had been bred for war. The man had a shield slung over his back and a very fine looking sword belted to his hip. He looked road-weary and somewhat lost. He slowed the horse when he realized the group had spotted him. Slipping his riding gloves from his hands, he reached up and removed his open-faced helmet and scanned the group. He was clean-shaven and had short, curly black hair.

The stranger clicked his tongue, and his steed moved forward, right up to where Elmo stood, axe in hand.

"By Cuthbert, it's true," the stranger muttered, half to himself. His eyes were wide, and they flicked back forth among the companions, studying each in turn. "I will not doubt again, m'lord," he added, still staring.

"Pardon?" Elmo said, staring back, a cautious, concerned look on his mien.

"Can we help you?" Shirral asked.

"I don't know," the man replied. "I hope so. I was sent to find you."

"Find us?" Ahleage said, half smirking. "By whom?"

"By Saint Cuthbert, my god and guiding hand."

"What?" Ahleage blurted, nearly choking. "Why would a god send you to find us?"

"I don't know," the stranger replied, smiling warmly. "I know it sounds bizarre, but he came to me in a dream, showed me your faces, and sent me here to find you."

"Find us?" Elmo repeated, still holding his axe.

"Yes. I have seen each of you. A wizard with a silver mane, a rogue with a sharp tongue, a big man with an axe, a hairy fellow with a bow and a song in his heart, and a woman, a druid. He said I would need you, and you, me.

There is work to be done, and I had to find you so that we can do it together."

"That sounds really noble," Ahleage said, looking at the rest of his companions out of the corner of his eye, "but as you can see, our work came to an abrupt end"—Ahleage nodded at Melias's body—"and we're going in different directions. Did your god tell you that?"

The man frowned. "Saint Cuthbert made it plain that there would be difficulties along this path, but I know his will is for me to bring us all together, so I hope you will reconsider. You *must* reconsider."

Shanhaevel glanced at the others in turn, and when he caught Ahleage's eye, the young man brought his hand to one side of his face to hide it from the stranger, then made a crazed look back at the elf. Shanhaevel had to keep from cracking a grin, but then he shrugged. Maybe this gets me more time with Shirral, he thought.

"You seem sincere," the druid said, "but we have no idea if you're telling the truth or not. Regardless, we don't even know your name."

The man started then shook his head in embarrassment. "By Cuthbert, I'm sorry! I am Sir Govin Dahna, knight of Saint Cuthbert. You can call me Govin. If there is a man of the church back in that town, I will go before him and allow him to conduct his test of truth on me to prove to you I am what and who I say I am."

"All right, then, Govin," Shanhaevel said, pointing from person to person. "That's Elmo, over there's Draga, there's Shirral, that's Ahleage, and I'm Shanhaevel—not Shadowspawn," the elf said, throwing a look toward Ahleage. "The unlucky soul on the back of the horse was Melias."

"Yes, that is one of your names, Shanhaevel. You go by another, however. *Faldurios su wel elmirel dwa sulis min anweilios su Shantirel Galaerivel, magiost.*"

Shanhaevel's eyes widened as he stared at the man before him. Govin had used the elf's own tongue—*Some who know you well name you Shantirel Galaerivel, mage.*

Shirral was staring open-mouthed at first the knight, then at Shanhaevel.

"Kilieria su delmeir, Kahvlirae," Shanhaevel finally replied, bowing slightly. *You speak the truth, noble knight.* "Your dreams seem to tell you much about us."

Ahleage shook his head, exasperated. "What in the nine hells did he just say to you?"

"He told me some things that only the people of the Welkwood should know, and he named me as a wizard."

Despite the discomfiture of this man knowing so much about him, Shanhaevel was beginning to warm to the knight. It was strange. He somehow felt . . . right—yes that was it, *right*—with Govin here. That's as odd a thing as you have ever thought, Shantirel Galaerivel.

Sir Govin bowed his head. "Forgive me. I did not mean to put you on guard. I only wish to prove that I am legitimate. This is a lot to accept, I realize. Perhaps I should withdraw and let you discuss things for a bit in private."

"I don't think that's necessary," Elmo said. He had that look on his face that had convinced Shanhaevel there was more to him than his story told. "You must be tired after riding here all the way from . . ."

"From Dyvers. I rode here from Dyvers."

"Yes, a long journey, indeed. Our unfortunate companion, here, Melias, needs a proper burial. We were hoping to get him back to Hommlet, but the day grows late. We should make camp and discuss this further. You are welcome to join us."

"I accept your invitation," the knight said with a small, appreciative bow.

It was nightfall by the time the group set up camp. They pitched their meager shelters and built a small fire in a secluded spot a fair distance away from the moathouse, on some high ground that was dryer than the surrounding marsh.

Everyone had gathered around the fire, and was consuming a fine stew of rabbit meat. Shanhaevel had just finished telling Sir Govin the tale of their exploration of the moathouse and of Melias's death. By mutual agreement with Elmo during a private conversation earlier, he left out many of the significant details of Lareth and the things they had found in his chambers. There was an expectant silence now, as everyone watched the knight while he ate, waiting for him to respond in some manner to the story.

Govin was wolfing down spoonfuls of stew, seemingly unconcerned that everyone was studying him. Finally, he sopped the last drops of broth up with bread and set the bowl aside. He leaned back against a tree and steepled his fingers.

Shanhaevel stole a glance in Shirral's direction. She had said little to him since their conversation before. Now, she had her head bowed slightly and was absently biting her lower lip, staring at nothing.

"I see now why I was sent here," Govin began. "Your task is not yet completed, yet your perseverance has faded away." He leaned forward again, warming to his speech. "This Melias—may his spirit rest—was the guiding hand. He brought you together, and he had the drive to see this through. Now that he is gone I have been sent, not by a mere lord, by no king or viscount, but by a power far stronger and more enduring."

Ahleage coughed at this point, and when Shanhaevel looked over, he could see derision written on the man's face.

"Perhaps," Ahleage said, "but I don't follow your god, so what's he want with me? I don't know that strange dreams really provide a good enough reason for me—probably not for my friend Draga here, either."

Draga merely shrugged and went back to whittling on a piece of branch.

"Of course not," Govin replied. "Not everyone hears or recognizes the call of Cuthbert. You need your own reasons for choosing your way. I can't give you what you want out of this, but I believe it will come to you, nonetheless. Success lies down this path, should we choose to follow it."

"Sir Govin," Shanhaevel said, folding his fingers together and leaning forward, "if everything you say is true, it would seem that something fairly profound will come of it. Why do you think Cuthbert wants *you* to lead us?"

It was a leading question, Shanhaevel knew, but he wanted to see just how much the knight might know about what was going on.

"I did not come here to lead you. That is not my place. You are already companions, having learned to rely on one another before my arrival. It is plain to me that I can only ask to join you, not presume to lead you.

"To answer your question, though, I cannot say in certain terms what will come of this, but I believe I have part of the answer. It is a poem, something else that came to me in a dream, though I do not know what it means, yet. Here it is."

The Two united, in the past,
A Place to build, and spells to cast.
Their power grew and took the land,
And people round, as they had planned.

A key without a lock they made
Of gold and gems and overlaid
With spells, a tool for men to wield
To force the powers of Good to yield.

But armies came, their weapons bared,
While evil was yet unprepared.
The Hart was followed by the Crowns
And Moon, and people of the towns.

The Two were split; one got away
But She, when came the judgment day,
Did break the key and sent the rocks
To boxes four, with magic locks.

In doing so, she fell behind
As he escaped. She was confined
Among her own; her very lair
Became her prison and despair.

The Place was ruined, torn apart
And left with chains around the heart
Of evil power—but the key
Was never found in the debris.

He knows not where she dwells today.
She set the minions' path, the way
To lift her Temple high again
With tools of flesh, with mortal men.

Many now have gone to die
In water, flame, in earth, or sky.
They did not bear the key of old
That must be found—the orb of gold.

Beware my friend, for you shall fall
Unless you have the wherewithal
To find and search the boxes four
And then escape for evermore.

But with the key, you might succeed
In throwing down Her power and greed.
Destroy the key when you are done
And then rejoice, the battle won.

When the knight had finished, Shanhaevel was certain his face was pale. He looked from companion to companion, realizing they all looked shaken.

"Melias begged us to find the key before he died," the elf said quietly. "None of us knew what he meant."

"So what?" Ahleage argued. "He could have been talking about anything—and that poem could mean anything! There's nothing to prove that they are the same."

Shanhaevel nodded, and then he remembered something. "Well, there might be one way to find out," he said, rising to his feet.

He moved over to the pile of gear, going through it until he found Melias's pack. Returning to his seat, he opened the pack and looked for the scroll case.

"Do you think that's such a good idea?" Shirral asked doubtfully. "He was an agent of the king. You might be breaking some law or other."

Shanhaevel looked at her then shrugged.

"It may be that those are his orders from the viscount or the king," Elmo said, motioning for Shanhaevel to open the scroll case, "and if there's something useful in there, we must find it. I think, under the circumstances, any transgression would be overlooked."

Shanhaevel eyed Elmo for a moment, wondering just how the big man might have come to that conclusion, then shrugged and twisted the seal from the scroll case. The roll of parchment inside was crinkled and weathered. Everyone gathered around as he stared at the words written on the scroll in a careful, neat hand. They were, word for word, the poem the knight had just quoted.

"I don't think there's any doubt, now," Shanhaevel said in a breathless whisper.

Ahleage's eyes were wide as he shook his head, agreeing with the elf's assessment.

"But what does it mean?" Shirral asked Govin.

The knight shrugged. "I don't know, but I am willing to accept Cuthbert's wisdom in bringing us together. I have faith that whatever it is we are to accomplish, it will be revealed to us when the time is right."

Shirral continued to chew her lip while Elmo frowned.

"I think the time *is* right," the huge man said. "It's time for a few explanations." Elmo rose from the ground where he had been seated as he spoke to the group. "You see, I am not merely an ale-swilling simpleton, although I have done little to maintain that guise in recent hours, so I suppose most of you already realized that. It is an image I have cultivated for many a year, now, and it has been very useful for throwing off suspicion."

Shanhaevel leaned forward, eager to hear what this huge man, whose mien was suddenly contemplative and intelligent, was going to say next.

"You see," Elmo continued, looking at his hands, "I, too, work for the viscount." There were a few gasps from the group. "I am a Knight of the Hart—a hunter, a tracker. It has been my responsibility to keep an eye on the activities around the area—the comings and goings of merchants, strangers, what have you. Few have passed through Hommlet without my knowing."

Shanhaevel found himself shaking his head in amazement, and he saw that everyone else around the fire shared his sentiment.

"I knew there was something up!" the elf said, grinning wryly. "When Ormiel told me you were speaking to him, I was confused. Every once in a while, you said or did something that seemed so out of character for the—pardon the expression—simple bumpkin farmer you seemed to be."

Elmo smiled and nodded. "Yes. You are extremely astute, 'whelp born of the shadow wood,' more so than most people I meet. There was a time or two that I slipped up, but most of the time, I was watching for your reaction. I wanted to know if I could trust you, each of you. I learned today that I can, and that's going to be a very important part of our relationship if we're going to see this through."

"How is it that you know my true name?" the wizard asked, not really surprised.

"I told you: It's my job to know as much as I can about everyone who comes and goes." Elmo smiled again as Shanhaevel nodded in acquiescence at the explanation. "In this case, though, there are two reasons. First: Ormiel told me. Regardless of what practical jokes your friend here likes to play—"

"I still like his nickname better," Ahleage replied, grinning but not looking up from the dagger he was studiously examining.

"And the second one reason is: *Estrumiel de sudri oltrinos*—'I, too, speak your tongue.' " Shanhaevel blinked in surprise, as did Shirral, but Govin only smiled. "In any event," Elmo went on, "Govin is right. We've only scratched the surface of this problem. I've known about it for a while, but I couldn't risk revealing myself until I was sure we could do something about it."

Elmo gazed into the fire for several moments. His brow wrinkled, and his visage turned grim. He seemed to be gathering his courage.

"The Temple of the Elements is flourishing once again," Elmo continued. "I have sources in Nulb, the next village to the east and the community closest to the sight of the place, that confirm this. I intend to stop it."

Elmo looked at each of the companions.

Shanhaevel sat quietly, reflecting. Is this why I'm here? he thought. It was one thing when we were just looking for a bandit lair, but now . . .

Still, the elf realized, there was that warm glow he was feeling, thinking about this. These people are my friends, he reminded himself. I trust them, and they me. And Shirral. Shanhaevel looked across at the druid, who was biting her lip, a worried look on her face. This is her home, he thought. She needs my help, too.

"I'm with you," Shanhaevel said. He had already made up his mind that he would stay and be a part of this, regardless of what Shirral did. "Well?" he asked her.

The druid gazed back at the wizard steadily, her blue eyes reflecting the flickering firelight as she studied him. Finally, she grimaced and shook her head, but she said, "All right."

Shanhaevel smiled despite himself.

"Well, I'm not," Ahleage growled, throwing a rock off into the trees. "This is as far as I go. Tomorrow, I ride for greener pastures. Draga, are you coming with me?"

The hairy bowman looked up from the object he was carving, which Shanhaevel now saw was a some sort of a flute or similar instrument, and frowned. "If we leave them, and they fail, who else will do this?"

"Who cares? It's not *our* problem!"

"Sooner or later, it will be," Shirral said. "If the temple grows and becomes too powerful to stop, there will be no greener pastures left."

"I know you don't follow my god," Govin said. "I cannot ask you to go on faith. But I can foresee this deed being a great boon to you."

Ahleage scowled, looking at all of them, then sighed and slumped in resignation. "Oh, what the hells. I'll stay and help." He glared at Draga. "Since when did you get all noble?"

Draga only smiled sheepishly and said nothing, whittling again with his knife.

"Excellent," Elmo said. "We ride to the temple at first light."

"Then it's official," Shanhaevel said. "We are an alliance."

"No," Govin said, smiling. "We are *the* Alliance. It is the name that came to me in my visions: The Alliance."

* * * * *

The fire had burned low at the campsite. The night air was cool and filled with the sounds of sleeping. Only Shanhaevel, Ahleage, and Draga were awake, keeping watch. The bowman sat a little off to the side, working on his flute, occasionally playing it softly, testing it before continuing to work on it.

"Mmm," Shanhaevel said, draining his mug as he looked up at the stars. "So, what's your story, Ahleage?" he asked quietly. "How did you get hooked up with Melias?"

Ahleage twisted his mouth around in a pensive frown. "Well," he said, playing with one of his ever-present daggers, "Let's just say I was getting tired of the street life in Verbobonc. Melias and I bumped into one another one night, and he offered me a job. It was a nice change of pace, so I accepted."

Shanhaevel chuckled. "You tried to steal something, he caught you, and then he gave you a chance to avoid going to the viscount's dungeons if you would come with him."

Ahleage grinned. "Well, not exactly, but close enough. My welcome was worn out back there, that's for sure."

Shanhaevel nodded. "What about Draga?" he asked, gesturing at the man sitting next to him. "Where's he from?"

"I don't know," Ahleage answered, shrugging. "He doesn't say much, but he's good for a laugh or two, and he's a damn fine shot with that bow," he finished loudly enough that Draga heard.

The bowman looked up and smiled, then played a little melody on his flute. It was not in tune, but Shanhaevel could tell it was getting better as Draga continued to work on it.

"Yes, he is," the elf replied, grinning.

Ahleage looked directly at the elf. "What about you? Why are you here? And what in the nine hells did Elmo mean when he called you 'whelp of the shadow wood?' "

Shanhaevel sat back, thinking. "When Burne called upon Lanithaine to aid him, it seemed to go without saying that would I come, too. When Lanithaine died"—the wizard swallowed hard, thinking of the incident; it seemed so much longer ago than a few short nights—"he bade me to come without him."

"So Burne wanted someone to come poke around the ruins of an old fort, and you just said, 'Sure?' " Ahleage looked skeptical.

"Well, I didn't know exactly what the favor would be when I agreed, but essentially, yes. It's something I had to do for Lanithaine's sake. And it's what my full name actually means."

"What?"

The elf looked at him. "My full name is Shantirel Galaerivel—'Whelp born of the Shadow Wood' is the truest translation, although I prefer 'child' to 'whelp.' 'Shanhaevel' is the short form, and it means 'shadowchild.' "

"Shadowchild?" Ahleage said, looking at Shanhaevel. "Why would your parents name you that?"

Shanhaevel smiled as Ahleage reached to refill his mug from the wineskin the two of them were sharing. "Actually, I was orphaned. A woodsman found me crying one day while he was hunting. He didn't like children very much, and it was in a deep, dark part of the Welkwood, so he gave me this unpleasant name in Elvish. He was from a community of humans and elves who managed to live together peacefully, which is how he knew the Elvish language."

"So you don't know who your parents were? They were never found?"

Shanhaevel shook his head. "They lived a little ways away from that community. They were slain by ettercaps, the spider people who live in the darkest part of the woods. No one is really sure how I managed to survive. Anyway," he continued, "my aunt Soli—she's not really my aunt, but I think of her that way—she's an elder on the council where I grew up. Aunt Solianturel made them shorten it to Shanhaevel. Shadowchild."

"So that's why you call yourself Shanhaevel," Ahleage said. "I like Shadowspawn better. Really, that's kind of what your name means."

Shanhaevel just shook his head in resignation. "Whatever makes you happy."

Shanhaevel turned to look up at the night sky. He stole a glance at Shirral, sleeping on the far side of the remains of the fire, wrapped in her thick cloak.

"She likes you more than she's admitting, you know," Ahleage said. "You're giving up too easily."

Shanhaevel nearly choked on his wine. "What? What are you talking about?"

"I'm not stupid, and neither is anyone else. We all know how you feel about her. Believe me, I can see it in your eyes when you look at her, and it's in her eyes, too. She's just stubborn, that's all."

Shanhaevel cocked his head to one side, studying Ahleage and mulling over the man's words. "She made it clear I should leave."

Ahleage snorted in derision. "That's what she *said.* That's not what she was thinking."

Shanhaevel shook his head, but he realized he was suddenly thinking about the possibilities again.

Hedrack's footfalls were soft against the flagstones, echoing in the near silence of the great temple chamber as the high priest of Iuz hurried toward the private chapel behind the writhing violet curtain. Once beyond the dais and in the room with three altars, Hedrack dropped to his knees and, taking a deep breath, began to pray, frowning slightly as he struggled to find the right words. It was not long before the priest felt his deity's presence in his mind.

"My lord Iuz," Hedrack said, the words tumbling forth. "I am your Mouth. I pronounce your wishes to the world you will tread beneath your feet."

I sense your unease, servant. The gravelly voice inside the priest's head grated down his spine.

Hedrack knew better than to hide this information from his master. "Yes, my lord. I bear unpleasant news. We have lost the moathouse. Lareth did manage to flee and is safe with me, but certain things were left behind that could prove troublesome."

There was no answer, but Hedrack nonetheless felt the waves of malevolent displeasure washing through him as Iuz seethed. Despite himself, the priest shuddered, a small part of him fearing that the god's annoyance would spill over to him.

How? Iuz finally asked, his voice more grating than ever. *How did this happen?*

"Lareth reported that a band of interlopers wielding substantial magic invaded the place. I'm still trying to find out the particulars." Hedrack's thoughts strayed to the handsome priest, bound in chains in one of his recreation rooms, awaiting his return for more questions. "I will know more soon."

It is his *doing,* the god said. *I warned you that he had sent meddlers to interfere. You must not take them lightly. For them to defeat one of our best commanders . . ."*

"I understand, my lord," Hedrack responded. He knew the group of adventurers that had managed to bring Lareth's forces down would follow the trail to Nulb, looking for more information on the temple. Hedrack's instructions had been clear: Destroy them when they arrived and bring their bodies to him.

What other news? Iuz asked, interrupting Hedrack's thoughts.

"Ah, good news, my lord. We have begun to bring forth creatures from the planes. I have witnessed three, and Falrinth and my other staff have moved several more from the planes to the nodes. Our army is growing, my lord."

Excellent, Iuz beamed. *What of my beloved? Have you located her yet?*

"Efforts proceed apace, my master. She remains only marginally aware, and communicating with her is arduous. She does not seem to know where she is, and thus far Falrinth's scrying efforts have revealed little. However, we have found the key she mentioned—a golden skull, although it does not appear to be intact. There are four sockets that seem to have been designed to hold something . . . gems perhaps. Once Falrinth determines its workings, we will use it to free her."

Of course! Iuz effused, waves of pleasure radiating over Hedrack from the god. *She was always clever. The sockets are, indeed, designed for gems, one representing each element. This is an item of power that she and I constructed before to aid in ruling the temple. She must have attuned it to herself, somehow. Find the gems, place them in their sockets, and you find her.*

"Excellent, my lord. I will notify Falrinth at once."

You must find her! Iuz said, the insistence washing over Hedrack like a wave of cold black water. *That is your main charge in my service. Discover her prison and bring her forth.*

Hedrack bowed lower, touching his head to the floor before him. "I hear and obey, my master."

With that, Iuz was gone, leaving the priest alone in the chapel, reflecting on his thoughts.

How much longer can I delay in unearthing her? he wondered.

Hedrack shook his head, dismissing the thought. He knew he would obey his god's commands in due time. Indeed, it was the timing that was important here. Too soon, and he would lose control of the feuding factions on the levels above. Too late, and he would risk his master's ire.

In the meantime, he had other matters to attend to, including dealing with this band of would-be heroes who had stuck their noses into something they shouldn't have. Thinking of these cretins as he returned to his chambers, as well as having been forced to report unpleasant news to his master, had put the priest in a foul mood. When he arrived, Deus and Ahma snapped to attention and saluted him. He dismissed the ettin and unlocked his chamber door.

Stepping inside, Hedrack surveyed the room. Mika was busy straightening the place, while Astelle was stretched out upon the bed, chin in hands, a petulant pout upon her face. She had been acting this way ever since Hedrack had brought the new girl in.

Sitting in the corner, the young woman stared at Hedrack with fearful eyes, her hands and ankles bound tightly. Her dress was torn and dirty, a result of her capture by Lareth's men the night of the field commander's last, fateful raid on Hommlet. Her dark hair was matted about her sweaty face. Hedrack smiled at her, which caused the terrified girl to shrink back further into the corner.

There was a knock upon his door. Hedrack turned back and unlocked it, swinging it open to admit Barkinar, the commander of the temple troops and Hedrack's second-in-command.

"We have a new batch of sacrifices," Barkinar began, peering at Mika as she hurried to fetch a cold drink for the visitor. "I thought you would want to witness their delivery to the nodes."

Hedrack sighed, thinking how much there was to do and how he wished at this moment to be left alone to brood. To brood and to spend time with his new plaything. He turned to look back at the young woman tied in the corner, then at Astelle, who was still flopped on the bed, not lifting a hand to aid Mika in making Barkinar comfortable. Perhaps, he thought, I could use a bit of spectacle.

"Yes," he said to Barkinar, "I would like that very much. I will be along shortly."

Barkinar nodded and took his leave.

Hedrack shut the door behind the man and turned to look at the girl in the corner. He strode across the room and squatted down in front of her, reveling in her terrified squirms to pull away from him. Smiling, he pulled a knife from his boot and sliced the bonds from the girl's wrists and ankles. As she cowered, he waved his hands in front of her and spoke a few words of prayer. As the girl's visage changed from fear to eagerness, the priest said, "Now, young thing, what is your name?"

"P-Paida," the girl replied, beaming that he had deigned to speak to her.

"Be a good girl, then, Paida, and go to Mika. She will help you learn what is expected of you."

Paida smiled and leaped to her feet, running to the other girl.

Hedrack turned to Astelle, who was still pouting.

"You," he said, grabbing her by the wrist and lifting her to her feet. "You and I are going to take a walk."

Astelle's face brightened as she fell into step beside her master. Hedrack led her out the door, locking it behind him. As the pair of them headed toward the staging area of the nodes, Hedrack smiled, thinking that Astelle would make a fine sacrifice to one of his precious elemental creatures.

During the night, Shanhaevel had a dream. Burne came to him, the wizard's face hovering insubstantially in front of the elf's field of vision.

"Shanhaevel, you must remember this when you awaken. I can only assume that something terrible has befallen Melias, for I cannot reach his mind. If Elmo still lives, he will be able to explain further. It is time you and the others knew the full truth. The forces of the temple are on the rise again, and you must stop them from releasing a terrible evil, an evil we could not destroy ten years ago. I am sorry we kept this from you before. Melias and I felt it best not to reveal this until the time was right, but now, there can be no more delay.

"You must find a golden key and return it to me. I will have determined the means to destroy it by then. The key is in the form of a skull, missing its lower jaw. It contains four gems, one for each of the elements, set into the crown line at the compass points. You must infiltrate the temple ruins, discover the whereabouts of this key, and return it to me. Whatever happens, get the key. Many lives depend on your success."

Burne's face faded from view, and Shanhaevel's dreams were troubled by looming golden skulls and demonic faces. When he awoke, the pink of dawn was just brightening on the horizon. Shivering, he sat up, remembering Burne's dream message with perfect clarity. When the rest of the Alliance had awakened, the elf shared the message with them.

Elmo nodded when Shanhaevel finished. "This skull is known to me, at least somewhat. It was created during the initial rise of the temple, as an object of power. It must be the orb of gold mentioned in the poem. So we must do this. We must find this key, before it's too late."

"What does 'too late' mean?" Ahleage asked, worry on his face.

" 'Too late' is when the temple leaders find this key and use it to release the demon."

"What?" Ahleage choked. "No one said anything to me about demons last night! This is way over my head."

"She was sealed there when the temple was defeated," Elmo explained. "Burne, Lanithiane, and others rode with the prince to combat her at the Battle of Emridy Meadows. Their losses were heavy, and when the time came to destroy her, they were too weakened. Instead, they sealed her deep within her own lair, trapping her and making it impossible for anyone to reach her again. Except that she must have seen it coming, and somehow she attuned this object, this key, so it became the means to free her. She knew it would be only a matter of time before someone found it and unlocked the seals on her prison."

"Boccob," Shanhaevel breathed. "Melias knew this the whole time. He and Burne. And Lanithaine. Why didn't they just tell us?"

"They felt that you would never agree to do this if you knew the full extent of the problem. I disagreed with their reasons, but it wasn't my expedition, so I acquiesced."

Despite Elmo's eagerness to be underway, the group had to bury Melias. They knew they had no time to return to Hommlet for a proper ceremony, so they chose a quiet spot near their camp. Govin spoke a few words in honor of the man he had never met. The grave was flanked by two large maple trees that were just beginning to leaf out, their buds blazing crimson in the morning sun. It was a fine marker, Shanhaevel decided as they mounted up and set out toward Nulb.

Nulb was a dirty, seedy, dangerous place, and since they wanted to attract as little attention as possible, the Alliance left the road and went around the town to avoid the place entirely. Instead they headed directly for the temple, hoping to find a safe and hidden spot close to the ruined structure in which to rest for the night. With most of the day gone, the sky had grown overcast, and Shanhaevel could smell the threat of rain as they rode.

Shanhaevel looked over at Shirral. She had been pensive and quiet the whole day, despite several efforts on the wizard's part to engage her in conversation. He had not yet found a good way to open up to her, to find out if Ahleage's comments from the previous evening would hold true. He shook his head and turned his attention back to the small track along which Elmo was leading them.

The route to the temple was little more than a rutted trail. The dense forest pressed in on either side, but it was obvious that some amount of traffic had been using it recently, which set the entire group on edge. Shanhaevel found himself shuddering on more than one occasion, his skin crawling from the sensation of being watched. Pulling his hood up as it began to drizzle, he hunched down as if he were shying away from prying eyes.

After about an hour of riding through the waning cloud-filtered light of the late afternoon, they reached the edge of the tree line and saw it. Dismounting and leaving their horses in a small copse of trees near the road, the group stealthily approached the ruined temple on foot, leery of guards. There seemed to be none.

The vegetation surrounding the place was sickly and warped, with a profusion of nettles, briars, and burrs. Many of the trees were dead and skeletal, and the scrub growth at their bases was stunted and unnaturally colored, yellowish with disease. Here and there among the weeds gleamed the bleached white remains of countless dead, skulls half-buried in the soil and other bones scattered among the brown grass.

Surrounding the main structure were piles of gray rubble with the occasional intact section of wall. At the northeast corner of these outer walls stood the stump of a tower. There seemed to be no signs of life there other than a handful of ravens perching atop the structure.

The main building itself was intact, an impressive bastion of arched buttresses and hideous leering faces carved into the stone. Disgusting creepers and vines clung to the entire thing, as though clawing at the building in an attempt to get to the rich source of malevolence inside.

Shanhaevel shivered. The light, already diffused in the overcast sky, somehow seemed even weaker and more ineffectual here. More than once, he saw a darting movement out of the corner of his eye, but when he turned his gaze in that direction, all he spotted was a shadow or a blackish bush, moving slightly in the breeze.

"By Cuthbert, this place exudes evil," Govin said. "My mouth is sour with the taste of it."

"Yeah," agreed Ahleage, "and I keep seeing things that aren't there."

"Come on," Govin said, loosening his sword in its scabbard. "Let's have a look around."

"Wait," Shanhaevel said. "Why aren't there any guards?"

"I've asked myself that question about a dozen times, now," Ahleage added.

"My suspicion," Govin responded, "is that the residual evil of the place is enough to discourage most would-be explorers, and there's a certain logic to giving the appearance of being abandoned, rather than swarming with guards."

"Well, even if we can't see guards, that doesn't mean there aren't some hiding somewhere," Shanhaevel warned. "Let's get a little unobtrusive reconnaissance, first. I'll call Ormiel to fly overhead and see what he can see."

"Good idea," nodded Shirral, her eyes wide. "Let's make absolutely sure before we go in."

Reaching out with his mind, Shanhaevel called to his hawk, summoning the bird. Ormiel swooped past and circled the ruined temple, but he peeled abruptly to the side and retreated to a nearby tree.

Ormiel, spy for me, Shanhaevel told him. *Fly and look.*

No, the hawk answered. *Bad place.*

"He won't go near the place," the wizard explained to everyone else. Shanhaevel sighed and shook his head. "He can sense the evil, too."

"Then we'll just have to trust our own wits and senses," Govin said, starting toward the temple, "and our faith in goodness to see us through."

"I was afraid he was going to say that," Ahleage muttered.

At Elmo's suggestion, they approached the ruined structure from the side. It would be wiser to avoid the main road, if possible. They soon discovered, though, that despite the fact that the walls were thrown down and ruined, the path was almost impassable. Everywhere the thorns, nettles, and creeping vines were too thick and high to move through.

"We could be out here all night, trying to hack through this," Elmo grumbled as he wiped blood from yet another thorn scratch on the back of his hand. The skin already showed a swollen red welt. "As much as I hate to come knocking at the front door, we're going to have to follow the road, I think. There's no other way inside."

Reluctantly, the companions made their way around to the south side, following the road until they were inside the barrier. Ahead of them, the great archway of the main doors loomed, casting dark shadows upon the portals themselves. Standing inside the destroyed walls set Shanhaevel's teeth on edge. The entire place reeked of hatred and malevolence.

What the hell are we doing here? he wondered. *This place must feed off our fears.*

The drizzle that had been falling began to transform, becoming a slushy sleet that grew heavier by the moment. It rattled off every surface, crackling as it hit the stonework of the ruins and pelting the huddled figures as they drew cloaks and hoods more tightly around themselves.

The companions approached the front entrance in the fading light of early evening, studying the twin bronze doors before them, which towered more than twenty feet high and were nearly as wide. The doors were held fast by huge iron chains, and Shanhaevel could see that every crack and crevice in the thing had been sealed with soft iron. More importantly, though, a set of magical runes had been etched into the portal, each glowing with a silvery radiance. Shanhaevel could make out only a little of what the runes said, although their effect was clear enough. None of the companions could muster the will to approach the doors any closer than about ten feet. Beyond that, they found the deed impossible to carry out.

"They are binding sigils," Shanhaevel said, turning away to escape the sense of opposition that washed over him when he tried to draw near. "They were put there by Burne, Lanithaine, and the others when the temple fell a decade ago. That must be how they sealed the demon inside."

"So there's no way to open them?" Govin asked.

"Not that I know of," Shanhaevel replied, shuddering still at the proximity to the temple.

"Come on, then," Govin suggested, heading around the side of the building. "There's got to be another way inside, some secret passage that they are using."

The rest of the companions followed the knight, who made his way carefully through the tall weeds and dead trees, following what seemed to be game trails criss-crossing through the bracken. As they approached the rear of the temple, Shanhaevel noted again the large number of ravens silhouetted against the steely gray sky atop the tower. Perching among the ruins of the upper floors, they made him shiver.

Ravens are never a good sign, he told himself, then rolled his eyes. That's silly, he chastised himself. They're just birds.

When the group got closer to the base of the tower, the ravens grew agitated, and fully a dozen or more of them arose from their perches. The birds swooped down upon the group, and as Shanhaevel watched, they appeared to grow larger in size.

"Look out!" Shanhaevel cried, bringing his staff up to swat at the first of the creatures that flew past him. It was huge, he realized, with a wingspan of nearly ten feet. It went soaring past, nearly knocking him down.

By now, the rest of the Alliance was aware of the attack, drawing weapons and crouching low as giant ravens swarmed and swooped all around. Elmo growled in pain as one of the beasts raked him with its claws, catching him across the back of one shoulder with a razor-sharp talon. Draga, Elmo, and Ahleage had their bows up and were firing arrows at the birds. Govin, Shirral, and Shanhaevel did their best to repel those giant ravens that swooped in to attack the bowmen.

At that moment, the group came under attack from arrow fire. One of the missiles tore through Shanhaevel's cloak, barely missing his leg. Another caught Ahleage in the arm. He cried out and nearly dropped his bow.

"The tower!" yelled Govin, turning his shield to ward off any more shots aimed at him. "They're firing from the arrow slits! Get into cover!"

The group managed to retreat from the tower and fend off the attacks of the ravens at the same time, moving into a grove of usks, short bushy trees usually prized for their sweet fruit. The pale blue, still-unripe fruit of these particular twisted, stunted specimens were tainted with angry red splotches, however.

From this protected spot, the battle continued in the sleet. At first, the ravens were everywhere, and Shanhavel suffered several cuts on his arms and hands from the flyby attacks, but the bowmen soon took their toll on the birds, dropping them out of the sky one by one. Finally, when but one or two of the giant creatures remained aloft, they turned and flew away, leaving the Alliance crouched among the sickly trees, wet, bleeding, and panting. A handful of giant birds that had been shot were only wounded, flapping their wings haphazardly and struggling to move across the ground. Elmo stepped out to dispatch the injured ones with his axe and to retrieve intact arrows. Shirral tended to everyone's wounds.

"Well, if they didn't know we were coming before," Ahleage snarled quietly in disgust, jerking a thumb back over his shoulder toward the tower behind him, "they sure as hells know now. There's no way to get over there without being turned into a pincushion. I might be able to sneak up there, but what then? I'm not going in there by myself."

Shanhaevel thought for a moment. A possibility occurred to him, but he wasn't sure how much he liked it. What choice do we have? he asked himself. Sighing, he said, "I have an idea, but it isn't terribly noble. It'll kill them, hopefully all of them, in one blow. Before I agree to do this, though, I want to give them a fair warning."

"I'll go order them to surrender," Govin said. "We'll see what happens."

The knight stood and walked out toward the tower. He approached the main door, his shield held before him. The rest of the group watched from cover.

"Hear me!" Govin called out. "In the name of Cuthbert and goodness, surrender! We offer you this one chance, or we will destroy you!"

In reply, several arrows hissed out from the arrow slits, causing the knight to flinch back behind his shield. Backing away hastily, Govin returned to the others.

"All right, I gave them a chance. Whether they think we're bluffing or not, they want a fight. What do you have in mind, wizard?"

"Wait and watch," Shanhaevel said, preparing to cast his magic. Taking a deep breath, he began an incantation to render himself invisible. As he finished the spell and faded from sight, Ahleage chuckled.

"I was hoping you'd do that," the man said.

"Shhh," Shanahevel said quietly. "I'm almost ready. Govin, give me about two minutes, then come out and make that same demand again."

"Yes, I like offering myself as an easy target," the knight grumbled. "All right, two minutes."

Shanhavel stood. "The rest of you, sit tight. This shouldn't take long."

He made his way toward the tower, trying to disturb as little of the grass and weeds beneath his feet as possible.

He crept along, using his staff for balance, checking to see if he was leaving easily discernable footprints in the mud. So far, so good, he told himself as he got to the base of the tower, near one of the arrow slits. Now, he only had to wait until Govin appeared again.

A moment later, the knight came out, his shield held in front of himself. When Govin reached the point where he had been previously, he called out again. "This is your last chance. Surrender now, or we will attack!"

Shanhaevel could hear a handful of snickers through the arrow slit, and then he heard movement from just on the other side of the opening. More arrows shot out at the knight, who was struck once in the arm and howled in pain as he backed away, eliciting more guffaws from inside the tower.

Grimly, Shanhaevel peeked inside the arrow slit and saw a scruffy looking bandit, a bow in hand, peering right at him. He had to fight the urge to jerk back away from the man, but it was obvious that the bandit did not see him. The man stepped away from the arrow slit, letting a piece of black canvas fall across the opening. Nodding and taking a deep breath to calm himself, Shanhaevel whispered his spell, bringing his staff up as he did so. When he neared the end of the incantation, he thrust his staff through the opening, forcing the canvas back out of the way, and pointed his finger inside.

There was a single surprised yelp from the other side of the arrow slit, but Shanhaevel, knowing that his spell-casting had negated the invisibility and that he was now visible again, had already ducked away, crouching low and pressing himself tightly to the base of the tower. A heart-beat later, there was a muffled but concussive thump as the elf's spell went off. Tongues of flame shot out of each of the arrow slits like fiery breath from some beast, and then vanished. Nodding in grim satisfaction, the wizard motioned for his companions to join him.

The rest of the group moved out of hiding and came running toward the tower. There was no arrow fire this time. When they reached the base of the tower, Ahleage stared at Shanhaevel.

"What the hells did you do?" the man asked.

"Flung a little magic their way," Shanhaevel replied.

"It looks like the whole inside of the tower exploded," Elmo said. "I've heard of spells like that. You did that?"

Shanhaevel nodded, but he didn't feel much like celebrating. "I did. I doubt anyone survived." The thought made him grimace. "It's a pretty brutal spell."

Govin, his arm apparently healed by Shirral, had his sword out. "Let's get out of the slush and see."

The door turned out to be barred and chained on the outside, but it didn't take Ahhaege long to defeat the lock.

"That's odd," Shanhaevel observed. "They must come and go by a different route."

"Perhaps they have a way to the temple inside," Govin suggested.

Inside, the acrid smell of sulfurous smoke and burned flesh was strong. Entering cautiously, weapons at the ready, the Alliance crept inside the tower.

None of the bandits remained alive. From their positioning, it was obvious that they had been lying in wait, prepared to ambush anyone foolish enough to enter the tower through the main doors. Two low walls flanked the entrance, designed to funnel intruders toward a central point where ranks of spearmen and crossbowmen would annihilate them. The bodies were still in those spots. The fiery burst of magic had killed them instantly and dropped them where they had stood.

Guilt washed over Shanhaevel. They never knew what

hit them, he thought. He tried not to imagine what it must have felt like, that instant of fiery death. They attacked us, he reminded himself, and they serve an evil so powerful that it's palpable. He shook his head, refusing to grieve for these thugs.

The group wasted little time exploring the interior of the tower, lighting a couple of lanterns and beginning to explore. The main room, where the bandits had died, held little besides rude furniture and some old cloaks and blankets, as well as some sacks of foodstuffs. The remains of a half-eaten meal still rested on the tabletops, burned to a crisp, now. From the rafters hung various smoked meats and sausages, along with some bags of herbs and onions. Beneath an ascending staircase—blocked at its upper end by the collapse of the upper levels of the tower—were several barrels filled with water, beer, and sour-smelling wine.

Off of the main room were two smaller ones, apparently quarters for the officers of the bandit troops. Ahleage rooted around in an oak chest in the first chamber, but all he came up with was personal clothing and effects. In the other chamber, they found a second chest, this one sealed tight. Ahleage knelt down to pick the lock.

"Ow!" the young man howled, jerking his hand away from the lock and sticking his finger into his mouth. "Something pricked me!"

Shanhaevel moved beside Ahleage and peered down at the lock. A small needle protruded from it. "Look what was set inside the lock," he observed, pointing.

"Whoa," Ahleage said, suddenly falling back on his backside, "I don't feel so good."

He was pale and had broken out in a sweat.

Shanhaevel turned back to the chest and examined the needle in the lock more closely. Oh, Boccob, he thought, as he saw the substance coating the needle.

"What is it?" Elmo asked when he saw the elf's stricken face.

"He's been poisoned," Shanhaevel said. "There's poison on the needle."

"Move out of my way. Now!" Shirral crossed from where she had been searching through some papers at a desk and crouched down beside Ahleage. "I need some room!"

Closing her eyes, Shirral prayed, placing her hands over Ahleage's chest. Shanhaevel listened as the druid beseeched the forces of nature, calling upon the spirit of the land to aid her. When she was finished, she sat back, peering intently at the man's face.

Ahleage lay with his eyes closed, not moving. His color seemed to be getting better to Shanhaevel's eye, but the elf had no sense in these matters. His heart thumped in his chest as he waited to see if Ahleage would survive. Everyone hovered over the fallen man, waiting.

"Ahleage?" Shirral called. Her eyes filled with tears. "Ahleage, can you hear me?"

Ahleage opened one eye, looking first at the druid, then swiveling it around to peer at each of the other faces gathered around him where he lay. "Yyyeesss?" he asked, drawing the word out.

"Are you all right?" Shirral asked, frowning.

"Actually, no."

"Tell me what's wrong, then," the druid said. "Whatever you need, if I can heal it, I will."

"Oh, that," Ahleage remarked dryly. "I'm fine, now. I'm just hungry. You don't have any roasted chicken, do you?"

"Oh for the love of—" Shirral snarled, leaping to her feet. "I thought I was too late. Damn you, Ahleage! You scared me to death!"

She kicked him on the side of the leg.

"Ow!" Ahleage said, laughing and holding his sides as

the druid stalked away. "You should have seen the looks on your faces! That was priceless!"

Shanhaevel rolled his eyes and sat back. "Damn, Ahleage. You know how sensitive she is after Melias. That wasn't funny."

"Yes, it was," he replied, tears streaming down his face. "At least, *I* thought it was."

Shanhaevel stood and moved over to where Shirral stood at the other end of the room, her arms folded across her chest. The elf could tell she was fuming.

"Hey," he said, "he's just a jokester, that's all. He—"

"Damn him!" Shirral said, and a single tear ran down her face. "I thought I was too late. I thought he was dying."

"Shh," Shanhaevel said, turning the druid to face him and then giving her a hug. To his pleasant surprise, she did not resist, melting into his embrace. "That's just the way he is. You know he's thankful for what you did, even if he doesn't say it."

"I know," Shirral replied. "It just scared me, that's all."

She buried her face in Shanhaevel's chest for a moment, then, just as abruptly, she looked up at Shanhaevel. The elf stared back at her, wondering what she was thinking.

"You all right, now?" he asked, brushing away the tear.

She nodded and pulled free from his hug. By this time, Ahleage was on his feet again, having managed to get his laughter under control, but he was still smiling.

"Don't you dare do that to me again!" Shirral punched Ahleage in the arm, but this time, Shanhaevel could hear a hint of laughter in the druid's words. "Chicken," she said, rolling her eyes and walking away.

Ahleage snickered and looked at the rest of the group. "See? *She* thinks it was funny."

Govin sighed loudly, and Shanhaevel gave a wry grin.

"Let's finish here and get moving," the elf said.

Despite a thorough search of the tower, the companions could find no way into the temple from the tower. They left it behind, hoping to find another entrance elsewhere. Outside, the sleet had turned to snow, although there wasn't enough to coat the ground, yet.

"This snowfall seems unnatural," Shirral muttered. "It never snows this late in the year."

Shanhaevel had to agree with her, although he wasn't sure if the eerie sensations crawling up his spine weren't just from the temple itself.

The companions completed their journey around the perimeter of the temple, stopping at the front entrance again. It was well after dark, now.

"Damn," Govin growled. "How do we get in?"

"We'll never find it in the dark and snow," Elmo said. "Let's get away from here and camp somewhere out of the way. We'll figure it out in the morning."

Everyone was tired, cold, and hungry, so no one argued. The Alliance moved quickly along the path, the last vestiges of malevolence still whispering at the edge of their minds. Once the temple was out of sight, everyone's spirits improved immensely. The sense of relief that washed over each of them was almost palpable. They had just moved back onto the trail after fetching their horses when Shanhaevel heard the sound of distant hoofbeats.

"Shh!" Shirral called from the rear. "I hear riders."

"Get off the road!" Elmo commanded, turning his own horse and riding into the trees along the side of the path.

Shanhaevel wheeled his own mount and trotted into the cover of the forest. When he was several feet back under the boughs, he halted the horse and listened. Sure enough, from the direction of Nulb, the sound of galloping horses grew louder. A moment later, the sound ceased.

Shanhaevel called out to his hawk. *Ormiel, are you there?*

Yes, came a sleepy reply.

Fly to me.

"What happened to them?" Ahleage whispered fiercely. "Where'd they go?"

"I'm not sure," Elmo replied. "Let's wait a moment longer. I don't want to run into any ambushes out here."

A moment later, Ormiel swooped past Shanhaevel's shoulder.

"Gods!" growled Ahleage, flinching as the bird shot past him. "What the hells was that?"

"Shh! It was just Ormiel," the wizard whispered, smiling in the darkness. *Men were riding this way. Find them.*

I find, the hawk replied, flying off into the night.

"Tell your bird not to scare me like that anymore," Ahleage huffed, hunching his shoulders.

"Did you send Ormiel ahead to scout for us?" Elmo asked.

"Yes. I told him to find the riders. Maybe he'll see where they went."

"Good idea. Let's stay quiet and keep an eye and ear out."

The group sat, waiting for Shanhaevel's familiar to report. The silence was broken only by the falling snow pattering on the branches around them. After nearly ten minutes, Ormiel called out to Shanhaevel. *Riders went into trees.*

We are coming, Shanhaevel replied. "Ormiel found where they left the road," he reported to the others.

"Let's go, then," Govin said.

As a group, they all moved back out onto the road.

Show yourself, the elf called, listening for the telltale sounds of the hawk. He caught sight of the bird perhaps forty yards ahead of them.

"Ormiel says the riders left the trail and entered the woods here," Shanhaevel told the rest of the group as they approached the spot where the bird perched high in a tree.

When they reached this spot, they discovered a faint side trail that they had missed before leading off into the woods. Elmo hopped down and examined the ground for a moment.

"Yep, there are fresh tracks here. Hard to see in the dark, but with the snow, they're discernable. This is where our visitors went."

As the group turned off the main path and followed this side trail, the snow stopped, and the sky cleared as the clouds blew out. Shanhaevel pushed his hood back. *Ormiel, are the riders nearby?*

They went into a man-nest.

He relayed this information to the others.

After a short while, the path opened onto a clearing. In the middle sat a ramshackle farmhouse with an equally dilapidated barn behind it. No one seemed to be around. At that moment, Luna broke through a long fringe of cloud, bathing the clearing and the woods around in pale light. Celene, Luna's blue little sister, was still hiding, though a deep blue fringe round a nearby cloud gave her away.

"Do you think they knew we were coming and are hiding?" Shirral asked, peering around.

Elmo shook his head. "Don't know," he replied. "But it looks like the tracks lead to the barn."

Everyone looked where the man pointed to the ground. Fresh horse prints ran past the farmhouse and toward the doors of the barn.

"There's no light inside," Govin said. "They're either hiding in there, or else they went somewhere else."

"I'll go check it out," Ahleage said, dismounting. "Everybody stay here unless you hear me yell, then come running."

Ahleage crept off in the darkness and was soon lost from sight.

"When he wants to disappear, he really disappears," Shirral breathed.

"Let's get back in the trees a little, out of sight," Shanhaevel suggested. "Even if the thugs aren't here, they may come back, and we don't want to be sitting in the middle of the path when they do."

The rest of the companions dismounted and led their horses a little way into the trees, tethering the mounts to low branches. They settled in to wait, listening to the dripping of the moisture from the melting snow on the tree branches.

Odd, thought Shanhaevel. The snow seems to come and go almost randomly. What could be causing that?

The last of the clouds disappeared, but the stars remained dull behind a thin haze. Even little Celene was little more than a blue blur trailing after Luna. The pale moonshadows had moved almost an arm's length before Ahleage returned.

"There's nobody in the farmhouse," he reported, still keeping his voice low. "There are a bunch of horses in the barn, though."

"Their horses are here, but they're not?" Draga asked. "Where'd they go?"

"Don't know," the man answered. "But we can wait and

find out. There are a few good hiding places around. We could even hide in the farmhouse."

"Did Ormiel see where they went, by chance?" Elmo asked.

"I don't know. I'll ask." Shanhaevel called to the hawk and posed Elmo's question, but the bird merely repeated what it had said before, that the riders had entered the man-nest. "He seems to think they're inside one of the buildings."

"Well, they're not," Ahleage insisted. "I checked."

"Maybe there is some sort of secret door," Shirral offered, "a trapdoor that leads to a tunnel or something."

"It's possible," Ahleage admitted. "I didn't look around for anything like that."

"So, what are we going to do?" Elmo asked.

"I like the idea of waiting," Govin said, and Shanhaevel nodded in agreement.

"Yes," the elf added, "we could set up a watch and see where they come from. I say some of us hide in the house, and we put some others out here, hidden in one of the good spots Ahleage mentioned."

Everyone agreed to this plan, and it was decided that Govin, Elmo, and Draga would wait inside the house, while Shanhaevel, Shirral, and Ahleage would remain outside, hiding behind an old well that sat near the edge of the clearing but faced the barn.

"I've got spells that will be useful out here," Shirral mentioned as the three of them made their way to the well. "Between the two of us, we should be able to surprise anyone coming into the clearing."

"Right," Shanhaevel said, squatting down behind the well and preparing to get comfortable. "Wherever they went, they won't be glad to see us when they return."

He stifled a long yawn with the back of his hand as his two friends found dry spots next to him. As the three of them sat there behind the well, Shanhaevel's eyes grew heavy. No time for sleeping, he told himself, but the long day's activities were wearing on him, and more than once he caught himself snapping his head back after nodding off. He rubbed his eyes and looked at both Shirral and Ahleage. They seemed to be fighting sleep as desperately as he. Maybe this isn't such a good idea, after all, he thought. What are we hoping to learn from these brutes, anyway?

At that moment, the wizard heard a distant sound, as though a bolt had been thrown back. Ahleage and Shirral both heard it, too. They each sat forward, peering carefully around the base of the well toward the barn and farmhouse. There was no one there. There came another sound, a scraping, and voices that seemed to echo oddly in the night. Shanhaevel looked this way and that, peering carefully in all directions, but he could not see anyone at all.

The elf turned to his two friends and mouthed "Where?" to them. Ahleage could not see well enough to read the wizard's lips, but Shirral shrugged her shoulder and gave him a look of confusion.

Ahleage suddenly rose, holding on to the side of the well and listening, then, his eyes wide, he dropped back down beside the druid, motioning for them to be still and quiet. Swallowing the lump in his throat, Shanhaevel froze in place, holding his breath and listening intently.

At that moment, a shadowy figure rose out of the well.

* * * * *

Hedrack scowled as he stared across the polished surface of his table at Falrinth, sitting on the opposite side. The high priest of the temple, the Mouth of Iuz, did not like what he was hearing from the wizard.

"You are sure," Hedrack asked again, wanting no more confusion, "that they have been there?"

"As I said," Falrinth repeated, recounting his tale to the armored priest. "When Grozdan did not visit me this evening as he should have, I sent Kriitch up to see what the trouble was. Through his eyes, I saw Grozdan and his men, all dead. Kriitch checked, and all of the men's valuables had been removed as well. I did not see who did it, but my guess is that it's the ones you have been looking for, although how they got past our spies in Nulb, I do not know."

"Hmm," Hedrack said, considering. The wizard was right, of course, although Hedrack hated making any assumptions. These meddlers Iuz had warned him of were growing irritating. The priest had expected to deal with them quickly and decisively—or rather, he had expected his underlings to deal with them quickly and decisively—and instead, they had been met with setback after setback. He had too many things on his mind and too many things for his commanders to deal with, to spare more time and effort on these mewling cretins who thought they might poke their nose into his plans, but it appeared that he had no choice.

"All right," Hedrack said at last, looking at Falrinth again. "It is obvious that they are a bigger thorn in my side than I presumed. I will not underestimate them again. I want no more problems. Find them. Use your scrying magic to figure out where they are, then I will send Lareth to deal with them."

"Of course," Falrinth replied, nodding in acquiescence. "I will let you know as soon as I discover their whereabouts."

The wizard rose to leave, drawing his heavy robes about him.

"What have you learned from the key?" Hedrack said, stopping the wizard in his tracks. "Have you determined yet how we may use it?"

"I know some of its workings, but not all. When I locate the four gems, then I will have the answers you seek."

"Find the interlopers, first. Do not fail me, wizard. And hurry," Hedrack warned, scowling. "The time grows nigh for us to move against our enemies. I want this resolved before then."

"I understand," Falrinth said as he stepped through the chamber door. "I will bring good news."

Hedrack, still deep in thought, shut and locked the door then returned to his chair. He sighed, feeling the heavy burden of command upon his shoulders today. The temples are fighting again, he reflected, and she gives little help in finding herself. Her own foolish pride let her be caught, and now I must dig her out again.

A soft noise distracted Hedrack from his thoughts, and he glanced across the room to where Mika and Paida stood, trembling. It was Paida who had whimpered, though both girls stared at their master with plaintive expressions on their faces. They both had been forbidden to speak, and Paida's own doe-eyed stare seemed particularly expressive. She kept her lips firmly closed, but she mewled softly nonetheless, obviously trying to plead with Hedrack for permission to break his rule of silence.

The high priest smiled and strolled over to where his two serving girls stood. He squatted down beside Paida, noting with satisfaction how her calves were corded with the strain of standing on her tiptoes. He checked Mika's, too, running his hand along the back of her leg, feeling the rock-hard muscle quivering there. The girl whimpered at his touch.

Each girl currently stood inside a box, her feet trapped there by a lid with holes in it that closed and locked about the ankles. Except where the girl's toes touched, the floor of each box was covered entirely with small, thin metal spikes that jutted up underneath each heel. Each girl had two choices: raise herself up on tiptoe or rest her heel, and thus her weight, on the spikes. The lid of the box was high enough up the ankle that the girl's leg was forced to remain perfectly vertical, and she could thus not sit down.

The wine that Mika had spilled upon one of Hedrack's silk robes had been a particularly good vintage, and of course the robe itself was now ruined. Hedrack had decided to punish both girls so that Paida would learn just how high her new master's expectations were for obedience, diligence, and care. He considered one quarter of an hour in the box a reasonable punishment, and the burning candle on his desk told him they had perhaps five minutes remaining.

Hedrack smiled at his two lovely maidens. "I must go out again for a while, but I will return soon."

The two imprisoned girls whimpered in unison, but they obediently avoided speaking. A single tear trickled down Paida's cheek, and her hands clenched and unclenched at her sides as she struggled to remain on her tiptoes. Hedrack nodded in satisfaction and departed.

Shanhaevel barely suppressed his gasp of surprise as he watched the man, holding a pair of throwing spears in one hand, fling his other arm over the side of the well and climb out. In the glow of the moonlit night, the elf could see that this unexpected visitor was wearing a chain-mail shirt and had a shield across his back. Amazingly, the fellow hadn't noticed either the elf or his two companions crouched next to the well. Swinging a leg over, the man scrambled out of the well, heading toward the dilapidated barn next to the farmhouse. Immediately, a second and then a third armored figure followed.

Shanhaevel counted six men by the time the last one was up and out of the well, all of them well armed and armored. Fortunately, it didn't appear that any of them carried bows of any sort. The six strangers were talking softly, discussing something in urgent tones as they moved across the clearing toward the barn.

Neither Shirral nor Ahleage had made a move yet, and Shanhaevel remained frozen, caught totally off guard by the appearance of these strangers.

Gathering his wits about him, the elf quickly chose a spell and prepared to cast it. He raised himself up and peered over the side of the well, but it was empty, nothing more than a dry shaft. Satisfied that no one else would be coming out of the well for the moment, Shanhaevel crouched back down.

"Nothing in there," he whispered to his companions. Pointing to the retreating men, he said, "Let's do it."

Both the druid and Ahleage nodded.

Shirral closed her eyes and mouthed a prayer. When she was done, she swept her arms out before her, gesturing in the direction of the line of men walking toward the barn.

At the same time, Ahleage rose and moved forward, his body slung low and his feet silent in the grass. Shanhaevel followed him, his own spell at the ready. There was a sudden shout from ahead as the men moving toward the barn halted, suddenly milling about in confusion.

That would be Shirral's spell, Shanhaevel noted with satisfaction, watching as the surrounding plant growth came alive, writhing and wrapping itself around the feet and ankles of the six men, holding them fast. Only one of the men managed to avoid the reaching, grasping grass and weeds, stumbling away from the others and nearly falling as he did so. Ahleage moved toward him, gaining the drop on the man and threatening him with a dagger to the throat before he knew the man was there.

"All of you surrender!" Ahleage ordered. "Throw your weapons to the side and do not resist."

Several of the men grumbled in defiance, trying to turn to better face the man, but when they realized they were helpless, trapped by the magic of the entangling plants, they reluctantly surrendered, tossing their weapons down.

Shirral had remained behind, her blade drawn, waiting to see if any more surprises appeared at the mouth of the well. Shanhaevel gave a shrill whistle as he collected the discarded weapons, signaling for the rest of the Alliance to come out of hiding. Elmo and Draga were already out the front door of the farmhouse, and

Govin appeared a moment later, carrying a lit lantern to guide their way. The other two had their bows out. Once they joined the other three, Govin gave his lantern to Ahleage and bound the captive so that Ahleage could join Shirral by the well. Holding the lantern high, he peered down inside the mouth of the well, studying the interior. Then, setting the lantern on the edge, he swung his legs over and disappeared inside.

Shanhaevel gathered what weapons he could, although a few had been tossed down in the midst of the area of Shirral's spell, and the wizard could not reach them without becoming entangled. By the time he was done, Ahleage had crawled back out of the well, and he and the druid had moved to join the rest of the group.

"What's down there?" Govin asked, gesturing toward the well.

"Looks like some sort of secret passage," Ahleage replied. "A set of ledges drop about halfway down into the thing, and then there's a ladder propped against the side. At the bottom, there's a door painted to look like the side of the well. I took a peek, and there's a tunnel that goes back a long way. The door bolts shut from the inside, but it wasn't latched."

After a nod from Elmo, Shirral told the trapped men, "I am going to release you from the entanglement. Don't even think about going for a weapon."

The six strangers glared at their captors, but when Shirral released the magic from the plants, none tried to resist. Govin, Elmo, Shirral, and Ahleage herded the men into the barn while Shanhaevel stayed behind, gathering the rest of the weapons. Draga took a position to watch the well, his bow handy. When Shanhaevel had collected everything, he joined his friends inside, leaving Draga alone to stand watch.

The men were quickly stripped of their armor and bound. Govin and Elmo led them off one at a time to question them before deciding what to do with them. While this was going on, Ahleage and Shanhaevel moved off to converse in private, leaving Shirral to stand watch over the men.

"We can't keep prisoners," the wizard said. "We want to be able to move fast and at a moment's notice. They'll slow us down and make us vulnerable."

"Then let's just kill them and be done with it," Ahleage suggested.

"No. Killing them is not an option."

"Why? We killed the men at the tower today."

"I'm not a murderer, Ahleage. This isn't like at the tower today. Those thugs had a chance to surrender and wouldn't." Shanhaevel felt as if he were trying to convince himself as much as the man standing next to him.

"It was the right move. They would have killed us if they'd had the chance. This is a war, Shanhaevel. It's kill or be killed. But if you won't let me kill them, I have another idea. Perhaps you have some magic up your sleeve that we could use to convince them to leave for good and never come back."

"Hmm," Shanhaevel mused. "Illusions aren't my specialty. Give me some time to think about it."

"All right. We'll see what Govin and Elmo find out and go from there."

After the other two men were done interrogating the prisoners, everyone gathered to discuss the situation.

"None of them want to talk," Govin began, "which isn't surprising. They seem frightened. Something has them shook up, something other than us capturing them."

"They did admit that they had instructions to watch for us in town and attack us with the intent to capture us,"

Elmo added. "They've been expecting us. How, I don't know, but it was wise of us to slip around town without them seeing us."

"So, what's beyond that door down in the well?" Shirral asked.

"They wouldn't say. Their lair, I suspect."

"So, in your estimation," Ahleage said, "what are our chances of convincing them that they can find greener pastures somewhere else?"

Govin and Elmo looked at one another and thought for a moment. "I suppose," Govin finally answered, "that if we could convince their leader, the rest of them would follow along."

"Their leader?" Shanhaevel asked. "You mean someone beyond the door? How many more men do you think we would find there?"

"Hard to say," Govin said. "I suspect they're hoping we'd go try to find out and get the bad end of it. But I meant the leader of these six. That fellow over there with the beard is their sergeant," the knight added, gesturing subtly. "If we can talk him into running and never looking back, he'd probably convince the others."

"That's easy enough to take care of," Shirral said. "Bring him off by himself and let me have a few minutes alone with him."

Shanhaevel turned and looked at the druid with surprise and dismay on his face.

When she saw his expression, she rolled her eyes and said, "No, stupid! I meant I could use a little of my magic on him, convince him that he'd be helping me out if he and his men could go far away."

Shanhaevel gave the druid a sheepish grin and nodded. "I hadn't thought of that," he said.

"It figures," Shirral replied, grimacing.

Shanhaevel, Elmo, and Shirral led the sergeant off by himself while the rest stayed behind, continuing to watch the prisoners.

Shirral squatted down in front of the man, who was still bound, and looked him in the eye. Then she chanted softly, invoking a spell. When she reached the end of her magical phrases, she flicked her fingers softly in front of the fellow's face, and Shanhaevel observed his expression change from sullen defiance to eagerness.

"Now," Shirral said, "I want you to tell me all about yourself." Her voice was soft and sweet, and she held a big smile, which the prisoner returned. Shanhaevel nodded in satisfaction and returned to the others.

After several more minutes, Elmo returned, leaving Shirral alone with the man.

"Any luck?" the wizard asked.

"Boy, did Shirral ever get him to talk," Elmo replied. "She's convincing him right now that it's best if he and his men ride on and never turn back. The tunnel leads all the way to the tower. There's a secret trap door up through the bedroom where Ahleage got poisoned. They're frightened because of all their dead companions."

"Ah," Shanhaevel said, nodding. "That would do it, I suppose. That would also explain how the troops came and went."

"They don't know much about the temple itself," Elmo continued. "They just raid and gather information. Their captain, somebody named Grozdan, would take off every once in a while, through the tunnel, to visit the temple itself and get marching orders. That's where they got their instructions to watch for us in Nulb and capture us."

"There's our way in," Shanhaevel said.

"Any traps along this tunnel?" Ahleage asked.

"No," Govin replied. "Shirral specifically asked him

how safe the tunnel was, and he said it was fine."

"After we were way past due to ride into town and didn't, they rode back to report," Elmo added. "When they discovered everyone at the tower dead, they hightailed it back here and were discussing what they should do next when we caught them."

"Should we expect anyone else to come through there tonight?" the wizard asked.

"I don't know," Elmo answered. "It doesn't sound like anyone but them uses this tunnel. They certainly don't know how Grozdan got into the temple itself from the passage, and they don't mention ever seeing anyone else coming or going."

"Just to be safe, I want to block that door from this side," Ahleage said. "I'll get Draga to help me."

"Sounds good," Govin said. "We'll get the men on their way."

The six bandits were given their armor and horses, but not their weapons. Based on the harrowing sight they had discovered in the tower, it must not have taken too much convincing from the leader, and they all fell in line, riding off in the middle of the night.

"I suggested that they could find better—and safer—work in Dyvers, and he completely agreed with me," Shirral said, a slight smile on her face. "He was convinced that he and his men were going to strike it rich there. I don't think we'll have any more trouble from them."

Ahleage and Draga had returned from blocking the passage by this time, and Ahleage sat, going through the goods they had pulled out of the tower earlier in the day. As Shanhaevel yawned and considered readying himself for sleep, Ahleage whistled softly in surprise.

"Hello! What's this?" he muttered, half to himself, as he pulled a blank sheet of parchment out from a small gap in the slats of the lid of a small chest.

"What have you got there?" Elmo asked, moving over beside Ahleage to look at the page.

"There's nothing on it," Ahleage murmured as he turned the sheet this way and that.

"Hey, look!" Shirral exclaimed, moving beside Ahleage and grabbing his wrist. She lifted the man's hand up into the air. "When you hold it up to the lantern light, there's a map here."

The rest of the companions gathered around the druid and looked at the faint traces of the map.

"The other end of the tunnel goes right to the tower, like they said," she noted, pointing.

"There's a second tunnel that goes underneath the temple," Govin said, pointing to a spot where the subterranean passage branched off in two directions. "Just as we suspected it might."

"The way it's marked on the map, it might be concealed," Shirral replied, "which also confirms what we thought: Those six didn't know it existed."

"That's got to be where this Grozdan went to meet with his superiors," Shanhaevel said. "It probably connects with the lower levels of the temple."

"Then the first thing to do tomorrow is explore that tunnel," Govin said.

By this time, it was well past midnight, and everyone was exhausted. Govin volunteered to stand first watch. The knight set an old chair on the porch and made himself passably comfortable while everyone else got ready to bed down for the night.

Shanhaevel was surprised at how little used the place was. In addition to a large open room that served as a sitting room, dining room, and kitchen, there were two smaller rooms that were presumably bedrooms, though there was very little furniture left. Shanhaevel leaned his staff into a corner in one of the bedrooms and pulled his bedroll out of his saddlebags, which he had brought in with him after they had stabled their horses. Shirral stood in the doorway for a moment, watching him.

"Is there room for me in here, too?" the druid asked, somewhat shyly.

Shanhaevel looked at her—silhouetted by the light of the single lantern in the other room—then nodded.

"It's cold," she said as she came in and tossed her own belongings near where he was preparing his blanket. "We'll stay warmer if we use both of our blankets together."

The wizard had already stretched his blanket out so that he could wrap himself in it, but Shirral layered her own woolen covering atop his and then dropped down, pulling half the covers over herself and leaving half for him beside her. She was yawning profusely, Shanhaevel saw, and he had caught himself doing the same several times since entering the cottage. Smiling and realizing he was going to be glad for the warmth, he crawled under the bedding beside her.

For a moment, Shanhaevel merely lay there, inhaling the faint fragrance of Shirral's hair near his face, but then he felt her shift, turn toward him, and he looked into her eyes, knowing she could see him, even in the darkness. She pressed her lips against his, just once, and then her eyelids closed. Soon both of them were breathing the slow, easy rhythm of slumber, huddled together in the coolness of the early spring night.

Hedrack smiled, pleased with what he was about to reveal to his master, Iuz.

"Your beloved grows more aware every day. Without knowing it, she has begun to affect the elements around the temple. I believe that I can focus her power and bring it to bear in a useful manner. She is not at full strength, to be sure, but she grows stronger."

That is fortuitous news. Iuz beamed, his malevolent pleasure washing over Hedrack. It was a welcome sensation. *You will harness this power, turn it against those damned interlopers that the mustached fop sent. Do not kill them, though. Bring them here, to the temple. I want them sacrificed to me.*

"I hear and obey, my lord."

Hedrack bowed, knowing the delight he would shower upon his lord should he manage to do such a thing. But Iuz was already gone.

Hedrack left the inner temple and visited the cell of his prisoner. Lareth stared at nothing, his eyes glazed. The burn marks on his face would never go away, disfiguring the once-handsome priest of the moathouse. As Hedrack had suspected, Lareth had been too wrapped up in his own beauty, too immersed in his own glory. Hedrack had made sure that would never be a problem again, and now, Lareth's feverish mind churned with hatred for those infidels who had cost him his glory. He would be good for little else anymore, but for what Hedrack now had in mind, Lareth was the perfect instrument.

"I have duties for you," the high priest said, signaling for the guards to release the prisoner.

Lareth's appearance was ragged, but there now burned a fire in the man's eyes that had not been there moments before.

Hedrack drew close and spoke softly. "They're out there, you know."

Lareth blinked and looked into Hedrack's eyes.

"They're close, too. And you remember what they did to you."

Lareth nodded slowly, his nostrils flaring. "Yes. . . ."

"The plans you had . . . the promises . . . They ruined all of that."

"Yesss. I hate them."

"The humiliation of defeat," Hedrack reminded him. "I know you want to right that wrong, don't you?"

"Yes. Please let me destroy them."

"No." Hedrack's tone was firm. "Not destroy. Capture. I have an army above. It is yours. You will take command, as you were meant to. You will lead them. You know where the enemy is. Lead that army, and exact your just revenge. Bring your enemies to me, so that they may be cast to the elements and properly sacrificed to Iuz."

Lareth's head was nodding vigorously, now, saliva flecking his lips as he breathed heavily, the hatred overwhelming him. He was a near-mindless machine, and he was ready to throw his life away for the privilege of capturing the six who were hiding in the abandoned farmhouse. He strained where he stood, eager to move forward, to begin his last, greatest quest, but he was unwilling to take his leave without permission from the one who had instructed him so effectively—with pain, horrible, horrible pain—about the error of his ways.

Hedrack knew that a small, rational part of Lareth's mind still clung to the notion that his own mistress, that spider bitch Lolth, would save him, would take him and make him whole and beautiful again. The high priest knew that the broken man before him still believed he was destined for greater things in her service and that he would gain the chance to exact revenge. In a way, Hedrack pitied Lareth for his false hopes. If there was one thing he was certain of, if there was one constant in the universe he believed above all else, it was the pettiness of gods.

Lolth would have nothing to do with a man such as Lareth, of that Hedrack was convinced. She would see the failures that tainted his damned soul, and she would not mend his ruined face. She might ignore him—or worse, betray him at the point when his belief was strongest. That was the way of Lolth, Iuz, and all of the masters. They did not accept failure, for it reflected badly on them. It was much better, Hedrack knew, for a deity to turn away, to find another champion. It saved face.

Still, Hedrack would exploit Lareth's faint hope. He would temper it, mold it, and forge it into something useful, if only for a brief while. He smiled and waved his hand, softly casting a spell as he did so. He would use his magic to transform the broken, defeated man and rid himself of a pest that had gone too long unchecked. Lolth, too-proud Lolth, would see her own meddling in the temple warped. Her power over this man would be tainted, transformed, and used in a way she never intended. Hedrack smiled as he thought of the spider bitch's displeasure at being thwarted. He almost wished he could see her face. Almost.

"Now, go, my friend," Hedrack said to Lareth at last. "Go mount your steed and command the army. Bring the hated ones back to me in chains, then you can help me punish them for all of their transgressions."

Hedrack gave Lareth a gentle shove, and the man who had once been beautiful almost stumbled in his eagerness to carry out the high priest's orders.

Hedrack left the cell shortly afterward, making his way back to the main temple. He passed through the writhing purple curtain and passed the three small altars of the private temple. He descended the stairs to the chamber of gems where the shaft of pearly white light softly illuminated the throne in the center.

Seating himself in the gem-encrusted chair, Hedrack reached out with his mind, seeking her. *Awaken, my lady. Your servants need your help.*

Why do you disturb my rest? she replied, less sluggish than before. *I am weary from answering your questions. Why do you not free me?*

Patience, mistress. Lord Iuz and I have a plan that will bring you to us very soon, I promise. But first, I have need of your services.

There was hope in the other mind, now, eagerness to be free. *What? How can I aid you, trapped as I am?*

Call on your power, my lady. Call on the forces of the elements.

But that is not my realm! I am the lady of fungi. The elements were his *notion.*

Hedrack frowned, having known this would surface sooner or later. In his mind, it did not matter who sat at the bottom of the temple, bound in that pit beyond his reach. In the end, what he desired had more to do with focusing the temples than the realms of power behind the energy. But eventually, the discrepancies between her love of all things fungal and the elemental bent of the temple would come to a head.

He cleared his mind of those thoughts and projected, *It does not matter, my lady. Funnel your energy into the temple around you. We will take care of the rest.*

He felt it: the hum in the walls, the vibration of energy. Yes, he thought, it's working.

Very good, my lady. Pour yourself into it. We will free you soon, I promise. Very soon.

Hedrack arose from the throne and hurried from the room. He was very pleased.

* * * * *

Shanhaevel woke shivering. He groaned and opened his eyes to see Shirral huddled next to him, shivering as well. She had the majority of the blanket wrapped about her, leaving only her neck and shoulders bare. Suddenly his mind cleared and he sat bolt upright.

"Why in the hells is it so cold?" he asked her.

"I don't know," she said, "but something's wrong. Can't you feel it? In the air?"

Shanhaevel rubbed his eyes and scrambled off the pallet.

"Boccob! It's freezing!" he muttered in the darkness. There was more to it than that, he realized. Shirral was right. Something *was* wrong. He could feel it. The elf hurried out of the room.

In the main living area, Draga was trying to stoke the fire higher, and Govin was pacing back and forth, half-dressed, rubbing his hands together and muttering. As Shanhaevel entered the room, Elmo came out of the other spare room, rubbing his arms. Upon seeing the wizard, Govin stopped pacing.

"This isn't natural," Govin exclaimed. "It's *springtime*, not winter! And that's not all—I can *smell* evil in the air."

Shanhaevel merely nodded and crossed the room toward the fire. "What time is it?" he asked.

"Almost dawn," Draga answered. "I just came in from my post, about ready to wake Elmo for his turn at watch, but Govin was already up. Now Elmo is, too."

Elmo joined the rest of them by the fire. "Who can sleep with this chill in the air?" he muttered. "Where in the hells did this weather come from?"

"You know where," Govin growled, jerking a thumb in the general direction of the temple. "You can feel it."

No one denied it.

"How long has it been getting cold?" Elmo said.

Draga snorted. "Only about half an hour. And there's no wind either, like when a norther comes in. It was calm and quiet."

"We need to get back out there on watch," Shanhaevel said. "We'd be easily trapped in here."

"I can go back out," Draga replied, "but I have to get a warm cloak first."

Shirral, the blanket wrapped around her, entered the room, but instead of moving close to the fire she crossed to the door, a grim look on her face. She flung it wide and stepped onto the porch.

Shanhaevel followed, sensing her extreme unease. He stepped behind her, wrapped his arms around her shoulders and hugging her against him.

"What is it?" he asked.

Instead of answering him, she pointed. He turned to look into the small yard. It had begun to snow again, more heavily than he had seen in his life.

"By Cuthbert!" Govin growled, following the two of them out. "They've awakened something."

"Yes," Shirral said quietly. "The demon. And she's powerful enough to thwart the Mother herself."

"All right," Elmo said, stumbling out onto the porch as he pulled on his boots. "Draga and I'll get out there and keep watch while the rest of you get ready. Shanhaevel, join us as soon as you can. We may need your eyes."

Nodding, Shanhaevel turned and headed back into the smaller room to gather his things. Everyone else began scurried about, dressing and preparing for whatever might come. Shanhaevel stifled a yawn as he grabbed his cloak and staff. As he was leaving the room, slinging his cloak about his shoulders, Shirral stopped him with a touch on his arm.

"Be careful," she said, and she leaned in to kiss him once, softly, on the lips. "I can feel something wicked stirring."

"I know. Everyone can feel it. I will be wary." He squeezed her hand and said, "You watch yourself, too."

Shanhaevel turned away and headed out of the room, but he turned back and drew Shirral to him, hugging her tightly. The scent of her hair filled his nostrils, and the warmth of her body against him made his heart race. Prying himself free, he left her to don her armor and hurried out the door to join Elmo and Draga.

Once outside, Shanhaevel hugged his cloak about his body, shivering in the cold. The snow was falling steadily, and the ground was already beginning to disappear beneath a blanket of white. The wizard shook his head in wonder and dread at the notion that such heavy snow would come so late in the season.

"Nice night for a little vigil, eh?" Elmo said with a smile, but the worry in his eyes belied his humor.

Shanhaevel snorted. "Whatever's going on, it has everyone spooked."

"Something's going to happen," Draga said, "and soon, too. I can feel it."

"Yes," Elmo replied. "We all sense an attack, and I can't explain that, which worries me. In battle, I like to base my planning on knowing where the enemy is, how strong he is, and what he's doing, not on malign feelings hovering in the air. This snowfall isn't going to help. *Everything* feels wrong. I don't like it."

"Elmo, you sound like a veteran who's been on many field campaigns," the elf said, a slight smile on his face. "Another little secret of yours no one knew about before now?"

Elmo laughed. "I told you, I am a member of the Knights of the Hart in Furyondy. I have received some training in martial tactics, you know."

"Hey," Draga cut them off, crouching low and whispering. "Do you see that?"

Shanhaevel and Elmo ducked down beside the bowman, gazing out across the snowy clearing into the woods beyond. Even with the elf's vision, the woods seemed gloomy through the falling snow. In the distance, threading their way through the trees, were figures—many figures. They were crouched low and coming toward the stronghold—men and other things, big things like ogres and trolls.

"Oh, gods." Shanhaevel's heart leaped into his throat. He tried to calm himself by taking a deep breath. "Boccob, Draga! You don't need me to help you keep watch. Your sight is almost as good as mine out here. There's an army of them, coming this way."

"That's what I was afraid you were going to tell me," Elmo said. "Draga, check that side. See what's coming from that direction."

Draga obeyed, while Elmo moved to the other corner of the farmhouse to have a look at the back side of the farmhouse.

Shanhaevel turned back to watch the advancing force, sweeping his gaze in either direction, tracking them. In his estimation, there were possibly a hundred or more, plus maybe a total of two dozen ogres, trolls, and even what looked like a giant. He tried to squelch the panic that was rising in his chest. A giant!

Draga returned from the side of the house, shaking his head. "It's no use. They've surrounded us."

"It's the same on this side," Elmo said. "We defend the house, then. Back inside."

The three of them retreated inside, and Elmo quickly explained the situation to the rest of the group.

"We're trapped," Ahleage muttered, flicking his wrists and producing two daggers. "What do we do, now?"

"We pray that the gods give us strength to hold them back," Elmo whispered. "Everyone, take a window. Keep the shutters closed except for a crack."

The members of the Alliance moved to various windows, taking up defensive positions and watching.

"Shanhaevel, do you have some of those spells of magical light ready?" Elmo asked from his vantage point by the front door.

"Yes," Shanhaevel replied. "Two of them."

"Get ready to light up the night, then, because I think they're about to charge."

As if on cue, a shout arose from outside, and the army surged forward.

"Light, now!" Elmo said, swinging the door open, an arrow nocked.

All around the farmhouse there began a howling from the advancing force, a war cry to begin the charge. From all sides they came, jogging forward with weapons in hand. Hurriedly, Shanhaevel muttered the words of his spell, aiming the effect into the air some thirty paces directly over the heads of the men charging on this side.

Elmo's bow sang as he sent arrows at the approaching hordes, dropping men as fast as he could. For every one he dropped, though, three more moved ahead, drawing closer.

As soon as his spell went off, Shanhaevel turned and darted across the room to a window on the other side. There, Draga and Ahleage were using their bows in much the same way Elmo was, though neither of them could see the oncoming enemy as well. Shanhaevel cast his second spell, illuminating the landscape for the bowmen.

"That's more like it!" Draga said, working his bow as fast as he could with deadly accuracy. Ahleage joined in, and soon, they were mowing down the front ranks of the onrushing attackers.

Shirral had positioned herself in one of the bedrooms, in a window facing the barn, and was using her sling to attempt to hold back the oncoming forces. Govin paced in the center of the main room, ready to take up a position anywhere a breach was imminent.

After a couple of furious rounds of bowfire, the first wave fell back, retreating back into the trees. Shanhaevel moved back next to Elmo, for that appeared to be the weakest spot in the defenses and the place where the most enemy troops were amassed.

"That was just a feint," Elmo said. "They just wanted to see how we'd react. They're going to regroup and come at us again where they think we're weakest."

Shanhaevel looked around, trying to determine what *he* thought was their weakest point. His gaze settled.

"There," he said, pointing toward Shirral, huddled by herself in the other room, her sling in hand.

Elmo looked and nodded. "Yes," he said, "that's where I would come, too. Of course, they haven't shown their true strength yet, so when they do come . . ."

"What haven't we seen?" the elf asked.

"Bowmen and magic," Elmo replied.

Shanhaevel nodded. "We should move around to keep them guessing."

"That's a fine idea." Elmo grinned and moved past Govin, motioning the knight to take his place.

As Govin approached, Shanhaevel explained, "We're mixing it up, hoping to catch them off guard a bit."

Govin nodded. "Hold back on the rest of your magic until they get really close."

"You know that magical light isn't going to stay too much longer. When it winks out, we're in trouble."

"I don't think we have to worry about that for too much longer," Govin said, pointing. The sky was just beginning to lighten in the east, although it was hard to see because of the snowfall, which was growing steadily heavier.

Shanhaevel realized he could barely make out the line of trees through the white curtain, which was falling in huge, thick clumps.

"It's like goose down," he said, wishing the circumstances were different so he could enjoy it.

A shout arose from the tree line, and again the horde advanced. This time, as Elmo had predicted, bowfire accompanied the onrush of troops, forcing the members of the Alliance to crouch low behind their defenses.

"What can you throw at them?" Govin asked, peering through the crack of the doorway at the oncoming men and beasts.

Shanhaevel risked a glance as an arrow whizzed close and a second one thunked into the wall a few inches to one side of the door frame. The elf ducked back in and said, "I have plenty, if I can get enough time to cast."

"I'd buy you time, if I could, wizard, but they're almost to the porch. Better do something quick."

Shanhaevel began. He drew on the magic from other planes, focusing the energy, then poked his head out long enough to spot a large contingent of men clumped together. He aimed his spell, and a single glowing cinder shot forth from his fingertip directly at the foemen. When it landed, it detonated, and a ball of flame blossomed, engulfing the troops in searing heat. The men caught in the inferno screamed, briefly, before dropping onto the scorched earth.

"Perfect!" Govin said. "There're more coming on the left."

Shanhaevel started casting anew, forming other magical energies and bringing them together. He hurled his new spell and ducked back inside.

Govin watched, but when there was no bright burst of flame, he turned to the elf and shouted, "What's wrong?"

"Nothing," Shanhaevel replied. "I just conjured a cloud of foul vapors and positioned it in a line about ten paces out, directly along this side of the house. Nothing will want to come through it for a few moments, at the very least."

"Hmph." The knight frowned. "Fighting with smell. You wizards . . ."

Shanhaevel smiled. "I'm going to see if anyone else needs me."

Govin nodded, and Shanhaevel shot across the room toward Shirral, who was standing with Draga while the bowman fired arrow after arrow. When she turned and saw him, she waved him away and pointed to Elmo and Ahleage. He turned to see the two of them trying to repel a substantial force that had managed to get to a window and were struggling to get inside. Elmo was using his axe to keep them at bay while Ahleage stayed clear of the wide arc of the wicked axe, his bow in hand.

Shanhaevel cast, and when the magic materialized, five of the figures slumped down, deeply asleep. That tipped the balance back in Elmo and Ahleage's favor, and they repelled the last few remaining enemies.

A shout from behind made Shanhaevel turn again, and what he saw made his heart skip a beat. A giant was approaching the front door with a fist full of burning logs and was preparing to fling the firebrands at the house.

Damn! The elf fumed. I forgot they would be too tall for the cloud of vapors. Govin seemed on the verge of charging out to confront the giant, but the immensity of the creature gave the knight pause.

"Govin, hold!" the wizard shouted. "Open the door and give me room!"

The knight nodded, flung the door wide, and leaped away.

Shanhaevel wasted no time, aiming the lightning bolt at the huge creature, but he wasn't as fast enough. The bolt that flashed across his field of vision was true, crackling all about the giant's body, but when the massive humanoid cried out in agony and tumbled forward, its momentum carried it into the front of the house. The ground shook, and the air exploded in shards and splinters of wood as the giant collapsed across the front porch and destroyed the front wall of the house.

Both Shanhaevel and Govin leaped away from the destruction, scrambling to avoid the jagged beams that had been ripped free by the impact. Already, the fire from the creature's burning timbers was spreading, igniting the dry wood of the farmhouse. Smoke filled the rest of the ruined structure. Nothing else seemed to be attacking them for the moment, so Shanhaevel sank down to the floor, coughing and gasping from the smoke.

"Unless you can put out this fire, we have to get out of here!" Elmo moved beside him, helping the elf to his feet. "Everyone! Gather outside before they charge again!"

Shanhaevel scrambled through the hole that was once the front wall, keeping himself pressed well back from the flames, which were quickly growing to a roaring inferno.

Too fast, Shanhaevel considered in a daze as he watched the tongues of fire leap from spot to spot, licking the wood. It's burning too fast. Elementals! he realized as he made it out into the snow of the yard. Creatures of flame were jumping round the ruin of the house, burning whatever they could. Dawn had broken, but the daylight was still weak and gray. Looking back, Shanhaevel watched as the rest of the companions fled the fiery farmhouse, which would be consumed in a matter of moments.

"Listen!" Elmo said, his voice loud in the early morning. The snow had stopped falling, at last, though now it was at mid-thigh on most of the group. In a softer voice, Elmo continued, "We make a stand here, right in the middle. Bow and sling fire first, and then we give them everything we've got left once they are in reach."

"It's no good," Shirral panted. "All I have left are some healing spells and a couple of other things not useful in battle. Nothing I can do to them."

"Then be ready with healing," Elmo instructed. "Shanhaevel, whatever spells you still have, use them wisely."

Everyone nodded and prepared for the final assault. Even though the snow had ceased falling, the smoke from the fire made the battleground just as hazy and difficult to see through as before. There was a guttural shout from in the distance, but it was not the order to attack. It was an angry sound, full of despair, hatred, and fury.

"Boccob! What was that?" Shanhaevel breathed, steeling himself for what was about to come, expecting some huge beast or thing summoned from the lower planes.

The first figure to appear through the thick, drifting smoke was not a terrible creature, however. It was a man upon a horse.

It was Lareth.

Shanhaevel stared at the priest. The once-handsome man was now horrible to look upon. His face bore scars inflicted by fire and sharp blades. Shanhaevel took an involuntary step back when he saw the feverish hatred in the man's eyes. The other members of the Alliance saw it, too, for the elf heard several of his companions gasp, and no one made a move for several moments.

"Yes," Lareth said, his once-honey voice now rough as gravel. Shanhaevel wondered what foul substances might have been poured down the man's gullet to ruin the dulcet tones he remembered from before. "See what you have wrought upon me, what maiming you inflicted through your interference! Now you will suffer, as I suffered at your hands."

Govin stepped forward, sword held high. "Nay, Lareth! These things you suffered were not our doing. You cannot blame us."

"Wrong!" Lareth screamed, his eyes burning fiercely. "The pain! All the pain! And it was *your* faces I saw! *Yours!* You were there!"

"Think carefully." Govin shook his head, apparently hoping he could still reason with the crazed cleric. "We did not defeat you, nor did we follow you from the moathouse. You fled, and someone else did these terrible things to you. We would not do those things. Only a cruel and hurtful master would visit such punishment, and a master like that does not deserve your loyalty. Cease this war, surrender to us, and we will help you. We will not mistreat you like the ones who scarred your face."

Lareth seemed to listen to the knight for a moment, but when Govin reminded the priest of how his once-beautiful face was now ruined with scars, Lareth's eyes blazed in crazed fury once more.

"Lies! I will not listen to them. You will die in the nodes of fire, water, earth, and air!"

Lareth's horse reared on its hind legs, and the priest had to grab hold of the pommel of the saddle with both hands to keep from falling. Shanhaevel peered around, awaiting the inevitable approach of more of the enemy, but they never came. Aside from the roar of the flames and the stamping of the priest's horse, it was strangely quiet.

A strong breeze wafted over the battleground, clearing the smoke and mist and giving the companions a better view of the carnage they had wrought. The land around the ruined farmhouse was literally piled with the bodies of the crazed priest's army. The few left alive were fleeing into the woods. Only Lareth still stood fast, trying to regain control of his panicked and bucking mount. He was alone, facing all six of the companions.

The hatred still burned in the priest's eyes, though it was now joined by something else, the elf saw. Lareth was afraid. He had witnessed six individuals defeat his army. Still, Lareth's insane desire to destroy those whom he believed had maimed him drove him to hold his ground. His horse still seemed skittish, but Lareth maintained his position, glaring at the six of them.

"I will see you dead," he spat, twirling his mace once. "I will destroy you and see your corpses delivered into the nodes!"

"Your lust for our blood will be your undoing, priest!" Govin roared, pointing an accusatory finger at Lareth. "We have defeated your army and bloodied your master. Do you think you, all by yourself, can hope to conquer us? We have the might of Saint Cuthbert to deliver victory into our hands! If you do not surrender, you will die!"

Snarling, Lareth stood in the stirrups and shouted at the top of his lungs, "Aid me, my mistress Lolth!"

Swinging his mace wildly over his head, Lareth spurred his horse forward. The six companions fanned out, weapons at the ready, as the crazed priest rushed them. Shanhaevel readied himself for the attack, but Lareth took his charge straight to Govin, who stood his ground, his body held low in a defensive crouch, sword ready to strike.

As Lareth reached the knight, Govin shifted to his right, darting directly in front of the charging horse. The mount whinnied and reared up, and Govin came in low, swinging his blade at Lareth. The knight caught the priest squarely in the chest with his blow, which shattered the man's armor and threw a spray of blood into the air. The force of the blow sent Lareth flying backward into the snow. As the frightened mount skittered away, Govin closed on Lareth, who was struggling to rise to one knee, blood pulsing from his chest and staining the snow the color of wine.

"Aid me, my mistress Lolth!" Lareth repeated, his voice cracking with the strain of his mad bloodlust. He began muttering—casting a spell, Shanhaevel realized as he heard the sinister words. Lareth raised one hand at Govin even as his lifeblood spilled away into the frozen ground.

Before Lareth could complete his diabolical conjuring, though, Govin brought his sword back and swung it forward, grunting from the exertion. The blade cut cleanly, slicing through Lareth's neck. The priest's head tumbled away, as his body hovered, kneeling for a moment longer, and then finally toppled over into the crimson-tinged drifts of snow.

* * * * *

Hedrack paced in his chambers as he watched Falrinth, impatient for news. In the middle of the floor, the wizard knelt upon several thick cushions, his hands clasped before him. He seemed to be in a trance, his eyes unblinking, focused on nothing.

The high priest felt a sudden tingling, a magical connection that made the hair on the back of his neck stand. Lareth was dead, Hedrack knew, and he smiled, wondering if the spider bitch knew what he had done to her servant. But first, Hedrack needed to know the outcome of the battle above. With an anxious growl, he spun on his heel and faced the wizard.

"What do you see up there?" he asked Falrinth. "How does the battle fare? Do we have victory?"

The wizard jerked as though he'd been awakened from dozing. "No. They stand, and the army has broken and fled. Lareth is dead."

"Yes, I know," Hedrack replied, pacing again. "How bad were our losses?"

"Perhaps half, but the company exhausted a lot of magic defending themselves. The remaining forces could be regrouped." Falrinth left the suggestion hanging.

Hedrack considered this, then shook his head. "No, let them flee. I anticipated this outcome, and I have already set into motion a contingency plan. I will have Barkinar round up the remaining troops and prepare them for the possibility, however slight, that the meddlers survive my little surprise and make their way inside."

Falrinth nodded, although the look on his face made it clear he did not understand what Hedrack meant.

"As you wish," the wizard said at last.

"Leave me," Hedrack instructed. "Keep an eye on the troublemakers. I want a report of their next moves the moment you know something."

Falrinth rose and moved toward the door. "They may very well find a way inside, you know," the wizard said as he opened the door. "They are proving more resourceful than we anticipated."

The high priest nodded, a half frown on his lips. "Perhaps," he said, "and that is why Barkinar will be ready."

Falrinth nodded and left, pulling the door shut softly behind him. Hedrack continued to stare at the closed portal a moment after the wizard's departure, pondering the possibilities. Let them come, he mused. Dangerous though it was, the idea of the meddlers roaming in his halls made him lick his lips in anticipation. If they get inside, it will be all the easier to snare them and present them to Iuz.

* * * * *

The morning was quiet except for the sounds of labored breathing. For a moment, the Alliance stood, unmoving, staring at the headless body of Lareth lying in the thigh-deep snow. The dead priest's fingers still twitched, perhaps struggling even in death to finish the casting that could not be completed in life.

Sword still in hand, Govin stood, feet slightly apart, and stared down at what he had done. He bowed his head, eyes closed, and softly muttered a few words of thanks to Saint Cuthbert for granting him the strength to achieve victory. When he opened them again, there was no regret in his visage—nor was there malice or glee, Shanhaevel noted—only the look of a man who did what he had to and would think on it no further.

Shanhaevel closed his own eyes for a moment, thankful that the battle was over.

Suddenly, a keening wail, an unnatural sound of death and despair, cut through the silent morning air. In a heartbeat, the wizard knew that death had been awakened in the woods. He blanched as a dark, shadow-like thing rose from the body of the beheaded priest—a horrible shade that extended eight wispy legs tapering to nothing before coming to rest on the ground. The head of the creature—a demonic, insubstantial spider form—was Lareth's.

"Boccob!" Shanhaevel cried, his blood turning as cold as the snow around him.

"To the well!" Elmo cried, already running.

In a terrified mad dash, the six companions darted across the yard, heading straight toward the well. Shanhaevel began a spell even as Elmo reached the lip of the well and scrambled over the side. Frantically, he worked to unblock the secret passage, clearing away Ahleage and Draga's handiwork from the night before. Scrap wood and debris flew until Elmo had cleared a hole large enough for a man to pass through.

Elmo ushered Shirral through the makeshift passage. Ahleage was next. By the time Draga, Govin, and Elmo had disappeared inside the well, the haunt was just beginning to separate itself from the body from which it grew, but there was no mistaking the message in the sound it made as it howled, intimating its craving for life, for souls. The shadow hungered, and Shanhaevel knew what it would mean to be caught. Its song hinted at darkness, terror, and everlasting pain and cold. The elf prayed that his spell, coupled with the heavy snowfall, would veil the Alliance's escape.

With a sharp gesture, the wizard finished his spell. Immediately, he felt the cold, whipping wind that he had summoned. It swirled through the clearing of the farmhouse, stirring up the smoke and snow in a blinding gray wash that masked all movement and whisked away any hint of footprints. Satisfied that their trail was covered, Shanhaevel ducked down into the well, pausing near the top of the ladder.

Ormiel, fly! Fly far away and wait for me to call you. I go to hide in the earth.

Bad thing in the woods. I fly away.

Yes, Shanhaevel responded. *I may be gone a long time. Wait for me. Stay warm.*

I wait.

With that, Shanhaevel dropped the rest of the way down and ducked into the tunnel. Govin shut the door, and Ahleage dropped the bar into place. The group stood panting and looking wide-eyed at one another in the light of one lantern, which Elmo kept partially hooded.

"What *was* that?" Draga whispered, his voice wavering.

"Death undying," Govin replied, his face grim. "It will be on us soon. It can sense our life-force, and it will not stop hunting until it finds us."

"I guess it's time to explore the inside of the temple, then," Ahleage said wryly, but there was no humor in his eyes.

"Lead the way," Shirral told him, her face pale in the dimness.

* * * * *

The tunnel descended steadily through the clay, shored up by stout timbers at regular intervals. Once the companions were sufficiently below ground level, they discovered that the tunnel had been cut directly through the limestone bedrock. It was narrow and cool in the passage, and the Alliance moved steadily, if cautiously, through it. After four hundred paces and a couple of slight turns later, they found themselves standing on the north side of a cavern perhaps forty feet across. A second tunnel led away east. According to the map Ahleage had found in the lid of the chest, the six explorers were now near the northwest corner of the temple, but still well below the surface.

"This is it," Ahleage said, holding a lantern up and peering at the sheet of parchment in his hand. "According to the map, the other passage heads out from right over there." He pointed toward the southeast corner of the oval-shaped cavern. There was nothing visible in the natural limestone wall.

"Let me take a look," Shanhaevel said. "I've got the eyes for it." The wizard stepped to the area Ahleage had indicated and studied the rock.

Shirral moved up beside him. "You're not the only one with keen eyes, you know," she muttered.

Shanhaevel glanced sideways at her. He nodded and continued to look.

"I'm going to follow the other passageway and see where it ends," Ahleage announced. "I'll be right back."

"I'll go with you," Draga said, "just to watch your back."

With that, the two of them departed, taking one of the lanterns with them. Elmo held the other light high, trying to give everyone a clear view of the limestone walls.

"It always makes me nervous when he goes off like that," Govin muttered, pacing in the middle of the room. "There's going to come a time when he doesn't come back, and . . ." The knight left the thought unfinished.

"Here it is!" Shirral proclaimed, running her finger along a faint vertical crack. "Right here."

The rest of the group crowded around her, looking at what she had discovered.

"Looks like a pivoting slab," Govin said. "Elmo, shall we?"

Nodding, Elmo stepped up beside the knight, and together they pushed on the stone. It swung open easily, revealing a narrow passage beyond.

Shanhaevel picked up the lantern Elmo had set down and shone it into the tunnel. The passage stretched straight ahead as far as the light would illuminate.

"Well, it agrees with what's on the map," Shirral said. "Too bad the map doesn't show what's at the other end."

"That's what we're going to find out," Govin said. "Just as soon as those two return."

"Are you sure that's such a good idea?" Shirral asked. "I burned off a lot of magic up there in the fight. I need to rest and meditate."

"I don't think we can wait," Elmo said. "That howling thing that rose up from Lareth will be tracking us, and we can't let it catch up."

Shirral nodded. "I suppose," she said.

A moment later Ahleage and the bowman did return, carrying a chest between the two of them. Draga also carried a rolled up piece of cloth and an extra quiver in his free hand.

"Look what we found," Ahleage said, setting the chest down and throwing the lid back. Inside were small containers, all ornate boxes and coffers trimmed in precious metals. "The tunnel goes for a long way, and at the end is a small room. All this was sitting at the base of a ladder. We didn't bother going up to the tower again."

Shanhaevel noticed the folded cloth in Draga's hand and asked to have a closer look. When he unfurled it, the elf realized it was a cloak made of a rare weave. He had only seen such a fabric once before, back home in the Welkwood.

"Elven!" he breathed. "This is a rare find, indeed. Watch."

He flung the cloak over his shoulders and moved beside the wall. The rest of the group murmured in surprise as he faded into the surrounding rock.

"Is it magic?" Ahleage asked as Shanhaevel removed the cloak.

"Partially," the elf replied. "That, and the elves have a way of weaving their fibers to reflect the surrounding light."

"What about these?" Draga asked, holding out the quiver he bore.

Shanhaevel walked over to the bowman and removed an arrow from the container. He examined it closely for a moment. His eyes caught what he was hoping to see: a faint sign engraved in the shaft.

"They bear the mark of magic," he told Draga. "Hang on to them. Use them carefully."

Draga nodded, a wry grin on his face, and stuffed the newfound arrows into his own quiver, then tossed the spare one aside.

"Leave the rest of that here," Govin said, pointing to the chest. "We'll take it with us when we come back this way."

"Assuming we come back this way," Ahleage said. "With an army overhead, it's only a matter of time before they realize where we went." He shut the lid and pushed the container over against the wall near the new tunnel the group was about to enter.

"Let's go," Elmo said.

One by one, the Alliance filed into the narrow opening and followed the tunnel, with Ahleage scouting ahead. It descended more sharply than the previous passage had, and it was so narrow that Govin, Elmo, and Draga had to turn sideways from time to time to squeeze through.

The going was slow, but eventually the tunnel widened and turned, becoming a better-constructed corridor. The ceiling was a rounded arch that ran the length of the passage, and torch sconces were set in the walls at regular intervals. Some of the sconces still held torches, though none were lit. The stonework itself was good, solid craftsmanship, and the walls and floors had been polished smooth.

After a while, Shanhaevel could sense slight air currents, deducing from such that the place was somehow ventilated.

"I think we're here," Shirral whispered, shivering and running her hand along one wall. The tunnel ahead turned once more.

"Oh, we're here, all right," Govin said. "I can feel the taint. The very walls ooze with evil."

"Stay here," Ahleage called softly over his shoulder, then he darted ahead into the darkness, stopping at the corner and peeking around. He waited a moment before disappearing around the bend.

Govin sighed, but everyone held their positions while they waited for Ahleage to return. Shanhaevel went through his remaining spells, considering which ones would be useful.

At that moment, they heard Ahleage shout, and the unmistakable red-orange light of bright flame suffused the corridor just around the corner.

Govin was around the corner of the passage instantly, his sword in hand. The rest of the companions followed without hesitation. Beyond Ahleage and around the corner of that intersection, a wide passage glowed with flame, while the passage they currently traversed continued past into darkness. When Shanhaevel saw the unmoving silhouette of Ahleage standing near another intersection a bit farther down, one arm raised before him as though to ward off some attack, the elf's heart skipped a beat. The man's form was stiff. In fact, it was absolutely unmoving.

"Hold, Govin!" the wizard called out, slowing and throwing himself against the wall of the passage. The knight paused and turned to look back at Shanhaevel, who motioned frantically for him to get away from Ahleage.

"Come here!" the elf hissed.

"By Cuthbert! What's wrong with him?" Govin asked, his teeth clenched as he stepped back beside the wizard. He took a half-step forward again, barely able to restrain himself from charging around the corner. From this vantage point, Shanhaevel saw that his worst fears were confirmed: Ahleage had been transformed into a statue.

"Easy, knight," Elmo said, moving up beside Shanhaevel. "Whatever happened to Ahleage could happen to you, too. We must be cautious."

"It looks like he's been petrified," Shanhaevel whispered.

Govin's eyes bulged. *"What?"* he growled. "We must do something!"

"Shh!" Shanhaevel said, motioning for the knight to keep his voice down. "We will! But if you don't be quiet, everyone in the entire temple's going to know we're here."

"What should we do?" Draga asked from behind the three of them.

"Let me think," the wizard replied. "Whatever you do, do *not* look at anything that comes around that corner."

Shanhaevel studied Ahleage for a moment, even as the flames around the corner flickered and cast the shadow of his form on the wall.

"All right," the elf said at last, handing his staff to Elmo. "Give me your shield, Govin."

The knight looked at him askance but handed the shield over. Shanhaevel gasped as he took hold of the thing, for it was heavier than he had expected. Hoisting it up with both hands, he moved down the hallway, holding the shield in front of him and keeping his back pressed against the wall.

"What in the hells are you doing?" Govin called out.

Shanhaevel ignored the knight and walked all the way to the corner, so that he was right behind Ahleage. Keeping the shield high in front of him so that it blocked his line of sight ahead, he moved around the corner, navigating by staring at the floor before him.

"Wizard! Stop!" Govin called again.

Shanhaevel continued to ignore the knight, instead concentrating on what he was looking at—or rather, what he was not looking at. Slowly, moving the shield around, he studied the passage in small sections.

The glow of fire came from several places, the brightest of which were two braziers set in the floor, one at each corner of a T-shaped intersection. The closer of the pair was mere inches away from Ahleage. A runnel of flame lit each brazier, igniting oil that flowed through shallow channels in the floor alongside each wall. The channels came from the far end of the passage, which hit a dead-end after perhaps thirty feet. At that far end, there was a great fountain. It, too, was filled with oil burning brightly. Flanking the fountain, set into the side walls of the short hallway, were a pair of doors. Between Shanhaevel and the fountain of burning oil stood a creature he'd only heard described in legend.

The beast, a dull brown in color, was vaguely lizard-like in appearance, although it sported eight legs instead of four. Shanhaevel was careful to avoid looking at the creature's face. It snorted and hissed, bobbing its head back and forth, as though it was trying to move into a position past the side of the shield and catch the wizard's attention. Shanhaevel kept his eyes averted, though, refusing to meet the thing's gaze.

Hurriedly, Shanhaevel shuffled backward, keeping the shield raised and cutting off his sight from the beast. He turned around and took a few steps toward the rest of the group, lowering the shield as he did so in order to speak.

"It's a basilisk," the wizard said quietly. "Its gaze can turn a man to stone. I read about one once, long ago. If it comes around the corner, don't look at its face!"

The group tensed and waited for a few moments, but the basilisk did not appear. Puzzled, Shanhaevel tried to recall everything he knew about the fabled basilisk. Finally, he said, "Just stay here and wait."

"What are you going to do?" Govin asked.

"I'm going to try to destroy it," the wizard replied, hoping his voice sounded more confident than he felt. "I still have some magic left, even after the fight above."

"Be careful," Shirral growled, flashing her icy blue eyes at him in warning.

Shanhaevel nodded, swallowed, and turned to cautiously advance toward the corner once more. None of this made any sense to him, though. Why would the creature be down here? How did it get here? He remembered that a basilisk's gaze reflected back at the monster could turn the creature to stone, but he was pretty certain none of the companions had anything even faintly resembling a mirror. Shaking his head, he reached the corner and, using Ahleage's frozen form as cover, began a spell.

Staying behind Ahleage's petrified form and keeping Govin's shield between himself and the beast, Shanhaevel leveled his free arm in the direction of the basilisk and uttered the final phrases of the spell. Instantly, he felt the magic forces slide through his arm, erupting as a stroke of lightning. Shanhaevel watched as his magic bolt flashed, spanning the length of the hallway between him and the far wall, where the flaming fountain still burned. The lightning fully engulfed the body of the beast as it crouched in front of the elf—and passed right through it.

Shanhaevel barely heard the surprised shouts of his companions behind him. The basilisk, apparently unscathed by the attack, continued to stand, hissing and shifting almost exactly as it had before.

"What in the hells are you doing?" Shirral cried.

Shanhaevel didn't answer. His eyes narrowed in suspicion. Even though the magic he had mustered into the lightning bolt wasn't on the same level as Lanithaine's, he was certain the beast should have been affected somewhat.

Perhaps the basilisk is immune to electrical magic, the wizard thought. *Then let's try a little fire.*

Setting the shield down—but still careful not to look at the monster's face—Shanhaevel mustered the magic of one of his familiar, reliable spells. From his spread fingertips, he sent a sheet of flame cascading across the body of the basilisk.

Nothing happened. The basilisk didn't react in the slightest and seemed completely unharmed by the wizard's attack. Shanhaevel, shaking his head, stepped back out of the way and thought. Behind him, Govin took a few steps forward.

"What in the hells is going on?" the knight asked insistently. "Is it dead?"

"No," Shanhaevel replied, his tone revealing his frustration. "It isn't even singed, so far. I have one more idea. Wait."

With that, Shanhaevel drew upon another reserve of magical energy, channeling the mystical forces and shaping them into the spell he desired. He stepped from around the corner and pointed his finger at the basilisk's flank, firing off two green missiles that he knew would fly unerringly at the beast and strike true. Only they didn't. The first shot straight ahead, but rather than striking the beast, it seemed to pass right through and hit the far wall, and the second missile sputtered and fizzled, flying haphazardly off to one side.

"Damn," Shanhaevel said in disbelief. "It's like it's just not there!" Then realization hit him. "Of course!" he said, snapping his fingers. "It's not! It's an illusion!"

With that, the creature faded from view.

"What are you muttering?" Govin asked, still standing behind the wizard.

Shanhaevel laughed. It all made sense! The creature was an illusion, which explained why it was down here in the first place, why it didn't come around the corner to attack the group in hiding, and why none of the wizard's spells had had any effect on it.

"It's all right," Shanhaevel said, picking up Govin's shield and then turning to face his companions. "It's not really there. It's illusory magic. As long as you are really convinced it isn't real, it will just disappear. But you have to—"

"Shanhaevel, look out!" Elmo shouted, bringing his bow up and drawing an arrow to his cheek in one smooth motion.

Shanhaevel spun around, acting before he realized that perhaps he had been wrong and that the basilisk had merely disappeared, reappearing directly behind him. But what he gazed on as he turned was not the magical beast, but an elf, a woman, smiling at him as she thrust a sword directly at his midsection.

Gasping in surprise, Shanhaevel swung the knight's shield up, not enough to block the blow, but enough to force the killing stab aside so that it sliced into his side, grazing his ribs rather than plunging into his heart. He felt liquid warmth on his side and a sharp, stinging pain as he stumbled away from his attacker.

At the same instant, an arrow buried itself in the elf woman's shoulder. She growled in anger and vanished. Shirral cried out, and Shanhaevel heard bowfire from behind him as two more arrows streaked across his field of vision and vanished in mid-air. The wizard heard a pained grunt from in front him as his own back hit the wall and he slid down, his entire side slick with blood now.

Govin raised his sword high and swung at the spot where the wizard's attacker had been. His blade passed through air. Reaching down and taking hold of the shield in Shanhaevel's hands, Govin lifted it from the elf's grasp and stepped forward in a defensive crouch. Deftly he swung his blade from side to side.

"Careful!" Shanhaevel croaked, trying to warn Govin. "If you don't believe the beast is false, it will still turn you to stone!"

Then Shirral was beside Shanhaevel as Elmo and Draga ran past, weapons in hand, to join Govin. The druid took the wizard by the shoulders and dragged him backward, away from the fight. Pain shot through Shanhaevel's side.

Shirral released Shanhaevel and let him sink to the ground as she dug through one of her satchels. "Here," she said, removing one of the vials the group had recovered from the chest in the tower, "drink this." She held the small bottle toward his mouth. He opened his mouth and swallowed the thick liquid as Shirral poured it down his throat. It tasted of cinnamon and ash.

As the potion settled in his stomach, Shanhaevel felt a tingling throughout his body. It seemed to start everywhere, but as it grew stronger, it coalesced near his injury, until he could feel the rent flesh knitting together, being made whole again. In a moment, Shanhaevel felt free of pain. He gazed down at his side, seeing pink scar tissue peeking through the cut in his black shirt. He stood, feeling clear-headed once more.

Shirral was already on her feet, moving close to Ahleage.

"Careful!" Shanhaevel called as he moved beside her. "It's not real, but you really have to believe it."

Shirral nodded but kept her focus on the hunt. Beyond the druid, Govin, Elmo, and Draga were all moving slowly, cautiously, trying to find Shanhaevel's invisible attacker.

As Shanhaevel picked up his staff, he realized he was almost spent. A substantial portion of his energy had been exhausted in the battle at the farmhouse, and now, after using even more spells dealing with the basilisk that wasn't there, he wondered if that hadn't been the intention all along. The basilisk was placed there to drain our resources, he thought. She—and anyone else down here—wanted to wear us down before attacking.

At that moment, movement caught Shanhaevel's eye, and he jerked his head around in time to see the elf woman dropping down from high up on one wall, her sword raised and ready to plunge between Shirral's shoulders. Shanhaevel opened his mouth to shout, but it happened too fast, and he watched the blade ram into the druid's back.

"No!" Shanhaevel cried out as Shirral crumpled to the ground. He was running in the direction of the attacker before he even realized it, his staff raised. The elf woman, standing over Shirral, turned and smiled malevolently at Shanhaevel before winking out of sight once more.

Forgetting the woman, Shanhaevel dropped to his knees next to Shirral, who lay facedown. He gently rolled her over, even though his heart was pounding.

Shirral was still breathing, but her whole body was limp. Her eyes were glazed and stared dully at nothing in particular. Shanhaevel cradled her head in his arms, fighting back the tears. There is still time, his mind screamed at him. Don't let her die!

"Govin!" The wizard cried out. "Shirral needs you!"

The other three men had moved in and surrounded the fallen druid. Their backs to her, they stood guard in case the invisible assassin attempted to strike again. Upon hearing his name, Govin stepped back into the circle of protection and knelt, opposite Shanhaevel.

"It's bad," Shanhaevel said, still holding Shirral. "We're losing her."

"Let me see," the knight said, pulling Shirral in his direction and rolling her over on her stomach.

The wound between her shoulders was jagged, long, and deep. Shanhaevel shuddered as he peered down, sickened by the sight of the exposed bone visible in the gash. It looked as if the druid's spine had been severed in the blow.

"I'll do what I can," Govin said, and he closed his eyes. He placed his hands upon the wound, heedless of the blood, and uttered a prayer to Saint Cuthbert.

As the knight prayed, Shanhaevel heard a door open. Looking up, he saw a man, dressed similarly to himself, step through one of the portals and into the room. The man began to gesticulate, his fingers weaving a complicated pattern in the air. Another wizard!

"Don't stop," Shanhaevel whispered to the knight, then he stood up, still watching the man's motions, trying to discern the nature of the spell he was casting.

Upon seeing the man enter the hallway, Elmo and Draga took a halting step or two away from their companions, but they both seemed reluctant to leave their posts. Shanhaevel realized the wizard opposite him was taking advantage of that, standing seemingly unprotected out in the open while casting.

"Hold fast," Shanhaevel muttered under his breath, resisting his own urge to dive out of the way of whatever magic was about to erupt in their direction. "Let Govin finish his healing, and then we can deal with the mage."

Whatever magic the wizard was conjuring, Shanhaevel did not recognize it. When the spell was finished, a faintly shimmering globe of energy appeared around the wizard, slightly distorting his image. Immediately, the wizard began a second spell.

"What's he doing?" Draga asked. His wide eyes darted back and forth, watching for the invisible attacker but not wanting to turn away from the wizard. He sheathed his sword, slid his bow free from his shoulder, and nocked an arrow. Drawing it back, he took aim at the wizard. "Shanhaevel? Should I?"

Shanhaevel nodded. "Yes," he answered. "Disrupt the spell."

He spoke a moment too late, for the other wizard completed his second casting, and suddenly there were five of him, all standing in the midst of the shimmering globe of magic. At the very same instant, the elf woman appeared next to Draga, swinging her sword at the bowman's weapon. The sudden arrival startled Draga, who loosed his arrow a moment before the assassin's strike snapped his bow in two. The arrow clattered harmlessly off the wall.

Elmo leaped across the distance, attacking the woman with his axe. This time, the elf woman had no chance to invoke her invisibility. All of her energy was consumed in defending herself from the blows of the huge axeman. Struggling to deflect the powerful swings aimed at her, the woman slowly fell back, desperately using her own blade to ward off the blows.

"Falrinth!" she shrieked, backpedaling. "Do something!"

Draga had tossed aside his ruined bow, drawn his sword, and was now advancing on the multiple images of the wizard. The wizard hastily cast again.

At that moment, Shirral cried out, and Shanhaevel spun around to look at the druid. Govin still knelt over her, his hands bloody, but it appeared that he had finished his prayer of healing. Shirral, still facedown, was writhing in pain, her fingers clawing at the coarse stone floor.

"By the Mother!" she howled as she rolled to her side, rocking back and forth. "It hurts so much! Oh, it hurts!"

"What's wrong with her?" Shanhaevel demanded as he dropped down beside Govin.

"I mended her as much as I could, but all I really managed to do was keep her from dying. She's still badly wounded."

"I can take care of her," Shanhaevel said. "Go help Draga and Elmo."

Govin hesitated, looking at the wizard, then nodded and rose to his feet. He took an instant to survey both situations and then moved to join Draga.

Let's just hope we don't have any more invisible friends about, Shanhaevel thought as he fished through Shirral's pack.

When he found another of the vials they had recovered, he carefully uncorked it. At his knees, Shirral was groaning softly, still sprawled on her side. Her eyes were shut, and a sheen of perspiration coated her face. Shanhaevel inhaled a whiff of the elixir and caught the scent of cinnamon and ash. He reached down and coaxed Shirral into a sitting position.

"Come on, drink this," he said, helping the druid to rise. "I know it hurts. Easy, just drink this and you'll feel better."

Shirral grunted and clenched her teeth. Slowly, awkwardly, she sat up. The druid opened her mouth and, as Shanhaevel poured the contents, she drank down the entire potion. When the bottle was empty, Shanhaevel watched for the effect of the magic.

A soft blue glow began to emanate from Shirral's body. She closed her eyes again, but this time, there seemed to be a look of peace rather than of pain on her face. When the glow subsided, Shirral opened her eyes again and looked at her companion.

"Feel better?" Shanhaevel asked.

Shirral nodded and smiled, her icy blue eyes twinkling. "Yes," she said. "Thank you."

The tone of her voice made Shanhaevel glow, for it resonated with heartfelt affection.

"Come on," Shanhaevel said, rising and helping Shirral to stand, as well. "We have a mess on our hands."

Together, they got to their feet and observed the battles taking place around them. Elmo had managed to press the elf woman down the length of the hallway, while Draga and Govin were desperately trying to attack the wizard whom the assassin had called Falrinth. Unfortunately, the elven woman had just managed to disappear again, and Draga and Govin were having little luck determining which image of the wizard was the real one, although they had succeeded in reducing the number from five down to three. Shanhaevel could tell, also, that Falrinth was casting another spell.

"Listen," Shanhaevel said, turning to Shirral. "We can defeat that wizard if we can get rid of Miss Invisible beforehand."

"Besides a few healing spells, I only have a couple of tricks left that might be useful," Shirral answered, "but I have to know where she is first."

"I have a spell that just might work," Shanhaevel replied. "Get ready."

He called up the magical energies easily, gesturing and waiting for the spell to take effect. When he was done, the view before his eyes changed substantially. He now saw manifestations of magic all about him, auras radiating from different places throughout the T-shaped intersection where the company fought.

The three images of Falrinth glowed brightly, as did the shimmering globe of energy, which was no surprise to Shanhaevel. The illusionary spell of the basilisk also glowed, which the elven wizard had almost forgotten. He had expected to see all of those emanations of magic. However, flanking the flaming fountain were two forms that also radiated magic, though they were unmoving. Shanhaevel, taken aback at their presence, studied them for a moment. They were vague in shape, not exactly human in form, and they stood motionless, as though waiting for some instructions of some sort. Puzzled but sensing that they were not immediate threats, Shanhaevel continued his sweep of the area.

Ahleage in statue form glowed, as did a handful of weapons and items in the possession of the various companions. That left only two more sources, one that he expected to find and one he did not. The first, of course, was the elven assassin. She was moving up the hall toward them, having managed to get past Elmo. She seemed to be coming toward the two of them, which suited Shanhaevel just fine. The final magical radiance came from a small creature sitting high on one wall of the wide passageway, near the door where the wizard had entered.

It appeared to be a centipede, about a foot long, and it rested in a crack in the wall, watching everything taking place below. This puzzled Shanhaevel, but he did not have time to dwell on it, for the woman was almost upon them.

"Keep your voice low, and pretend we're watching the wizard," Shanhaevel told Shirral. "She's close. Are you ready?"

"Yes," the druid whispered. "Tell me where."

When the assassin had closed so that she was slightly to the side and behind Shirral, Shanhaevel tensed. When he saw the woman draw her weapon back, ready to stab at the druid, he swung around, blocking the blow with his staff as the woman became visible. Surprised at Shanhaevel's quick reaction, the woman blinked. Shanhaevel took advantage of the situation to hit her hard, right in the midsection, with the other end of his staff.

Shirral turned and pointed to the woman, shouting a single word and summoning magic of the earth. Immediately, a faint purplish glow sprang up around the woman, who had stepped away from Shanhaevel's attack and was straightening up once more. Shirral had her scimitar out and was advancing on the elven assassin, who smiled and deftly stepped to one side. When Shirral turned to face her, the other woman's smile turned to a frown, and she backed away, confusion plain on her face.

Elmo, having seen the commotion by the two spellcasters, hurried to join them, and he closed with the woman, who now had a panicked look on her face, realizing she was no longer invisible.

Shanhaevel turned to see what was happening with the others. What he saw shocked and dismayed him. Draga had taken a stand between Govin and the wizard, who was now down to one image. Draga was defending against the knight's attacks. Govin, refusing to strike his own companion, repeatedly tried to move around the hairy bowman, but Draga would not allow it.

He's been charmed in some way, Shanhaevel realized. The bastard is using Draga against us.

Shanhaevel moved forward, ready to strike the man down, when Govin stopped pressing his attack and giggled. Shanhaevel faltered in midstep, wondering what the knight could possibly find funny in the midst of a desperate battle. Govin was rooted to the spot though, and his giggle turned to a full laugh. Dropping his sword and shield, the knight grabbed his sides, doubling over and guffawing, hardly able to breathe.

More magic, Shanhaevel realized. I'm going to get my hands on this bastard's spellbooks for certain. But first . . .

Shanhaevel closed with the other wizard again, then stopped, realizing that the spell he had cast to detect magic emanations had reached its limit and winked out, leaving his sight normal again. However, the giant centipede in its niche was still quite visible, though well camouflaged.

Shanhaevel suddenly had a very good idea what the horrid insect was.

Quickly, the elf cast. He had only a couple of spells left, but the one he was about to invoke might still prove useful. Summoning the supernatural energies once more, he flung his hand out in the direction of the centipede, which, upon seeing the elf's gestures, had turned and was trying to retreat into the wall. But it was not fast enough.

In a flash, a long glowing arrow streaked forward, trailing a stream of liquid as it went. The magic arrow struck true, embedding itself in the giant insect and spraying the liquid over it. The centipede writhed in agony and fell free of the niche, dropping to the stone floor below and transforming as it did so. Distantly, Shanhaevel heard the other wizard shriek, and he knew his assumption had been correct.

When the creature hit the floor, it lay still, but it was no longer a centipede. Shanhaevel did not recognize it precisely, but he had no doubt that it was an imp of some type, summoned from the lower planes. Its flesh smoked and sizzled as the liquid, which was a potent acid, soaked and burned it.

"Thank you, Melf," Shanhaevel muttered, acknowledging the creator of the magic arrow of acid he had just used to slay the imp.

By this time, Govin had ceased his laughing, and Draga was his own self again. Both of them were advancing on Falrinth, whose face looked slightly burned, as if from acid, and who was desperately trying to cast one more spell.

"Get him!" Shanhaevel yelled. "Don't let him cast again!"

The two warriors were not quick enough. Behind Falrinth, a glowing portal appeared, a doorway framed in strange light, and the mage backed through it, avoiding the oncoming warriors. As soon as he was through, the doorway winked out of existence.

"Damn!" Govin growled, flinging his sword through the space where the doorway had been a moment before. "Damn that wizard to the hells!"

The knight spun around, looking for something, anything, to attack. When he saw that there were no enemies, he sighed loudly, and his shoulder sagged.

"If I ever track that wizard down . . ." he swore, leaving the vow unfinished. "Shanhaevel, I don't know if you know the spell he used on me, but don't you ever make me cackle like that. Ever."

Shanhaevel suppressed a smile. He could only imagine the indignation the knight must feel at having to endure such an ignoble thing. "I would never do that to you," the elf said, his smile leaking through. "I promise."

Govin glared at the wizard for a moment, then nodded curtly and pointed behind Shanhaevel. "What in the hells is that?"

Shanhaevel turned and saw that the knight was pointing to the dead imp.

"Exactly," he answered. "It's a thing from the hells themselves—an imp of some sort, perhaps a quasit. It was the wizard's familiar, as Ormiel is mine. I discovered it watching us, and when I killed it, the wizard suffered accordingly. There is a strong bond between mage and familiar. When one suffers, the other suffers also."

"That's why he seemed suddenly in agony?" Govin asked. "Why his face seemed burned?"

Shanhaevel nodded. "I would suffer great injury, too, should anything happen to Ormiel."

"Hmm, well, I guess I know how to get even then, should you ever cast that infernal laughing spell upon me."

Shanhaevel raised one eyebrow, but the twinkle in Govin's eye made it clear the knight was merely teasing.

"Let's see how the others fared," the knight said.

Shanhaevel turned to see Shirral and Elmo examining the body of the elf woman. Shirral pulled something off the woman's face and suddenly straightened and stepped back, flinging the item away in disgust.

Govin stepped closer, and Shanhaevel and Draga followed. "What is it?" the bowman asked.

"She's no elf," Shirral replied, glaring at the body.

"What do you mean?" Govin asked.

"She was only disguised as an elf," Elmo explained, his face grave.

"Well, then, at least we know one of our own wasn't besmirching our good name," Shanhaevel quipped, moving beside the druid to gaze down at the body. "So what's bothering you?"

Shirral grimaced. "Oh, nothing, except that she looks like she's got some orcish blood in her."

"Oh, a half-breed, huh?" Govin said, nodding. "Figures."

"What does that mean?" Shirral said, turning to face the knight, her eyes smoldering.

Shanhaevel winced, dreading what was to come.

Govin blinked a couple of times, a look of puzzlement on his face, then his eyes widened. "No! That's—" he sputtered. "I mean, I—That's not what I meant!" He took a deep breath. "I was trying to point out that I was surprised an elf would be here at all. Many half-orcs are angry with their lot in life, shunned by both of their lineages. It made more sense to me that a half-breed would have fallen in with the temple than an elf. That's all I meant."

Shirral's glare didn't lessen much. "It's not just half-orcs that are shunned by both lineages. In most people's eyes, a half-breed is a half-breed, regardless of the blood mixed together."

Govin's face grew very serious. "Shirral of the wood, daughter of the earth and sky, you have my solemn word as a servant of Saint Cuthbert that your lineage is of no concern to me. You are a steady and true companion. I respect your friendship and would never disparage your heritage."

Shirral's countenance softened. "All right, Govin. Thank you."

"Well, regardless of her bloodlines," Elmo said, standing, "we have a bigger problem on our hands."

The huge axeman still looked shaken.

"What's wrong?" Shanaevel asked.

"It could have just been coincidence," Elmo replied, shaking his head, "but she"—he pointed at the dead half-orc—"called him Falrinth."

"So?" Shirral asked, removing a pair of earrings and a belt from the woman.

"Falrinth was the name of a wizard who rode with Thrommel ten years ago," Elmo answered. "Burne told me once that Falrinth was a key to their efforts to destroy the demon. When he fell during the battle and was carried off by temple forces, the rest of them were forced to revise their plan, sealing the demon inside the temple rather than confronting and destroying her. They all grieved for the loss of their friend. Burne has presumed all these years that Falrinth was killed."

"And now you think this might be him?" Shanhaevel asked. "The same Falrinth?"

"It's quite possible," Elmo replied. "They might have broken him instead of killing him, turned him to their cause. He may be one of the main resources the temple leaders are using to hunt for the key. His knowledge of the demon's power was extensive."

"Burne must know of this," Shirral said. "We have to figure out a way to get him a message."

"If we can get to the surface," Draga cut in, "one of us could ride for Hommlet."

"That's a big if," Elmo said. "First, we have to find a way past that army. Plus, we must see what can be done about Ahleage."

Everyone turned, suddenly remembering their petrified friend. A wave of despair passed through them as they beheld Ahleage's frozen form. It seemed as though the palpable evil of the temple weighed even more heavily upon them.

No, Shanhaevel insisted to himself. *Don't let it wear you down. Fight it!*

"I don't understand," Govin said. "You told us the image was false. Why, then, is he cursed so? Would not the effects also be fake?"

Shanhaevel nodded. "Except that the image seemed real enough to him. He believed he was going to be petrified . . . and so he is—at least in his mind." Shanhaevel considered. "If that's true . . ."

Shanhaevel hurried over to where Ahleage stood, frozen in place. He examined the man carefully, studying the skin and clothing. To his surprise—or rather lack of it, now—Ahleage was not made of stone at all. The wan light cast from their lanterns had only made him look like stone. He was only totally and completely rigid.

"Of course!" Shanhaevel said. "He's only petrified in his mind."

"Then he can be saved!" Draga said, the relief evident in his voice.

"Well, maybe." Shanhaevel frowned. "Actually, even had he truly been turned to stone, there are ways to reverse it, but it still requires special dispelling magic to do so. I know of such a spell, but I would have to spend some time studying before I cast it."

"I could do it," Shirral said quietly. The druid stepped forward as Shanhaevel turned to her, one eyebrow raised. "I think I can reverse the condition."

"Your magic allows for dispellings?" the wizard asked.

Shirral nodded, closed her eyes, and prayed. Shanhaevel took a deep breath, hoping this would be the right course. As Shirral muttered her prayers, the rest of the group gathered around, waiting expectantly. After several long moments, Shirral placed a hand upon Ahleage's rigid arm and murmured the final words of her prayer.

There was a faint blue flash that cascaded across Ahleage's body, and in the next instant he was yelling and backing up, his shield still in front of him. He backed right into Draga, who caught hold of his companion and held him steady. Ahleage's head whipped about when he realized his whole frame of reference had changed in what for him had been a mere instant.

"Wha—? What happened?" Ahleage asked, regaining his balance. "Where's the, the *thing?*" He gestured in the direction where the basilisk had been.

Shanhaevel sighed in relief and joy—more joy than he thought he could feel in this accursed place. On impulse, he decided to tease Ahleage. "Thing? What thing? We heard you yell, we ran around the corner, and we found you like this."

"No! There was a thing, a *beast!* I saw it!"

"Hmm," Elmo said, playing along. "There's nothing there. You must have been seeing things."

"I was not!" Ahleage growled indignantly. "It was right there!"

"Easy, Ahleage," Draga said, patting his friend on one shoulder. "It probably scurried under the door right before we got here."

The bowman snickered, and Shirral covered her mouth with her hand to hide her smile.

"Oh, I get it," Ahleage said, turning from companion to companion, seeing the smiles on all their faces. "Just having a little fun with me, huh?"

At that, everyone grinned openly, born of both the humor and the relief that their companion was safe and recovered.

"You were affected by powerful magic," Shanhaevel explained, still grinning. "You were tricked by an illusion to believe you had been petrified. Shirral returned you to normal."

Ahleage blinked, looking around at the group, and finally settling on the druid. "Th-thanks," he muttered at last.

"Oh, you're more than welcome," Shirral said sweetly. "It's the least I could do for those friends of mine who pretend to be dying of poison."

Everyone chuckled, but the oppressiveness of the temple caused the mirth to subside quickly, and the group returned to the business at hand. Ahleage accepted a magical weapon and armor obtained from the dead assassin.

As they were preparing to move on, Shanhaevel remembered the two vague forms standing near the flaming fountain. With a little study, the elf determined that they were magical constructs, invisible servants that wizards often summoned to perform menial labor. These two had worked together to light the oil in the fountain, which had lit the place upon Ahleage's arrival.

"I'll wager that the half-orc woman was Falrinth's bodyguard," Shanhaevel commented as they prepared to check the doors leading off the wide passage.

"Perhaps we'll find out beyond these portals," Govin said as he opened the first of the doors.

"Just go slowly," Shanhaevel warned. "Both Shirral and I have burned off a lot of our spells. If we run into trouble, we'd better be ready to turn back fast."

"Caution is the word," Govin replied. "Falrinth may still be lurking around here."

"Or some more of his pets," Elmo added from the back of the group.

The first door they passed through led to what appeared to be the half-orc's chamber. It was furnished with a simple cot, a table with a chair and bench, and a wardrobe. The walls, however, were decorated with various sorts of unusual weapons, mostly wicked-looking daggers—the tools of an assassin. The group spent some time poking around the place, turning up a few gems and small pieces of jewelry, as well as some vials of thick poison in the wardrobe.

Once they were done, they moved across the hall to the door through which the wizard had arrived. The chamber beyond was obviously Falrinth's lair. The walls were lined with shelves, each of which was laden with books, scrolls, stuffed and mummified animals, and so forth. In addition, there was a small bed, a writing table, some cabinets, and a second door leading out. A cloak with many strange runes hung upon a peg near that second door, and next to it was a piece of parchment with more odd symbols. Attached to the far wall was another sheet of parchment, this one larger. It seemed to be a map of some sort. Of the wizard himself, there was no sign.

Govin led the way into the room, and Shanhaevel called softly, "Careful, Govin. Wizards are known for their fondness for magical traps. Don't touch anything until I have a chance to examine it first."

Nodding, the knight continued in, cautiously, followed by the rest of the group. Everyone fanned out, checking for signs of possible danger.

When they were certain that the wizard truly was gone, the members of the Alliance relaxed. Shanhaevel moved to examine the cloak and the parchment with the runes near the door. The cloak seemed plain enough, just elaborately decorated, so he moved over to the parchment.

As the elf read, he heard Govin say, "Remember, Ahleage, the wizard said not to touch—"

At that very instant, Shanhaevel's eyes roamed over a symbol he immediately realized as magical. Unfortunately, the very act of reading the sigil triggered its effect.

A powerful explosion knocked Shanhaevel backward, engulfing him in a blast of searing flame as he fell to the floor. The explosion was over in an instant, but Shanhaevel was in agony, his face burned and his eyes blinded. He clawed at the burns and realized a heartbeat later that his throat was going hoarse from screaming.

Suddenly, there was cooling relief. The pain faded, and as he pulled his hands back from his eyes, Shanhaevel found that he could see again. The first sight that greeted him was Shirral's face, creased with worry, looming over his own.

"Are you all right?" she asked, her voice tremulous.

Shanhaevel nodded, not trusting himself to speak.

"I didn't do it," Ahleage was saying, somewhere nearby. "I didn't touch a thing."

Shanhaevel smiled slightly as he tried to move up into a sitting position. Shirral gave him a hand and rocked back to give the wizard some room. "You didn't do it, Ahleage," he said. "I did it myself."

"See!" Ahleage said adamantly. "I told you!"

"That may be," Govin replied, "but I saw you about to—"

"All right, all right," Elmo interrupted. "Shanhaevel seems fine, so let's quit arguing over who actually triggered it."

"Hey," Shanhaevel said, standing. "I said it was me. And I didn't touch it. Don't read anything in here. That's how it was triggered. Don't even *look* at that map until I get a chance to check it for more runes."

"Are you sure you're whole again?" Govin asked.

"Yes," Shanhaevel replied. "I'm all right." He looked at Shirral, who smiled back, but her worry lines were still evident.

"That, however, was the last of my healing power," Shirral said. "So we must stop and rest, soon, so I can meditate and pray."

"We should at least check this other door," Govin argued. "If Falrinth is still around, I'd rather face him now than when he's had time to heal and regain his spells."

"I agree," Shanhaevel added, "and I do want to examine that map, first."

"Are you kidding?" Ahleage said. "You almost had your head blown off from the last thing you examined."

"I'll be all right," Shanhaevel responded. "I know what to look for, now. I'll need a mirror. Look around and see if there's one anywhere in here."

The group searched the place, but no one could find a reflecting glass anywhere, so Shanhaevel reluctantly agreed to leave the map for later. "I hope it's still here," he said wistfully.

Leaving the map behind, the group turned its attention to the door. After allowing Ahleage a chance to examine it for possible traps, Govin opened it. Beyond the portal was a small workroom, obviously the wizard's laboratory. Beakers, bottles, and tomes covered a table in the center of the room, while more shelves along the walls were filled with wands, staves, and rods of all sizes and shapes. Again, Falrinth himself was nowhere to be found.

Shanhaevel's eyes almost bulged out of his head. "Boccob!" he muttered, looking around the chamber. "Look at this horde!"

Elmo whistled. "Is all of this magical?" he asked, pointing to the various items on the walls.

Shanhaevel nodded, scarcely able to speak. "I imagine so," he said, "but there's no way to tell for sure without some divination, and I just don't have any more of that spell left. Look around for Falrinth's spellbooks. They might be here somewhere, too." The elf's face felt hot from his excitement. "Remember, just look. *Don't* touch anything."

"Maybe we can find a mirror in here," Shirral suggested.

"Good idea," Draga replied.

The group spread out and searched the place. Shanhaevel was almost giddy with excitement as he examined in detail the various devices on the shelves and worktable. What a mother lode, he thought. With this kind of magical power, I could be—

"Here's one," Ahleage said, pointing to an item on the other end of the table, careful not to touch it.

Shanhaevel hurried to see what he had found. It was a small polished mirror. The elf carefully picked it up, even as Ahleage practically dived under the table to get away from any impending blasts.

"Take it easy!" Shanhaevel chuckled. "No wizard is going to trap a mirror."

"I don't care," Ahleage said as he rose, wide-eyed, from the floor. "Standing too close to you when you mess with things appears to be dangerous."

Shanhaevel just smiled and pocketed the mirror.

"Why would a wizard keep all of his best magic stored away in here, rather than with him?" Elmo asked, looking around. "You'd think he'd want to use all of this stuff."

Shanhaevel frowned, for the axeman's words made sense. If this were mine, the elf thought, I wouldn't keep it stored away. In fact, if I had been Falrinth, I would have had at least two or three of those wands with me out there in the hallway.

"Good point, Elmo. Very good point."

"So, what are you saying?" Ahleage asked.

"This place seems to have been a little too easy to find," Shanhaevel replied. "Maybe we were supposed to find it." His heart was sinking. Of course Falrinth wouldn't leave all of his prized possessions just sitting out like this. I'm a fool to think he would. His true treasure trove must be hidden somewhere else. "Come on, let's at least get that map."

Shanhaevel led everyone back out into the main room. Standing with his back to the map, he scanned its contents through the mirror, looking for more of the magical sigils that he knew would trigger an explosion. Sure enough, they were there.

Damn, the wizard thought. Falrinth was quite the protective fellow.

Shanhaevel put the mirror away, removed the map from the wall, and rolled it up. As he did so, an oddity in the stonework caught his attention. Looking more closely, he found a continuous crack running up the wall. Following it with his eye, Shanhaevel realized he was looking at another secret door.

"Hey!" he called to his companions, his voice filled with excitement again. "I think I found another hidden portal."

"That figures," Draga said as the companions all gathered around. "Shall we push?"

"Let Ahleage do his thing, first," Govin advised, stepping aside to make room.

Rolling his eyes, Ahleage stepped to the wall and went over it carefully, looking, as usual, for any signs of danger. "Looks clean to me," he said, stepping away again.

Together, Elmo, Govin, and Draga placed their shoulders against the wall and pushed. Nothing happened. The three men redoubled their efforts, but to no avail. The wall did not swing open.

"Gah!" Draga said at last, easing up from his exertions. "Must have just looked like a secret door, Shanhaevel. That's nothing but solid wall."

"Maybe," Shanhaevel said thoughtfully. He frowned. "Maybe not. There might be some other way of opening it—a trigger of some kind. Look around and see if you can spot a switch, a lever, or something disguised as one of those things anywhere in the room."

Somewhat reluctantly, the group spread out, checking every item of furniture, every square foot of wall, every last item in the room carefully. This went on for a number of minutes, until Ahleage sighed and knuckled his back.

"This is getting us nowhere," Ahleage complained.

"I hate to admit it, but he's right," Shirral added. "I think we've found everything we're going to find."

"Just a few more minutes," Shanhaevel pleaded. "If we leave, Falrinth could come back and clean the place out."

"Besides," Elmo said, "we may not have many other options. That thing that crawled out of Lareth might be waiting on the surface."

"It's possible that Falrinth is still around here somewhere," Govin added. "We hurt him today. If we can catch up to him before he has a chance to seek healing and regain his strength and spells, so much the better."

"Hey!" Draga said, standing next to a wall and holding a torch cresset in his hand. "Look at this!"

The bowman pulled the cresset free of the wall, but where a normal hole should have been, a tiny lever projected instead.

"How does that work?" Ahleage asked, puzzled, as everyone crowded around Draga's discovery. Carefully, he reached out and touched the metal protrusion.

"Try to turn it," Elmo suggested.

Ahleage twisted, pushed, pulled, and generally fussed with the metal rod for half a minute or so before giving up.

"If it's supposed to do anything, it's too hard for me to move."

"Wait!" Shirral exclaimed. "Use the cresset!"

"Ah!" Shanhaevel said, nodding eagerly in agreement with the druid. "Put the cresset back on and then try it."

Draga handed the cresset to Ahleage, who slipped the thing back on the rod. There was a tiny click, and then Ahleage twisted the device. It rotated easily this time, and behind them, the section of wall that had held fast before swung free.

"That did it," Ahleage said.

"You were right, after all," Draga told Shanhaevel as he drew his sword.

The space beyond the hidden portal turned out to be exactly what Shanhaevel had been hoping: a second laboratory. This one looked far more lived in, and there was an amazing amount of clutter everywhere. However, the thing that drew everyone's attention was a small iron box sitting in the middle of the table. It made all the companions uneasy, and Govin refused to touch the thing. Carefully, Ahleage examined it from the outside, and when he found nothing to indicate mundane traps, Shanhaevel took a turn. Satisfied that nothing untoward would happen, the elf flipped the lid open.

Inside was a small golden skull with no jaw. It had four empty sockets at the compass points of the crown line that appeared to be designed to hold gems.

"Boccob!" Shanhaevel breathed. "The key. We have the key!"

"Don't touch it!" Govin hissed, jerking the elf away from the box. "I can feel its wickedness from here."

Shanhaevel nodded, carefully shutting the lid once more and picking up the box.

"Let's get out of here," Govin pleaded. "I am suddenly overwhelmed with dread at the thought of staying."

"The knight is right," Ahleage added as the group began to depart. "We have what we came for. It's long past time to go."

The Alliance made its way out of the wizard's chambers and back into the T-shaped intersection. Just as they were about to head back out through the tunnel that led to the tower and well, a forlorn keening faintly drifted down from that direction.

Shanhaevel shivered at the sound.

"It's Lareth," Ahleage breathed, "or the thing he has become."

19

Hedrack paced back and forth, his steps hammering on the stone floor of the meeting chamber. The high priest was angry, truly angry. And, he had to admit, more than a little afraid. Every careful plan he had made of late had gone awry. Underlings had failed in their duties, and those damned meddlers had caused him untold amounts of trouble.

He was seething, ready to have Falrinth cast into one of the elemental nodes for this latest disappointment. To have lost the key—the very golden key that would free Zuggtmoy!—was unforgivable. And to those interlopers . . . !

Hedrack wondered just how much longer Iuz would be willing to put up with such blunders. The high priest knew that, regardless of whose fault it was that these mishaps continued to occur, Hedrack himself would be held responsible.

Lord Iuz will not tolerate such incompetence, he thought, just as I do not. It is the way of the world.

Falrinth shifted in his uncomfortable position, kneeling as he was with his hands and feet manacled behind his back. He remained silent, however, dutifully waiting for his superior to speak again.

Good, thought Hedrack. He must fear for his very life, now, for I will not be a patient man any longer.

"So, you are certain this will free her? Even without the *key?*" He hotly emphasized the last word, making it clear that Falrinth's new proposal for freeing the demoness would not alleviate his extreme displeasure at the wizard's foolishness.

"Yes, my lord. I had been studying this for a while, even before we knew of the existence of the key. The wards on the doors will be of no consequence to my servants. They can place the items and ignite them at the proper moment while we watch from a safe distance. I am certain it will work."

"Never mind that. What I want to know is, are you certain this will free her? There is no danger to her well being?"

Falrinth attempted to shrug, but having very little mobility due to his bindings, it was barely more than a flinch. "I cannot say without *any* doubt at all, my—"

"That is not the answer I want!" screamed Hedrack, crossing the distance between them in a single step and slapping the wizard across the mouth.

Falrinth grunted in pain as his head whipped to the side, the fierceness of the blow causing him to lose his balance and topple over onto his side.

The two attendants—tall, mangy bugbears with matted fur and sour-smelling leather armor—immediately reached down and righted Falrinth once more. The wizard stared at the floor, a trickle of blood running down his chin. He worked his jaw slowly before speaking.

"I am convinced that it will free her unharmed, my lord," the wizard said at last, forcing the words through clenched teeth.

Hedrack smiled, bending slightly at the waist to stare straight into Falrinth's eyes. "That's much more satisfying to hear." His visage sobered again. "For your sake, you had better be right. If even the slightest harm comes to her as a result of this, I will not be tossing you into one of our private little sanctuaries below. Instead, I will offer you directly to Iuz, as a toy, a plaything, and I will make mention that you have been secretly consorting with the spider bitch behind my back."

Falrinth's eyes bulged at this revelation.

"Oh, yes," Hedrack continued, his voice dripping with honeyed acid. "You did not think I knew, did you? I am aware of much. You and Lareth both have been inviting trouble, playing lackey to others besides he who will trample the Flanaess beneath his feet. Perhaps, if I mention that fact, he will not be so quick to blame me for all the trouble your incompetence has caused."

Falrinth was shivering slightly, as evidenced by the faint clinking of the chains that bound him.

Excellent, Hedrack thought, smiling. Now, I have his attention.

With a nod from the high priest, the bugbears moved to flank the prisoner, lifting him between them and bearing him away to his cell once more.

Once alone, Hedrack let out a deep and mournful sigh, for he did not relish his next task. Making his way down to the central temple, he passed beyond the writhing purple curtain and prepared to contact his lord and master. Dropping to his knees, he prayed.

Almost immediately, he felt the presence of his god in his mind. "My lord Iuz," he intoned, "I am your Mouth, I pronounce—"

What news? the presence demanded, its evil washing over him, mingling with impatient anger.

Hedrack flinched, knowing this was going to be most unpleasant. "My lord," he began, looking for the right words, the best way to honey-coat the news. "We have encountered more setbacks, and I am afraid I have unfortunate news."

I grow tired of your excuses, priest. Perhaps it is time I find another, someone more capable of carrying out my wishes.

"This humble servant begs your indulgence for a moment longer, master," Hedrack pleaded, truly groveling now. "I also have encouraging news that I pray will offset the unpleasantness of the other."

Iuz's malevolent displeasure washed over Hedrack, sickening the high priest in the core of his stomach and making his limbs weak and numb. But after a moment, the sensations of ill ease subsided. *Very well, speak.*

Sighing in relief, Hedrack began. "My lord, the golden key has been lost. To the meddlers, unfortunately."

You incompetent idiot! Iuz cried, his gravelly voice grinding into Hedrack's brain and driving him hard to the floor. *The one thing that would free her, you have lost!*

His head pounding from the pain of Iuz's wrath, Hedrack struggled to speak. "N-No, my L-Lord," he managed to utter through clenched teeth. "There is another way."

The waves of hatred crashing over the high priest subsided once more. *Go on,* Iuz insisted.

Catching his breath, Hedrack continued. "Falrinth believes he knows where she is, and he thinks he has a way to free her without the golden orb. He thinks we can free her from her bindings."

Iuz was silent, as though considering for a moment. *Interesting. Tell me more.*

"If you recall, my lord, he was a part of the company that planned to destroy her ten years ago, before his capture and conversion to the beliefs of the temple. He believes he knows how the bindings work. He thinks he knows a way to circumvent and destroy them. I have but to give the order, and he will try."

Is there a danger to her?

"He has assured me there is not," Hedrack said, hoping beyond hope the wizard was right.

He has failed you before, Iuz grumbled, blackness roiling with the words. *Why should you trust him, now?*

"Because he bargains with his life, my lord. Because he now knows that I am aware of his other allegiance, his servitude to the spider bitch, and he believes that it is only through my machinations that you do not yet know. I hold that over his head."

Hmm, well played. Very well, proceed with this new plan.

Hedrack smiled despite the pounding in his chest. "Yes, my lord," he answered, but the god was already gone from his mind.

* * * * *

Hedrack returned to the cell and loomed over Falrinth, who was kneeling in one corner, still bound in his chains, and glaring back sullenly. He knew better than to open his mouth in open disdain to Hedrack. The high priest understood all too well the wizard's resentment, though. After all, Falrinth had attempted to save his own pitiful life with the plan, and in return, Hedrack had thrown him back in his cell.

If only he understood, thought the high priest, how much anguish he truly did save himself. His stay in this prison is a welcome alternative to what might have been.

The high priest signaled for the guards to release the wizard. As Falrinth stood, stretching too-long-bound muscles, Hedrack clapped the wizard on one shoulder.

"Iuz likes your plan, my friend. We are going to put it in motion at once. You should go and prepare."

Falrinth blinked, hesitating. Then, seeing the earnest look on Hedrack's face, the wizard nodded and, with a last sidelong glance at his jailers, hurried from the room.

"Come on!" Elmo urged as he turned and headed down the passage they hadn't yet explored.

As Shanhaevel swung around to follow, Ahleage skidded to a stop and stared after them. "Are you *crazy?*" he growled. "We can't go deeper into the temple. That's suicide!"

"We don't have a choice!" Shirral hissed, trying to grab Ahleage's arm and pull him along. "We can't stand and face that *thing* right now. We're tired and our magic is all but exhausted."

"No!" Ahleage insisted through clenched teeth, yanking his arm free from the druid's grasp. "We could hide! Maybe the wizard has a spell that will turn us all invisible. Anything is better than going deeper into this hell hole!"

"Ahleage," Shanhaevel said, taking his friend by the arms and forcing the man to look him in the eye. "If we don't get out of here, right now, we are going to die! Don't let the temple beat you down. It's evil, and it preys upon your mind, making you feel defeated before you've even fought. Whatever's down that corridor, it can't be any worse than what's coming this way. Now, come on!"

With that, Shanhaevel released Ahleage and turned to follow Elmo into the gloom of the passage. It seemed to be some sort of a dead end, but then the elf spotted a steep set of steps at the very end, leading up. Elmo was perched near the top, pushing open a trapdoor set into the ceiling. The huge man poked his head up through the opening and paused to look around, then motioned for everyone to follow. He ascended out of sight.

As Shanhaevel reached the bottom of the steep steps and waited for Draga, Govin, and Shirral to make their way up, an unnerving howl rose up from the opposite direction. The sound made the wizard's spine crawl, and he shuddered. Ahleage ran up beside him.

"I can't believe I let you talk me into this," he growled as the elf started up the steps.

"It's that or face that horror that was Lareth," Shanhaevel replied, reaching the top and beginning to climb through the trapdoor.

"Not this," Ahleage whispered as he crowded up behind the elf. "I mean two nights ago, around the campfire. I can't believe I let you all talk me into coming to the temple in the first place."

As soon as Ahleage was through the trapdoor, Elmo settled the lid back into place. Shanhaevel made a quick inspection of the new space in which they found themselves. It was a small, circular room, very dusty and with many cobwebs. Only one passage led out. The only light was the group's own lanterns, but at the far end of the passage, the elf saw the faint glow of torchlight emanating from around a corner.

"Come on," Govin said, drawing his sword and proceeding cautiously down the passage out of the room. "That thing'll figure out where we went soon enough."

"Wait," Ahleage called softly. "Let me take the lead. Istus knows I'm a fool, but I can keep a sharp eye out for"—he shrugged—"whatever."

Acquiescing, Govin let Ahleage move a little ahead of him, and the group proceeded down the hall.

Shanhaevel, padding along beside Shirral, was trying very hard to keep from scuffing his feet along the floor. Despite his efforts, it seemed to him that every footfall was a thunderclap in his ears. This isn't like walking on the floor of the forest, he reminded himself. Shaking his head, he redoubled his efforts at stealth.

The gloom of the place weighed down upon him. The mass of earth and stone overhead seemed somehow to be slowly sinking, pressing down, threatening to crush them all, to trap them them in the darkness. Even the lanterns Elmo and Shirral carried seemed to do little to banish the menacing shadows, and Shanhaevel found that he was hearing faint noises just beyond the range of the light. He shuddered and pressed on, staying close to Draga, who was right in front of him.

The passage ran straight for a ways, then turned to the right. There was a door to the left, currently shut, and the tunnel continued on into the gloom. It was here that the torches were lit, and the cobwebs and dust of before were absent.

"Which way?" Shirral asked, her voice barely above a whisper.

"No doors!" Ahleage replied just as softly, turning to head the other direction. "As long as we don't open them, we're not surprised by anything on the other side."

Shirral looked at Shanhaevel, who only shrugged and nodded. They continued to pad along, and more than once Shanhaevel realized he was holding his breath. After a short while, this next passage opened into another circular room, although this one was larger than the first, and far from being empty, its rounded walls were lined with statues. Ahleage pulled up short of entering and peered around.

There were nine statues in total—strange and fantastic creatures, only some of which Shanhaevel recognized.

Nearest was a great spherical beast with but a single giant eye in its middle, gaping jaws below that, and ten tentacles, also containing eyes, on its top side. It had been carved so that it appeared to float. Next to that was a rearing dragon, much smaller than Shanhaevel imagined a real one would be. The other forms were hidden by the gloom, although four odd, glowing bronze spheres set into the walls lighted the place. Two other passages led out of the room.

"Now what?" Ahleage asked over his shoulder, not turning his back to the chamber. "How much farther are we willing to go?"

"We need a place to rest," Elmo said, "some place where we can hide and wait for a chance to go back and get out of here."

"That way," Govin said, pointing across the round room to the passage on the left.

"How do you know?" Ahleage insisted, scowling. "What makes that one better than the other?"

"I don't know, but it is," the knight answered. "I can *feel* it."

Ahleage raised one eyebrow at Govin as if the knight were crazy, but finally he shook his head and crept across the open floor of the round chamber, heading for the passage Govin had indicated.

As Shanhaevel followed, he noticed that the glowing spheres had detached themselves from the walls and were floating, hovering. He looked more closely and realized the lights were closing in on the group.

"Uh, let's hurry," he said softly. "I don't think this room is safe."

When Shirral looked in the direction he was staring, she gasped, "Will o' wisps!" She shoved Govin, who was in front of her, so he would move faster. "Don't let them touch you!"

Ahleage looked over his shoulder, and when he saw the advancing balls of light, his eyes widened. He turned and jogged out the far side, the rest of the group close behind.

The Alliance hurried down this new corridor, which was once again kept in darkness, although it lacked the dust that might indicate disuse. It ran for much longer than the more recent tunnels had, and after a few moments, Shanhaevel heard running water ahead. Ahleage slowed, cautious once more, and the elf stole a glance behind them. The will o' wisps, as the druid had named them, were not following, although they still bobbed and weaved in the now-distant chamber.

The water flowed from a horrid fountain set back in a slight alcove. Leering demonic faces spewed nasty smelling water from mouths, eyes, and open sores on their faces. The rancid water fell into several basins blackened by some sort of aquatic growth.

Ahleage shuddered and gave the fountain a wide berth, skirting along on the opposite side of the passage. "Still think this is a great idea?" he asked Govin over his shoulder as they continued. "How much longer does our luck hold out?"

"Ahleage is right," Elmo said, slowing. "This is getting us nowhere but lost. We should stop and rethink this."

"No," Govin insisted. He pointed again. "I can't explain why, but this is the way we must go."

"Look, knight," Ahleage said, turning on Govin with a fierce look, "we're mad to be doing this. We found the key, and we should be trying to leave, not go deeper. And where is everyone? Why aren't we running into temple forces? It scares me that it's so empty in here."

"I understand your reluctance," the knight said. "I feel so many bad sensations from this accursed place that I want to retch. But for some reason, I can sense something else ahead."

"What?" Ahleage insisted. "What do you sense?"

"I don't know. I can't quite put my finger on it, but it feels . . . *holy,* somehow."

Ahleage rolled his eyes and whistled. "I think your brain has been poisoned by this place," he said in disgust.

A sensation of frigid blackness suddenly ran up and down Shanhaevel's spine. Shuddering from the unnerving feeling, he turned to peer back down the hall, half-expecting to see one of the will o' wisps nearby. Instead, a shadowed thing reared up not two paces away and turned his blood to ice.

"Boccob!" the wizard yelped, jerking back instinctively and slamming into Draga.

Lareth's face stared balefully at him and hissed, malevolence radiating from its spectral, spidery body. It shambled forward, its two front legs curled upward, reaching for the elf.

Shirral screamed, and Shanhaevel felt someone grab his collar and jerk him back as one of the tendrils swiped at his face, barely missing. They were running, Govin leading the way, all of them scrambling madly, desperately away from the shade that had crept up on them.

Shanhaevel paid little attention to the twists and turns of their progress, concentrating only on staying close to the rest of them and making sure Shirral was still beside him. He did not dare turn around to see if the animate shadow was still there. From farther back, the creature let out its keening wail, which both terrified the elf and relieved him. As horrifying as it was, it meant they were putting distance between themselves and the monster.

As he rounded another corner, still making certain he was keeping up with Draga, Shanhaevel nearly collided with the bowman, who had stopped to stare at Govin. The knight was standing in the middle of a hallway, once again a dust- and cobweb-covered passage, staring around uncertainly.

"Here," the knight said. His voice was filled with doubt. "Somewhere right here . . ." His words trailed off as he peered at the floor, then moved to the wall and pressed it experimentally with his hand. A frown pursed his lips as he looked, then, shaking his head, stepped back and pointed, saying, "A door. It is here somewhere. Find it!"

Shrugging, Shanhaevel stepped up to where Govin had indicated. He looked, feeling his spine crawl from increasing panic at the thought of the shadowy creature catching up to them again. Suddenly, he spotted the seam Govin had somehow known would be there—the outline of a door!

"Here!" the elf cried softly, pointing. "It's right here. Push!"

As one, the companions found places and pushed. Slowly—far too slowly for Shanhaevel—a section of the wall pivoted inward.

Nodding his head in satisfaction, Govin was the first one through, gesturing for the others to follow him. When the last person was safely beyond the portal, Draga pushed it shut again.

When it finally closed with a slight *click*, the bowman sank down with a weary sigh. "That was close," he said, looking at his companions. "Too close."

Everyone nodded as Shanhaevel peered around. It was an odd-shaped room, all uneven angles and corners, and it had the appearance of not having been used since the temple fell ten years ago. The place had the look and feel of a chapel, and it even had an altar covered with a snowy white cloth that had been inscribed with red runes:

Venerate This Shrine of Good.
Then Haste Away, All Ye
Of True And Good Faith!

A statue of Pholtus, god of the blinding light, had been placed in a niche in the wall. A large silver staff topped by a large disk—known as the Staff of the Silvery Sun, the symbol of Pholtus—hung upon the western surface. Other wall hangings gave the room a peaceful feel that seemed out of place after the oppressive dread of the temple.

"How did you know?" Ahleage gasped, sinking down to the floor and stretching his legs out before him. Perspiration beaded on his forehead.

Govin shook his head. "I don't know. I just felt it." He closed his eyes and whispered, "Thank you, Saint Cuthbert, for your guiding hand."

"It might be Pholtus you should be thanking," Elmo replied dryly, pointing to the symbols.

Govin nodded. "The energies of many holy beings may lend a hand during times of true need. My thanks extend to all of them."

"So," Shirral said, slumping down in her own spot, "what now?"

"We wait, rest," Elmo answered, finding a spot of his own and setting his lantern down before laying his axe gently on the floor. "Are we safe here?"

"Yes," Govin replied. "That thing will not enter, I think. This place feels consecrated, and Lareth's spirit may not pass into it."

"That won't stop something else," Shanhaevel pointed out. "Something . . . alive." He shuddered.

"That something has to find us, first," Ahleage muttered, closing his eyes. "But damned if I know how to get back out again."

The group fell silent, and eventually, everyone caught their breath. They broke out a meager meal to share, and when they were done, they settled in to wait.

Draga pulled out the small wooden instrument he had been working on. He played a few notes, but somehow, the tones sounded hollow and weak, and he put the thing away again, looking forlorn.

Shanhaevel, in an effort to pass the time, paced through the room, examining the various trappings of the chapel, wondering how anyone might have managed to transport all of this into the bowels of the temple without notice. As he was studying the silver symbol, he caught sight of a tiny ring of metal that had been partially hidden behind the intersection of the staff and disk. Reaching up, he took hold of the ring and tried to pull it free. As he drew the ring out from its hiding place, he discovered that it was connected to a length of steel thread that went back into the wall. Upon pulling on it, there was an audible click, and a section of the wall swung open next to the elf.

"What did you do?" Ahleage exclaimed, jumping to his feet, his sword in his hand. "Another one! You found another one!"

"Careful," Govin said, rising to his feet as well. "I have a great sense of unease about whatever's beyond there."

Collecting themselves, the six friends moved cautiously toward the secret door and peered inside.

The six-sided chamber beyond was inky black, and it appeared to be empty except for a lone skeleton stretched out near the door. Shanhaevel shuddered. The place had an eerie feel to it, something he could not quite put his finger on. As the group moved farther into the chamber, the elf spotted a coffin resting against the far wall, its lid closed and buckled. The rest of the companions spotted this, too, and the whole group approached the sarcophagus cautiously. The lid had a silver cross inlaid into its surface, and there was a scroll case lying atop it.

"How strange," Shirral breathed, reaching out to gently poke at the scroll case with her blade. "Why would there be a tomb here, hidden behind that chapel?"

"And who was the poor fellow by the door?" Ahleage asked.

"I don't like this," Govin said. "It doesn't feel right."

"Should we open it?" Ahleage asked, flicking daggers in and out of his sleeves in nervousness.

"Yes." Govin nodded. "I think we should. But let's be prepared. Draga and Ahleage, be ready with your bows. Elmo, Shirral, and Shanhaevel, you open it on the count of three."

Surrounding the sarcophagus, they took a collective deep breath, unfastened the locks, and prepared to remove the lid.

"On the count of three," Govin whispered, "we flip it open. Ready?"

Everyone nodded and took hold of an edge. Shanhaevel half-expected something to rise out of the coffin and lunge at him. Tightening his grip, he waited for the knight's countdown.

"One," Govin said.

Shanhaevel took a deep breath.

"Two."

"Three!"

The lid went tumbling to the side, and three companions scattered while the other three prepared to attack. Govin tensed, then paused and stared curiously down at the inside of the coffin.

Shanhaevel peered inside from several feet away, rising up on tiptoe to get a better look. It was a man—a very handsome man, in fact. Far from being dead, the fellow looked healthy and strong, if unconscious. He was clad in fine mail with a white surcoat, and it took the elf a moment to register the crest upon the breast. The arms of Furyondy and Veluna, as well as the Knights of the Hart were there.

Two royal houses and a knightly order, the wizard realized.

"My god!" Elmo said, stumbling to one knee and getting a closer look.

"What is it, Elmo?" Shanhaevel moved beside him. "Who is this?"

"I don't believe it," the big man said, reaching out to nudge the comatose form. "It's him."

"Him, who?" Ahleage demanded as he and the others crowded around.

Elmo took a deep breath before replying, "Prince Thrommel. It's the missing prince!"

Shanhaevel fell back, stunned. *Thrommel?* In here? In the bowels of the temple? Boccob!

Govin shook his head in disbelief, and Draga grinned from ear to ear. Shirral checked the man, feeling to see if he was injured or ensorcelled in some way.

The prince stirred. His chest rose ever so slightly, then fell, and Shanhaevel thought he saw the eyelids flicker. For the first time, the elf noticed the finely tooled gold belt around the man's waist and the gold medallion around his neck with the emblem of a crown and a crescent moon inscribed upon it.

The prince's eyelids fluttered open, blinking in the light of the lanterns. He reached out, grasped the edges of his coffin, and tried to rise. Govin's strong hand was there to aid him. The knight lifted the man into a sitting position, from where the prince blinked repeatedly and peered about, studying the faces of the six companions surrounding him.

"Where—? Where am I? Who are you?"

"My lord," Govin began, "I am Sir Govin Dahna, servant of Cuthbert. These are my companions and friends. Are you injured in any way?"

The prince blinked several more times as he focused on the knight's face. "I—I don't think so," he said, moving his arms and legs experimentally. "Who are you, again? And where in the hells am I?"

"We are the Alliance, my lord," the knight responded, "and you are in the bowels of the ruined Elemental Temple."

"The temple! What am I doing here? What alliance? What are you talking about?"

"We are—" Govin began, but Elmo interrupted him.

"My lord, I am a Knight of the Hart, like yourself. These companions and I have banded together in the service of the viscount of Verbobonc and your father, at the behest of Burne of the tower. We were exploring the ruins of the temple and discovered you sealed away—magically preserved it seems. We apparently broke the spell."

"I see," Thrommel replied, rubbing his eyes. "Burne, you say? What dire circumstances would cause him to send you all into the ruins of the temple?" Then, shaking his head in dismissal, he continued, "I must get to Mitrik so I can let everyone know I am alive and well. Jolene must be beside herself with worry. The wedding! Tell me they haven't cancelled the wedding!"

The prince tried to rise, but he was unsteady on his feet, and several hands reached out to aid him as he slowly and carefully climbed out of the coffin.

"My lord," Elmo said gravely. "You have been missing for seven years. It's the spring of 579."

Thrommel stared, swaying unsteadily on his feet. *"Seven years?"* he breathed. "They must all think I'm dead."

"No," Govin interjected. "Not all."

"My lord," Elmo said. "Somehow, through some means of scrying, members of your father's court knew you still lived, but there appeared to be no way to determine your location. Jolene has refused to marry, although there have been a number of suitors."

"Ah, Jolene," Thrommel said, smiling gently. "Always the loyal one—fiercely so. I hope she is well."

"And Melias," Govin added, "who served with you at the fall of the temple ten years ago, held out hope that he would someday find you."

"Hmm," the prince mused, nodding his head absently as he listened to the unfolding tale. "His dedication honors me."

Elmo looked at the rest of the Alliance, from face to face, his own visage grave as he spoke "Sadly, my lord, Melias was leading this expedition, but he fell in battle not three days ago. I am sorry."

"No!" the prince said, his unsteady legs betraying him at last. He sat down hard. "Not Melias. I would have welcomed seeing him again."

"And he, you, my lord," Shanhaevel said. "As would have my master, Lanithaine. He was on his way here when he also fell."

The prince looked at Shanhaevel and frowned. "Lanithaine, the wizard?"

Shanhaevel only nodded.

"Two of my company, fallen in battle, and I, missing for seven years? What is going on? Why are we in the depths of the temple? Tell me your tale, and quickly."

Shanhaevel blinked once at the man's commanding manner, but then the elf remembered that he was, after all, a prince, used to commanding *and* to getting what he wanted with but a word.

With little fanfare, Elmo explained the situation to Thrommel. When he was done, the prince sat thinking for several long moments. Finally, he spoke again.

"This key . . . you now have it?"

"Yes, Prince Thrommel," Shanhaevel said, retrieving the box from his pack and opening the lid to display to the prince.

Both Thrommel and Govin recoiled from the thing, and the prince said, "Ugh! It is foul with evil. I can feel its corruption even from here." He turned back to Elmo. "You say that you recovered it from a wizard named Falrinth? The very same who also rode with me at the Battle of Emridy Meadows? He fell in battle that day."

"Perhaps he was taken prisoner instead, my lord," Elmo replied. "He might have been broken in some way and made to serve the temple."

"That is very grave news," Thrommel said, "but it shall be addressed, just as soon as we return to the surface. You say that Burne is researching the means to destroy this key?"

"Yes," Shanhaevel replied. "We must take it to Hommlet, at once. Once the key is destroyed, the demon will be forever imprisoned in this place."

"Yes," the prince said, "and I must ride to Mitrik, this very day. My sword! Where is Fragarach?" Thrommel looked about frantically, glancing into the coffin as well. "Was there a sword here, with me?"

"I see only your shield, prince," Ahleage said, pointing to the crested shield that had lain beneath Thrommel's feet in the coffin. "There is no sword."

"Ah!" Thrommel cried, pointing to the lid of the coffin.

Shanhaevel turned his gaze to where the lid rested upon the floor, cast away when the Alliance had awakened the prince. Where the inlaid cross had been, there now rested a fine broadsword, its hilt wrapped in silver and gold wire, its pommel set with brilliant emeralds. The blade shone brightly even in the dim light of the lanterns, gleaming with an almost unnatural bluish hue.

"Fragarach!" Thrommel shouted, holding forth his hand. The sword leaped free of the lid of its own accord, crossing the distance to the prince's outstretched grasp. Thrommel held the blade aloft, closing his eyes in contentment, as though some unseen power coursed from the blade into his body.

When Prince Thrommel opened his eyes again, they were clear with determination and purpose.

"We must leave this chapel and find our way out of the temple," he said. "You must deliver the key to Burne, and I must ride to Mitrik."

Shanhaevel sat with his back against the wall of the chapel, keeping an eye on the others while they slept. Despite the prince's eagerness to move quickly, the lack of sleep and the exertion of battle had caught up with the members of the Alliance. While Shanhaevel, Shirral, and Draga rested, Elmo, Ahleage, Govin, and Prince Thrommel kept watch.

Burne had visited Shanhaevel in his dreams again. The wizard's floating visage had appeared, and the words Burne had spoken remained with Shanhaevel even upon waking.

Shanhaevel, I have discovered the means to destroy the key. As soon as you retrieve it and are able to return to Hommlet, we can conduct the procedure together. If, for some reason, you are unable to reach me, or if something happens to me before you can return, I will pass along the steps for the key's destruction now.

You must expose the key—complete with its four gems—in quick succession and in the proper order, to the forces of each of the four elements. First comes air—a gust of wind should do nicely. Follow that with a hard strike from stone, preferably granite. Exposure to searing flame is next, to be followed, finally, by complete immersion in cold, black water. Only after these four steps are followed will the orb crack and its magical energies dissipate.

Hurry, Shanhaevel! Return to me with the key!

When Shanhaevel awakened several hours later, the dream remained in his consciousness, and the import of

Burne's words had horrified him. The key could not be destroyed unless it was whole, and the Alliance did not possess the four gems. We're not done, yet, he had realized. He had hung his head in dismay, dreading to tell the others, but tell them the elf did, and his words had been met with many groans and disconcerted looks.

"We have no choice but to continue to look for the gems," Govin had said grimly.

"First, we see to it that the prince reaches the surface," Elmo had added.

Thrommel had shaken his head. "No. Your task is far more important. I will make my own way to the top, guided by the wisdom of Cuthbert. You continue your quest. Seek the gems."

Elmo had opened his mouth to protest, but the prince would hear none of it, so the huge axeman had finally given in.

"I shall depart a little before you," Thrommel had announced. "With luck, your fiendish spidery friend will not be there, but if it is, I will lure it away from you so that you may escape." When he had seen both Govin and Elmo shaking their heads and opening their mouths about to protest, the prince had silenced them with a gesture. "Do not worry, my friends. Fragarach will protect me from this fiend."

Now Shanhaevel sat, awake, thinking about all that had transpired. It seemed like many years ago that he had set out with Lanithaine to ride to Hommlet. He had been almost a different person, then. Certainly, if he survived this terrifying escapade and ever managed to return to the Welkwood, he *would* be a different person, a far different person.

Shaking his head, Shanhaevel turned to his spellbooks and spent the next several hours meticulously studying, memorizing the formulas he would need to cast his spells. When he finished, he sat pondering the coming trials within the temple. Shirral was still in some sort of reverent trance, communing with the forces of nature, bringing the powers of the earth into herself in order to shape and form them as she desired.

Shanhaevel sighed softly. Though we draw upon powers that are vastly different, he mused, in the end, we both become vessels, channeling that power *from* somewhere *to* somewhere else. Why is it, then, that neither of us can comprehend the method the other employs to garner that power?

The wizard looked at his own pack, bulging with gear. He noticed a particular bulge and frowned. It was the smallish box, in which was the small golden skull, the key to either free or destroy the demon. Shanhaevel frowned because the thing made him uneasy. Every time he picked the box up, he was overcome with a sense of dread and foreboding. He just didn't like the thing.

Half grumbling, he leaned over, flipped the pocket of the pack open, and retrieved the box. He shook off the unease that washed over him as best as he could and set the box in his lap. He remembered Burne's explanation of how to destroy the thing and wished he could carry out the ceremony here and now.

Shanhaevel opened the box and stared down at the small golden skull. The thing was nestled in a padded, velvet-lined depression in the middle of the box, staring up at him. If he let his imagination run, he could almost sense the skull smiling at him.

Very carefully, and with no small amount of trepidation, Shanhaevel reached down and tugged the skull free of its form-fitting depression. Almost immediately, he was overwhelmed with visions—horrible visions of agony, torture, and death. He tensed, suffering through the stinging pain of ice and wind as he fell endlessly through a colorless void, his body buffeted cruelly by a howling storm that carried him away. White light seared him, blinding him. He tumbled into nothingness, and suddenly he was buried beneath a million tons of dirt and stone, his body pinned deep beneath the surface of the world. Trapped, unable to speak, to move, to even open his eyes, he was crushed by the pressure of the earth itself. His ribs cracked, his heart constricted, and his breath was squeezed from him.

Then he was elsewhere, free to move again, gasping for the blessed air—only to discover that it was searing hot, scorching his lungs. Flames licked at his body, burning away his hair, his skin, boiling his blood in the span of a heartbeat. He opened his mouth to scream and felt his flesh scorched to nothing. He swallowed a briny mouthful of cold water. Choking, he flailed about once more, drowning in darkness, feeling himself sinking deeper and deeper, the pressure of the brackish sea enveloping him and bearing him down and down and—

Shanhaevel blinked, gasping a deep lungful of air. The elf's heart raced, and his face and hands were covered with a cold sheen of sweat. He felt his face drawn back in a fierce snarl of pain and tension.

The chapel. He was back in the abandoned chapel. With only one shuttered lamp burning, the small room was very dim.

Shanhaevel sighed and relaxed, feeling the ache in his tense muscles slowly drain away. He shook his head, clearing the visions that still flickered in the corners of his mind, and he wondered how long he had been sitting there. He looked around at his resting companions. The chapel seemed quiet, but—

In half a heartbeat, Shanhaevel was no longer there but in a great and terrible temple, one decorated with horrible images carved into stone the color of death and decay. Standing in the middle of the great room, looking at him, was an older man, dressed in crimson robes and leaning upon a staff. The man's face was wrinkled and leathery, and he wore a smile as he gazed at the wizard, though the grin was far from benign. Slowly, almost languidly, the man reached a hand out toward Shanhaevel and opened his mouth to speak.

"Give me the orb, whelp," the man said.

The hatred and malevolence that washed over the elf as he heard these words made him cringe and shudder. He shrieked in horror and tried to back away, but, overwhelmed with loathing and terror for this figure standing before him, he slammed into a great column and crumpled to the floor.

The old man walked toward him, but no matter how hard he tried, Shanhaevel could not move.

The old man reached for the orb, grasping it and taking it from Shanhaevel. Still smiling, the old man backed away, the key grasped in his hands. He moved to the front of the temple, where a great raised dais spread out before a rounded alcove. In the center of this alcove sat a huge black throne, carved of stone. The old man sat down upon the throne and *sank*, disappearing into the very floor of the temple.

Shanhaevel found himself pulled along, following the man as the throne descended, slipping deeper into the depths below the temple. Finally, the throne stopped, and the man stood and walked to the center of a large room filled with earth and the smell of rot. Fungi thrived everywhere. In the center of the room, next to the elderly man, was an immense blob, a being of putrescence and decay. Looking as much like a bloated mushroom as anything, the creature stood upon four immensely thick legs. A pair of strange armlike extensions protruded from its sides. The fungus-thing stank of rot and mold. Slowly, inexorably, the fungus creature reached for him.

Shanhaevel screamed. . . .

* * * * *

Shanhaevel's cries clamored through the chapel. When the wizard opened his eyes, Govin was on his feet, standing before him, sword in hand, looking down.

Prince Thrommel stood close by, Fragarach in his hand, apparently ready to do battle with any foe.

"What is it? What's wrong?" the knight asked. He looked ready to strike at whatever unseen menace threatened his companion.

Shanhaevel raised his hand to point at the foreboding figures standing before him, threatening him, and blinked. The old man and the fungus creature were both gone. He peered around the chapel, looking for the horrific beings, but the figures were nowhere to be found.

"A vision," Shanhaevel breathed, looking down at his hand, which was still firmly clasped around the golden skull. "They were standing right there." He understood now how the golden key functioned, could feel the unwanted knowledge flowing into him from the item.

"Who?" Govin demanded, looking around once more. "Who was here?"

Shanhaevel swallowed and shook his head. He knew what he had just seen, for the orb itself was telling him, even though his mind rebelled at the implications of it.

"Iuz," the wizard croaked, his hands shaking. "Iuz the old. Iuz the terrible."

"What?" Govin cried.

"Yes," Thrommel muttered, "the Old One's hand was always behind the rise of the temple. You did not know this?"

Govin shook his head, his frown intense.

The other companions were stirring now, moving over to see what the commotion was about. They all seemed perfectly fine, oblivious that anything might have been out of the ordinary in the chamber.

"I— I saw them," Shanhaevel said. It had seemed so real! "They wanted this." He held up the orb.

Govin drew back from it, repulsed by the evil it embodied.

"He fashioned it," Shanhaevel continued, "he and his mistress, the demoness Zuggtmoy. I saw them both standing there, in the middle of the room. He smiled at me"—Shanhaevel shuddered, remembering—"and told me to give him the orb."

The rest of his companions looked around, doubt showing on their faces.

"There is no one here now," Draga said.

"I never saw or heard anyone," Ahleage added, wrinkling his brow, obviously convinced that the wizard had been seeing things.

"No," Shanhaevel replied, shaking his head. "You don't understand. I don't think they were really here. I felt their presence through this." Again, he gestured at the golden skull still clasped in his hand. Subtle waves of nausea seemed to wash over him whenever he was reminded that he still held it. "She definitely wasn't really here, and I don't think he was either."

"How do you know?" Elmo asked as Shirral knelt beside Shanhaevel and took his free hand in hers.

"I know she wasn't here because I know she's still trapped, sealed behind the doors. I don't think he was actually here because she wasn't here. Besides, in this vision,

I was somewhere else—some temple with a great throne made of black stone. I think it was a vision triggered by touching this wretched thing."

Blanching, Shanhaevel shoved the golden skull back into its form-fitting pocket and slammed the box lid closed. Instantly he felt great relief.

"How do you know all of this, all of a sudden?" Shirral asked. She was huddled close to Shanhaevel and caressed his face soothingly. Worry filled her eyes, and her mouth frowned in a way the wizard had never seen before.

"Because it told me," Shanhaevel replied, closing his eyes and suddenly feeling very weary. The druid's caresses were cool and gentle against his skin, washing away the last of the taint of evil still lurking in his being.

"It . . . it *told* you?" Govin gasped, obviously disturbed. "It speaks? We must find those gems and destroy this thing soon!"

Shanaevel opened his mouth to answer, but just then there was a deep rumble that reverberated all around them. The ground shook as shock waves rattled the chapel and sent dust cascading from the walls.

"What on Oerth was that?" Draga growled, his legs braced wide to hold his balance.

Shanhaevel imagined his face must have been a pale personification of his own fright, for when Shirral returned his look, her eyes widened in fear. When he spoke, his words were soft.

"I don't know."

22

Hedrack moved forward eagerly, ignoring the dust that hung in the air of the demolished stairway. The swirling, floating detritus was so impenetrable that the high priest was unsure if the blast had, in fact, demolished the magical portal. Pushing past chunks of stone, he worked his way down the steps, moving closer, determined to find out. When he reached the bottom of the stairway where the great doors had once stood, there was nothing. The last few steps had been destroyed, leaving only a scarred and shattered hole in the floor. The walls to either side had been ripped away, and a large portion of the ceiling had collapsed. Where the magically sealed doors had once stood, barring passage or even approach, there was now only a great gaping hole. Beyond, Hedrack could see a portion of the dirt floor of the Temple of Earth.

The high priest grinned in delight. "Yes," he murmured softly. "Excellent. Her power must be returning now, with one of the four sundered." He turned back to face his small retinue of experts, including the wizard Falrinth.

"You will begin preparing for the destruction of the second door. Prepare the one at the front entrance. I am going to visit the chamber of light and speak with her."

Falrinth bowed low as the rest of the men and humanoids scurried to carry out the high priest's orders. "We will assemble the oil and flash powder at once," he said, genuine eagerness evident in his own voice. "I will prepare the door first, then send for you when we are ready."

Hedrack nodded absently, immersed in thoughts of the glory that would be his once she was freed. Iuz would laud him with praise and power for certain. "Yes," he said at last, "when you are ready."

With that, he returned to the main temple below, dismissing Falrinth and the others with a casual wave of his hand.

When he reached the chamber of light, he passed through the pearly column of illumination and seated himself upon the throne.

The bonds are slipping away, she said, startling Hedrack. She had never spoken first during their contacts before. *It feels so good. Free me! I want to rise, to roam my halls once more and scour the land.*

We hurry, my lady, Hedrack replied, amazed at how aware the demoness was. He was pleased. With the destruction of the first doorway, her power was returning to her, and her awareness with it. *The next portal will fall in a matter of hours.*

Hurry! I feel others seeking me, seeking my death.

They are of no consequence, the high priest projected soothingly. *They cannot muster the wherewithal to do more than annoy. We will be triumphant.*

Fool! she radiated malevolently. *They have the key, the golden key! They can destroy me with it. You must recover it, for it is the power of this temple. Without it, we can never fully command the elements.*

Hedrack did not answer immediately. Her vehemence startled him, made him mentally retreat from her. He sat for a moment in thought, contemplating what her ire meant, what changes would exist in the power structure of the temple once she was freed. A decade ago, he had been nothing, a minor servant in the cause of the temple, charged with trivial duties. She had never taken notice of him, and she did not know him now. Would she respect his position as commander of the temple once she was returned to power, or would she seek out others, those whom she considered to be more loyal, more trustworthy? He did not relish the idea of surrendering his position of authority. The situation would require careful cultivation. He would speak to Iuz about it, he decided.

Realizing he had not answered the demoness, Hedrack hastily projected, *The orb will be recovered from the interlopers. They will fall and become sacrifices to the elements, as have all others who have come to oppose the might of the Elemental Temple. I will see to it personally.*

Yes, she replied. *See to it personally. They must not be allowed to enter my sanctuary with the key. The danger to me would be great.*

I understand and obey, Hedrack acknowledged. He arose from the throne then, not wanting to give the demoness another opportunity to find fault with any of his actions. Frowning, he strode out of the chamber and up the stairs toward the greater temple, pondering the machinations he would have to put into motion to ensure his position would remain intact.

* * * * *

Shanhaevel's view was far away from his body, drifting effortlessly over the deep snow of the surface, near the front doors of the temple. A spell made it possible, one in which he could see things far away—an invisible eye he guided with a thought. He peered toward the front doors of the temple. What he saw made him gasp. A crowd had gathered, standing back from the front of the temple. He recognized at least one of the men as Falrinth. The wizard seemed to be directing some sort of invisible magical force, moving a large quantity of kegs to the great door. The kegs already there were stacked against the portal, and additional ones were being added to the pile.

Shanhaevel recognized the magical forces as more of the invisible constructs he had spotted in the chamber near the flaming fountain—magical servants, shapeless beings that could carry out simple commands. They were stacking something against the door without seeming to be affected by its powerful warding magic. When the last keg was placed atop the pile, one of the invisible servants removed the lid. Shanhaevel couldn't hear what was being said, but Falrinth had turned to talk to another—a man in black armor with a hideous helm. Embroidered on the back of the man's cloak was the skull of Iuz.

Shanhaevel shivered. Iuz the terrible joining forces with a trapped demon! The elf was beginning to think this whole expedition was a horrible mistake. *We should go. Get out of here right now. They're too powerful. Too strong. If we got far enough away, the temple wouldn't affect us.*

The man in the dark armor nodded, and he and everyone else stepped back even farther from the doors. Falrinth cast. Shanhaevel watched the wizard with a critical eye, trying to determine what was about to happen.

"What's going on?" Ahleage hissed from somewhere beyond, back in the chapel where Shanhaevel's body sat. "What's happening?"

Suddenly, the elf recognized the spell Falrinth was conjuring, and he realized with terrible certainty what was about to happen.

"Oh, Boccob!" Shanhaevel muttered. "They're going to destroy the doors!"

Falrinth completed his spell and sprinted in the opposite direction, retreating from the doors as a small, streaking cinder went flying toward the stack of kegs. There was a sudden concussive blast accompanied by a blossoming ball of fire that was quickly overwhelmed by an even larger and more destructive detonation.

Shanhaevel felt the blast as it occurred, even though in reality he was far away. As before, it shook the temple to its foundations. Chunks of stone, earth, and wood exploded with vehemence. The particles of what had once been the front of the temple showered down upon the surrounding woods.

"That cannot be!" Thrommel whispered fiercely as the vibrations faded. "The warding magic of those doors is too powerful. It was placed there to prevent just such an occurrence. There should be no way to destroy them."

"Perhaps there shouldn't be," Shanhaevel said, "but that's exactly what they just did. They intend to destroy all of the doors and free the demon."

"Well, then, we've got to stop them!" Elmo growled.

Shanhaevel nodded and released his hold on the spell, bringing his frame of reference back to the chapel once more. "Yes," the wizard replied, blinking as he adjusted to the difference in lighting. "Forget the gems. We must stop them before they destroy another door."

"Yes, but how are we to find where they will strike next?" Shirral asked. "We don't know where the other doors are."

"I do," Thrommel said quietly.

Everyone looked at the prince.

"I was there when the doors were sealed," he explained. "Shanhaevel, you were observing them working on the front doors, right?"

The elf nodded.

"Start there, once we leave this place. You must go to the surface and track them down from there. I can leave first, as I suggested before, and hopefully lead any threats away. You follow. Get to the great temple just inside those outer doors. Follow the large staircases. Each door gives way to another, deeper in the temple structure. Eventually, you will find one that they haven't destroyed yet."

"We can waste no more time," Govin said. "We are rested. We must depart at once."

"Give me a few moments, then follow," Thrommel repeated. "Just tell me the way out."

An idea occurred to Shanhaevel. "Hold on," he said, reaching for his pack once more and rummaging through it. He retrieved the rolled-up map he had found in Falrinth's chambers, the one with the dangerous glyph on it that he had removed from the wall. "Perhaps this can help," the elf said as he unrolled the parchment. "When I was studying it before, some of it looked familiar. Give me a moment to remove the explosive symbol."

"If you're going to do that in here, I'm going in there," Ahleage said as he retreated into the other room. The rest of the group and the prince moved a safe distance, as well.

Shanhaevel pinned the corners of the map down with things from his pack. Careful to avoid looking directly at anything written on the map, he cast a magical dispelling, similar to the one Shirral had used to free Ahleage from the effects of the illusory basilisk. Muttering the words of the spell, he centered the magic on the map and released the energy bound there, and a portion of the markings disappeared.

"All right!" Shanhaevel called out, studying the map. "It's safe to come see now."

The group clustered around the large sheet of parchment, examining it carefully. It did not take them long to determine that it was, indeed, a depiction of some of the temple. It included Falrinth's chambers, plus most of what the Alliance had traversed to reach the chapel, although it did not show the chapel itself. Shanhaevel traced the path backward from where they were now to Falrinth's and the tunnel to the well beyond, showing Thrommel how to return to the surface. The prince studied the route carefully for a few moments, then stood up to leave.

"I cannot stay to aid you, though I consider the cause worthy enough. I must return to Furyondy and to Jolene, but I will get word to Burne. He will know what is happening here. Find Falrinth and stop him, then destroy the orb. The people of many lands are counting on you. May the hand of Cuthbert guide you to victory."

With that, the prince slipped out of the hidden chapel and was gone, leaving the Alliance to seal the secret door behind him.

The group sat for a moment, letting the prince's words sink in and giving the royal progeny time to get ahead of them. Then it was time to go. The companions gathered their gear and prepared to set out.

"Let's hope he was successful in luring the spider-shadow away," Govin said. "May Cuthbert go with him. Let's go find that wizard."

With Govin leading the way, the Alliance slipped into the darkness beyond.

The horrid undead thing that had resulted from Lareth's death was nowhere to be found. Shanhaevel watched every shadow as the group retraced its steps back along the path. The elf could only imagine what horrors prowled through these passages when the temple flourished ten years ago. He was surprised that so much of the place was empty now, and yet, he was grateful, too.

The companions managed to return to the tunnels between the well and the tower without incident, but as they reached the cavern, Govin hesitated.

"Which way should we go?" he asked as everyone else passed through the secret door. "I imagine either direction will be watched."

Frowning, Shanhaevel nodded. "You're right," the elf said, considering. "But I have something that just might solve that problem. Come on."

The companions moved toward the well, and just before they reached the door leading into the side of the shaft, the wizard gathered everyone together in a small group and gathered the magic forces within him. He summoned the arcane energies and cloaked the group in them, causing the Alliance to disappear from view.

"Hey!" Ahleage said. "That's pretty damned handy."

Slowly, so as not to bump or trip one another, the group

made their way into the well. Ahleage moved up the shaft to the top and peered over the lip.

"There doesn't seem to be anyone around," he whispered, "although they could be hiding in the barn or the ruins of the house."

"It doesn't matter," Elmo called back up. "Let's just get to the temple."

"Wait!" Shanhaevel said, then called out to Ormiel.

Friend! the hawk greeted. *You hide beneath the ground a long time.*

Yes, the elf replied. *Are you well?*

Hungry, the hawk projected. *Hunting food.*

Do others prowl the woods? Any bad things?

No. Not for a while.

"Ormiel says nothing is around, but just to be safe, let's go through the woods instead of taking the path."

Holding onto one another so as not to lose track of each person's position, the group moved up and out of the well into bright daylight. They avoided the barn and ruined farmhouse, choosing instead to cross the small open space between it and the woods. Leaving footprints in the half-melted snow, they picked their way through the woods, finding the going slow because of their invisibility. More than once, someone stepped on another's heel or bumped into the back of a companion who halted without warning.

Eventually, however, they reached the temple. Stopping at the opening that had once been the main gate in the long-ruined wall, they stopped and peered around, checking for guards. There were none to be found, which surprised Shanhaevel.

"They've blown away the front door," the wizard pondered aloud, "and yet they don't set some sort of watch?"

When they were satisfied nothing was going to attack, they filed inside, passing through the gaping hole that had once been the sealed doors. Inside, they examined the place thoroughly. They stood within a vestibule, which opened to the nave of the temple. It still appeared that no one was about, so Shanhaevel dispelled their invisibility so that everyone could function normally again.

The whole place was garishly decorated with vile scenes. The floor of the vestibule was set with reddish brown slate squares, and the walls were plastered and painted with images of murder, destruction, enslavement, and even worse deeds that made Shanhaevel blanch and turn away. He realized this was the place from his vision, when he had held the skull key.

Beyond the vestibule, in the main part of the temple, the floor was set in greenish stones. The light streaming through the high, narrow stained-glass windows that flanked the main entryway fell upon that green, creating a ghastly mixture of hues that hurt the eyes.

"By Cuthbert, what vileness!" Govin breathed, clenching his sword so tightly that his knuckles turned white. "Why didn't they raze this place and bury it beneath the ground? It should never have been allowed to stand in even this condition."

"Agreed, knight," said Elmo, shaking his head, "but they did what they could, and now we must do the same. Come on, let's see where they went."

With that, Elmo turned and headed into the nave, a huge room that might have been forty paces wide and easily three times as long. Strong pillars of pinkish stone, shot through with worm-colored veins, held up the high, vaulted ceiling. They were worked in bas-relief—more images of vile and damnable acts. The companions' footfalls echoed sharply in the place as they walked, peering this way and that. Stained-glass windows were the only source of light, though Shanhaevel wouldn't allow his gaze to linger on any of them long enough to discern the images portrayed there.

Ahead, Shanhaevel saw an altar cut from a large block of the pinkish marble with a depression on the top surface. As he drew nearer, he saw that the depression was in the shape of a man, legs splayed apart and arms held away from the body. The stone was stained a darker shade of red here. Shanhaevel shook his head and moved on, but Shirral, having also spotted the telltale depression, gasped and stood rooted to the spot, staring.

"No, don't linger," Shanhaevel said, moving to her side. "Look at me. Look at *me!*"

She finally pulled her gaze away from the altar and stared, wide-eyed, at the elf.

"You must block it out, Shirral. If you let it get to you, you will not survive."

"I—" she said, at last, nodding. "All right."

To either side of the altar were two wings of the chamber, projecting out at an angle back toward the front of the building. Both of the wings held an altar, and each was decorated in a different color scheme. The wing to the left was in greens, and the one to the right was all browns and blacks.

"The colors of the elements . . ." Shanhaevel remarked, peering more closely at the wing to his right. He spotted a door against the far wall. Curious about the symmetry of the place, he walked back across to his left and looked in that direction. There was an identical portal there. "Everyone, look! There are doors in these wings."

"Let's keep to this main area for now," Govin said, having moved ahead of the central altar to a large circular pit in the floor. "We want to find that staircase the prince mentioned." The knight stood on the edge of the pit and was peering down into its depths. "If that doesn't work out, or if he isn't remembering correctly, we can consider taking alternate routes down."

Beyond the pit, the group came to a wide staircase leading down. It was perhaps twenty feet wide, and each step was both broad and tall, made of a gray stone flecked with white, blue, red, green, and black.

"This is what we're looking for," Shirral whispered, peering down into the darkness below.

Govin shuddered. "My senses are overwhelmed with the taint of the evil once wrought here. I can still feel the suffering of those who were sacrificed to these elements. It seeps from the very stones."

"Easy, knight," Elmo said. "We all feel it. Keep your wits about you."

Beyond the staircase was a railing, and beyond the railing was what might have been the high altar of the temple. The entire area beyond the railing was decorated in reds, oranges, and golds, and scenes of fiery torture abounded. In the middle of the place was a large bronze pot, perhaps eight feet wide. Hanging down from the ceiling directly over the vessel was a long chain.

"The temple of fire," Shanhaevel breathed, looking around as his companions stayed close together. "They revered the flames above all other elements, I presume."

"I don't care what they revered," Govin said, shuddering again. "This place should be blasted from the face of the lands."

"Look," Ahleage said, crossing the distance from where the group stood to the farthest region of the temple. "Look at this throne."

The rest of the group joined him, spying at last what he had seen. A great throne sat upon a high dais, which was made of four different colors of stone—the shades of the elements. The dais, in the shape of a semicircle, was actually set into the northernmost wall of the temple farthest from the blasted entrance at the other end. Inscribed in tall, bold letters across the back wall were words that made the hair on the back of Shanhaevel's neck stand out:

The Power of Elemental Death
Brings Mortals Low
But Raises The Nameless One
High

"This is the throne from my vision," Shanhaevel said, flinching in memory of the vile hallucination. "With the four gems in place, the key will take you directly down. To *her.*"

"The nameless one . . ." Draga gasped.

"I pray to Saint Cuthbert that no one ever manages to free her," Govin said, "but should we meet her, we have the strength to prevail." Spinning away from the throne and walking toward the back of the temple, he said, "The staircase down. It's time."

24

They descended the staircase into the depths of the temple once more, still seeking Falrinth, hoping to catch the wizard before he could destroy a third door.

Shanhaevel swallowed nervously. Ahead of him, Ahleage moved along, following the stairs, while behind the wizard, Elmo held a lantern high, helping everyone to see.

As the group, moving single file, reached the end of the stairs, Shanhaevel saw that a second opening had been blasted in the structure of the temple. He could easily imagine that a second set of doors, also sealed with magical sigils, had been placed at the foot of the stairs, but now there was only a gaping hole.

"The second door," the elf said quietly, "or what once was."

"We only felt two blasts," Elmo said.

"Then the third must not be far beyond," Govin said, motioning for Ahleage to push on.

Beyond the blasted remains of the second portal was a patch of earthen floor—what once might have been a large area. Now a large portion of the room had collapsed, and a great wall of rubble blocked their way.

"Damnation!" cursed Govin, smacking his hands together.

"So, now what?" Shirral asked. "One of those other ways down?"

Govin, his mouth twisted in a snarl of frustration, nodded and headed back up the stairs as the rest of the group followed him. He stopped at the pit he had been examining earlier. "We try this next. We must find another way down, get to the next door, and stop them. Look there, about fifteen feet down. There is a ledge and, if I'm not seeing things, a set of stairs that spirals down from it." The knight pointed down into the shaft.

Ahleage, who had lain down on his stomach to peer over the edge of the pit, turned his head sideways and stared at Govin. "You just got through saying that you hope we never meet this 'Nameless One,' and now you want to go straight down a gaping shaft that probably leads to one of the nine hells itself."

"I think I can see light from the very bottom," Shirral said, hunched over and peering down, herself. "It's just a faint white glow, but I'm almost certain something is lit down there."

"I could be in Hommlet right now," Ahleage muttered, even as he uncoiled some rope and tied one end to a post of the railing. He tossed the other end over the side of the pit and continued his tirade. "Leah could be on my lap. I could be eating some of Glora's fine roast chicken, but nooooo, I'm here, about to go down a hole with a crazy knight and you four, all insane enough to follow him."

"Are you finished?" Elmo asked.

Ahleage pursed his lips, as if thinking. Finally, he replied, "For now. Give me a few moments though. . . ."

"Well then," Govin said as he sheathed his sword. "Let's get moving."

"Let me go first," Ahleage suggested. "I can check to make sure the ledge is solid and safe enough to stand on. Hold tight until I get down there."

Ahleage sat down and dangled his legs over the side. He took hold of the rope, twisted around, and lowered his body so that he was hanging freely in the shaft with only his head above the surface of the floor.

"Don't wait too long, though. If some demon tries to grab me, I sure want the rest of you to be there, too."

With that, Ahleage lowered himself.

Once he had determined the safety of the ledge, the rest of the group descended into the shaft. Shanhaevel swallowed nervously as he peered between his feet over the edge of the narrow ledge. The drop made him sweat. Far, far below, he could see the faint glow of light that told him how far he would fall, should he slip. Ahead, Ahleage moved along, following the ledge around to the stairs that descended lower into that shaft. Behind the wizard, Elmo held a lantern high, helping everyone to see.

As the group descended the stairs, moving single file, Shanhaevel used his staff to make sure his footing was sound. The steps spiraled downward, but fortunately, they seemed to be stout and intact. The group took a couple of turns around the perimeter of the shaft, and then the steps just ended at a small platform hanging from the side.

"Great," Ahleage said. "Good idea, Govin. Let's head back up and try those doors, I guess."

It was then that Shanhaevel felt a strange, cool breeze against his cheek. "Hold a minute!" the elf said just as everyone was about to reverse direction. "I think there's something here."

"What? Did you find another secret passage?" Ahleage asked, having turned to face Shanhaevel as the elf examined the wall.

"Actually," the wizard replied as he pushed a section of wall so that it suddenly slid downward, "yes."

"Istus's mother!" Ahleage breathed. "You give me the creeps, the way you always find those things. Elmo, shine your light down in here."

The huge man held the lantern forward as Ahleage squeezed past Shanhaevel and moved through the portal opening. He stopped halfway through.

"What is it?" Shanhaevel asked, peering past the man into the area beyond. The floor immediately before Ahleage was covered in bones. Skulls mingled with femurs, and rib cages tumbled together with fibulas in a jumble of remains. Many of the skeletons were roughly intact, still wearing armor of some sort in several cases.

"A great battle was fought here," Shanhaevel surmised. "Maybe when the temple fell."

"So that's supposed to make me feel better?" Ahleage said, still frozen in his spot. "I don't want to go in there."

"Wait a moment," Shanhaevel said, then turned and looked back along the line of companions strung out on the stairs. "We've found a secret way into some tunnels, but it's full of bones."

"What's beyond the bones?" Shirral asked.

"It looks like a hallway, but I can't tell for sure."

"We don't have a choice," Govin said. "Keep moving."

"All right," Shanhaevel said, then turned back and relayed the answer to Ahleage.

"Did you *tell* them about the bones?" Ahleage asked testily.

"Yes."

"Lots of bones?"

"Yes."

"Was this Sir Govin Dahna's, Sir We-must-stop-them-at-all-cost idea?"

"Ahleage," Shanhaevel replied, sounding each word slowly and distinctly to drive home his urgency. "Go inside the door. Now."

Ahleage sighed and skulked into the chamber. Shanhaevel followed close behind. The area was indeed a hallway, or rather, a T-shaped junction of two hallways, each several paces wide. The covering of bones stretched beyond the lantern light in both directions. The passageway straight ahead went about that distance before it ended, a door to either side.

As the last of the members of the Alliance filed through the secret door, it abruptly slid upward, closing. Ahleage lunged at the portal, trying to stop it from completely sealing shut, but he was not quite in time. With a solid *thunk*, the door slammed shut.

The echo of the door had scarcely faded when there was a clattering at each end of the hallway. In horror, the companions watched as several intact skeletons arose from the heaps. Wearing armor from their days among the living and brandishing weapons in their bony fingers, a half dozen or more of the undead charged the group from both sides.

"This way!" yelled Elmo as he cut across the corridor into the central part of the intersection. The others followed him, all except Ahleage, who was clawing frantically at the door. When he realized that his friends had left him there, he turned and sprinted into the safety of the side hall.

Elmo, his axe held ready, motioned for Shanhaevel and Shirral to get behind him and the more battle-capable members of the group. Draga, Govin, and finally Ahleage took up positions across the mouth of the hall, ready for the onslaught. The first of the animated horrors turned the corner, their bony grins silently laughing as they clattered down the hall toward the waiting defenders.

It was at that moment that the door beside Shanhaevel and Govin opened. An ogre stood there, a club raised in its hand, ready to bring its weapon down upon the head of some enemy. Behind it, a second ogre waited with a feral grin on its ugly, wart-covered face.

Shanhaevel was too surprised to move when the ogre's club came crashing down on him. The elf was only able to twist his body out of the way enough to avoid being brained. The weapon caught him across the back of the neck and shoulder and drove him straight to the ground. All of the elf's extremities went numb, and he could scarcely breathe. He lay on the floor, his mind unable to register what had happened. The ogre stepped into the corridor where the members of the Alliance were already battling a line of skeletons. The creature raised its weapon to strike the wizard again, and behind it, the second ogre waited eagerly to get into the fray.

As Shanhaevel watched the huge wooden weapon loom over him, its face set with sharp stones, he found himself suddenly thinking of Lanithaine. His old mentor's face seemed to hover in the elf's field of vision, smiling down on him, and Shanhaevel wondered if Lanithaine would be proud of him, of what he had been a part of. I came and served, the wizard thought. I honored his name and helped to protect the people of Hommlet from harm . . . at least for a little while.

Shanhaevel smiled back at Lanithaine, hoping his teacher *was* proud of him, and then the vision dissolved, and it was the ogre again, about to kill him. But the beast never got the chance. Govin was suddenly there, jumping between the huge creature and the fallen wizard, warding off the intended blow with his shield and driving his sword deep into the ogre's midsection. At the same moment, Shirral dragged Shanhaevel away, giving Govin room to fight.

Shanhaevel tried to twist his head around, to smile at the druid as she pulled him to safety, but he could not move his head the way he wanted to. He heard the scream of the ogre as the knight's sword eviscerated it, and out of the corner of his vision, he saw Elmo bull-rush a skeleton, shattering the undead with his shield while he swung his axe around to strike at another. Shanhaevel's vision blurred as a jolt of pain shot through his neck and down his back. Agony coursed up and down his spine, so much so that he could not even scream. The searing pain faded to a dull throbbing, and he could feel his fingers and toes again.

"Shhh," Shirral told him, trying to press her hands against the back of his neck. "Hold still!"

The liquid fire that coursed down every nerve in his body immolated him, forcing him to cry out with the little strength he could find, only a hoarse croak. Suddenly, there was blessed coolness. He felt it radiate through him like a frozen stream melting in the spring sun. Shirral's fingertips gently caressed his skin, sending quiet ripples of healing magic through him until the pain from the ogre's blow was reduced to a vague throbbing in his neck and shoulder muscles.

Shirral sat back, looking at Shanhaevel, who blinked and realized he could sit up.

"Thank you," he said, not knowing what else he could say.

Without a word, she leaned forward, grabbed him roughly by the collar of his cloak, and kissed him, pulling him to her lips and holding him tightly. He blinked in surprise and then kissed her back.

Just as suddenly, Shirral pulled away from him and uttered a few words of prayer so that her flaming scimitar ignited in her hand. Raising her weapon high, she leaped in beside Draga, who was being pushed back by no less than three skeletal warriors, their spears coming dangerously close to the bowman's flesh time and time again.

Shaking his head to clear his senses, Shanhaevel rolled to his feet, noting that there was still some stiffness where he had been struck.

Govin was locked in a battle with the second ogre, while the rest of the companions fought skeletons. Now that Shirral stood with Draga, it looked as if Ahleage was bearing the worst of the fight, with three of the skeletons surrounding him. The man danced and feinted, trying to keep from getting pinned, but he was tiring.

Shanhaevel moved up behind Ahleage and said, "Keep them busy for just a moment more!" Then, he began a spell, drawing the magical energy and directing it outward as a sheet of flame from his spread fingers. He caught two of the skeletons in his magical fire. The scorching flame crackled and licked over the bones of the skeletons, igniting them like dry wood. When the jet of fire finally dissipated a moment later, the skeletons were nothing but a heap of smoldering bones.

"Thanks, wizard," Elmo grunted, using the broad, flat blade of his axe to smash skeletons now, shattering them with his ferocious blows.

Ahleage said nothing, but he did take the offensive again, battering the lone skeleton still facing him with the flat of his own sword. Shanhaevel assisted with his staff where he could, swinging the stout weapon about and cracking bones when he saw a clean shot. After Elmo knocked the last skeleton backward to shatter against the wall, Shanhaevel turned to see Govin, his shield arm hanging awkwardly at his side, standing over the second ogre. Blood dripped from his blade.

Shirral was already moving to the knight's aid, preparing to use her magical healing powers to mend his arm. Despite his injury, the fire in Govin's eyes told Shanhaevel that the holy warrior was ready for more. Leaning on his staff to catch his breath, the elf looked around at the rest of his companions. Each of them had wounds, some worse than others. Draga had a nasty gash across the side of his face that had barely missed his eye. Elmo had a gaping rent in his armor across the ribs on his left side, and he was bleeding. Even Shirral walked with a slight limp. Yet none of them seemed cowed or subdued. Instead, he sensed an eagerness about the group, despite the oppressive feel of the temple, as though they felt they were close. Even Shanhaevel felt the excitement coursing through his limbs.

When Shirral finished her healing work, the companions turned their attention to their surroundings, trying to determine which way to go. At either end of the great hallway were other passages, and, of course, there was the room from which the ogre had come. They were just beginning to debate which way to go when Ahleage held his hand up for silence, his head cocked. In the distance, Shanhaevel could make out muffled sounds, a discussion it seemed, accompanied by footsteps. Motioning for the rest of the group to follow him, Ahleage padded forward, in the direction of the sounds.

"My lord Hedrack, we are almost ready to destroy the third door," a man in the distance was saying. It sounded as though the voice carried from just a bit beyond where they were, around a bend in the passage.

Hedrack? Shanhaevel thought the name was familiar. The name from the papers in Lareth's lair! *Was this the man in the armor I saw today?*

"Very good," another voice replied, one that was rich and deep and carried the weight of authority—Hedrack's, Shanhaevel knew. The power that radiated from that voice left no doubt in the elf's mind. The footsteps had stopped. "You may proceed. I shall be in the main temple, preparing for her arrival. Notify me when the last doors are sundered."

"As you wish," the first voice answered, then there was a commotion, as though several others were scurrying somewhere.

"Hedrack!" Govin hissed. "We take them now, before they can destroy the door!" With that, the knight dashed around the corner.

"No!" Shanhaevel called after Govin, cringing at the thought of charging recklessly into battle unprepared, but it was too late. Shaking his head, the wizard followed as the rest of the Alliance charged after the knight.

The bend in the passageway deposited them in a wide corridor that ran at an angle and ended in another wide staircase leading down. A second passage, as wide as the first, branched off in the other direction, so that the whole of the intersection was in the shape of a Y with the staircase as the vertical line at the bottom. Falrinth and a small host of men and bugbears stood near the top of the stairwell, looking down into its depths. They were turned away from the onrushing knight and other members of the Alliance, and there was no sign of anyone else.

Upon hearing Govin's heavy footfalls, Falrinth spun, bringing his hands up instantly, and cast a spell. The wizard stepped back as the bugbears brandished weapons and stepped forward, blocking Govin's advance. Grunting from exertion, Govin charged into the fray, raising his sword high and swiping at the mangy humanoids. Ahleage and Draga hit the wall of bugbears a moment later, and quickly, the wide corridor was a broiling sea of weapons and blood.

Falrinth was on the verge of casting a spell that Shanhaevel recognized—the flaming ball of fire the elf had used several times before. Shanhaevel opened his mouth to shout a warning, but before he could utter a word, Ahleage threw a dagger, and the blade blossomed in the other wizard's shoulder. Crying and stumbling backward in pain, Falrinth lost his concentration, and the spell he had been about to unleash failed. Snarling in anger, Falrinth reached inside his robes and removed a small length of wood, polished dark with age, and ducked to avoid further injury.

Shanhaevel frowned when he saw the wand in the other wizard's hand. He quickly cast a spell of his own, summoning three of the glowing green missiles and directing them unerringly toward Falrinth. As the other wizard raised his arm to use the wand, the missiles struck him in rapid succession, causing him to howl in renewed pain.

Shanhaevel followed with a new spell, launching the acidic arrow that he had used to slay Falrinth's imp, but Falrinth had taken enough. He turned away and scampered into the darkness of the opposite corrider. The magical arrow of acid fell harmlessly to the floor where he had been only moments before.

Her flaming blade in hand, Shirral was battling a pair of grim-looking men, each of them wielding a short spear. Govin and Ahleage, meanwhile, had waded through the thickest clump of the enemy and found themselves pressing the attack against the force of temple followers from both sides, trapping them.

With practiced ease, Shanhaevel summoned his spell of sleeping and put the few remaining combatants down. As the handful of men-at-arms and bugbears slumped to the ground, Ahleage moved in to finish them with his dagger. Shanhaevel gaped at him.

"No, Ahleage!" the elf cried out, causing the man to pause.

"They would release a demon on the world!" Ahleage said. "We can't leave them here to destroy the door after we're gone. If there was another way, I'd take it, but there isn't. Blood for blood, wizard."

Shanhaevel shook his head. "They cannot get near the door to ignite the powder. Only Falrinth can do that, with his magic. Leave them to their fates."

"I won't risk it," Ahleage replied. "A flaming arrow, a hurled lantern or torch . . . You convinced me to come here, to save the world from this festering evil. Well, I'm here, now, and I'm going to make sure it gets done. Turn away if you cannot watch."

Resigned, Shanhaevel turned away, trying hard not to listen. He concentrated instead on Shirral, who was looking at him with sorrowful eyes.

"Does the evil of the temple wash over us?" he asked her softly. "Does it win in the end, then?"

"The lesser of two . . ." the druid whispered, taking his face in her hands and kissing him. "Our sorrow at committing even the lesser evil is what separates us from evil."

Shanhaevel nodded, feeling great sadness in his heart, because he realized Shirral was right. "I understand, now, why Lanithaine never talked about his experiences during the war," the elf said quietly. "In war, the line that separates the two sides of conflict grows perilously narrow."

Govin looked back at his companions, and his gaze fell finally on Ahleage, whose bloody dagger was still grasped in his hand. The knight frowned. "There will be too much killing before this day is over," he said. "May

Cuthbert have mercy on us all."

"Come on," Ahleage said, wiping the dagger on a dead bugbear's cloak. "We still have a wizard to catch."

Shanhaevel and the rest of the Alliance crept through a wide corridor decorated with gruesome murals. The elf's stomach roiled as he passed images of demons frolicking upon some great battlefield, dancing and playing among their vanquished foes—suffering humans, elves, gnomes, and dwarves. The defeated lay in agony, battered and broken. Claiming the bodies of the victims were horrid growths—great pools of vile substances, fungal sprouts of every conceivable shape and color, molds, and other things the wizard could not identify. Shanhaevel forced himself to stare at the floor, avoiding the hideous imagery.

The passage led gently downward, bisected occasionally by sets of broad stairs and smaller side passages. Falrinth had escaped, fleeing through several winding passages and stairwells, deeper into the temple. His wounds had left a discernable trail of blood, and the chase led the group to this vile passageway. Now Shanhaevel could see the faint glow of light where the hallway opened into a much larger space ahead.

Elmo, who was now in the lead with Govin, held up a hand, signaling the group to halt. Shanhaevel paused in midstride, listening intently. After a long, breathless moment, the word was passed back: *A great chamber lies ahead. Be ready for an attack.*

Sorting through the magic he had prepared, Shanhaevel selected a couple of useful spells and steeled himself for the coming conflict.

Quietly, Elmo started forward again, treading softly upon the great black flagstones of the corridor and into the vast chamber beyond. One by one, the rest of the Alliance followed him in, fanning out. The warriors took the lead. Shanhaevel and Shirral remained near the back, out of harm's way but ready to cast spells when needed. The place was obviously a temple, and Shanhaevel scanned the great room, taking in the details and looking for hidden threats.

The vast chamber was a rough U shape, with the hallway through which the group had entered connecting to the bottom of the curve. Several smaller passages led off, four to a side, along the outer perimeter. A great altar atop a raised dais, with steps leading up to it, dominated the center of the chamber. A great red cloth, embroidered with the elemental symbol for fire, covered the altar. Behind the altar was a great purple curtain that writhed and undulated in some unfelt breeze. To either side of the altar and set back a little were two great statues, each twenty feet tall. To the left, the statue was of an old man, except that the head was that of a horned and grinning skull. The right-hand statue was the great bulbous fungal thing Shanhaevel had seen in his vision. He cringed, realizing that the two statues depicted Iuz and his demoness consort, Zuggtmoy.

Flanking the altar were a pair of golden columns that rose to the ceiling, well over fifty feet above the floor. The ceiling itself had been decorated to appear as a night sky full of bright, twinkling stars. All along the walls, near the ceiling, were a series of flying buttresses, atop which sat hideous gargoyles that leered down at everything below. The walls, as well as the floor, were of the deepest onyx, unblemished with any further decoration. Torches flickered along the walls at even intervals, casting weak light throughout.

At that moment, a lone figure, dressed in the blackest armor with the stylized symbol of Iuz painted in bright gold upon the breastplate, stepped into the room, passing through the shimmering curtain and walking past the altar. It was the same man Shanhaevel had seen through his spell, out in the snow, when the second door had been demolished.

Upon seeing the six intruders, the figure stopped, contemplating the group for a moment. Slowly, almost casually, the figure removed its helmet.

The man behind the helmet wore his hair short and his face was clean-shaven. He smirked slightly, though his fingers drummed frantically upon the helmet under his arm.

"Well, at last we come face to face," the man said, his rich and deep voice echoing strangely in the large chamber and confirming that this was, indeed, Hedrack. "Falrinth told me you were on your way. You do prove yourselves time and again as more than a mere annoyance, don't you? I, Hedrack, Mouth of Iuz, high priest of the Elemental Temple, salute you." Hedrack bowed low, sweeping his arms out to either side.

Govin, who was standing the closest to the man, took a couple of steps forward and said, "I am Sir Govin Dahna, knight of Saint Cuthbert. I bring the light of truth and goodness into this unholy place. Surrender, Hedrack, and be spared my wrath."

"Surrender?" The high priest laughed. "To you? I think not. You have done nothing, proven nothing! This is the Elemental Temple's finest hour! The elements will feast upon your souls before this day is through, Sir Govin

Dahna." He laughed again, turned, and disappeared through the curtain once more.

Govin growled and took two more steps forward, intent on pursuing the man, when chaos erupted.

From out of nowhere, a torrent of ice rained down upon the group. Thin, cutting shards sliced through the air, shredding clothing and skin alike. Govin dropped to one knee and held his shield over his head. Shanhaevel spun away from the center of the storm, shielding his face with his arm as the splinters of ice slammed against him. He could feel the stinging needles stabbing at him from everywhere, and the pain was fierce. Suddenly, he found himself free of the attack, and he spun around again, looking for evidence of where it had come from. He could spot nothing.

Frowning, the elf drew upon the energies he was so used to shaping and molding now, hoping they would reveal to him where magic was being used. As he opened himself to the magic and spoke the words of the spell, he was struck as something dark and swift shot past him, raking him with horribly sharp claws. He felt the talons drag across his back, trenching deep gouges in his flesh.

The wizard cried out and fell forward, losing control of the magic he had been gathering. He tumbled and rolled onto his back. He brought his arms up to ward off the next attack and saw something dart past, only inches away from his face. As the thing circled and turned to come at him again, he saw now that it was a gargoyle—a flying abomination, magically animated, from the buttresses overhead.

Scrambling to his knees, Shanhaevel waited for the next attack, and when the gargoyle soared close, he swung his staff up hard, catching the thing across the front of the wing. There was a sickening crack, and the gargoyle swerved away, flying haphazardly to the floor and landing hard. Shanhaevel saw other gargoyles swarming about, but he ignored them for the moment as he rose to his feet, trying to see what was happening to his companions.

Everyone was engaged in a fierce battle. A host of ogres and trolls had rushed in during the ice attack to swarm the companions. Shanhaevel turned to put his back against a wall, hoping to secure some bit of defense against the flying attacks of the gargoyles. Pressing himself firmly against the wall, he cast, praying to Boccob in the back of his mind to allow him time to make good use of the magic.

He prepared a bolt of lightning to catch several ogres that had formed up in a rank opposite Govin, Draga, and Shirral. As he completed the final words of the spell, he took aim with his line of sight, but a troll suddenly loomed over him, seemingly appearing from thin air. Both of its huge, clawed hands drew back, ready to strike. In his surprise, Shanhaevel yelped and fell back, unable to set the lightning where he had intended. Instead, the bolt struck from above. The troll raked out, snapping Shanhaevel across the head with one claw an instant before the lightning engulfed it. The creature shrieked as the electrical energy coursed through its flesh, killing it.

Shanhaevel was knocked sideways and tumbled to the floor, his vision blurred and hindered with streams of light. His ears rang from the thunder of the lightning, and his whole body felt numb. Even as he tried to rise, he was knocked sideways again as something plowed into him, scoring a direct hit on his ribs. With the air knocked from his lungs, Shanhaevel gasped and dropped to the floor once more, breathless and defenseless. As his vision was just beginning to clear, he saw yet another dark form hurtling toward him from overhead. He tried to roll away, but his muscles would not work.

At the moment it seemed that the flying gargoyle would plow directly into him, a blade slashed out—a blade of flame that ignited Shanhaevel's vision all over again, arcing through the air and slicing the gargoyle cleanly in two. The two parts of the flying beast tumbled apart and bounced like stone as they hit the ground and bounded away into some dark recess of the chamber.

Shanhaevel blinked, trying to clear his vision. His head throbbed from the blow of the troll, and his breath was still shallow. He was pretty certain one of his ribs was cracked, and the wounds across his back were bleeding.

In front of him, Shirral stood her ground, brandishing her blade of flame at anything that moved close. As Shanhaevel rose painfully to his feet, he caught sight of a new streak of light out of the corner of his eye. From behind the terrible statue of Iuz, three glowing green missiles shot into view, blazing across the distance and heading straight toward Shirral. The druid saw the attacks coming, but she was not fast enough to avoid them. All three of the missiles slammed into her chest, knocking her backward and making her cry out in pain.

Growling in frustration and anger, Shanhaevel managed to get to his feet even as Shirral sank down to one knee. He moved beside her, even though he saw an ogre approaching them. Reaching down, the elf grabbed the druid's shoulder and tried to help her stand. Shirral struggled to her feet, still wielding the blade of flame, and turned to face the ogre as it neared, a large axe in its hands.

Working quickly, Shanhaevel cast, muttering the words to a spell and aiming his own missiles at the beast rearing up before Shirral. Guided by his sight and mind, all three of the green missiles shot from his finger and hammered into the ogre's arm and shoulder. Shirral darted in and cut low, raking her blade of flame across its knees and sending it staggering back, howling in pain. The druid pressed the attack, cutting again and again as the beast reeled from the onslaught and finally fell.

Shanhaevel turned to see who else needed his help and spotted Ahleage, surrounded by two ogres and a troll. Pursing his lips, the elf rushed between them and set off another spell, summoning magical black tentacles and positioning them behind the two ogres. Immediately, the tentacles sprang up and writhed outward, seeking anything to grab. They found the ogres' legs. As the tentacles enveloped the beasts' limbs, the ogres screamed and tried to beat them away, flailing at the magical constructs with their clubs. Ahleage darted away, free at last to engage the troll.

As Shanhaevel turned, looking where his help was needed next, he spied a movement at the huge purple curtain. Narrowing his eyes, Shanhaevel saw an arm holding a thin wand that was stained dark with age. The wand was aimed at where Elmo, Draga, and Govin were engaged in a running battle with several large foes. A thin white beam sprang forth from the wand, and Shanhaevel saw his three companions engulfed in another of the magical storms of ice.

Grimacing, Shanhaevel prepared a spell of his own, waiting and watching. When the arm appeared again, he let his spell fly. A tiny cinder shot forth from his fingertip and streaked across the room to the figure hiding behind the curtain. When the cinder reached its target, it detonated, blossoming into a mammoth ball of flame that expanded in a heartbeat and then vaporized almost as quickly.

Falrinth staggered out from behind the curtain and fell

forward, his burned and smoking form tumbling against the base of the altar. Nodding in satisfaction, Shanhaevel started forward to determine the wizard's condition, when out of the corner of his eye, he saw another movement. Ahleage darted forward, daggers in his hands.

"Ahleage, no!" Shanhaevel cried out, but the man was too fast and did not hesitate. Reaching the downed wizard, Ahleage raised his daggers high, but he never finished the killing blow. The curtain sprang to life, writhing violently and shooting forth several dark tendrils that struck his leg.

Ahleage cried out and stumbled away even as Shanhaevel came to him. The man fell to the floor, trembling. To Shanhaevel's horror, Ahleage's leg atrophied before the elf's eyes, shrinking and darkening almost to nothing in a matter of seconds. Ahleage, almost delirious from the pain, rolled about, clutching his rotting limb futilely and screaming for someone, anyone, to help him, to make the pain go away.

Govin reached Ahleage and knelt down to tend to his tormented companion. The battle seemed to have come to a halt, and the rest of the companions gathered around their fallen friend.

Shanhaevel turned his attention back to Falrinth. The wizard was alive, but he was burned almost beyond recognition and did not seem long for this world. The elf grabbed Falrinth and dragged him away from the curtain, then knelt close to his face.

"My druid companion can heal you, but you must help me. Where are the gems?"

Falrinth stared unblinking at Shanhaevel's face and said nothing.

Shanhaevel shook his head and tried again. "She can make the pain go away. The temple will fall, but you can serve goodness once again, as before, when you rode with Prince Thrommel. Redeem yourself. Find it in your heart to rise to goodness once more. Tell me where the gems are!"

Very faintly, almost imperceptibly, Falrinth nodded. "Hedrack," he gasped. "Hedrack h-has them."

Something—Shanhaevel could never explain it later—made the elf flinch back at that moment. Perhaps it was a reflection in Falrinth's eyes, or maybe it was a rustle of cloth or the swish of a weapon through the air, but whatever it was, flinch Shanhaevel did, and it saved his life. The crushing blow of a mace that had been intended for his head instead fell upon Falrinth's face, spattering Shanhaevel with blood. Stumbling away from the gruesome sight of the other wizard's pulped face, the elf stared up to see Hedrack looming over him, bloody mace in hand.

"You won't be able turn him back to goodness, now," Hedrack said, his voice filled with malevolent glee. He took a step forward, raising his mace once more.

Elmo snarled, leaping between Shanhaevel and Hedrack, lunging into the air with his axe held high. Hedrack spun, sliding easily out of the way, and swung a fist around, pummeling Elmo in the ribs. At the same instant, Hedrack barked a single word—something Shanhaevel did not comprehend, a word of power. At the moment of contact, Elmo's eyes went wide. He spasmed, gasped in midair, then his body went limp as he skidded across the floor. Hedrack grinned down at the axeman's unmoving form, sniffed, and turned away again, casting another spell.

Before Shanhaevel could react, he lost track of Hedrack. His attention seemed to be forced elsewhere. One moment the high priest was standing there, and the next, Shanhaevel just didn't care. He could still see the high priest's movements, but it no longer mattered that Hedrack was walking across the room, retreating from him. Unable to shake off these disconcerting sensations, the wizard turned his attention back to Elmo.

Elmo lay perfectly still, his eyes staring at nothing. Shirral had already rushed to his side, rolling him over before Shanhaevel could even touch the man.

"Get up!" she pleaded, tears welling up in her eyes. "Elmo, get up!"

Elmo's still form told Shanhaevel well enough that he was dead.

"Noooo!" the druid wailed, realizing the terrible truth, too. She buried her face in Elmo's chest, huge sobs wracking her frame.

Shanhaevel reached out a hand to console her, but Shirral shoved him away, a crazed look in her eyes. "No!" she screamed, leaping to her feet. "Come back here, you bastard!" She took off like a shot, running after Hedrack.

"Shirral, wait!" Shanhaevel yelled, forcing down his own horror at Elmo's death and scrambling to his feet to try to catch her, to slow her from her mad, headlong charge. She was too fast, though, and he could not catch her. "Come on!" he cried out to Govin and Draga, who were still kneeling over Ahleage, watching with stricken looks on their faces.

Shanhaevel didn't wait to see if they would follow. He sprinted out of the temple after Shirral, praying he could catch up to the grief-stricken druid before she caught Hedrack.

The winding passages Shirral followed led to a series of well-appointed rooms—living quarters, from the looks of them. Shanhaevel saw Shirral dart ahead of him, around a corner and out of sight. Panic rising in his chest with every footstep, he ran after her, charging around the corner and almost into the flank of a huge creature—a two-headed monster that loomed over the fallen body of Shirral. The monster held a great axe in each of its hands.

Shirral moved, though she seemed woozy, languishing on a thick carpet with a gash across her forehead. The two-headed creature, an ettin, turned to Shanhaevel. Before the elf could react, though, a glowing hammer of dark blue light swooped in, hovering before him in midair. The wizard backed away from the levitating weapon, ready to dart out of the way should it attack, but the magical hammer was quick, and it caught him squarely on the chest. Coughing from the blow, Shanhaevel stumbled back and down, landing hard on his rump. His vision swam with spots, and he found it difficult to breathe. He tried to bring his staff up but discovered that he was sitting on it, and as he worked to get it free, the hammer hit him again, catching him in the temple. Everything faded to black.

"Wizard, come on! Get up!" It was Govin's voice, although it seemed far away. It came through a haze of pain, a throbbing, pounding pain that bounced around in Shanhaevel's skull. He considered speaking, but the idea of opening his mouth seemed to make his head pound worse, so he decided against it.

"Come on, Shanhaevel." Draga's voice cut through the throbbing. "Wake up. They've taken Shirral."

The elf's eyes opened, then, almost involuntarily. Nothing was in focus, but he blinked several times, willing them to work, and soon enough, several faces swam into view. Govin hovered over him, as well as Ahleage and Draga.

Shanhaevel was lying on his back, looking up at the ceiling. He tried to speak and found that his jaw was incredibly sore. He only managed a feeble croak.

"Can you drink?" Govin asked, holding up a small vial and lifting Shanhaevel's head.

The elf nodded feebly. The knight pressed the vial to the wizard's lips and dribbled a bit of the liquid. The familiar taste of cinnamon and ash confirmed its healing nature. Shanhaevel swallowed the thick fluid and felt some of the pain leech out of his jaw. Pushing himself up with one hand, he reached out, took the vial from Govin, and quaffed the remainder of its contents, swallowing it hurriedly. He felt the familiar feeling of the magic at work, the coolness spreading through his body as the potion did its trick, soothing away many of the pains he felt.

When the healing was done, Shanhaevel felt much better. Sitting up fully now, he looked from face to face at the three men around him. "What happened to Shirral?" he asked, strangely calm.

"Hedrack grabbed her," Ahleage said, his voice wavering the slightest bit. "He managed to get away before we could get past that"—he motioned with his head back in the direction of the two-headed ettin, now lying dead in a spreading pool of blood—"to reach and aid either of you."

Damn! Shanhaevel thought, furious. Another part of his mind was strangely surprised that this was his reaction. "We've got to find her," he said, trying to stand. He wavered on his feet, still a little light-headed from the beating he had taken. "Where did he go?"

Ahleage gestured back through the doorway where Shanhaevel had come in. "He threw her over his shoulder and went that way," he said. Gesturing at his now healthy leg, he added, "Govin managed to cure me." He shuddered once but that was all.

Shanhaevel saw how pale the man looked, recognizing the mark of having survived a harrowing experience. "You all right?"

"I'll survive." Ahleage nodded once. "But Shirral may not, if we don't go now."

"Elmo?" Shanhaevel tried to swallow but found that he couldn't.

Ahleage shook his head and pointed to a wrapped body a little bit beyond the dead ettin.

"We will avenge him," Govin said.

Draga, standing next to the knight, nodded and tightened his grip on his sword.

"Then let's go find him. Where might he have gone?" Shanhaevel looked around the room, seeing for the first time the richly furnished chambers. On a great bed on the far side of the room, two young women, covering their nakedness with furs, trembled as they stared at the group crouched in the doorway. Shanhaevel could tell they were scared to death.

"Paida?" Ahleage took a couple of halting steps toward the two, who shrank back, cowering. His eyes widened in recognition. "Ralishaz's mother, it is!"

"We must get them out of here," Govin said flatly, "and figure out where Hedrack has taken Shirral."

Ahleage tried to approach Paida, but the girl screamed and scrambled to the far side of the bed, covering herself completely with the furs.

"Hedrack must have charmed them in some way," Shanhaevel said. "I'll see if I can break it."

He began his spell, watching to make sure neither of the girls tried to escape before his spell coalesced. When he was done, he felt sudden burst of dispelling energy flash across the two women. For a moment, Paida and the other girl blinked in confusion, and then recognition dawned on the serving girl's face.

"Oh, thank the Mother!" Paida cried out, trembling anew.

"Please, don't let him come back," the other girl sobbed. "I want to go home!"

Ahleage smiled softly. "We'll take you home. What's your name?"

"Mika," the other young woman said. She followed Paida as the two of them, still clutching the furs about themselves, climbed off the bed and came toward the companions.

"Paida, Mika, do you know where he went?" Ahleage asked.

Mika blanched and shook her head.

Speaking to Shanhaevel, Paida said, "After you were hit by the glowing hammer, he dug something out of your belongings and grabbed the elf-woman. He carried her out, telling Deus and Ahma"—she pointed to the dead ettin—"to keep everyone from following."

Shanhaevel's heart leaped in his throat. He reached for his satchel and snarled in desperate frustration when he confirmed what he feared: The box with the golden skull was gone.

"He has the key!" the elf said, panic rising in his voice. "He's going to free Zuggtmoy!"

"We cannot let that happen," Govin said, his voice low and intense. "Where will he do this?"

"Back on the surface level, at that great throne," the wizard replied, gesturing upward with his thumb.

"Come on, then!" Govin said, motioning for the women to join them. "Let's go before it's too late."

Gingerly, the two women, using the furs from the bed to cover themselves, joined the four companions, and they exited the chambers, ready to return to the surface.

Just as Govin passed through the doorway and crouched to pick up Elmo's wrapped body, a dark form lunged out of the shadows. The face of Lareth glared as it let out a keening wail. It rushed forward, eager to consume them all. In an instant, two of the eight spidery legs of the undead creature struck, one glancing off Draga's shoulder and the other raking Mika's torso. There was no physical contact from the creature, but nonetheless, the poor girl's shriek died in her throat as the color left her body and she slumped to the floor, pale and unmoving.

Paida screamed even as Ahleage grabbed her arm and yanked her away from the horrid death spirit. Draga, holding his limp arm, fumbled for his sword, but Govin was there before the undead thing could strike again.

"Bless this weapon, Saint Cuthbert!" the knight shouted, and he swung his sword through the shadow spider. The blade slipped unhindered through the wispy apparition, but the face of Lareth grimaced in pain, and it howled as it stumbled back a step, trying to avoid the blessed blade.

Shanhaevel dropped to one knee, checking Mika, but the young woman was dead, her life drawn away by the touch of the cold spirit.

"Go!" Govin shouted, advancing a step toward the monster. "Get up there and save her! I will follow!"

Hesitating only a moment, Draga, Ahleage, and Shanhaevel hustled Paida from the chambers, scurrying away as Govin swung his blade again, eliciting another pained howl from the ghostly creature.

"May Saint Cuthbert protect him," Shanhaevel breathed as they ran.

"Why would Hedrack take Shirral?" Draga asked as they moved through the now-empty hallways. "What could he want with her?"

"Sacrifice for the demoness, most likely," Ahleage said as they hurried along.

At the man's words, Shanhaevel flinched, but he said nothing. He didn't want to think about such a thing, and he thrust it firmly from his mind. It's not going to happen, he told himself firmly. We'll just stop him before he gets the chance.

As the group moved ever upward, Shanhaevel noticed that the place seemed vacant. Many of the troops have either died at our hands or deserted, he decided. It was really no comfort. If she is freed, it won't matter how many of the enemy died. The elf quickened his pace a bit more.

* * * * *

When at last the four of them reached the top of level of the temple, entering the horrible chamber they had first explored, there was no one there either.

Shanhaevel motioned toward the blown-out front entrance and whispered, "Draga, take Paida and go. Get her somewhere safe."

Draga opened his mouth to protest, but as he looked back and forth from the wizard to the terrified woman, he nodded at last. He turned to go, leading Paida away. "I'll be back," he said.

Shanhaevel turned away from the exit and pointed at the front of the great room where the great semicircular wall faced out past the large throne of stone. Hedrack was there, his back to them. His rigid stance and quick, precise movements showed that he was working on something urgently. At the sound of their footsteps, the high priest turned, and Shanhaevel saw that he held the skull in one hand. The four depressions circling the top of the skull had been filled. Each hole contained a gem, one for each color of the elements. Shanhaevel groaned, realizing the key was now a powerful weapon in the hands of Hedrack.

Shirral slumped in the seat of the throne, her legs and arms bound, her face covered with a blindfold and a gag. She turned her head at the sound of the approaching footfalls, and Shanhaevel breathed a soft sigh of relief, knowing she was still alive.

"By Iuz, you will not go away!" Hedrack snarled, his face darkening in anger. "I would not have thought the wretched servants of the fop to be so persistent."

"Persistent is a fair enough word, Hedrack," Shanhaevel said coldly, moving steadily toward the man and preparing to rip the high priest apart with his bare hands, if necessary.

"Whatever your choice of terms, it changes nothing." Govin's voice echoed from behind the elf.

Shanhaevel turned to look at the knight, who stood a little way back, the body of Elmo lying at his feet. The knight's face looked a bit drawn, but he was smiling. Shanhaevel returned the grin, thankful to see his friend still alive.

"Victory is ours by the might of Cuthbert," Govin said. "You cannot stand against us. You must know that. Lay down your arms. One chance. No quarter will be given unless you surrender *now!*"

The knight strode forward as he spoke, closing with the high priest. Shanhaevel and Ahleage fanned out beside him, ready to finish this once and for all. Shirral, upon hearing the voices of her companions, struggled, trying to shrug off her bonds.

"So be it," the high priest spat, whirling to face them. "All of you, die!"

Without looking back, Hedrack slammed a fist into the druid's face, drawing a muffled grunt from her. She slumped down, groaning once and lying still. Hedrack held forth the skull in his other hand and spoke softly.

Shanhaevel, upon seeing the punishing blow the high priest had put upon the druid, swore furiously. He stepped forward, ready to fling a spell at Hedrack that would hurl the man back and slam him against the wall. Out of the corner of his eyes, he saw the others react similarly. All of them were ready to pummel the man standing at the far end into oblivion.

Before any of them could close on the high priest, there was a swirl of wind in the vast chamber, and suddenly, four loathesome creatures swam into view, summoned from some nether plane. Shanhaevel and the others drew up short.

Hedrack grinned, turned back to the throne, and sat upon it. As the planar creatures stepped forward to attack, Hedrack held the skull aloft, and the throne slowly sank into the floor.

Shanhaevel stood frozen in place for a moment as the horrible realization of what was transpiring hit him. Hedrack had summoned creatures from deep in the abyssal planes to cover his departure. The foul beasts advanced as the high priest disappeared, sinking down into the floor of the dais and taking the captured druid with him. If he were allowed to go unhindered, Zuggtmoy would be freed and the lands around the temple would fall prey to her.

Trying to watch all the creatures at once, Shanhaevel backed away from the horrors, which were now advancing eagerly. The first, a tall, gaunt creature that resembled a skeleton with reddish leather stretched tightly over its frame, grinned malevolently as it darted forward, swinging both of its long, bony claws at the wizard. Shanhaevel stumbled away from the attack and nearly rolled within range of the second creature, an ebony monstrosity with the head of a slavering, fanged dog and four arms, which was threatening Govin. The beast's eyes glowed a sickly violet, and Shanhaevel could smell the stench of rot as it lunged at the knight, swiping at him with two of its arms, both of which ended in snapping pinchers.

Another of the summoned creatures, a giant spike-backed toad with grotesquely human arms, loomed close to Shanhaevel, who rolled again, desperate to get away. It landed where he had been only a split-second before, bowling the dog-headed demon over. The two beasts tumbled to the side, snapping and hissing at one another. Govin waded in between them, swinging his sword with a well-practiced aim.

Shanhaevel scrambled to his feet and considered a spell that would harm these fiends. The two creatures Govin occupied ignored the wizard, but the tall, gaunt, skeletal monstrosity pounced forward again, causing the elf to fall back once more.

"Go!" Ahleage roared as he plowed into the red-skinned creature, slicing at it with his sword. "Save her!"

The skeletal demon swiped at Ahleage with a claw, but the man was quicker, severing its arm with a rapid strike.

Shanhaevel used the distraction to turn and run, sickened at the stench of rot, sulfur, and disease that radiated from the monsters. The last of the beings, a particularly horrid vulturelike monstrosity, also with humanlike arms, took flight and pursued him. The elf sprinted away, running past the great stairwell in the center of the temple and toward the throne in the distance. He kept running, even as he waited for the inevitable feel of claws raking across his back and a sharp beak ripping the flesh from his head and neck.

The vulture creature shot past Shanhaevel rather than attacking him, seeming to prefer to toy with him. It landed to block his path, near the huge hole in the floor where the Alliance had descended what seemed like an eternity ago. It spread its wings wide and screeched triumphantly, a sound that made the elf cringe as he drew up short, breathing heavily. Behind him, the other creatures howled, sending shivers down Shanhaevel's spine, as they did battle with Govin and Ahleage. Shanhaevel glanced around desperately, looking for some means of escape.

He has Shirral! a part of him screamed. Hurry! There might still be enough time to save her. You must try! If you don't reach her—

He couldn't make himself think of what might happen to the druid if he didn't reach her. But it won't matter, he told himself, for Zuggtmoy will be freed, and we'll all suffer the same fate. Panting, he wiped his sleeve across his eyes. His vision blurred with the sickening weight of the temple's evil pressing in on him.

It's the temple that makes you lose hope, he reminded himself. Focus! Don't let it win!

Shanhaevel cleared his thoughts. The vulture-thing was closing with him, now, clacking its beak and screeching in delight. The wizard kept his staff in front of him, holding it in a defensive stance, waiting to see if he might get a chance to dart around the beast and reach the throne. No opportunity presented itself, though, and the wizard grew more and more frustrated as time slipped away.

There was a blur of motion in the corner of the wizard's eye, and Draga slammed into the creature, driving it backward.

"Save the druid!" he roared as he stepped back, his sword in his hand. "Go, wizard! *Go!*"

The demon screamed at the newcomer before it, and when Shanhaevel darted forward, trying to slip past the two combatants, the fiend tried to cut the wizard off. Draga lunged again, sword up, slamming himself full force into the creature and driving his weapon into the vulture-thing's chest. His momentum cracked the thin, hollow bones of one wing as he drove it back. The fiend stumbled, crying from the pain inflicted by the warrior and slashing at Draga with its talons and beak. It gouged Draga's flesh in a spray of blood.

In one terrible instant, Shanhaevel realized that both friend and foe were about to tumble over the edge of the great pit. The planar beast was overbalanced. Tumbling backward, it flailed with its one good wing, trying to right itself as Draga continued to push it, drive it, oblivious to his own danger.

"Draga!" Shanhaevel cried out, taking a faltering step forward, hoping to catch his companion before both he and the abomination went over the edge. But the elf was much too far away and as his friend took that final step, the embraced combatants seemed to hang in empty space for a heartbeat before slipping down and away, lost.

Shanhaevel could only stare in horror at the dark pit. The final wail of the maimed monstrosity echoed as it fell to its death.

"Draga!" the elf shouted, devastated. *Make it count!* the wizard chided himself, shutting his mind off from the horror he had just witnessed. *Make his sacrifice worth something! Move!*

Shanhaevel shook off his despair and ran toward the dais once more. He brought into being a spell that he had never tried before, another of the potent magicks he had gleaned from studying Lanithaine's tomes. Weaving the magical energies, the elf transformed, changing from the familiar form of an elf into the very odd and unfamiliar form of an owl. His heart pounded as he transformed, fearing he might lose his mind to the process, becoming an owl in thought as well as in body. But it did not happen. When the spell was complete, he was still Shanhaevel.

Spreading his arms wide, Shanhaevel discovered they were now feathered wings, and instinctually he took flight, rising swiftly. He soared toward the now-concealed throne. The elf prayed that some means of ingress was still available. He spotted a square hole where the throne had been and made directly for it, beating his wings furiously before the shaft could close.

Shanhaevel did not contemplate the consequences of his actions. He did not consider that he was flying straight toward a bloated, horrifying demon or the angry, vengeful high priest who was trying to free her. All he could think about was the deaths of his friends, retrieving the golden key, and rescuing Shirral. As he dived into the hole and winged his way down that black shaft, his mind burned with fury for Hedrack, and the hatred seemed to give him strength.

The shaft descended a fair distance. The bottom was faintly lit with unsettling purple, green, and sickly yellow light. Shanhaevel could see the throne resting on the floor directly below him. The seat was now empty. He wondered if Hedrack lay in wait at the bottom, ready to attack anything that appeared from above, or if, in the high priest's pride, he assumed the abyssal creatures he had summoned would suffice to stave off any further interruptions. Regardless, Shanhaevel thought, Hedrack would not be expecting an owl to spring forth, and the elf hoped that would provide him with enough surprise that he could steal away the golden skull before Hedrack knew what had happened.

As the transformed wizard dropped out of the shaft and into the wider chamber at its bottom, he drew up from his plunge and banked to one side, darting away from the entrance to the place.

He found himself in another strange throne room, but this one faced at right angles to the one above, and unlike the chamber overhead with its harsh reds, browns, and greens, this one was inky black, with strange, glowing gray runes inscribed along the walls. The bizarre writing seemed to twist and writhe at the edge of Shanhaevel's vision as he scanned the place. The only light issued from flickering torches set in cressets all about the perimeter of the room.

At the near end of the long chamber, close to the shaft opening through which he had dropped down, a broad set of stairs led up into another chamber, currently unlit. At the far end, just before the throne, Hedrack knelt with his back to Shanhaevel, working at something on the floor before him. Sitting upon the throne was a horrid crone, a frightful woman whose gaze seemed glazed and distant.

Uncertain of how to proceed, Shanhaevel swooped in closer on silent wings, hoping to gain a better view of what the high priest was doing. As the transformed elf circled overhead, he saw that Hedrack knelt at the edge of a great symbol inscribed in the floor—a hexagon inside a circle. The tips of the hexagon, radiating out past the circle, glowed in the colors of the rainbow—red, orange, yellow, green, blue, and indigo—while the center of the device pulsed with a faint purple light. The various hues somehow seemed sickly and wrong, but the wizard gave it little thought, for Shirral was lying on her back in the center of the device. She had been stripped bare, and Hedrack was attaching iron manacles to her ankles and wrists, obviously preparing her for some sacrifice. The druid seemed sluggish, her eyes only half open and her jaw slack as she stared vacantly up toward the ceiling. Resting on the floor between Hedrack's knees as he leaned out over the druid was the golden skull.

Shanhaevel banked again, preparing to dart in and steal the golden key out from under Hedrack's nose. The transformed elf had been swift and silent to this point, and the high priest had not noticed him at all. Hedrack secured both of Shirral's ankles and began to work on her left wrist. It would be such a simple matter to fly in, grab the key, and soar to the far side of the room before the high priest knew what had happened. Shanhaevel came around low and fast. He was approaching his target when the crone sitting upon the throne shrieked and pointed.

Shanhaevel's heart sank as Hedrack's head whipped around and spotted the owl even as he snatched up the key and clutched it close. Shanhaevel tried to pull up and fly out of reach of the high priest, but he had built up too much momentum, and it was an easy thing for Hedrack to swing out with his mailed fist and strike the wizard hard.

The blow sent Shanhaevel sprawling across black marble the floor. He came to rest against the wall a good distance away, his vision blurred red with pain and anger at his own failure. One wing was broken. Wide-eyed, he triggered the magical effect that would cancel the spell, and he felt himself shapeshift back into his normal form. His arm hung uselessly at his side, his staff at his feet.

Hedrack stood, facing the wizard, an unpleasant smile on his face.

"That was daring," the priest said, grinning. "I applaud your efforts. Since you managed to come down here, you can at least watch as I send your companion screaming into the abyss. My Lady Zuggtmoy will enjoy entertaining her, I'm sure."

At this, the crone cackled with crazed glee.

Shanhaevel clenched his fists and immediately regretted it, for pain shot through his injured arm. Gritting his teeth, he snarled, "Save your mocking for someone who cares to listen to you, you bastard. I came down here to put an end to this."

The wizard drew a deep breath and prepared a spell.

Hedrack laughed, seeming to find the elf's words genuinely funny. Shanhaevel paused in his casting, taken aback by the high priest's unexpected display. Hedrack chuckled softly at first, openly amazed, but he was soon bent halfway over, howling with amusement, gasping for air. Tears of mirth ran down his face. Shanhaevel could only watch, dumbfounded.

"You honestly still think you have a chance!" the high priest gasped between fits of laughter. "You think you might still be able to stop me! Oh, that is rich!" Finally regaining control, Hedrack continued. "Don't you understand? It's over! You've lost! The moment I gained control of the key"—he held up the small golden skull to emphasize his words—"victory was mine. What do you expect to accomplish now? How do you expect to stop me, when I can do *this?*"

The high priest gestured, and a scintillating coalescence swirled in the air near where he stood. The disturbance grew and solidified until it was a whirlwind, hovering beside the high priest. The thing of air seemed alive, shifting and spinning, sending a cascade of dust through the room. It towered almost to the ceiling. Shanhaevel swallowed and took an involuntary step back, thinking desperately through the magic he had left, trying to come up with something he could use to defeat the air being.

Hedrack gestured again, and another disturbance appeared, swirling into the form of a huge pile of earth and stone, vaguely manlike in shape. It swayed on its feet. Two massive arms that ended in great, rocky fists hung at its sides.

Obviously enjoying his grandiose demonstration of power, Hedrack made a third, and then a fourth gesture, bringing into existence two more elemental creatures, one of fire and one of water. The two new beings danced with energy, seeming to lean forward against the forces that bound them, eager to scurry forward and strike at the awed elf standing on the opposite side of the chamber. Behind Hedrack, the crone cackled in mad glee, delighted with the summonings the high priest had performed.

Gloating and proud, Hedrack lowered his arms. "So tell me, wizard, did you honestly think you had a chance? Did you really believe you could defeat the temple in its finest hour? I will give you credit. You are amusing." He gestured once more, and as one, the four elemental creatures lurched toward Shanhaevel. "Destroy him. Now."

As Hedrack watched, standing casually, with one arm folded across his chest and the other hanging easily at his side, his four new pets made for Shanhaevel unerringly, moving to consume him in their essence, to freeze, crush, burn, and drown him utterly.

The air elemental spun crazily, whipping about the room, gliding rapidly along one wall until it was behind the elf, trapping him and preventing escape. The creatures of fire and water moved to flank Shanhaevel, their bodies a sheet of flickering flame and a trembling, surging wave. The creature of earth came last, making the hall shake with its slow, deliberate footfalls.

Shanhaevel had nowhere to go. He was trapped between the four elemental forces, surrounded by the powers of nature and doomed to suffer their effects. Desperately, the elf looked at Hedrack, hoping beyond hope that there might be some reprieve from the high priest, some sudden notion from the man that death like this was beyond even his desire, but Shanhaevel knew in his heart that Hedrack delighted in this. Shirral would die, and Zuggtmoy, strong in her own plane, though she had manifested as a cackling crone here on Oerth, would be freed to ruin the lands around the temple.

"Now, you will die." Hedrack gloated, still watching the destruction he was visiting on his foe. "As soon as my men destroy the last of the doors, my Lady Zuggtmoy will be free, and this lovely sacrifice will be sent to an abyssal plane to await the demoness's attentions there."

Shanhaevel felt a familiar lump grow in his throat, felt the overwhelming sense of sadness that produced it. He thought of Lanithaine, grieving again for his teacher and friend. The wizard's sense of sorrow seemed bottomless as he contemplated his own failings. He had been unable to save his mentor, he could not now save his love, and in the end, he would not be able to save even himself. Shanhaevel hung his head even as he felt the forces of the four creatures closing in. He sank down to one knee, his wounded arm still limp at his side, and bowed his head, surrendering to the inevitable at last.

Hedrack's gasp of surprise forced the elf to look up in the high priest's direction. The golden skull was skittering across the floor toward Shanhaevel, knocked free of Hedrack's grasp. Shirral had done it. With one arm still free of the shackles, she had managed to reach up and knock the key loose, sending it clattering in the direction of the elf. The golden skull bounced a couple of times as it rolled across the floor, sliding between the massive foot of the earth elemental and the roaring flames of the living fire creature. The small bejewelled orb rolled to a stop at Shanhaevel's foot even as Zuggtmoy screeched in horror and anger from her chair.

Hedrack snarled and backhanded Shirral, knocking her back with an audible *thunk* that Shanhaevel could hear even over the roar of wind and fire around him. The druid slumped back with a pitiful cry and lay still. Spinning, Hedrack looked to see where his treasure had rolled to a stop. When he saw the object of his desire resting near the toe of Shanhaevel's boot, the high priest's eyes grew wide.

Rage, still smoldering in the elf's heart, now flamed. Snatching up the golden skull with his good arm, Shanhaevel stood up. The four creatures surrounding him were now no more than a couple of paces away. Each of them stopped, however, as their quarry rose before them, holding aloft the source of their summoning and the icon of their subservience. Presenting the skull, Shanhaevel felt the link of command to the four elemental creatures, and he knew that they were under his influence and would obey his commands.

For a moment, Shanhaevel considered sending the elemental beasts to attack Hedrack, to drive him against a wall and to destroy him as he had intended to destroy the wizard, but he realized it would be fruitless and would most likely harm Shirral in the process. The only way to defeat Hedrack was to destroy the key before Zuggtmoy could be freed—except that he needed Shirral's aid to do that. Even if Shanhaevel could manage to free his companion, Hedrack would slay the druid before he would allow her to participate in such a ritual. Even with the orb in his grasp, defeat still seemed imminent to the wizard.

Unless there is another way . . . the elf thought. Going quickly through the steps of the process Burne had explained before, he realized he might have an alternate way to perform the rites of destruction. Wind and earth, then fire and water. It could be done. Maybe.

Hedrack spun on his heel, pulling a knife from his boot and kneeling down next to Shirral, who still seemed groggy. Her head was bruised, and blood leaked from a wicked gash on her temple. Hedrack squatted so that Shanhaevel could see him clearly, could witness what he was about to do. Shanhaevel had seen it coming, had braced himself for it, yet he still felt the panic rise in him as the high priest grasped the druid by the hair and pressed the blade against her throat.

"Give me the skull or she dies right now!" Hedrack commanded.

Fighting the urge to comply with the high priest, Shanhaevel responded, "You will kill her anyway, but"—the wizard held the golden skull aloft, so that Hedrack could see it—"do you realize what will happen if I do this?"

Shanhaevel plunged his arm into the center of the creature of air, his grasp on the magical key making him immune to the effects of its buffeting winds.

Hedrack's eyes widened a second time, suddenly aware of what Shanhaevel was thinking. Releasing the druid's hair, he raised his arm and pointed beseechingly.

"*No!* Do not! You must not!"

Hedrack leaped to his feet and charged the distance between them.

Quickly, Shanhaevel spun on his feet and darted across to the creature of earth, commanding the beast to strike at the key with one of its rocky, powerful stone fists. The monster brought its thick hand down hard, almost knocking the orb out of the elf's grasp, but Shanhaevel managed to hang on with his one good arm. There was an intense clanging sound from the blow.

"Stop him!" Zuggtmoy shrieked. "Stop him, you fool!"

Hedrack was closer now, no more than a dozen long strides away, though he was walled off from reaching Shanhaevel by the creature of earth and stone. Wasting no time watching the high priest, Shanhaevel spun away and thrust his arm into the heart of the hot, licking flames of the creature of fire. He held the orb in its center, though he himself was not burned because of his hold on the key. As the blood pounded in his ears and the stones beneath his feet trembled, Shanhaevel felt the gold grow hot in his palm and heard a scream of agony from Zuggtmoy.

Hedrack was but a couple of paces away, now, pushing past the creatures that blocked his way, squeezing between the earth elemental and its flaming counterpart, ignoring the scorching flames that licked at him and singed his hair. The high priest lunged for Shanhaevel, trying to grab the elf, but he was not fast enough. The wizard darted away, launching himself at the last creature in the sequence, plunging his fist, still holding the orb, deep into the murky recesses of the water beast.

"No!" Hedrack screamed, and the roaring in Shanhaevel's ears intensified. He felt the orb crack in his hand, shattering into a dozen jagged pieces of gold. The gems around the skull's crown slipped free and shattered. In the distance, Zuggtmoy screamed once more, but it was not the cry of the old crone, but rather the pained roar of the great bulbous demon—her true form. Shanhaevel's momentum carried him into the depths of the creature of water, and as the golden key cracked, he felt its magical protection over him slip away. He felt the intense cold of the water.

The water itself subtly changed, too. It no longer undulated with life. Instead, it turned into a torrent of water, a cascade that spilled to the floor as Shanhaevel passed through it, tumbling unharmed to the other side and sliding across the floor, soaking wet. Shaking his head to clear the streams of water that poured down his face and wiping the damp, bedraggled hair from his eyes, the wizard tried to sit up, but the floor beneath his feet rumbled and shifted. With only one good arm, he lost his balance.

Behind the elf, Hedrack screamed, a plaintive, terrified shriek. Shanhaevel heard a sickening sound of stone clattering upon the floor, a wet smacking sound, and the high priest was quiet. He turned to see what had happened.

The creature of stone, its magic undone by the destruction of the golden skull, had fallen lifeless—right atop Hedrack. The high priest's body was pinned beneath a great slab of marble. A twisted and mangled leg stuck out at an unnatural angle. He was still alive, though his face was white with shock and terror. He gazed up at the ceiling, muttering softly.

Shanhaevel approached the high priest, even as another rumbling shockwave shook the chamber.

"Kill me." Hedrack pleaded softly. "Kill me, p-please kill me. D-d-do-don't let him g-get me—"

"Who?" Shanhaevel asked, shifting unsteadily on his feet as the chamber crumbled around him.

"My lord and m-m-master." Hedrack's tone was fevered and crazed. "He w-will torment m-me. He . . . w-will punish me. Please kill me. Don't leave me to h-him, I beg you."

Shanhaevel considered for a moment, then reached for the knife that was just beyond Hedrack's grasp. He stood for a moment, looking down at the high priest.

"Yes, please," Hedrack said. "Kill me . . . quickly. D-do it, I beg you."

Shanhaevel raised the knife, preparing to plunge it through Hedrack's eye, wondering why, after all of this, he would grant the high priest's request, would help to spare the man his fate. He raised the dagger, but a cry stopped him short.

"Shanhaevel!" Shirral cried. "Help me!"

The elf turned to see the druid, still chained to the floor, although the symbol beneath her had vanished. Pieces of stonework were falling now—bits of the ceiling and walls tumbling down around her. Shirral was helpless to dodge the shards, imprisoned as she was.

Dropping the knife and leaving Hedrack, Shanhaevel scurried across the floor. He dropped to his knees beside

Shirral and began frantically working with only one hand to unlock the manacles that bound her. In the throne nearby, Shanhaevel could see the image of Zuggtmoy, still trapped in the chair. She was in her true form now, but she was insubstantial, fading in and out of view. Occasionally, she would materialize so solidly that the elf could hear her howls of pain and agony, as she was being ripped from this plane and dragged back to her own.

Finally, Shanhaevel managed to unbind Shirral's hand, and he worked to free one of her ankles. The druid leaned forward, working on the binding that encircled her leg. Around the two of them, the chamber shook and heaved, dropping huge chunks of masonry and stonework around them. One particularly large piece shattered near the two, spraying them both with shards of stone that stung their skin.

We're not going to make it out of here, Shanhaevel silently fumed as he struggled to release the catch on the manacle.

"Release, damn you!" he commanded the shackle, frustrated that one arm still hung useless at his side.

As if responding to the elf's demand, the manacles clicked open, and Shirral was finally free. Shanhaevel tried to help her stand, but the floor beneath him shifted suddenly, rocking and cracking so that it buckled in the middle of the chamber. Both of them went sliding toward a crevasse that had opened in the middle. Foul fumes belched up from the rip in the stone, spewing up and filling the air with smoke, gasses, and heat.

"No!" Shirral yelled, clinging to Shanhaevel as they both edged closer to the chasm.

With one arm wounded, the elf had a difficult time controlling his inexorable slide, but the druid managed to take hold of his shirt in one hand and grab an outcropping of buckled floor stone with her other. Slowly, straining, she pulled them both away from the shifting, widening gap in the rock.

The two companions rolled to the side, panting, but the collapse of the room was growing in intensity. Scrambling to his feet, Shanhaevel helped Shirral to stand, yanked his tattered cloak free, and gave it to her to cover herself.

"This way!" the wizard said, taking her by the hand and leading her toward the bottom of the shaft. As they passed the point where Hedrack still lay, pinned beneath the stones of the dead elemental, the high priest reached his free hand out, desperately straining for them.

"Please!" he called, turning his head as he saw them pass just beyond his grasp. "Don't leave! Don't let him take me!"

Shanhaevel ignored the high priest as he reached the point where the shaft was directly overhead. The shifting collapse of the temple had fractured the earth, however, and the hole leading to freedom was now sealed. There was no way to escape. Shanhaevel whirled around in frustration, knowing their time was running out. As the walls of the chamber sagged inward, his gaze settled on the broad stairs leading up into the darkness. It was the only way out of the room.

"Come on!" Shanhaevel growled, taking Shirral's hand once more and dragging her up the stairs.

"Nooo!" Hedrack howled, and Shanhaevel paused for the briefest of moments, turning to look back at the high priest. As their eyes locked, as the elf saw the desperation in Hedrack's own visage, he knew his own face was a cold mask of contempt. He felt no compassion for the man. Without remorse, he turned away just as a great mass of one wall tumbled downward, burying the high priest beneath it. Hurrying with Shirral up the stairs and out of the chamber, Shanhaevel never looked back.

The area at the top of the broad steps was another wide throne room. It, too, was on the verge of collapse, and there was but one way out—a large pair of bronzewood doors, sealed tightly with both silver and magic, that faced the throne. When Shanhaevel saw the portal, his despair was complete. As the earth shook and the stonework of the temple continued to fall all around him, he sank to his knees, shaking his head.

Shirral settled beside him and pressed her face against his chest. Tears and blood streaked her cheeks. "We did it, though," she sobbed, struggling to smile. "We stopped them." She took his face in her trembling hands and kissed him. "We kept them from freeing her."

Shanhaevel nodded at her numbly, thankful that they would have that to cling to, to give them some measure of solace in these final moments. He drew the druid to him with his good arm and held her tightly as the thick columns of the throne room collapsed, sending deadly shards of stone scattering in all directions. As the ground bucked and quaked, Shanhaevel watched death close in on them.

Suddenly, there was bright blaze of blue light that emanated from the sealed doors. With a loud crack that reverberated above the noise of grinding stone and trembling earth, the doors flew apart, each half of the portal slamming hard against the stone wall in which it was set.

Shanhaevel gaped in open amazement for a heartbeat before lurching up to his feet, pulling Shirral, whose face was still buried in his chest, along with him. Pointing, he staggered forward, dragging her along behind him. When the druid saw where he was headed, she gasped then scrambled to catch up with him. A column smashed hard into the floor where they had been crouched, stinging them with slivers of shattered rock as it hit. Turning, they both fled through the open doorway and up the stairs they found beyond.

Running as fast as he had ever thought possible, Shanhaevel scrambled up the stairs, into a wide hallway, then turned and found the next portal, also gaping open. Without hesitating, he charged through and clambered up the next set of steps, still holding Shirral's hand. At the top, though, he found the way blocked by collapse. Groaning, he turned back, thinking desperately.

"The shaft!" he said, praying the pit would still be open and the ledge intact. "Come on!"

He pulled Shirral along behind him. His broken arm ached horribly, but he tried to put it out of his mind as they sprinted together, struggling to maintain their balance as the whole place rumbled and shifted violently. Dust filled the air, and passages were crumbling, sealed off.

Desperately, Shanhaevel ran down the long hall of bones, scattering the remains of long-dead warriors as he charged through. When he reached the spot where the secret door had been, he began the desperate search to find the release and open it.

"Help me!" he cried to Shirral.

Together, they fumbled for the catch, and when Shirral found it, the two of them slammed the hidden panel down and peered through. Fortunately, the ledge was still there, and the two of them slipped through the small opening and into the shaft beyond. The tremors of the collapsing temple continued, and the companions had to brace themselves against the wall of the shaft to maintain their balance.

Hold together just a little longer, Shanhaevel prayed. Taking Shirral's hand, he began the ascent to the top, to blessed escape. He knew of a spell that would aid him, a bit of magic he could use to levitate upward, but he refused to think about it. *I won't leave her,* he insisted.

"Shanhaevel!" Shirral cried as the world pitched and rocked. "It's not going to hold!"

As if in response to the druid's words, the stairs cracked and crumbled beneath their feet.

"Do you have any magic?" Shirral asked, desperation in her eyes. "Anything that could—?"

"I won't leave you!" he cut her off, shaking his head. "We can shout for help!"

"Use it!" Shirral said. "Cast something and get yourself out!"

"No! I can't take you, and I won't go without you!" The steps they were on suddenly shifted, and Shanhaevel was forced to leap back and away as the section dropped away into the darkness. He and Shirral were now separated by a large gap. Shanhaevel choked back a sob.

"No!" he screamed, reaching across to Shirral. *Not when we're so close!*

Shirral looked at him, and in her eyes he saw the love she felt for him. She smiled, even as the section of stone beneath her gave way, and she fell.

"Noo!" Shanhaevel screamed, wanting to lunge after her, but he leaned wrong and was unable to get his legs under him. As he watched her slip away, he thought his chest would burst, but then, an amazing thing happened. As he watched, horrified, he saw the woman he loved transform, taking the shape of a small bird. In the blink of an eye, she was a sparrow, her wings beating furiously as she swooped up the shaft to the surface.

Laughing in delight and relief, Shanhaevel watched her go, gladness filling his heart. The earth shook, and before more of the stonework could break away, he began his spell. As he finished weaving the magic of the levitation spell, the stairs he was standing on gave way, and he found himself hovering in space. Trembling in relief, the wizard rose steadily as the walls of the shaft cracked and tumbled into the darkness below.

At the top, Shanhaevel found Shirral waiting for him, once again in human form.

"Why didn't you just go?" he asked as they both ran toward the front of the temple, to the gaping hole where the front doors once stood. "Why didn't you just fly out of here?"

"Because you were still down there," she said simply.

When they were but thirty paces from the exit and freedom, a good portion of the ceiling crashed down around them, narrowly missing Shirral and grazing Shanhaevel's leg. He tumbled forward, losing his balance, and felt his breath leave his body as he landed hard on his back. Sharp pain coursed through his wounded arm, and he fought to remain conscious.

"Come on!" Shirral urged, grabbing the wizard by the shoulders and helping him to his feet. Together, they stumbled the last few feet toward the exit, leaping through it and out onto the ground just as the remaining structure fell to ruin behind them.

* * * * *

Multiple rumbles shook the ground—aftershocks from the total destruction of the temple. Dust hung thick in the air, and the earth groaned. Shanhaevel lay panting in the snow, feeling it soaking into him as it melted rapidly, heated by the warmth of the spring sun. With a final exhausted sigh, the wizard rose to a sitting position.

A few feet away, Govin, Ahleage, and Paida stood, grinning at him. Between the knight and Ahleage, Draga reclined on a makeshift litter. His face, chest, and arms were a weave of bloody scratches. Though almost as pale as the surrounding snow, Draga was also grinning. Shanhaevel blinked in surprise, then laughed, smiling widely at Draga.

"I did not think we would see you again," Govin said, genuine pleasure in his voice. "You have the blessing of Cuthbert himself, it seems."

"So it would seem," Shanhaevel agreed, finally feeling his breathing returning to normal.

"I thought we'd lost you," Draga said, beaming at Shirral. "I was already imagining what I'd have to say to Jaroo when we returned to Hommlet."

"Yes, well," Ahleage interjected, "now she can imagine telling him what happened to her clothes."

Ahleage squinted, watching the druid warily, but the grin on his face was broad and joyful. Beside him, Paida, who had Govin's cloak wrapped around her, turned and furrowed her brow, glaring at the man.

Shirral scowled at Ahleage for a moment, her icy blue eyes flashing, but then she cracked a smile and laughed. Her laughter faded, though, when she saw the wrapped form of Elmo lying on a second litter behind them all. A single tear rolled down the druid's cheek as she moved toward the huge axeman. She knelt beside his body and lowered her head.

Shanhaevel was tempted to move to her side, to try to comfort her, but something held him back. He sensed that she needed a moment alone, a chance to say good-bye by herself. Instead, he turned and looked at Draga, shaking his head.

"I thought I was seeing the dead when I first spotted you there. How on earth did you survive?" the wizard asked.

Draga merely shrugged, but Ahleage was quick to answer. "Somehow, this lucky son of a sailor managed to land on the ledge of the shaft when he went over. After Govin and I managed to kill those other *things*"—Ahleage shuddered at the memory of the fiends— "we heard him calling. We had just pulled him back to the surface when the whole place crumbled down around our ears."

"We waited for you as long as we could," Govin added, "but when that last, strange flash of blue rippled through the place and everything began to come down, we could stay inside no longer." The look in the knight's eyes told Shanhaevel he wasn't terribly proud of having left them behind.

"It was the right decision," Shanhaevel said, and he meant it. "It would have been senseless for you to die if we had never come out."

"I am thankful you did," Govin said, "though I can't imagine how you managed it."

"That, my friends, is a tale to be told on the way back to Hommlet."

Epilogue

The taproom at the Inn of the Welcome Wench was boisterous this evening. The five companions sat around a table piled with platters of food. Steaming meat pies, roasted chicken, huge hunks of cheese, cold milk, fresh bread, eggs prepared several different ways, potatoes, and assorted fruit covered the surface, and the members of the Alliance were heartily consuming the delicious food.

It had been three days since the fall of the temple, and everyone was healed and refreshed after recuperating from their exploits. Shirral snuggled next to Shanhaevel as they ate, feeding him bites of cheese between the occasional kiss. Paida and Leah joined them, Leah sitting with Ahleage and Paida relaxing between Draga and Govin.

Glora Gundigoot continued to bring fresh dishes of her wonderful cooking out to replace what was already consumed. Around them all, the local inhabitants of Hommlet, including the members of the council, drank, sang, and celebrated the Alliance's victory.

Only Hroth did not participate in the festivities, sitting off to one side, nursing a cold mug and staring into the large fireplace. When Shirral spotted the captain of the militia, she slipped from the table and moved to the man's side. Shanhaevel watched as the druid sat next to the captain and whispered something to him. She reached out a hand and took the older man's in her own. Hroth smiled at her, and she leaned in and rested her head on his shoulder. He took her in his arms and hugged her tightly, then, a tear sliding down his cheek.

Finally, Shirral pulled away and stood, saying one last thing to Hroth. The man smiled and nodded, patting her hand before letting her leave his side and return to the table. When she sat down next to Shanhaevel once more, the wizard looked at her questioningly, and she leaned close and kissed him on the cheek.

"He's a very sad man who will miss his son very much. I just told him Elmo had honored him with his bravery, and he should be proud."

Shanhaevel nodded and took her hand in his own. He turned his attention back to the table, where Govin now stood, preparing to speak.

"By the grace of my god, Saint Cuthbert, we successfully saw our way to the end of this monumental victory. For the first time in a long while, I don't really know what lies before me. I do know, however, that there are no finer people than the four of you I would rather be with when I follow that unknown path. I—"

The banging of the front door cut the knight off in mid-sentence. A young man was standing there, dressed in the finery of court. He wore a tunic of blue and red, and the coat of arms of Furyondy was embroidered upon his right breast. He swept into the room, muddy boots and all, and bowed low to no one in particular.

"I bear a message for certain distinguished members of an alliance—including one Sir Govin Dahna, loyal knight of Saint Cuthbert, and his companions, Shantirel Galanhaevel, Shirral, Ahleage, Draga, and Elmo—from his lordship, marshal of Furyondy, Prince Thrommel. Can anyone direct me to these individuals?"

For a long moment, there was perfect silence. Everyone in the room stared at the liveried courier, unable to speak. At last, Govin recovered his wits and stepped around the table toward the young man.

"I am Sir Govin," he said with a bow, "and the others you speak of, with the exception of Elmo—may his spirit find peace—dine with me here." He gestured to his friends. "What is the message?"

The courier handed Govin a scroll case, saluted the knight, turned on his heel, and strolled out the door and into the evening. Staring after the courier for a moment, Govin held the scroll case until Ahleage coughed loudly.

"Uh, knight, you can open it any time you'd like," Ahleage suggested, tapping his fingers on the table.

Shaking his head, Govin turned his attention back to the others and cracked the seal on the case. Pulling the curled parchment free, he unrolled it and read. When he finished, he let his hands fall to his sides, staring off in wonder.

"Well, what does it say?" Shirral insisted, reaching for the message.

Govin let her take it from him, and Shanhaevel looked over the druid's shoulder as she read aloud.

" 'My good and faithful subjects and friends, I trust this message finds you all in good health and successful in your efforts to dispatch the elemental temple. I have returned home in triumph and have been received gratefully by both my father's court and my beloved, Jolene, princess of Veluna. Unfortunately, civil war in her nation threatens our impending marriage. Several in her father's court challenge my claim to her hand and would see our union destroyed.

" 'I require your assistance. If this notice has reached you, I must assume that you have achieved victory over our mutual enemies. Come with all due haste to Chendl. I have a special task that requires your unique talents. Further explanations will have to wait until your arrival. Thrommel.' "

Shanhaevel looked up and saw everyone around the table staring wide-eyed at Shirral.

"By Cuthbert," Govin said, that look of amazement still on his face, "what a great honor this is, serving the prince. Tomorrow, it seems, we ride for Chendl."

Shanhaevel shook his head, realizing he had already made up his mind to go, to ride with his companions, his friends, the Alliance.

"What was it you were saying about unknown paths, Govin?" he asked, a smile appearing on his face.

Queen of the Demonweb Pits

Paul Kidd

Master and apprentice lay in the heather, side by side. Recca wore flamboyant armor and a helmet fashioned like a screaming eagle, and his apprentice was in gear rugged, tested, and unadorned. Recca was thin and rakishly handsome with amber eyes and golden hair as soft as silk. His apprentice, almost invisible in the weeds beside him, was a huge human. When they'd first met, Recca had thought the boy too big and too powerful to move in stealth, yet he was always somehow silent as a cat. No, not a cat—a bear, dark, terrifying, and immense.

The war had taught him failure, hate, and emptiness. He had a stark brilliance with the sword, which Recca found annoying. No flamboyance, no style—merely a brutal, unforgiving efficiency. Recca's reputation had been founded on his brilliance, his merciless speed, and his raffish charisma. But in dark times, men looked to tireless, efficient men for comfort. Men like Recca's apprentice.

With the turning of the war, decent targets had become fewer and fewer. The only troops of Iuz to be seen were armies in retreat, but here, all of a sudden, a mistake had been made. A demonic general was bringing labor troops to build field fortifications. There would be a general, officers, officials—and they were guarded only by shambling, rotting zombies armed with shovels and stakes. There were no abyssal bats, no demons. A general of Iuz would fall—the greatest coup achieved by any band through the entire war. Recca's reputation would be immortalized.

The war was ending, and it was time to look to the future. A new generation would be searching for heroes—for kings. As the hero of the resistance war, Recca's name would ring upon a hundred thousand tongues. . . .

Recca thought the new attack would be easy, but his apprentice failed to agree. The big human studied the scattered parties of zombies digging ditches and hauling rocks. He looked at the general's tents and the few guards set on hills and ridgelines, and he drew back into cover.

"Withdraw. It's a trap."

His voice was bass—quiet, grim, definite. The elf rolled to look at his apprentice and raised one brow.

"And we know this *how?*"

"It smells wrong."

"What? Have you become part man, part hell hound?" Recca slid an amused sidewise glance at his apprentice. "The problem with humans is that they cannot accept being clever! There is a superiority that comes with intelligence and training. I have trained you superbly. Every movement you make is properly honed." Recca smiled. "Remember—evil may have cunning, but it never has wit or style."

If the apprentice had been a bear, he would have growled. The big man made to speak, but Recca had already slithered back down from the ridge to give orders to his men.

They collected there under cover—painted men, camouflaged and almost invisible. Eleven of them sat and listened, trusting their leader to give shape to their lives. Recca looked about the empty wilderness and filled his mind with images of his victory—his glory.

"They're coming! More Iuz vermin to kill! A general, and without an escort in sight!" The elven warlord infected his men with his confidence. "We'll slaughter a general!"

An Iuz general. The only demonic warlord to be slain in this war, and its head would fall to Recca! Recca parted the weeds and showed his men his plan for victory.

"They're fortifying this valley. That means their army is coming, so we must work fast." Recca looked the scene over with all the care of a true artist at work. "They'll survey this ridge. This is the obvious point to use as the crest of their line. So we hide, and when the general comes, we fight. I want you all to attack the workers in one group. This will draw attention to your position. I will then slay their general. We flee down the gully, here into the trees. So lay traps to kill the pursuit. Usual mix. Rendezvous at broken pine an hour after dusk." He slapped his men on the shoulders and bade them go. "Good hunting!"

The apprentice did not leave. He hovered, huge and unsmiling beside his teacher. He never smiled, never laughed, and never tired. His sword jutted through his belt, always poised for a lightning-draw.

"I will cover your back, Master Recca."

"I do not need you." The elf rested one hand languidly on his sword—the black sword of the swordmaster of the elves. "My sword and I have work to do."

The apprentice was utterly unmoved. "Then I will make sure you are free to do it."

He led the way into the best possible cover—not the obvious place to hide, it was a place in which only a ranger could disappear. The apprentice used his sword to slit a thin carpet of the dead, dry grass, and he slid beneath it, disappearing totally from view. Unwilling to follow a mere student's lead, Recca stood proud and alone on the hilltop until prudence dictated that he hide at last.

Soon, shambling footfalls sounded on the turf. The undead servants came to build their masters' wall. With them came their overlords—a general, his scribes and advisors—all feeling perfectly safe so far behind their lines. Soon the sounds of the attack came—rangers' war cries and the sounds of spells. Recca saw his target standing and staring at the commotion. The elf rose in silence, sliding forward to strike from behind—

And then everything went wrong.

Eleven of Recca's men engaged the undead in battle, and suddenly the air rang to the sound of piercing screams. Shambling, rotting corpses on the hillside split open as shapes inside the dead flesh exploded into the air. The zombies burst and took shape as filth-spattered, howling monsters with dead grey skins, fangs, and claws. Carnivorous and mad with rage, they flung themselves on the freedom fighters, fighting in a frenzy of speed.

Wights!

Recca cut with his sword, but his target was merely an illusion—a spell sent by an enemy that mocked him and laughed. From within the enemy tents, more shapes exploded into the sky—abyssal bats and huge rotting demons, skull-headed and spewing acid as they flew. A blast of fluid ploughed through Recca's men, turning three into skeletons and scattering the others in fright.

A laughing toadlike demon lurched up the hillside toward Recca. The huge demon was covered in pustules and bristled with fangs. It struck sparks from the boulders with its claws. Towering over the elf, the demon leaped and capered on the hill, bellowing in lust and glee.

As the monster drew near, three of the wights attacked Recca. He spun past one, cut, spun, cut again. The sole surviving monster threw itself at him. Recca ran and jumped, twirling like an acrobat. He landed behind his prey, lanced backward with his sword and felt it strike home. He jerked his blade free, turned and decapitated his enemy in a single blinding stroke.

Behind him, he heard a blade striking at incredible speed—one, twice, thrice—strokes that struck home with massive force. Recca saw his apprentice standing, smeared with soil and dust. Two wights lay dead at his feet, each one almost sheared in two. Seeing the abyssal bats and wights charging into his men, his apprentice turned and lunged toward the valley with its gully and its traps.

"Retreat!" Recca bellowed. *"Now!"*

Recca ran. He sped as only a grass elf could—the swiftest runners of the Flanaess. Recca reached safety amongst thick brush and boulders too thick for the titanic bats to penetrate, ducked past traps, and then looked back up the hill.

His apprentice had obeyed him, running with the heavy, lumbering stride of a big man. He reached the boulders, turned, and saw his comrades fighting not far away. There were now only five survivors, but they were making for the gully, and the enemy had left themselves open to attack. The apprentice flicked an eye over the fight, then moved forward.

"Master, I'll go left. You can hit from behind once they see me charge."

Recca looked at the fight and sheathed his blade.

"No."

His apprentice stared, his eyes searching Recca for an answer, unable to comprehend.

"Why?"

Honor! Men like Recca and his marauding rangers could not afford the luxury of honor. Leave that for the foppish knights in their castles. Survival was a practical art, and only survivors returned to fight and kill and win. Recca raked his apprentice with a glance that despaired of the human's petty intellect.

"You suffer from an overdeveloped sense of justice."

"We can save them!"

"We can't save them!" Recca shoved his apprentice onward. "We've lost, so we go while we still can, and we live to avenge them!"

The apprentice stared, shocked and lost.

"They did what you asked them to!"

"Because they were sworn to!" Recca's voice rose in anger at his student looming over him in the gully. "They are soldiers, and soldiers are tools! You leave them when you're done with them!"

Recca turned to go. His student watched him leave, turned . . .

Then charged.

He was young, but he had a violence in him that could detonate mountains. The big man burst through the weeds and ploughed his sword through an abyssal bat, cleaving off its wing. The bat screamed and spurted out a column of acid. The apprentice dived and rolled, and the acid missed him, blasting a second bat off its feet. The huge man lifted a hand, and a spell made grass burst into life and grapple a bat to the ground. He stabbed down with his sword in one swift blow—and two bats were dead and down.

The rangers fled, fighting their way back to the gully. Wights sprang like javelins from the grass, but the apprentice cut them down, sheltering injured comrades as they helped each other walk. He fought as he had never fought before—swift, punishing, and precise. He was death—swift, pitiless, and unyielding. Recca watched his student fight, and he simply stared.

His apprentice was holding them back. He was holding them. If survivors returned with tales of Recca fleeing the battle, his ambitions of leadership would be dead. Recca snarled and charged into the fight. He spun in a spectacular acrobatic flip over the enemy, spinning to cut a shapeshifter through the spine.

Far beyond its warriors, the toad demon watched the fight. The beast reared, its great yellow gut swelling as it roared in challenge. It was a demon none would dare to fight except a swordmaster. Recca sped away from the combat and ran at his chosen foe. He gave an ululating scream, feeling the glory of the eagle in his veins. He was Recca, he was a blademaster, and he was invincible!

The demon had a sword of its own, but the monster never bothered to draw. It suddenly blinked out of sight. Recca stopped, looking wildly about, then staggered as something ripped into his back. The demon stood behind him, bawling with joy. Recca spun and cut, but the monster had gone, and again claws ripped him from behind, tearing through his armor and gouging his flesh. Recca lurched, lashed out—then had the sword smashed from his grasp. The demon croaked, its throat pouch puffing. Recca dragged a dagger from his belt and blundered forward, screeching in hatred as the demon laughed.

Smiling, the demon struck, punching through the golden eagle, claws ripping into Recca's chest. The elf collapsed to his knees and stared in horror. The demon flexed, Recca felt his lungs tearing—and then suddenly the monster fell back with a roar. A sword hacked at the creature. The demon dodged, only to be caught by a kick from a massive boot. The demon staggered, and suddenly Recca's apprentice was there, huge with rage.

The toad flickered out of sight. The apprentice whirled and swung, but the screaming monster had appeared behind him. It caught the human's sword and snapped the blade in two. Snarling, the apprentice turned and tore the black blade out of Recca's dying grasp. He cut, the blow fast and vicious, but the demon disappeared an instant before the blade struck home.

The apprentice reversed and jammed his sword behind him, striking the demon as it reappeared. Black, steaming blood burst from the fat toad's guts. The monster screamed, wrenched free, then flashed out of sight again. Whirling, the apprentice brought his sword down in a massive blow aimed at empty air behind him.

The demon flickered back into view. The blow smashed the demon in two, plowing through skull and chest. Other monsters backed away as the bisected monster fell aside. The warrior bellowed, and his enemies fled into the gloom.

Somehow, Recca still lived. He lived long enough to see his apprentice win the fight that he had failed.

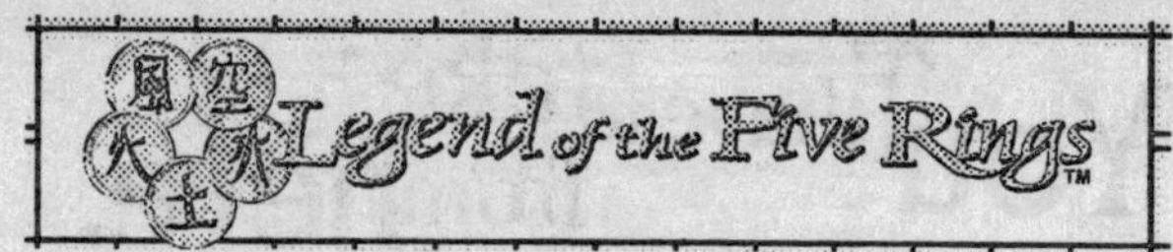

The Phoenix

Stephen D. Sullivan

The five Elemental Masters—the greatest magic-wielders of Rokugan—seek to turn back the demons of the Shadowlands. To do so, they must harness the power of the Black Scrolls, and perhaps become demons themselves.

March 2001

The Dragon

Ree Soesbee

The most mysterious of all the clans of Rokugan, the Dragon had long stayed elusive in their mountain stronghold. When at last they emerge into the Clan War, they unleash a power that could well save the empire . . . or doom it.

September 2001

The Crab

Stan Brown

For a thousand years, the Crab have guarded the Emerald Empire against demon hordes—but when the greatest threat comes from within, the Crab must ally with their fiendish foes and march to take the capital city.

June 2001

The Lion

Stephen D. Sullivan

Since the Scorpion Coup, the Clans of Rokugan have made war upon each other. Now, in the face of Fu Leng and his endless armies of demons, the Seven Thunders must band together to battle their immortal foe . . . or die!

November 2001

Invasion Cycle J. Robert King

The struggle for the future of Dominaria has begun.

Book I

Invasion

After eons of plotting beyond time and space, the horrifying Phyrexians have come to reclaim the homeland that once was theirs.

Book II

Planeshift

The first wave is over, but the invasion rages on. The artificial plane of Rath overlays on Dominaria, covering the natural landscape with the unnatural horrors of Phyrexia.

February 2001

Book III

Apocalypse

Witness the conclusion of the world-shattering Phyrexian invasion!

June 2001